Praise for *New York Times*

bestselling au

andre

Kane

"Andrea Kane expertly juggles suspense and romance."
—Iris Johansen

"Kane is a skilled writer, so the romantic complications… between her intelligent and driven main characters never get in the way of the suspense."
—*Milwaukee Wisconsin Journal Sentinel*

"Andrea Kane delivers the kind of edgy suspense and romantic tension that will rev up your pulse and keep you turning the pages."
—Jayne Ann Krentz

"Tautly written, high-octane thrillers! Andrea Kane sets new standards for suspense."
—Lisa Gardner

"Andrea Kane delivers a spine-tingling tale."
—*Strand* magazine

"A real page-turner! A keep-you-up-all-night romantic suspense."
—Karen Robards on *Run for Your Life*

"This chilling page-turner is a winner, with an atmosphere of terror that escalates to a stunning conclusion."
—*RT Book Reviews* on *I'll Be Watching You*

"Part brilliant character study, part icy thriller, here is a novel laced with romance and suspense."
—James Rollins on *Dark Room*

"Kane is an adroit master at romantic suspense, and she keeps the reader guessing to the very end."
—*Booklist*

Andrea Kane's groundbreaking romantic thriller, *Run for Your Life*, became an instant *New York Times* bestseller, paving the way for a series of smash hits focusing on the various cases investigated by NYPD detectives and FBI special agents. With a worldwide following and novels published in nineteen countries, Kane is also the bestselling author of fourteen historical romance novels. She lives in New Jersey with her family, where she is learning new ways to sharpen her firearms and investigative skills like a true FBI agent. Between target practices, she is researching and writing her next supercharged romantic thriller.

www.AndreaKane.com

andrea

Kane

THE GIRL WHO DISAPPEARED TWICE

First published in Great Britain 2011
MIRA Books, Eton House, 18-24 Paradise Road,
Richmond, Surrey, TW9 1SR

ISBN 978 0 7783 0501 9

59-0811

MIRA's policy is to use papers that are natural, renewable and recyclable products and made from wood grown in sustainable forests. The logging and manufacturing processes conform to the legal environmental regulations of the country of origin.

Printed in the UK
by CPI Mackays, Chatham, ME5 8TD

To Freddy,
the heroic FBI Tactical Canine Dog
who was killed in the line of duty.
Thank you for protecting our country.
I hope my bloodhound, Hero, is a fitting tribute to you
and all the other brave service dogs like you.

PROLOGUE

Westchester County, New York
Summer, thirty-two years ago

When six-year-old Felicity Akerman went to bed that night, she had no idea that life as she knew it was about to change forever.

She settled under the light cotton blanket and put her head on the pillow, her long blond hair tied back in a ponytail because of the heat. She was wearing her favorite short-sleeve nightshirt with the bright orange soccer balls on it. She *had* to wear it tonight. It was like a gold star on a perfect spelling test. A prize. A big win.

That's what today's game had been. The doctor hadn't been too sure about letting her play. Neither had her mom and dad. But she'd talked them into it, and gotten the okay she was holding her breath for. No one understood how miserable she'd been, sitting on the sidelines all summer long since she broke her arm. But it was better now. No more cast. No more pain. No reason to wait.

She'd proved that today on the playing field at Pine Lake Soccer Camp. She'd scored three out of her team's four goals.

With a happy smile, she rolled onto her right side, reflexively protecting the left arm that had been in a cast for seven long, hateful weeks. Her smile widened as she remembered she didn't have to do that anymore. She wriggled her fingers and bent her elbow. Free. She was finally free. *And* finally her team leader again.

The bedroom curtains rustled as a warm summer breeze blew in through the window. Her mom had left it halfway open before she went out. The summer air felt good. It swirled around the room. It smelled like flowers. It acted like a lullaby.

Felicity shut her eyes, her fingers still wrapped around a fold in her nightshirt. Next to her, her sister said something in her sleep and flopped onto her back. She hated sleeping alone when their parents were out. Normally Felicity liked her room to herself—sharing the same face, same hair, and same birthday with her sister was enough. But tonight she was so happy that she didn't mind. Besides, they weren't alone. Deidre was right down the hall, listening to her cassette player and singing along. Her voice was really awful. The two girls giggled about that all the time. But they never said anything to Deidre. She was their babysitter, and she was very bossy. She was also eighteen and starting college. That made her practically a grown-up. And their mom and dad always told them they had to be respectful of grown-ups.

Even Deidre's bad singing wasn't enough to keep Felicity

awake. Lots of physical activity after lots of sitting around had really worn her out. She drifted off to sleep.

She didn't see the window slide open the rest of the way. She didn't see the silhouette of a figure climb inside and cross silently over to the bed, going straight to her sister. Nor did Felicity see the intruder force a damp handkerchief over her face. But she did hear a whimper.

Groggily, Felicity rubbed her eyes and turned over. Still half asleep, she could vaguely make out a human form dressed in a long, loose black hooded sweatshirt. The person was leaning over the other side of the bed. As Felicity watched, her sister's whimpering stopped, and she went very still.

Felicity's small body went rigid, and her eyes snapped open. She was suddenly and fully awake. Who was in their house?

But there was no time to find out. The intruder straightened, and a gloved hand was clamped down over Felicity's mouth. She started to squirm, fighting with all she had. The sleeve of the sweatshirt brushed her forehead. Damp, with a funny smell. Like orange medicine.

The gloved hand lifted, and a wet handkerchief with that same orange medicine smell was pressed down on Felicity's nose and mouth. The smell was awful. Felicity wanted to scream. She couldn't. And she couldn't break free.

The room started spinning. Felicity caught a glimpse of her sister. It looked like there were two of her. And Deidre's singing sounded far away.

The stinky smelling handkerchief won.

Everything went black.

CHAPTER ONE

Manhattan, New York
Present day

The bar smelled like stale beer and sweat.

Casey Woods shifted in her seat, which was situated far away from the social hub of the place. She rolled her glass between her palms. It was filled with whatever was on tap that the waiter had brought her. Taking a sip, she looked nervous but wistful among the slew of college kids milling around the East Village hangout.

She was one of those kids. Or trying to be. She was a wannabe—a shy and naive misfit, on the outside, looking in. Hungry to be welcomed into the inner circle.

She reached around and fiddled with a strand of her long red hair, which was tied back, giving her a more youthful appearance. Her gaze darted around, flickering, every so often, over her target. He was in his early thirties, perched on the first bar stool. Whenever she glanced his way, he was usually staring at her.

The time ticked by slowly. Casey made sure to openly, if shyly, eye the hunkiest-looking guys, changing her demeanor from hopeful to unsure or dejected. Every guy she focused on eventually left, either with a group of friends, or with a girl he'd hooked up with.

At just past three-thirty in the morning, the bartender started closing up, and the bar emptied out. With just a few stragglers left, Casey's hopes for the night were ostensibly dashed. Her lashes lowered in an expression of utter defeat.

Slowly, she rose, reaching into her messenger bag for some cash. As she'd planned, the bag slid off her shoulder and plopped on the floor, contents spilling everywhere. Flushed with embarrassment, she squatted down and began stuffing things back into her bag—her wallet, makeup, and fake student ID.

From her peripheral vision, she saw the man at the end of the bar rise, toss some bills on the counter and walk out with the last few stragglers.

It was 4:00 a.m. Closing time.

Despite the pointed glare of the bartender, Casey took her time replacing the contents of her bag, rearranging them as she did. She kept her wallet out long enough to slap some bills on the table. Then she made her way to the door.

The bartender locked it behind her.

Casey sucked in her breath and turned, making sure to follow the same route she'd been taking all week. She'd set the pattern. But tonight she'd stayed at the bar later. The streets were emptier. The timing was right.

She steeled herself as she walked past the alley near Tompkins Square Park. She kept her gaze fixed straight ahead.

She heard Fisher's footsteps an instant before he grabbed her. His arm clamped around her waist, his free hand pressing a knife to her throat. Too hard. Too fast. No taunting. This was *not* how she'd planned it. And now he had her.

"Don't fight. Don't scream. Don't even breathe. Or I'll slit your throat."

Casey complied. She didn't have to fake her trembling, or the fear that stiffened her body. Silently, she talked herself down, reminding herself why she was doing this. She offered no resistance as Fisher dragged her into the alley. The psychopathic SOB shoved her down on the filthy concrete ground, kneeling over her, a glittering look of triumph in his eyes. He kept the knife at her throat, using his other hand to tear at her jeans.

The button popped. But the zipper never gave.

Marc Deveraux made sure of that.

Emerging from the shadows like a predator in the wild, he lunged at the would-be rapist with all the strength of his powerful build. He yanked Fisher's knife-wielding arm up and away from Casey, then slammed down on his forearm until Fisher's bones made a cracking sound and the knife clattered to the ground.

Fisher howled with pain.

"I'm just getting started," Marc promised menacingly. He dragged Fisher up and slammed his back against the wall. "You okay?" he called out to Casey, who was scrambling to her feet.

"A hell of a lot better than I was thirty seconds ago," she managed.

"Good." He turned his attention back to Fisher. "Talk," he

ordered, one knee pushed into Fisher's groin and one elbow digging into his windpipe.

"The girl came on to me," Fisher said, then yelped, sweat beading on his forehead. "She—" His breath caught as Marc increased the pressure of his knee.

"Wrong answer. Tell me about your plans for this girl—and what you did with all the others." He leaned closer, until his face nearly touched the other man's. "You don't want to know what I am or what I'm capable of. Compared to me, you're a Girl Scout." His elbow shoved deeper, cutting off most of Fisher's oxygen. "Now tell me about the girls—all of them. And don't spare any details. I'm a captive audience."

It took longer than expected to get Fisher's confession. It took a Navy SEAL's thumb dug deeply into his collarbone, causing blinding pain that persisted long after the pressure was removed, and the threat that a repeat performance would increase the pain tenfold if that's what it took to make the perp talk—assuming his neck didn't snap first. The bastard's cold-blooded confession had made bile rise in Casey's throat. He might be going to jail for a long, long time, but Casey wished they were throwing away the key for good.

"I'm done here, Marc," she told her rescuer. "Otherwise I'm going to be sick."

"Go," he urged quietly. "I'll wrap things up here and head over to the precinct. The bodies will be found. Any claim of coercion will be tossed. It's a murderer's word against ours. The confession will stick. Go home."

Home was a four-story Tribeca brownstone that was residence and office combined. There was no beating that. One mortgage. One place that held all her worldly possessions. And no commute. It was ideal.

Of course, she rarely made it up to the fourth floor, which was supposedly where she slept. Her bed was a casual acquaintance, if not a stranger. She virtually lived in her office. That was her choice. One she made every day. And she wasn't sorry.

With a quick glance around the reception level, she turned left and climbed the L-shaped staircase to the second floor. Directly ahead, she'd had French doors installed—doors that led out to a balcony overlooking the manicured garden in a gated backyard. Colorful flower beds. A maze of closely trimmed shrubs. And a pair of graceful willow trees on either side, rippling in the breeze. The entire effect was both serene and eye-catching.

Pushing open the doors, Casey stepped outside for a moment, quickly shutting them behind her. She hoped the cool air would revive her. Sighing, she noted that the sun was now well above the horizon, and climbing rapidly into the sky. Her watch told her it was nine-thirty. The unofficial coercion Marc had inflicted had taken a lot longer than expected to work. To Casey, it had seemed like an eternity before they'd pulled it off and extracted a full confession from Fisher.

She could still feel the perv's slimy hands on her. He'd really freaked her out.

With a shudder, Casey reminded herself that they *had* pulled it off, and gotten both—Fisher *and* his confession regarding the other victims. Not a pretty business. Still, the haunting, disturbing feelings inflicted by such men were the very reason she'd formed Forensic Instincts, LLC to begin with.

She walked across the balcony and reached the second set of French doors that led back into the brownstone. She held her access card up to the card reader and punched her security code into the Hirsch keypad. Pushing the doors open, she stepped inside and shut the doors behind her. No time for rest—not yet. It was time for her team's post-op meeting.

Forensic Instincts had been just a dream at first. Now it was very much a reality.

It all started four years ago, and was still in its fledgling state. Casey had begun her quest to assemble an awesome team, with herself at the helm. Thanks to her extensive credentials working with both behavioral and psychological profilers, her innate talent at reading people, and her years of working in both law enforcement and the private sector, Casey had easily transitioned into an independent profiler. She held a master's in Forensic Psychology from John Jay College of Criminal Justice, and a bachelor's in Psychology from Columbia. Most importantly, she was a natural at figuring out what made people tick.

Her two other team members were impressive as hell. She should know. She'd meticulously selected them. Assessed them. Recruited them. They were very different from each other. Both brought specialized capabilities to the Forensic Instincts team. The result was a growing track record of successfully solved complex criminal cases.

Their trio was unique, but still formative. Which meant they were sometimes welcomed, and other times regarded as a huge pain in the ass.

But, overall, they were earning a growing respect among law enforcement agencies and, more important, among their expanding client list. To those who hired them, they were the ultimate beacon of hope.

Her rules were few, but absolute. Unwavering loyalty, both to the company and to one another. One hundred and ten percent of themselves when they were on the job. Total candor, regardless of the cost—but only when they were behind closed doors. A low profile—which meant staunchly avoiding the limelight. As mavericks who pushed the boundaries more than conventional bureaucracy would allow, it was best to be unrecognizable. They were an eclectic trio, each of whom believed absolutely in his or her specific methods.

Three egos were involved. And none of them shy. That meant frequent debates, tons of constructive argument and—sometimes—stubborn unwillingness to budge. With the Fisher case, Casey had wanted to nail their perp by studying his interactions with college-aged women, then combining behavioral observations with her experience and sheer instinct. Marc had argued in favor of using statistics and past research to form a solid scientific base from which he'd work up a profile before going in for the kill. And Ryan was adamant about implementing game theory—getting inside Fisher's head, figuring out his sick reasoning—where he chose to hunt, and the strategies he used to go after his prey. The twenty-eight-year-old guy was an awesome combination of technology genius and strategic thinker. He studied behavioral patterns through complex computer programming and crunching enormous amounts of raw data, and then applied it to his analysis of human dynamics.

Each team member believed fervently in his or her methods. Fortunately, the whole was greater than the sum of its parts.

Yes, they made quite a team—strong willed, but the best. Casey expected nothing less as she expanded the operations, and Forensic Instincts grew. Her grandfather would have been proud. She'd used her trust fund wisely and well.

Smiling faintly, she looked around. The second set of French doors had granted her entry to the second-floor conference room. It was the largest and most elaborate space in the brownstone.

As she walked in, an entire wall of floor-to-ceiling video screens began to glow. A long, green line formed across each panel, pulsating from left to right. Then, a soothing voice, that seemed to emanate from every cubic inch of the room, said, "Welcome back, Casey," bending each line into the contour of the voice pattern. It continued, "Warning. Heart rate elevated."

Casey started. She just couldn't get used to being greeted by Yoda, the latest incarnation of Ryan McKay—Forensic Instincts' brilliant techno-wizard—and his artificial intelligence system. Somehow the damned thing knew who was in the room. It even knew when something was out of the ordinary. Like now. No matter how many times Ryan tried to explain to her how Yoda worked, to Casey it still sounded like magic.

The conference room was pure class. Polished hardwood floors. A plush Oriental rug. An expansive mahogany conference table and matching credenza. And, most crucial of all, a technology infrastructure that was light-years ahead of its time in both design and operation, all hidden from view. Only the gigantic video wall was visible, covering the longest side of the room and allowing Ryan to assemble a dizzying array of information into a large single image or several smaller, simultaneous data feeds. Videoconferencing equipment, an elaborate phone system, and a personalized virtual workstation available to each member of the group completed the elaborate system.

And it was all controlled by Yoda, who unwaveringly responded to requests made by team members. Behind the "shock and awe" of Yoda was a server farm located in the office's secure data center downstairs. Like a proud papa, Ryan had named their custom-built servers: Lumen, Equitas and Intueri, from the Latin words for light, justice and intuition. The names had become so much a part of Forensic Instincts that they'd incorporated them into the company logo.

Casey still found herself awed by the sophistication, power and pervasiveness of the technology. Truthfully, she didn't understand the half of how it worked. But Ryan did. And that was all that mattered.

Heading across the hardwood floor, Casey paused at the edge of the rug, then pulled back a chair and sat down at the long, oval conference table.

Leaning back, she called out, "Yoda, please show me TV news."

"Would you like world news, national news or local news?" Yoda inquired pleasantly.

"Local."

"CBS, NBC, Fox, ABC or all?" Yoda asked.

"All."

Yoda carried out her command by simultaneously showing all four channels, each occupying one-fourth of the wall.

Casey pivoted her chair around so she had a direct view. Staring intently, she tugged off the hair band she'd worn tonight, shook out her long red mane and combed her fingers through the tangled strands. When Glen Fisher appeared on the Fox News screen, she instructed, "Yoda, Fox News full screen."

Instantly, Glen Fisher filled the entire wall. He was sweating and agitated, and quickly bent forward to hide his face as the cameras zoomed in on him being hauled out of the alley and into the squad car.

It was a media feeding frenzy. The female newscaster on the scene was superanimated, as excited about delivering the story as she was upset by its occurrence. Casey read the signs on her face, heard them in her voice, saw them in her body language.

Acute energy—but mixed reasons for it. Chin held high, back ramrod straight, eyes bright with pride, but flickering away every now and then—she was already executing the steps necessary for her next promotion. But she felt guilty with her methods. She was a woman. Capitalizing on the violations and murders of other women wasn't sitting well with her.

She was talking way too quickly, rambling on about Fisher's shocking crimes, being sure to exaggerate all the colorful details—like the fact that he had a twisted, obsessive mind despite having had a stable childhood and an equally stable adult life. A decent job in a difficult economy. A wife who was devoted to him, though oblivious to the monster she was married to. And a lovely apartment in Manhattan, with neighbors who had no idea of the danger and depravity living among them. Even worse, he'd somehow found a way to elude the NYPD for months, staying so invisible that he wasn't even a blip on their radar, much less a suspect. Astonishing that it had taken the uncanny initiative of a young private organization like Forensic Instincts to zero in on Glen Fisher, and to set things in motion so this day of reckoning could come.

Irked by the melodramatic presentation and the digs at the NYPD, Casey cursed out loud and curled her hands into fists, making her nails bite into her palms. She was taking this whole case *way* too personally, which was unusual for her. But there were reasons for her lack of objectivity—what Fisher had done brought back memories that made her sick.

"Like the proverbial fly in the spider's web," said a masculine voice, interrupting her thoughts. "Clearly, you made the ideal bait."

Glancing over her shoulder, Casey watched as her trusty backup and fellow team member Marc Deveraux strolled into the room, eyeing the newscast and making a quick mental assessment. Not a flicker of emotion crossed his face, just an icy satisfaction in his eyes. Marc was Special Ops to the core.

He was also Casey's most heavily credentialed recruit—former FBI, former Behavioral Analysis Unit, former Navy SEAL. His heritage was diverse: Asian grandparents on his mother's side, and an extensive French lineage on his father's. As a result, he spoke three additional languages fluently: Mandarin, French and Spanish. With such a desirable, multifaceted background, Marc had been snatched up by the Bureau. At thirty-nine, he'd done it all and he'd done it fast. He was the sexy, brooding type—single and happy to stay that way. Most of all, when it came to the job, he was the real deal.

"I had an endless cosmetic makeover to become that ideal bait," Casey informed him. "You have no idea."

"A makeover?" Marc repeated with dry humor. "I'd sooner guess an acting coach. The thought of you as a socially inept wallflower…that's a reach."

"Very funny, smart-ass. But I haven't been eighteen in a long time. I needed a professional makeup artist to wind back the clock."

"Nope." Marc was never one to mince words. "For authenticity, all you needed to do was put on some teenage face gunk, and pull your hair back with a rubber band. Trust me, the rest of you worked. Just ask the horny frat boys ogling you. I saw them. I know the drill. If you hadn't been playing the scared virgin, they would have been on line to score."

"Sounds like you had a front-row seat."

"I did."

Casey shook her head in amazement. "I never even saw you."

"That's the point, isn't it? I'm good at making myself invisible. *And* at making sure no one's invisible to me. Including horny frat boys who—"

"Okay, enough on that subject," Case interrupted, bringing the topic to a quick close. She was in no mood to be razzed. Actually, she was more interested in giving Marc the praise he deserved. "Let's get to you. However you pulled it off, your timing was perfect. The delivery was terrifying. Even *I* almost lost it when you charged into that alley with murder in your eyes. And I have to admit I enjoyed watching Fisher freak out and humiliate himself—wetting his pants while he spilled his guts. It doesn't get any better than that, catching the psycho *and* extracting a full confession. Kudos."

Marc pulled back the chair beside Casey and dropped into it, folding his hands behind his head. "Sorry things got so ugly before I got everything I needed."

"No apology necessary. It's what the cops 'unofficially' asked us to do."

"Yeah, but they're not the ones who had Fisher's knife at their throats and his hands ripping off their jeans."

"Let's drop it, okay?"

Marc shot her a quick sideways look. Then he pivoted toward the TV, watching and listening to the details he already knew firsthand. Three redheaded college girls, all reported missing, now found raped and murdered. Three seedy pickup bars with alleys half a block away. Girls who hung out at bars hoping for normal college experiences, but who always left solo.

Through Fisher's confession, additional unknown victims had been identified and their bodies recovered. They were all kids new to Manhattan, either visitors or transfer students. Girls Fisher had done just enough research on to know that they had no friends or families to report them missing, but all of whom matched the descriptions of the known victims.

Marc blew out his breath. He was glad this case was solved. He hoped Fisher rotted in his cell. Now it was time to move on.

To Marc, moving on meant getting a few hours' sleep, and then—before the next case descended on the team—enjoying some recreation time. And *that* meant recapturing the adrenaline rush of his days as a SEAL by taking on extreme sports that other people would consider insane. His current favorite was BASE jumping—the acronym of which said it all. Buildings, antennae, spans and earth—all the wildly dangerous fixed objects that Marc would plummet from, not just for the thrills, but for the knowledge that he could master the precarious free fall before opening his parachute and floating to the ground.

Eager to get going, Marc shifted restlessly in his chair. "Where's Ryan?" he asked. "Down in his lair?"

"Nope. Upstairs. Right behind you. Ready to wrap things up so we can call it a day." With that announcement, Ryan McKay strode into the room. The complete antithesis of every computer geek stereotype, he was not only a technical genius, he was also a gym rat, who worked out two hours each morning and whose athletic prowess included being a mountain biking pro and running ultramarathons—his preferred ones being in Death Valley and the Moroccan desert. Thanks to Marc, he'd recently earned his skydiving certification and was enthusiastically starting to join him for several of his sports.

Besides his six-pack abs, Ryan was tall and broad shouldered and boasted those smoldering Black Irish looks that made women drool. The ironic part was that the gushing types and the lavish attention-givers irked the crap out of him. In fact, the very few women Ryan found the time for, and cared to pursue, were strong, independent and unimpressed with his physical attributes and accomplishments.

"Good," Casey greeted him. "Does that mean you've left your precious robots long enough to deliver our visual wrap-up?"

"No robots. Not this time. I was testing our new digitally encrypted wireless communication system. So far, so good." Ryan was already setting himself up at the touch-screen. His presentation would highlight the case details and emphasize areas that could impact future investigations, something he did at the conclusion of every case.

He lowered himself into a chair, shooting Casey a quick glance.

Like Marc, Ryan knew about their boss's past. And, like Marc, Ryan knew that, whether or not she admitted it, this was exactly the kind of case that would bother her.

The room had grown deathly silent. There was nothing to say, and Ryan wouldn't insult Casey by trying.

Casey jerked awake from a fitful sleep filled with violence and nightmares, startled by the ring tone of her cell phone. Her gaze fell on the clock. Four-thirty in the afternoon. A perfectly normal time to call someone—assuming that someone hadn't been awake for over fifty hours. She wished she'd turned off the damned phone before going to bed.

Well, she hadn't. And now she was awake so she might as well answer.

She leaned over and picked up the phone.

The last thing Casey Woods wanted right then was another gut-wrenching case.

Unfortunately, that's exactly what she got.

CHAPTER TWO

White Plains, New York
Day One

Family Court Judge Hope Willis had finished up the last case on her docket, made her ruling and dismissed the court. She was in and out of her chambers in minutes, pausing only long enough to shrug out of her judicial robe, gather some files and say a few words to her court clerk. Then, having made the transition from judge to mom, she blew out of the office and exited the building in record time.

She hurried through the parking garage, delighted to be on her way home earlier than usual. She'd actually get to spend some time with Krissy—hearing about her day at kindergarten, helping her with her homework and just seizing the opportunity to be silly together.

That was a rarity these days. Since Sophia Wolfe, the other

family court judge in White Plains, had transferred, Hope's caseload had increased. So had her hours, thanks to the fact that Claudia, her former court clerk, had broken up with her fiancé. She'd then weirded out on Hope, becoming difficult and snappish, and so out of it that she kept screwing up the docket. Because of their long history together, Hope had given her scads more chances until, finally, she'd had to let her go. Training a new clerk was brutal, and taking up far too much time and effort. There was only so much of Hope to go around.

Which meant that her hours with Krissy were limited.

And Edward? Talk about a strained marriage, and an equally strained family unit. Hope's husband was almost never home. A defense attorney for a large, prestigious law firm with offices in both Midtown Manhattan and in White Plains, he worked obscene hours. In fact, other than an occasional and unplanned meeting in the courthouse, Hope seldom saw her husband, and Krissy saw him even less.

There was a definite void there. So today was about Hope spending quality time with her five-year-old.

She'd hurried through the parking lot, slid behind the wheel of her GMC Acadia and driven off toward Route 287 and their Armonk home.

Naturally, there was traffic. These days, getting out of White Plains was almost as bad as getting out of Manhattan.

Hope crawled along, finally reaching the highway, where she took advantage of the opportunity to rapidly accelerate. Eager to get home, she exited 287 and cruised onto Route 684 North.

It was at that precise moment that Hope's life changed forever.

Everything might have been different.

If Hope had glanced out her window. *If* she'd spotted the other SUV passing by, headed in the opposite direction. *If* she'd seen the small passenger in the backseat, slapping and yanking at the door handle in an attempt to escape—and failing, the door secured with a childproof lock.

If...

But Hope did none of these. Her mind was on getting home to Krissy.

So, like two ships passing in the night, the two SUVs went their separate ways. Hope never saw the other driver. And the other driver never saw her.

Focused on the road, Hope had no way of knowing what she'd missed, or how close she'd come to averting the hell that was about to begin.

She was almost at the Armonk exit when her cell phone rang. A quick glance at the navigation system display told her that it was Liza Bock calling. Hope frowned. Liza's daughter, Olivia, was in Krissy's kindergarten class. And it had been Liza's turn to drive the afternoon car pool that day.

With a mother's sense of unease, Hope pressed the button that connected the call. "Liza?"

"Oh, Hope, thank goodness I reached you. I was afraid you'd still be at work." Liza's agitated tone did nothing to calm the growing distress knotting Hope's gut.

"What's wrong?" she demanded.

"Is Krissy with you?"

"With me?" Waves of panic. "Of course not. I assumed you'd picked her up after school today, and dropped her home with Ashley." Ashley was the Willises' nanny, and had been since Krissy was born.

"She's not." Liza's voice was trembling now. "I just spoke to

Ashley. She was very worried, so she called me. Krissy's not there."

"What are you talking about?"

"When I got to school, the kids all said you'd picked her up," Liza explained. "I double-checked with the faculty members on bus duty, and they confirmed. Everyone saw Krissy leave the school, and everyone heard her call out, 'My mommy's here!' and run to your car. They recognized your silver Acadia. It never occurred to them…or to me…"

"Are you saying Krissy's gone?" Hope could hardly breathe.

"I don't know. I called all the other kids' houses. No one's seen her. I don't understand."

"Liza, hang up and call the police. Tell them what happened. I'm calling Edward." Hope disconnected the call.

Twenty minutes later, she arrived home to mass pandemonium. Cops. Friends. Neighbors. Ashley, weeping when she ran up to Hope and announced that Mr. Willis had spoken with the U.S. Attorney, who'd contacted the FBI. As a result, specialized agents were on their way, both to the house and to Krissy's school. Local police were already at the school, questioning everyone, including all the car pool parents, who'd been summoned back to the crime scene.

Hope barely heard her nanny's words. She pushed past everyone—including the cops who were clearly waiting for her to show up so they could talk to her—and raced upstairs. She ignored the yellow tape that read "Do Not Cross," ducked under it and burst into Krissy's bedroom.

Pristine. Nothing disturbed. Nothing missing.

Nothing anyone else would notice. Only Krissy's mother. She noticed.

Oreo, Krissy's beloved stuffed panda, was gone. She slept with it every night, and left it on the center of the bed, covered by a tiny fleece blanket, while she was at school.

Hope raced over to the bed and flung the pillows aside. Then, she dropped to her knees, peering under the bed to see if the panda had toppled beneath it. She groped around, praying. When she found nothing, she tore off the comforter and sheets, shaking them out like a wild animal. Nothing. She began rummaging through the closet. She opened the bureau drawers and dumped clothes onto the rug.

"Judge Willis—stop it! We've sealed off this room." Officer Krauss, a member of Armonk's North Castle Police Department, hurried in. Having overheard the commotion coming from Krissy's bedroom, he sized up the situation, stalked over to Hope and blocked her frantic motions with his forearm. "You're contaminating personal items that could lead us to your daughter. We need her linens, her clothes—whatever we can use to find her. We also need you to provide us with a recent photo, a description of what she was wearing today, a full health history—and any information that might tell us who abducted her. We need you to focus and talk to us, not go ballistic."

Hope shoved his arm away and whirled around, whipping her head back and forth. "Talk to you? You're supposed to be finding my child. Why are you all here instead of combing the streets looking for Krissy? She's only been gone an hour. *Now* is the time to find her—before it's too late. You need her personal things? Take whatever you want. Photos, yesterday's clothes, her toothbrush. Check her comforter for prints. I doubt there'll be any. This SOB is too smart not to wear gloves. But try. And what about Krissy's school? That's where she was abducted. Did the outdoor cameras pick up anything? Do you *know* anything?"

"Nothing from the security cameras. But we have an entire team interviewing every member of the faculty." Krauss narrowed his eyes and stared at Hope. "But I have to wonder why you're tearing Krissy's bedroom apart and insisting we check her comforter for fingerprints, when you yourself just said she was kidnapped from her school. What aren't you telling us?"

"Nothing you shouldn't already have figured out!" Hope snapped back. "This was no random kidnapping. It was meticulously planned. For God knows how long. Obviously, the monster who abducted my baby researched the make, model and color of my car so he could pass it off as mine. He also took the time to study Krissy, and to learn what meant the most to her. Then he got his hands on it, and used it to dupe her into getting into that car with him...."

"What did he get his hands on—specifically?"

"That's why I'm tearing up her room. To find it. But it's gone...." Hope's voice cracked as she stared at the overturned bedding. "He was here. Today. But not to take Krissy. To take..." Hope buried her face in her hands.

Before Krauss could demand that she finish her sentence, Edward swung his legs over the tape and strode into the room.

"Hope?" His gaze darted wildly around, as if by visually covering every square inch of the bedroom, he'd spot his child. "What have you found out?" He turned to the cop. "Officer...?"

"Krauss," the other man supplied.

"Officer Krauss," Edward echoed. "Have you heard from the kidnappers?"

Krauss didn't ask why Edward Willis assumed this was a ransom case. He just filed the information away for later and shook his head. "No contact whatsoever. But it's early."

"Early?" Edward snapped. "We're not talking about a morning stroll. My five-year-old daughter's life is at stake."

"We're aware of that, sir. Our sergeant and two officers are at your daughter's school, as are detectives from the Westchester County Police and FBI agents from the White Plains Resident Agency. They're all questioning Krissy's teacher, principal and the entire staff. More FBI agents from Violent Crimes are on their way over here to join us locals. So is the county's CSI team. We'll comb through your house for clues, and branch out to widen the investigation."

"I called the U.S. Attorney. He alerted the FBI's New York Field Office," Edward announced. "I also made my own personal call to the field office. I have a contact there who specializes in Crimes Against Children."

"That wasn't necessary, sir. As I said, we notified the FBI to request their assistance as soon as we got Mrs. Bock's call. They were already aware of the situation. The hotline reached the local RA, who contacted the CAC squad in New York. Their Assistant Director in Charge contacted FBI Headquarters, and requested a Child Abduction Rapid Deployment Team. That team is en route. So is the team from the New York Field Office. They'll be setting up an off-site command post, and working with us to safely recover your daughter. Plus, an Amber Alert's been issued."

"What about the NCIC Missing Person File?" Edward pressed on, referring to the National Crime Information Center's entries. "Did you—"

"An entry was made immediately," Krauss interrupted quietly. "Being an attorney, sir, and familiar with the law, I'm sure you're aware that there's no waiting period in a child kidnapping. Our police department may not be the size of the NYPD, but we know our jobs. And we do them—well."

Krauss's point struck home, and, abruptly, Edward realized what an overbearing tyrant he was being. "I apologize. I didn't mean to attack you. But under the circumstances..."

"I understand. You're going through hell."

"Ed." Hope interrupted, clutching her husband's forearms. "Who would do this? Who took our baby?"

"I don't know." He drew Hope closer in a protective gesture. "But we'll find out. And we'll bring Krissy home." Again, his gaze swept the room. "Who trashed her bedroom?"

"*I* did."

Ed drew back, his brows knit in confusion. "I don't understand. You told me Krissy disappeared at school. That she was taken right after the bell. So why...?"

"Your wife was about to answer that very question for me," Officer Krauss interceded. "We checked this room out first, before we sealed it off for the Westchester County Forensic Investigation Unit. Everything seemed to be in order and completely untouched—at least until your wife turned the place upside down. Your nanny confirmed that she arrived right after you left this morning so she could do the laundry, bake cookies for your daughter's after-school snack, and catch up on her own studying. She assured us that no one was at the house, or in this room, today."

"Ashley's wrong," Hope countered. "So are the police." Tears glistened on her lashes. "Whoever took Krissy *was* in this room. *Today.* During the time that Krissy was in school. Ed—" she turned to command her husband's attention "—I looked everywhere. Oreo's gone."

His gaze snapped back to the bed. "Are you sure?"

"Positive. He and his blanket are both missing. The kidnapper must have come specifically to get them."

"Dammit." With a hard swallow, Edward turned to explain to Krauss. "Oreo is my daughter's stuffed bear."

"Panda," Hope corrected.

"Panda. She drags him all over the house. The only time she puts him down is when she goes to school. Then, she covers him with a little blanket. It's…" He paused to think.

"Lavender fleece," Hope supplied. "It came with one of her dolls. She gave it to Oreo. She said she was afraid he'd get cold when she went to school and wasn't there to hug him, so she tucked him in every day…on her bed…." With that, Hope finally, completely broke down. She bowed her head, her shoulders shaking with sobs.

Edward touched his wife's shoulder, but she backed away, wrapping her arms around herself in a determined attempt to withstand this emotional ordeal on her own. Still weeping, she drew inward, seeking comfort where none existed.

It was like reliving a nightmare. Only worse. Now she was grown. And now the victim was *her* child, her precious little girl.

Officer Krauss was scribbling notes onto a pad. "You're sure the bear was here when Krissy left for school?"

"Positive," Hope managed. "I saw him when I came in to get Krissy's jacket. She was already waiting for me at the front door. We were running late. I took her directly to school. She never went back upstairs."

"Which means she never reentered her bedroom." Krauss double-checked the bedroom windows. "As I said earlier, no sign of forced entry." He was already heading for the door. "My men and I will recheck the security system and every door and window in the house. Then, I'll need those personal items and information we talked about."

There was a long silence when Hope and Edward were alone.

"The FBI should be here any minute," he said at last.

"I'm sure they will. They'll set up Command Central, waiting for a ransom call, while they grill us. They'll start with our relationship, since we're Krissy's parents and the primary suspects. Then, they'll move on to every human being who holds a grudge against us—which will take days, given our careers. Meanwhile, Krissy's out there somewhere. Scared. Alone. And God knows what else." Hope's hand was shaking as she whipped out her cell phone. "So, yes, I'm glad we have the police and the FBI on board. But it's not enough." She punched in directory assistance.

"Who are you calling?"

"Forensic Instincts."

Edward blinked. "The profilers?"

"Yes," Hope confirmed. "You know their track record. It's unbelievable. Five cases. Five successes. They find criminals. Serial killers. Rapists. And kidnappers. They're on the fast track. And they don't have a dozen other cases they have to work at the same time."

A scowl. "We should check with the FBI first. What if the involvement of an independent organization puts Krissy in more danger?"

"It won't." Hope was talking so fast she was tripping on her words. "I've followed their work. They know just how to handle things. Your friends at the FBI might not like it, but I don't give a damn." A hard look at Edward as her index finger hovered over the send button. "I've been through this nightmare before. I'm not losing Krissy."

"I know what you went through. But you can't compare the two traumas. It's over three decades. Law enforcement's capabilities have grown by leaps and bounds."

"I don't care. I can't survive this again. Especially not when it comes to my daughter."

"I understand. But—"

"Look, Edward, three decades ago or not, some things haven't changed. Like the fact that an investigation can remain active for only so long. The last time the case went cold after two years. I'm not chancing that again. Not with my baby. Don't bother arguing with me. I'm doing this. I'll get them to drop anything they're doing. I'll pay them whatever fee they ask for." Hope was finished waiting. She punched the green button and put the call through.

"In Manhattan, I need the number for Forensic Instincts, LLC." Hope reached for a pad and pen.

"Fine. If you feel that strongly about it, go ahead," Edward reluctantly conceded. "But I want them working with law enforcement. Not independently."

"If that's possible, great. If not—" Hope shrugged, scribbling down the number. Having gotten what she wanted, she disconnected the call, and began furiously punching in the telephone number. "The truth is, I don't give a damn about the cops' or the FBI's internal politics. I don't give a damn about *anything*—except getting Krissy home safe and sound. So if Forensic Instincts' methods are too unconventional to suit you—hello?" Hope put her lips to the mouthpiece, her throat working as she spoke. "Is this Casey Woods?"

"Speaking," a weary voice answered. "And this is...?"

"My name is Hope Willis. Judge Hope Willis. I live in Armonk. An hour and a half ago, my five-year-old daughter was kidnapped from her elementary school. The police are here. So is the FBI. But the minutes are ticking by. And the suspect list is way too long for them to tackle alone."

"Really. And why is that?"

"Because I'm a family court judge, and my husband is a criminal defense attorney. We've racked up more grudge-holders and enemies than we can recall. We'll try to compile a list, but it'll be long. Plus, there are special circumstances involved that make this even more unbearable. I need to hire Forensic Instincts. Now. On an exclusive basis."

There was a prolonged silence at the other end of the phone.

Special circumstances. An interesting and succinct choice of words. Plus, Casey could hear the repressed note in Judge Willis's tone. The woman might be going through hell, but she was clearly holding something back. Half-assed candor didn't fly for her—no matter how dire the circumstances.

"I'm terribly sorry about your daughter," Casey responded. "But my team and I are just coming off a very intense, draining investigation, and we have other cases that have been back-burnered because of that, and now require our attention. I'm sure the FBI and the police will be on top of—"

"They're not enough," Hope interrupted. "I need more than conventional methods. We can't afford to waste a second. Please. You know how crucial these first three hours are."

"Yes," Casey replied soberly. "I do." *And they're slipping away,* she mentally noted.

"Then will you come? I'll do anything. Pay anything. Follow your instructions to a tee." The last semblance of Hope's facade cracked. "Please, Ms. Woods. I'm begging you. Find my baby."

Casey had to cave. And not just because this case would mean big bucks for the company. But because instinct told her that the honesty and trust would come when they met in person. If not, the team would walk.

For now, a five-year-old child was missing.

"Okay. Stay calm. We'll do everything we can," she assured Hope, her entire demeanor softening. "Hang on." A rustle as she snatched up a Post-it and pen. "Give me your address. Then give us an hour."

CHAPTER THREE

Forensic Instincts showed up at the Willis house at the same time as the FBI. Watching them pull into the driveway, Casey immediately recognized the four special agents who'd been contacted and deployed by the Crimes Against Children Unit at FBI Headquarters in D.C. They were one of the two Child Abduction Rapid Deployment teams in the Northeast, and consisted of specially trained agents from several different field offices, each of whom had dropped everything and taken off the instant they'd been contacted. Aware of how crucial these first post-abduction hours were, the CARD team was here to assist C-20, the New York Field Office's CAC squad, in tracking down Krissy Willis and bringing her home.

The team members now jumping out of their car consisted of Supervisory Special Agent Don Owens, and Special Agents Will Dugan, Guy Adams and Jack McHale. And Casey knew exactly which of them would be smiling at the sight of her team's arrival, and which of them would be exceedingly pissed off to see them.

"Hey, Don." As she climbed out of the driver's seat, Casey waved at the seasoned agent who had to be nearing fifty-seven and mandatory retirement. He was hard-core, married to the Bureau, and yet he was more open-minded about Casey's team than some of the younger squad members. Go figure.

"Casey Woods. Why am I not surprised to see you here?" Owens acknowledged her with a slight smile, his trim gray mustache curving with his lips. "I'm lucky I sped to Logan, and that my shuttle flight from Boston arrived early. Otherwise, you would have already set up the FBI's Command Post and canvassed half the neighborhood."

"Damn straight," Ryan muttered under his breath.

Casey rolled her eyes. Ryan was cranky. He hadn't gotten any of the sleep he'd anticipated after closing the last case. Functioning on zero rest was Casey's specialty. She could operate on empty and make it seem full. She was able to push past her fatigue and get the job done. And Marc was a Navy SEAL to the core. He could run on sheer adrenaline. So Ryan was the cheese who stood alone. He was a royal pain in the ass when he went without sleep. At times like this, barring essential needs to communicate, Casey and Marc avoided him like the plague.

"This place is going to be a circus," Ryan continued to mumble. "The CARD team. The Feds. The county police. The locals. Can't we send them all back to their desks?" A grunt. "You know, leave us alone…. I'll hack into the little girl's computer. Casey, you can run down the list of suspects, interrogate the right ones. Marc can beat the crap out of the scumbag who did this. Then you'll size up his reactions until we figure out where he hid the poor kid. And Krissy Willis will be safe in her own bed before the miserable prick who took her can do his worst. After that, we can all go home and crash."

Before Casey could reply, Ryan spied the tall, slender woman who was squatting down just outside the Willises' garage. Her brow was furrowed in intense concentration, and her delicate fingers were gliding over the streamers that dangled from the handlebars of what was clearly a little girl's bicycle.

"Oh, great," Ryan complained more loudly. "Look who's here. It's Claire-voyant—the cops' favorite psychic, doing her thing. Now, we'll be grilling suspects, and she'll be clutching Krissy Willis's dirty socks trying to get up in her head. I can hardly wait."

Casey stifled a smile. Claire Hedgleigh—Claire-voyant, as Ryan insisted on calling her—was a noted, self-described intuitive who consulted with several police departments, using her special skills to help solve cases. Casey and her team had crossed paths with her on a couple of cases. And Casey was more than impressed. She'd done extensive background research on Claire, both educationally and professionally.

Academically, Claire held a master's degree in Human Development and another in Transformative Theory and Practices. In addition, she had teaching accreditation from schools in the U.S., England and Australia in everything from psychic development to metaphysical sciences. And professionally, she had an A+ reputation and a three-year track record with the police. She was so good, in fact, that Casey was determined to lure her over to Forensic Instincts. She'd be a great addition to the team—once Casey broke the news to Ryan and pried the chip off his scientific shoulder. Instinct told her it wouldn't be as hard a sell as Ryan pretended. He and Claire interacted in a way that only masqueraded as combat. But both Marc and Casey recognized it as a smoke screen for something more.

At this point, Claire was rising to her feet. Tall and willowy, with pale blond hair and light gray eyes, Claire had a gentle, ethereal quality about her that suited her calling. Now, she released the bicycle handlebars, brushed a strand of hair off her cheek and spotted them. An exasperated expression crossed her face when she saw Ryan. Clearly, she was not in the mood for a verbal sparring match. And Ryan was practically vibrating to start one.

Casey's grin widened. An electrically charged tête-à-tête was definitely on the horizon. And Casey and Marc had already placed their bets on a timeline—and an outcome—for that.

For now, some barbed banter would be fine with her. The moments of levity would feel good. More than good. It would be like Novocain before a root canal. Because the latter was what they were about to walk into. Child abductions were among the toughest crimes to swallow.

"Play nice, Ryan," she said drily as they approached the garage. "Claire knows what she's doing. So don't give her too much crap."

"Who? Me?" he replied with mock innocence.

"Yeah. You look like a lion who's been prodded with a sharp stick. Relax. You can go back and hole up in your lair as soon as we get the lay of the land here." Casey reached Claire and stopped. "Hi, Claire. You're working this case?"

A friendly nod. "And, obviously, so are you. Anything I can do to help out, let me know."

Ryan made a derisive sound. "I think we'll rely on science. Messages from inanimate objects just don't cut it, at least not for me. But thanks anyway, Claire-voyant."

"Ah, Ryan. More obnoxious than usual, I see. What happened? Did you forget your Batman lunch box?"

"Ignore him," Casey advised. "He hasn't slept in a few days."

"Well, that explains it." Claire looked more amused than bothered—which pissed Ryan off even more. "Thanks for the news flash. I'll consider myself forewarned."

With that, she headed into the house. "Time to commune with inanimate objects," she called over her shoulder. "You'd be surprised how much talking they do—in a world that's realer than cyberspace."

Ryan definitely had an answer for that one, but he pressed his lips together and refrained from spouting it, as he, Casey and Marc reached the CARD team.

"So, the Willises hired you already." Special Agent Guy Adams looked even more unhappy than Ryan about the prospect of working together. Adams was a trained hostage negotiator, in his mid-thirties, sharp, and as competitive as Ryan and Marc. And he had little regard for approaches other than those he'd learned through the Bureau—least of all Forensic Instincts and their out-of-the-box methods.

"Is that a problem?" Marc asked in a cool, probing tone.

"Not as long as you don't overstep."

"We're here to work with you, Guy. You and C-20." Casey nipped the tension in the bud. "We all want the same thing—to bring Krissy Willis home, safe and with as little trauma as possible. So let's not turn this into a pissing match."

"Our special agents are already inside," Guy informed her, purposely sidestepping her attempt at detente. "The New York Field Office sent Harrington and Barkley. They're with the parents now, working on the Child Victim Background Questionnaire. The rest of the New York team is at Krissy's school, along with a couple of agents from the White Plains RA. Harrington and Barkley are about to debrief us. Harrington is lead case agent on this one."

"Good choices," Casey replied.

"Glad you approve."

"I do." Casey ignored his sarcasm. She was mulling over the agents she was about to deal with in the Willis home. Peg Harrington and Ken Barkley were both seasoned agents who'd been working CAC cases for over a decade. They were intelligent, and they were self-assured—which meant they didn't trip over fragile egos. That made working with them tenable. And having Peg at the helm would be great. She was cool under pressure and effective as hell.

"Did your clients supply you with all the facts?" Guy was asking Casey.

She wiggled her hand in an ambivalent gesture. "I checked in with Hope Willis from my car. I got the basics. Anyone happen to catch the license plate on the Acadia the kidnapper was driving?"

"Just a letter or two. Nothing solid to go on. The cops put out an APB. So far, nothing's turned up. They also notified the Westchester hotline, issued an Amber Alert and entered the case into the NCIC. Officers are at both scenes—here and at the child's school, along with the county police and CSI."

It dawned on Casey that Guy was being unusually chatty and informative, given his preliminary hostility. She glanced past him, and spotted McHale and Dugan head into the house. So that was Guy's plan. To keep her talking while the rest of the CARD team agents joined their C-20 counterparts and got a jump start on the case.

She had to admire their tenacious attempt to outmaneuver

her, even if it had been feeble. She also had to admit she'd have done the same thing in their place. The fact was, C-20 had every right to run the show. They were law enforcement; she and her team weren't.

Nonetheless, she was getting into the house and meeting the Willises. The FBI couldn't deny her that—they were her clients. The truth was, she didn't just want to meet them, she wanted to study them. She needed to know what Hope Willis was holding back. And she needed to get a firsthand look at how Hope and Edward Willis were coping—both individually and as a couple—with these initial hours after their five-year-old child's abduction.

Body language was a powerful revealer.

The FBI and the police had already conducted official interviews with the Willises, and were about to turn their efforts toward debriefing the CARD team. The usual procedure. Eliciting the usual response from Forensic Instincts. While the doors were firmly shut in their faces, they'd take full advantage of the opportunity to get information from their surroundings and the people in them. Each of Casey's team members would accomplish this in his or her unique way.

"Playtime's over, Guy," Casey stated bluntly. "You can shut us out of your debriefing sessions, but you can't shut us out of the house. Hope Willis hired us. We're going in to meet her and her husband. We'll be discreet. And we won't interfere with your investigation."

"That's fine," Don said, though with a bit of a sigh. "Any insights you glean would be a welcome addition to our efforts. We're talking about the life of a five-year-old little girl. I've got a granddaughter that age. Let's pool our resources and solve this one—successfully."

"Agreed." Casey gestured for her group to follow Don and Guy inside. This was great. They'd made peace with the CARD team supervisor. Barkley and Harrington had worked with them a lot, and they respected them. Ditto for the Violent Crimes squad in White Plains, and the Westchester County Police.

"Sweet," Marc murmured quietly. "Now we just have the locals to convince. Unfortunately, that's the hardest part."

There was no argument from his coworkers. The locals, especially the smaller precincts, were often skeptical of what and who they didn't know. Some were also determined to prove themselves, which made them territorial and leery of Forensic Instincts' independent status.

"We might get resistance, but we won't get beginners," Ryan said. He'd done a brief computer search on the North Castle P.D. "They're pretty solid."

Marc edged him an inquisitive look. "What did you find out?"

"They're got a retention rate that's sky-high. Their cops and detectives just stay on. They like their jobs. They're well trained and dedicated. There's not a lot of major criminal activity for them to deal with—mostly car and house break-ins. But they're ready for big stuff, too. They've got an impressive Emergency Service Unit. It's been around for over a dozen years. They've also got a strong community spirit. They take care of their own."

"Sounds good," Marc responded. "Unless they're insular and uncooperative."

"Only one way to find out."

Casey nodded. Best possible scenario. Best investigators. Best police support.

Now if she only knew what Hope Willis was hiding.

* * *

Hope was in the living room of her sprawling house, pacing around and tucking strands of blond hair behind her ears in erratic, repetitive motions, when Casey first laid eyes on her.

It took about ten seconds for Casey to feel convinced. The woman with the haunted eyes and the inability to sit still had had nothing to do with her daughter's disappearance.

Edward Willis was a little tougher to read. Stiff by nature, Willis was a polished attorney who was accustomed to hiding behind a well-established veneer. But beneath that veneer a fine tension rippled the surface. Just as there was obvious tension between him and his wife. Physical and emotional distance. Separate entities instead of one frantic unit. Edward was edgy, and way too knowledgeable about the law not to know he was a suspect.

Casey walked directly over to the couple. "Mr. and Mrs. Willis? I'm Casey Woods."

Instantly, Hope stopped pacing. She closed the gap between herself and Casey. "There's been no word," she blurted out. "No ransom note. No phone call. Not even a threatening email." Hope looked helplessly from Casey to the FBI agents she'd just spoken to, to the CARD team now moving in. "Does that mean he's hurting her? Worse? If he doesn't want money, what else could he want besides...oh God." Hope drew a few sharp breaths, her features contorting with fear.

"Let's not get ahead of ourselves, Judge Willis." Don stepped in front of Casey and introduced himself, keeping his voice quiet and calm. "I'm Supervisory Special Agent Don Owens. These are Special Agents Will Dugan, Guy Adams and Jack McHale. We're part of a specially trained child recovery team. We're here to help find your daughter. Have you given Special Agents

Barkley and Harrington, as well as the police, a full description and photos of Krissy, along with clothing samples…?"

"Yes." Edward Willis moved to his wife's side. "Thank you for coming, Agent Owens. I'm Edward Willis, Krissy's father. In answer to your question, we filled out a background questionnaire. We gave the police and the FBI a preliminary list of neighbors, friends, relatives, Krissy's friends, classmates and teachers—and we're working on a list of all of Hope's and my potential enemies. We also provided the photo and clothing you just mentioned, along with Krissy's comb and toothbrush, and all the details of the abduction that we have—which aren't many. What else can we do?"

"Make yourselves available for whatever's necessary," Don replied. "Media broadcasts. Following our lead when we ask you to prolong any phone calls we're recording. Working with us to separate what's real from what's bogus as the public starts to communicate potential leads. Which they will. Some through our hotlines. Some through the National Center for Missing and Exploited Children. Some through tips to law enforcement. You'll both be required to submit to polygraph tests. I assure you, it's routine. Don't be insulted—just do it. Eliminating suspects can be as important as pursuing them. And, most of all, have faith."

"Pursuit," Hope echoed, reminded for the umpteenth time of the potential flight risk involved. "What about roadblocks?"

"Taken care of county-wide and beyond," Don assured her. "And highway patrols are combing the area. Trust me, Judge Willis. We all know what we're doing."

Hope nodded, lowering her eyes as tears slid down her cheeks.

It was clear from the expression on Don's face that he

empathized with Hope's fears. It was also clear that he knew there was only one way to alleviate them.

"If you'll excuse me, my team needs to be debriefed," he informed her. "The quicker the better. That way we won't lose a minute. What room can we use?"

"My home office," Hope said at once. She pointed. "It's down the hall, second door to your right. The other FBI agents are in there with the police. There's a conference table and more than enough chairs."

With a brief nod of thanks, Don and his CARD team disappeared in that direction.

Hope turned back to Casey.

"I picked up on a certain evasiveness in your voice," Casey stated without preamble. "You're hiding something. Before we go any further, I want to know what that something is."

Inhaling sharply, Hope responded to the obvious first. "Do you honestly believe I could harm my child? Is that why you think I was being evasive?"

"Initially, it was one of the explanations I considered." Casey continued to be frank. Simultaneously, she was watching an interesting scene taking place diagonally across from them, in the kitchen. But the answer she provided Hope was definite and direct. "But after seeing you in person, my suspicions are gone. However, that doesn't answer my question. You *are* holding something back. What? And why?"

"Because it has no bearing on our daughter's disappearance," Edward Willis inserted abruptly.

With a quick glance over her shoulder, Casey signaled for Marc and Ryan to go do their thing. Once they'd complied, she leveled a direct stare at Edward.

"Tell me if I'm wrong, Mr. Willis, but I get the feeling you're not much in favor of your wife's decision to hire us."

"You're not wrong. I'm a firm believer in the legal system."

"As an attorney, I'm sure you are." Casey kept her tone respectful. But she didn't like this man. He was judgmental and controlling. And it was no surprise that he believed in the legal system—*his* legal system. He specialized in putting violent criminals back on the street in exchange for high visibility, a rush of self-importance and a hefty fee.

Aloud, all she said was, "I understand where you're coming from. Rest assured, my group won't be abusing law enforcement or whatever decisions you make with them. We're here to follow their lead—*if* our discussion with you now results in a mutual decision for us to work together."

"If?" Now Edward was taken aback. It was clear the man was used to getting his own way—even if, like this time, it meant Casey and her group vanishing into thin air.

His jaw tightened. "I don't understand, Ms. Woods. My wife hired you."

"True. But there's a stipulation. I need my answer. What is it I'm not being told?"

Hope stared at the floor for a minute. The hard swallow that she gave, the way she steeled herself, and the way she shifted into autopilot told Casey that she'd relayed this story countless times, but that it never ceased to hurt.

"My sister Felicity was kidnapped thirty-two years ago," she said quietly, her voice quavering from emotional strain. "We were six. She was sleeping next to me when it happened. I was chloroformed. So was she. Only it was Felicity the kidnapper chose to take. I've never understood why. We are—" a painful pause "—*were* identical twins. Very few people could tell us apart—unless they were familiar with our personalities. Which, to me, says the kidnapper was someone who knew us at least fairly well. And before you ask, Felicity's body was never recovered. The case was labeled cold, and closed two years after the abduction. Now, history is repeating itself…with my baby." Choking up, Hope pressed a fist to her mouth to stifle a sob.

"*Now* you see why I didn't want you to pursue this line of questioning," Edward snapped, once again putting an arm around his wife. The gesture seemed oddly stiff, even staged. "Dredging up a painful incident from Hope's past is pointless."

"I disagree." Casey quickly processed the implications of what she was being told, even as her gaze flickered once again to the kitchen doorway. "It explains that this terrifying crime is even more terrifying for your wife than it might be for another woman. Two treasured loved ones kidnapped in a lifetime—the first unsolved, and occurring when your wife was an impressionable, young child? Scars like that don't heal, Mr. Willis. Especially when the victim is an identical twin, who most people claim is like half of a whole. And now, a child—the very heart and soul of a mother. I can see why Judge Willis would be coming apart at the seams, reliving the past, and willing to go to any extreme to avoid a repeat of it."

"So you understand." Hope scrutinized Casey, her gaze filled with agonized pain.

"I do," Casey said without hesitation. "I understand your fear. And I understand what you weren't saying on the phone. Consider yourself our top-priority client."

Hope literally sagged with relief. "Thank you."

Casey wasted no time in getting down to business. "Your babysitter—it's Ashley, right?" She gestured in the direction of the kitchen.

Startled by the abrupt change in subject, Hope looked up and followed Casey's stare. Edward's head snapped around, too.

"My babysitter?" Hope repeated. "Yes, it's Ashley Lawrence. Although she's not really a babysitter. She's been Krissy's nanny since the day Krissy came home from the hospital. So we don't think of her as an employee. She's family. And she adores Krissy."

"All the more reason for my curiosity. If everything you're saying is true, why has she spent the entire time since I walked in here on her cell phone, arguing with someone?"

"It's probably her boyfriend." Edward waved away the observation. "I'm sure he's unhappy about her decision to stay here until we have news about Krissy."

"I see." Casey could sense Edward's escalating tension. "So he's a serious boyfriend. What's his name?"

"Frank. Frank Barber."

Casey jotted that down. "You mentioned that Krissy's stuffed panda was stolen from the house sometime today. Did the police find evidence of a break-in?"

"None."

"And no one had access to the house except Ashley, who claims that nobody came by here all day, and who's now arguing with her boyfriend."

"Oh, no." Vehemently, Hope denied the notion that Ashley could be involved. "As I said, Ashley adores Krissy, and the feeling is mutual. The poor girl was crying hysterically when I got home. She's in shock. She's probably talking to her boyfriend for emotional support."

"I don't think so. She seems more agitated than distraught. Agitated and, if I'm reading her body language right, scared." Casey pursed her lips thoughtfully. "Maybe she just realized she bit off more than she could chew, and that events are spiraling out of control."

"You're barking up the wrong tree, Ms. Woods," Hope insisted. "Ashley's not capable of harming Krissy."

"Maybe she doesn't have to be—at least not directly." Casey's gaze shifted to the pile of sophisticated-looking textbooks sitting on the kitchen table. "It looks like Ashley's in grad school. Unless you're paying her a fortune, I assume she has outstanding student loans. What does Frank do for a living?" The ensuing silence gave her her answer. "Nothing lucrative, I take it."

"He dabbles," Hope replied, reluctance and wavering trust evident in her tone. "He's a part-time bartender, and a part-time bouncer. Nothing concrete."

"And nothing a huge windfall wouldn't help in a big way." A poignant pause. "Think about it—a vulnerable young woman in love with the wrong man. A young woman who has direct access to your home, your schedules and your daughter."

For the first time, Casey's gaze flickered coolly to Edward, who—as Casey had anticipated—had gone very, very still. "I'd say that's a solid enough lead to check into, wouldn't you, Counselor?"

His jaw was working, but his gaze pierced hers with laser intensity. "I'd say that's your call, Ms. Woods."

CHAPTER FOUR

It's been a terrifying day. I know you're scared. But you're such a special child.

Unique. Precious.

The sleeping pill is working. Your eyes are shut. Your breathing is even. Your long blond hair is tousled, spread out on the pillow. I wish your lashes weren't spiky and wet with the tears you cried for hours, or that your neck wasn't damp with the perspiration caused by your struggles.

You look like you belong here. Which is good, since there's no escape. Even though right now that's all you'll want to do.

When you wake up, you'll cry. Beg. And finally withdraw. You'll have that haunted look in your expressive blue-green eyes.

It's my job to erase that. To change your mind about being here. To make you want this to be your home.

I will. I'm the only one who can.

I got all the tools I need from your book bag. You'll have nothing to do but comply.

Sweet dreams, Krissy. It will all begin when you wake up.

★ ★ ★

Ashley hastily disconnected her call the minute Casey walked into the kitchen. She looked jumpy—like someone who was either at the end of her rope, or had something to hide—as she met Casey's stare.

"Hi..." she said in a tentative voice.

"Hello, Ashley." Casey extended her hand. "My name is Casey Woods, and my organization is working with the Willises to help find Krissy."

"Organization?" Ashley shook Casey's hand, her own skin warm from holding the cell phone, and damp with nerves. "You're not with the police or the FBI?"

"Nope. I'm with Forensic Instincts. We're a private company, specializing in solving cases like these. I'd like to ask you a few questions."

Ashley's tongue wet her lower lip. "I've already told the authorities everything I know."

"I'm sure you have. But since my colleagues and I just arrived, I'd appreciate if you could fill me in, as well." Casey didn't have to turn around to know that the Willises had come up behind her and walked into the kitchen. Nor did she have to hear their footsteps. She could read it all over Ashley's face, see it in her eyes as her gaze darted past Casey, filled with a mixture of uncertainty and an appeal for help.

"It's all right, Ashley," Hope assured her, although Casey was quite certain that Hope wasn't the Willis she was appealing to. "Tell Ms. Woods whatever she needs to know."

Casey turned to Hope. "May I speak to Ashley alone? Maybe in a den or comfortable setting? I'm sure she's overwhelmed by the events of the day."

"Of course. There's a Florida room behind the kitchen." Hope pointed. "Take as much time as you need." She went to the fridge, pulled out two bottles of water, and handed one to Casey and one to Ashley. Edward stood to the side, his features and posture stiff.

"Thank you." Casey followed Ashley to the Florida room. The girl was definitely on overload. Maybe it was just a meltdown from the day. Or maybe it was guilt.

Casey suspected it was both.

"I'd like to start out by going over some basics with you," Casey began as soon as they were seated on the comfortable lounge chairs in the glass-enclosed Florida room. "I hope you don't mind if I take notes." She pulled out a pad and pen.

"I don't mind." Ashley spread her hands in confusion. "But wouldn't it be easier for you to get a copy of my police interview?"

"I'll do that, too. But my group tends to focus on the personal rather than the procedural. So there might be things you can tell me that will help us help the authorities."

"Like what?"

Casey clicked on her ballpoint pen and leaned forward. "Like giving me a mental picture of Krissy. Not her appearance—I can study the cops' photo for that. I can also read the victimology report her parents supplied. But often those aren't as in-depth as I'd like. Not where it comes to Krissy's hot buttons, her private likes and dislikes, her subtle behavioral traits. In many ways, you were her primary caretaker. The Willises have busy, high-powered careers—especially Mr. Willis. That doesn't mean they're not exceptional parents but you've spent the most time with Krissy, ever since she was born. There might be nuances you're familiar with that are fresher in your mind than they are in theirs."

A faint smile touched Ashley's lips. "Krissy's always been special. She's happy, she's bright and she's so precocious that even I have trouble staying a step ahead of her."

Ashley went on to describe a bouncy, enthusiastic child who loved books, drawing and Disney's Club Penguin, had lots of playdates and friends—including a little boyfriend named Scotty—was a Daisy Girl Scout, wanted to play the tuba when she reached third grade and who wished her straight blond hair was red and thick like her friend Erin's, whose hair reached all the way down her back without getting even a little thin and pointy.

"Krissy would love your hair," Ashley told Casey in a tone so filled with fondness that it couldn't be faked. "She'd ask you a million questions about who in your family is a redhead and how you managed to inherit it." Another small smile. "She'd also ask if you had a boyfriend, and if he liked red hair. Then she'd tell you all about Scotty and how much longer she can hang upside down on the monkey bars than he can. She's not what you'd call shy or quiet."

Casey put down her pad. "She sounds like a great kid."

"She is. Everyone likes her."

"What about her parents? Does everyone like them, too?"

An uncomfortable flush stained Ashley's neck. "That's a hard question for me to answer. They're wonderful to me, and they always have been. They have tons of friends. But they both also have these jobs that produce enemies. So I can't say...."

"I didn't expect you to know details about their work lives. I was referring to any major disputes in their personal lives—with others, with each other."

"Not that I know of," Ashley answered quickly, defensively.

Casey could see the pulse at her neck start beating a little faster. Nerves? Maybe.

Casey continued to speak in a calm, reassuring tone. "Ashley, my questions aren't meant to hurt the Willises. They seem like lovely people. I just want to find Krissy. I'm not interested in uncovering any family skeletons. Those are none of my business. But family arguments can lead to outside confidences. And outside confidences can lead to angry, bitter friends. You practically live here. So I'm asking you if there are any internal or external conflicts you know about."

That calmed Ashley down. "No, none."

"Okay." Casey switched gears. "I understand you were here at the house all day today, and that there were no visitors,"

The swift change in subject caught Ashley by surprise. "That's right."

"Do you keep the burglar alarm on?"

"Not during the day. But I do keep the doors locked. I'd know if someone broke in. Plus, I would have heard them."

"True," Casey agreed. She pursed her lips. "What about the mail?"

"What about it?"

"I noticed the mailbox is at the foot of the driveway, which is winding and long. Did you bring in the mail today?"

"Yes," Ashley admitted. "I already told that to the police. And, yes, the door was unlocked during that time. But I was only gone for two, maybe three, minutes. So if you're wondering if someone could have slipped in and out of the house, I doubt it. Is it possible? I suppose so. I'd like to think I would have spotted them. Not to mention how unlikely it is that they'd have had time to go upstairs, take Oreo, and leave—not to mention knowing the layout of the house, where Krissy's room is—"

"Unless someone drew them a diagram," Casey interrupted quietly.

"Who would—" Ashley broke off, her eyes widening as she realized where Casey was going with this. "Do you mean *me?* You think *I'm* part of this kidnapping?"

"I don't know what to think." An offhand shrug. "I can see how much you care about Krissy, and how torn up you are by what's happened. But you were the only person here all day. So you could be lying, or you could be involved on some level—maybe as an accomplice."

The shock that registered on Ashley's face was unmistakable. "An accomplice to who? My God, I'd never, ever hurt Krissy. I'd never take her from her family. I'd never put her through this."

"After everything you've said, I believe you." Casey softened her expression—and her tone. "But I had to ask. Especially because of Frank."

"Frank?" Again, Ashley was on the defensive. "What about him?"

"The Willises tell me that your boyfriend is kind of a drifter, and that he's far from rolling in cash. And you're in grad school. You have tuition and textbooks to pay for. The Willises are rich. It occurred to me that Frank might have pressured you into doing something you'd never ordinarily do, and convince you it was harmless. He'd make sure Krissy never knew who took her. You'd make sure he never hurt her. He'd just keep her long enough to get a huge payment from the Willises, then get her back to them. You'd both be rich. And no one would be any the wiser."

"And Krissy would be scarred for life." Ashley was trembling.

"I'd *never, ever* be part of such a sick scheme. Not for a million dollars."

"Would Frank?"

"Absolutely not. Frank's not exactly a go-getter, but he's not a thief. And he'd never kidnap a child."

"It's not a great theory," Casey murmured. "Considering there's been no ransom call—yet. But I had to ask. Not so much about you, but about Frank. That *was* him you were just arguing with on the phone, right?"

"Yes."

"Was it about Krissy?"

"Yes…no…I mean, it was about Krissy, but not in the way you mean." An uneasy pause. "He's upset about how much time I'm spending here. I know that sounds horrible. But he's a guy. He feels bad about Krissy, but he's had enough. He's been questioned by the police. He's listened to my hysteria all afternoon. And now he's dealing with my saying I'm not leaving this house until Krissy comes home safely. He's not a bad guy. He's just impatient and pissed off."

"Sounds like most guys," Casey said with a smile.

"I know." Ashley was clearly relieved by Casey's reaction.

"So you and Frank are tight?"

"Pretty much. We've been together for a year." Ashley opened her bottle of water and took a gulp. "I don't see us walking down the aisle or anything. But, like I said, he's a good guy."

"He just wishes you'd spend more time with him."

"Yes." Another swig of water. "And I wish he'd work a little harder. Want to be a little more. I doubt that's in the cards."

Casey gave an understanding nod. "Ambition's one of those qualities you're either born with or you're not."

"Exactly." Ashley shifted on her chair. "If there's nothing

else, I'd really like to get back inside. Maybe the FBI's heard something."

The concern, the worry, the freaked-out look in Ashley's eyes—all that was real.

"You really love Krissy a lot," Casey said.

"You can't imagine." Ashley rolled the bottle of water between her palms. "Corny as it sounds, I feel like a second mother to her. Like you said, I've helped Judge Willis raise her since she was born, and because of the Willises' long hours, I spend tons of time with her. And she really is the best kid in the world. Cheerful. Smart. She's only in kindergarten, but she's got a second grade reading level. She adds and subtracts faster than I do. And you should see what a whiz she is on the computer. She spends hours on Club Penguin. She chats on it. She colors pictures on it…she's awesome. And her penguin avatar is super cool."

"I'm sure it is." Casey rose. "I think we've covered everything. Let's go inside for an update. Oh, and Ashley…" she added as the younger woman stood up. "Krissy's lucky to have you in her life. You're a wonderful nanny."

"Thank you." Ashley gave a wan smile. "Now if I could only bring her home."

The debriefing session was breaking up when Casey walked into the house. The first thing she did was to seek out Special Agent Peg Harrington.

"Hi, Peg."

"Casey." The trim, forty-two-year-old woman with the short dark hair and intense expression greeted her. "Don told me the Willises had hired you. I don't need to tell you the rules."

"No, you don't. This is your case. My team and I are here to help my clients, and to support you in any way we can. All I need to know is how you're laying out the chain of command."

Peg cleared her throat. "Mr. Willis would prefer that the leadership came from the New York Field Office. So I'll be heading things up, with Ken Barkley as my co-case agent. But the White Plains RA's Task Force and the North Castle Police Department have good people on board, as well. And, of course, you saw the CARD team arrive. Plus, two agents from BAU-3 should be here in an hour," she added, referring to the division of the Behavioral Analysis Unit that dealt with crimes against children. "We're leaving no stone unturned."

Casey nodded. "Anything from the crime scene yet?"

"No. The entire school staff is being interviewed, particularly those who witnessed the incident, and the car-pool mom who had a bird's-eye view. So far, we've come up empty. The Willises are about to release a statement to the media, and issue a plea on TV. We're setting up a tip line for anyone with a potential lead to call in—anyone who might have spotted a silver GMC Acadia with a child inside and the letters 'X' and 'M' in the license plate."

"A suburban car in a suburban neighborhood," Casey mused. "Doesn't exactly raise any red flags."

"Unfortunately, you're right. Not only that, we've got two parents who have more than the average number of grudge-holders who'd love to strike them where it hurts. And what's more powerful than taking their only child?"

Casey grimaced. "Not a thing." She glanced around and watched the FBI team coordinating plans. "Look, Peg, we're probably going to overlap in our suspect interviews. So if there's anyone you want us to talk to, anyone on that list you think we're well suited to gain insights from, just say the word. Like I said, the list of potential suspects is a mile long. And we all want the same thing—Krissy's safe return. So use us as you need to."

"I will." Peg had seen Casey in action enough times to know that she didn't give a damn who got credit for the win. On the flip side, she was equally unmotivated by the rules of bureaucracy. And that sometimes ruffled feathers. "Right now, we're dividing up the list. Once we do, I won't hesitate to take you up on your offer. Count on it."

Once Peg had headed back into the tense huddle that was her team, Casey scanned the area for her own people. Marc was in the hallway, talking to a couple of C-20 agents. Ryan was nowhere to be found, but Casey suspected he was upstairs in Krissy's room, probing things with the agent assigned to analyze Krissy's computer for forensic evidence.

Hope and Edward were currently being prepped for the statement they'd be issuing within the hour on TV. Ashley was right beside them, listening intently. Her physical positioning and her body language were very telling. Casey made a mental note of both.

She then turned and made her way through the lower level of the house. She planned to wait until she could talk to Hope and Edward before she left. After that, when she and her team were armed with enough details to kick into high gear, she planned to drive over to Krissy's school and start conducting some in-depth interviews.

Strolling from room to room, she didn't expect to enter the eerily quiet playroom only to find Claire Hedgleigh sitting cross-legged on the carpet, rolling a crayon between her fingers while her other palm was pressed to a partially finished picture in an open coloring book.

Tears were trickling down her cheeks.

CHAPTER FIVE

Mommy?

Where are you? I'm scared. I don't know where I am. I don't know how I got here.

The picture I finger-painted for you in school is drying. My book bag zipper got stuck. So the bell rang two times before I came out. I was surprised to hear you honk the horn. Surprised but happy. You left work early. You left that bench you always sit on just so we could play. You hadn't even changed out of the black suit I helped you pick out this morning, so you could get to school before Olivia's mommy took me home.

Now I remember that smelly scarf. I tried to tell you it was stinky, but you were talking. Not to me. To somebody else. The car kept moving. I woke up a little. You gave me a drink to make the yucky taste go away.

I feel funny. Am I sick? This is not my bed. And these aren't my pajamas. I don't like pajamas. I get hot and they stick to me. I like nightgowns. Where's my nightgown?

I don't like it here. Was that Daddy's voice before? Is he still here? Are you?

What if you both left?

What if there's no one here but me and Oreo?

I keep calling your name, but you don't come. I called Ashley, too. She didn't answer. I don't want her anyway. I don't want Daddy either. I want you.

Where are you, Mommy?

Please come.

Claire squeezed her eyes shut, reflexively recoiling as the little girl's fear and confusion flowed through her.

The child was becoming more aware. The cobwebs were clearing from her head. And from Claire's. Afraid. So afraid.

Krissy was crying. Big droplets on her eyelashes, cheeks and chin. She was wiping them away with the backs of her hands. The top of Oreo's head was wet from the tears she couldn't catch.

Panic. She was starting to panic. Yelling for her mommy. Sobbing…begging…

"Claire?"

At first the voice didn't penetrate. Then Claire heard it, realized someone was calling her. She jerked back to her current surroundings, blinking as she glanced behind her and saw Casey.

"Are you okay?" Casey asked.

"No." Slowly, Claire rose to her feet, unaware of the dampness on her face. "Krissy is terrified. She doesn't know where she is. And she keeps calling for her mommy."

Casey didn't bat a lash. "You could sense what she was feeling. Was she reliving anything that happened? Anything you could pick up on?"

A slight nod. "Whoever took her was wearing a classic black

suit similar to the ones her mother wears to work. Her hair was blond and parted on the side, just like Judge Willis's."

"Was it real? Or a wig?"

"I don't know. Krissy didn't have a feeling about that...." Claire spread her hands wide in an uncertain gesture. "The woman was wearing dark sunglasses. She was clearly disguising her appearance. But, more important, she was doing her best to impersonate Krissy's mother. Her car. Her hair. A big smile. A welcoming wave."

"And a kidnapping." Casey's mind was racing. "Was Krissy remembering what happened in the car? Was the kidnapper alone? Did she hurt her?"

"I think she chloroformed her, and later drugged her again. And Krissy heard her talking. I didn't sense anyone else in the car, so I'm guessing she was on the phone."

"Probably talking to whoever she's working with—or for." Casey pushed on. "What else did you sense? Where's Krissy now? Could you see her surroundings? Who was with her? Anything at all that could help us find her?"

This time Claire hesitated. "Casey, I really should talk to the police first."

"You probably should. But it's freshest in your mind now. The cops are in meetings, getting their assignments so they can head out and start interviewing. I'm here. I'll memorize everything you say. I can be there when you talk to the task force, so that just in case a detail starts to fade, we'll ensure you give them the clearest and most comprehensive picture possible." A pause. "Claire, you've worked with me before. All I want is for that little girl to be found before it's too late. So tell me what you remember."

"She wants her nightgown," Claire replied quietly. "She

doesn't like pajamas, but she's wearing flannel ones. She's in a downstairs bedroom, behind a door with a lock on the outside and a separate one on the inside for when the kidnapper is with her. No one's there now. She heard voices before, but now it's silent, and she's frantic for her mommy."

"The room—did you see it?"

"Flashes of it, yes. It's bare. Quiet. There's a canopied bed with a white bedspread that has little gold crowns on it and pink ruffles all around the sides. There's enough light in the room, but it's from a lamp on the nightstand. No sunlight. And no window. Just four pale pink walls and a bare carnation-pink carpet. Like an institutional room, but with a few personal touches."

"No surprise," Casey responded. "The main offender is most likely a man. He'll want to put Krissy in an environment where she feels totally vulnerable, but surrounded by enough personal touches to lower her defenses and convince her that he cares. That'll provide him with the greatest sense of control. As for the little-girl decor, I'm sure that's courtesy of his female accomplice. She'll do it for him, but I'm hoping that a small part of her will also do it for Krissy. That would mean the woman feels a shred of pity or compassion—up to the point where she'd be crossing the line and jeopardizing her own safety. If that's true, we can use her emotions to our advantage."

Claire nodded, walking over and picking up the coloring book and crayons. "I'm going to find the North Castle detectives."

"Assuming they're still here," Casey reminded her. "It's possible that everyone's out doing their job and that the only law enforcement here are whoever Peg assigned to the Willises and the phones."

"Then I'll talk to them."

"Do you want me to be there?"

"No." A raw pause. "In this case, my recall is one hundred percent—unfortunately."

"I can imagine." Casey didn't envy Claire's gift. It had to be enormously painful at times like this. "Whoever you talk to, just don't do it in front of the Willises. They're about to give a media statement, and the BAU isn't here yet to coach them. The last thing they need is to hear that Krissy is terrified and locked up—for God knows what purpose. We can talk to them later. We'll make sure to emphasize the fact that Krissy is alive."

Halfway to the door, Claire paused, looking at Casey as if she were truly seeing her for the first time. "You're very insightful."

"So's my whole team," Casey replied. "It's something that you and I should discuss—when the time is right."

Claire's eyebrows drew together in puzzlement. "Okay. We will."

Just after Claire left the room, Casey's BlackBerry rang. She glanced down at the caller ID. No surprise at what she saw.

She punched on the phone. "Hey."

"Hey, yourself," said a deep, masculine voice. "I wanted you to know that I'm in your neck of the woods. I've got a case in Westchester County. I'm not sure when I can break away, but when I do, can we get together? Maybe later tonight?"

"Oh, a lot sooner than that," Casey assured him. "I'm at the Willises' house right now. I assume that's where you're headed?"

A sharp intake of breath. "They hired you already?"

"What can I say? They've got good taste. Just like you." Casey's light banter vanished. "I'm glad you're coming. We've got to find Krissy Willis before she's killed—or worse. Hurry."

* * *

Casey got the Willises alone before the BAU-3 team arrived to prep them.

"After your TV statement, my team and I are going over to Krissy's school," Casey told them. "We'll be interviewing a few specific staff members."

"Why just a few?" Hope interrupted. She leaned forward, lowering her voice. "Please, Ms. Woods, don't skim the surface just because the authorities are pressuring you. I hired you because of your creativity, your track record and your freedom to push the boundaries. Edward and I are both lawyers. We know the drill. Law enforcement is bound by rules that you can circumvent. So circumvent them. Do whatever you have to. Do it thoroughly. And do it fast."

"I intend to." Casey spoke as quietly as her client. "Don't confuse specificity with reticence. If I think someone on your list is a person of interest, I'll delve into their background, even if our investigation overlaps with the FBI's. But if my instincts tell me they're a dead end, it would be a waste of time to pursue them when I could be devoting my attention to more likely suspects, or people who could lead me in the right direction. I especially want to talk to Liza Bock, the car-pool mom who saw Krissy jump into the kidnapper's car. I also want to talk to her daughter, Olivia, and all Krissy's other friends. Kids very often know more than they think they do. The FBI task force will cover the gamut." *Particularly the sex offenders,* she thought silently and grimly. "Let us cover the probable."

Hope nodded. "All right." She handed Casey a stack of papers, including everything she'd given to Peg Harrington: a full list of personal names and each individual's relationship to Krissy, and pages and pages of professional names that Hope and Edward had come up with as potential enemies, resentful plaintiffs and/or defendants, parents who'd lost custody of their children, and all the other people who might hold a grudge against them.

"I'll review all this and get started," Casey said. She thumbed through the pages. "First come the angry parents. An eye for an eye would be strong motivation. Ferreting through that part of the list and interviewing the right candidates will be my job. I'll have Ryan concentrate on trimming down the list to the most logical thinkers among those. Whoever orchestrated this was sharp, focused and intelligent. And Marc will zero in on those who have the greatest access to you, your home and your day-to-day lives, plus anyone with a criminal record. You have no idea how fast and thorough we are. Have faith."

"I'm trying." Tears slid down Hope's cheeks. "But she's my baby."

"I know," Casey replied gently. "And, on all fronts, you've got the best of the best working for her safe return."

"Hey." Marc came up behind Casey. "Speaking of which, the BAU's here. They sent Hutch."

Casey half-turned. "Yes, I know. He called a little while ago." She watched as the familiar, commanding presence of SSA Kyle Hutchinson filled the room. For a man who epitomized the word *reserved,* Hutch managed to take charge without even trying. There was a natural, compelling quality about him that screamed leadership. From the power of his build, the innate confidence he exuded, even the jagged scar across his left temple—a souvenir of his days as a Washington, D.C., police detective—the whole package yanked everyone's gaze his way and told them he was someone of significant importance.

He never gave credence to those reactions. As always, he had just one purpose in mind. Doing his job.

He pressed forward, his sharp blue eyes focused on the Willises. Right behind Hutch was his partner, SSA Grace Masters, who was every bit as formidable as her partner. Anyone fooled by her slender build or wavy, light brown hair was an ass. She had a steel-trap mind, guts and grit to spare and an unflappable personality. Hutch's expressions were unreadable. Grace's were well thought out and executed. The two pros had worked together for years, and now brainstormed with the ease of a long-term partnership, and the precision of a surgeon's scalpel.

"Marc. Casey." Hutch nodded at each of them, then shifted his attention to the Willises. "I'm Supervisory Special Agent Kyle Hutchinson and this is my partner, Supervisory Special Agent Grace Masters. We're from the FBI's Behavioral Analysis Unit." He and Grace shook the Willises' hands.

"You're here to profile the bastard who took my daughter," Edward stated.

"We're here to behaviorally analyze the crime to help the investigative team do their job," Grace replied. "But, yes, we'll zero in on motivation, personality types, number of offenders—anything that will lead us to your daughter's kidnapper or kidnappers."

"Let's put off the details for now." Hutch nipped Edward's questions in the bud. "We've got to deal with the immediate. You're going on TV in ten minutes. So let's get you prepped and ready."

CHAPTER SIX

Claudia Mitchell was ironing and watching a rerun of one of her favorite TV comedies when a special report interrupted. Breaking news. An Amber Alert had been issued. Krissy Willis, the five-year-old daughter of Family Court Judge Hope Willis and prominent defense attorney Edward Willis had been kidnapped.

The parents appeared on-screen, ready to speak.

Quickly, Claudia turned off her iron and set it down on the stand, hurrying over to turn up the volume. The Willises were issuing a statement, a plea, begging for their child's safe return. Claudia stared at Judge Willis, the woman to whom she'd been court clerk for years. In all the time she'd known her, Claudia had never seen or heard her like this. No makeup. Panicked. A lost look in her eyes. Choked sobs in her voice. For a woman who was always put together and in complete control, it was a startling sight.

But why shouldn't she look like death warmed over? Her little girl was missing. The most important person in her life had been taken away, and could be lost forever.

It was a terrible ordeal, one that elicited great sympathy. It made Claudia wonder if maybe Judge Willis would have gone easier on her, shown her more compassion, if she'd already endured this life-altering trauma before she'd fired Claudia. At that time, Claudia had felt just the way Judge Willis felt now. Terrified and helpless. Alone. Joe had just ended their engagement and walked out of her life. Claudia had believed the decision was permanent.

Joe was her whole world. So, yes, she'd gone to pieces. And Judge Willis had tolerated it for a month, maybe two. Then, she'd let Claudia go, saying her work was unsatisfactory and that her improper management of the docket was compromising courtroom procedure.

So Claudia found herself not only alone but unemployed. And, given the state she was in, she was in no condition to seek employment elsewhere. Her entire life was in shambles.

Now maybe Judge Willis would understand. But, actually, how could she? Krissy wasn't her whole world. She was barely a part of it, given the number of hours the judge worked. The precious child was raised by a nanny, not a mother and father.

And Judge Willis would never be alone. She had a husband. Money. And now she was saying something about taking a leave of absence until her daughter was found and brought home safe and sound. A leave of absence? Her job would still be waiting for her. Her career would be intact. And she'd be held in high regard for her maternal commitment, rather than stared at like an emotional basket case.

Given the circumstances, Claudia felt a wave of guilt, which dissipated beneath the weight of an overwhelming sadness. She could still remember the first time Krissy had visited Judge Willis's courtroom, her wide-eyed excitement when she'd sat in her mother's chair and held her gavel. She was a wonderful child. None of what had happened was her fault. The poor little girl. She needed love, security. She didn't need—

The front door swung open, and Joe walked into the house. Claudia rushed out of the kitchen to greet him. She still couldn't believe her good fortune. He'd come back to her. The circumstances didn't matter. He'd come back.

"Joe." She put her hand on his arm, stopping him before he could pass by on his way to the basement.

He looked annoyed, glancing up from the video game he'd purchased and was now reading a description of. "What?"

"Judge Willis is on TV. She's announcing that her daughter was kidnapped, and she's pleading for her safe return."

"I heard about it on the car radio," he replied. "The little girl will be fine. And I wouldn't get any pangs over the judge—not after what she's done. I'm heading downstairs. You start dinner."

"But, Joe..."

His gaze hardened. "I'm not in the mood, Claudia. Let it go. I don't want to repeat myself. Do you understand?"

"I understand." Quickly, she released his arm and backed off. "I'll peel the potatoes."

"Good."

"When will you be coming up?"

"I'm not sure. I have a new game to try out."

It was almost midnight.

The Forensic Instincts team gathered around the brownstone

conference table, reviewing their notes, their accomplished tasks and their plans. The Willises' TV statement had gone off without a hitch. The FBI task force was utilizing the lower-level media room of the Willis house as their command center. In addition, all the telephone recording devices and the toll-free tip line were in place, and concerned citizens—along with the usual cranksters—were starting to call in. The interviewing process had long since commenced and would be continuing round-the-clock.

Casey had spent another hour with the Willises—including a half hour alone with Hope—filling in some crucial blanks.

Armed with their individual information, it was time for the team to regroup.

Ryan began by describing what he'd learned in conjunction with the forensic computer specialist who was doing a cursory sweep of Krissy's computer before removing it for a thorough evidential analysis. No real surprises. As expected, Krissy was a normal, if precocious, five-year-old whose only computer activities appeared to include games, crafts and chats via her avatar.

Whether or not one of her chat buddies was, in fact, a child predator laying the groundwork to get his hands on her remained to be seen. Once the computer reached the lab, an in-depth investigation would be conducted.

Marc reported in next, telling them that he'd used his FBI clout to gain info that would cross a chunk of suspects off the list—although he was still bugged by Sal and Rita Diaz, the Willises's gardener and housekeeper, who happened to be husband and wife and who the BU had ruled out due to confirmed alibis. Alleged alibis or not, Marc still viewed them as a couple who'd maxed out on all their credit cards and who were in debt up to their eyeballs. A couple who constantly had their noses shoved in the Willises' affluence, and who might very well feel they wanted a piece of it. A couple with a husband who had a history of bar fights, and a wife who was clearly cowed into submission.

It was a classic setup for a kidnapping—except for the fact that two separate employers had vouched for their whereabouts all afternoon, and that no ransom demands had come in. Still, Marc wasn't ready to let it go.

Casey had talked to all the car-pool mothers, particularly to Liza Bock. And, while she hadn't learned anything glaringly new, the evasiveness she'd encountered—on a whole different front—had raised her antennae and convinced her that her earlier suspicions were well-founded.

"I think Edward Willis is sleeping with Ashley Lawrence," she announced.

"The nanny?" Marc arched an eyebrow. He looked more intrigued than surprised. Very little about human nature surprised him these days—certainly not an affair.

"Yup." Casey leaned forward and propped her elbows on the conference table. "All the signs are there—Ashley's body language and her bickering with her boyfriend. Edward's antagonism toward us and absurdly forced show of protectiveness toward his wife. The weird dynamic that permeates the house. Affection mixed with tension and a hint of desperation, not to mention a healthy dose of anger and mistrust. Hope cares for her husband, but she's resigned herself to his career-immersed absence from her life and from Krissy's. Judging from the way she pulls into herself and away from her husband, I'd be shocked if she doesn't suspect there's another woman—and equally shocked if she thought it was Ashley. As for Ashley, she adores Krissy, but feels guilty as hell about something. And Edward is an arrogant, egocentric powermonger, who's perfectly suited for his job, and for screwing over his family."

"Does that include grabbing his kid and his hot young nanny and taking off for parts unknown?" Ryan asked.

"Uh-uh." Casey shook her head. "He loves his daughter—as much as he's capable of loving anyone—but he sure as hell doesn't want full responsibility for her. Any more than he wants a life with that hot young nanny. What he wants is exactly what he's got—the whole nine yards. A perfect little family. Great sex from a young woman who worships him. And a prestigious legal practice that he'd never in a million years leave. It feeds his bank account and his ego. Nope. Edward's got a good thing here. He just doesn't want us to blow it by telling Hope. As it is, he knows he's under the FBI's microscope, since he's Krissy's father and, therefore, a prime suspect. So he's not a happy camper."

Marc was tapping his pencil against his leg. Now he hunched over and drew a line through two names. "So we're crossing off the nanny and her loser boyfriend. What about other relatives—grandparents, siblings, aunts and uncles?"

"Edward's an only child. Both parents deceased," Casey responded. "Hope, as you know, has a much more complicated past. After her twin sister, Felicity, was kidnapped and the trail went cold, her parents' marriage fell apart. Her father started drinking heavily. He and his wife divorced. He took off, never to be heard from again. The wife, Vera, came close to a nervous breakdown. Having a six-year-old who needed her kept her from going over the edge. She still lives in the same house the twins grew up in. Hope says that part of her mother never gave up praying that Felicity would come home."

"Where is this house?"

"New Rochelle. A solid half hour away. Vera Akerman is

too shaken and heavily medicated to drive herself. For obvious reasons, Krissy's kidnapping is bringing back the worst memories of her life. But she needs to be with her daughter. So Hope's arranged for a car service to pick her up and bring her to Armonk."

"Do you plan to interview her?" Ryan asked.

"Gently, but yes. Tomorrow afternoon. I want to give her some time alone with her daughter."

"I agree," Marc said with a nod. "It's doubtful she can cast any light on Krissy's kidnapper anyway. In the meantime, let's move on. I scanned some internet articles on recent cases Edward was involved with as defense counsel. A few of them raised some red flags. Wealthy, white-collar scumbags, with backgrounds that scream violence. I'm sure they're guilty of the crimes they were charged with committing, but are instead free as birds, living the good life, thanks to Edward Willis. I already called in a few favors. I'll be getting a look at the court transcripts. Then, I'll be paying a few visits."

"How soon?" Casey asked.

"Tomorrow morning. I'll be pounding the pavement by noon."

Casey's head dropped back against the chair's backrest, and she blew out a frustrated breath. "We're fighting the clock. Krissy's already been missing for longer than the first crucial hours. Peg told me they have nothing solid from the call-ins. And there's been no contact about ransom. None."

"Child predator," Marc muttered. "You know that's what Hutch and Grace are going to come up with."

"Yes," Casey said quietly. "I know. But there are too many unique personal details here for our kidnapper to be a random sex offender, even one with a fetish for little girls. He specifically wanted Krissy. Why? We have to tie the two together." A pause. "I plan on being at Krissy's school tomorrow, and talking to her friends during recess. The parents all gave me permission, as did the school. It's a comfortable environment, and the kids won't feel pressured. I'll keep it light. But I'll get what I can. Tonight, I'm running through the list of disgruntled parents from Hope's family court. I'll talk to as many of them as I can tomorrow. Oh, and I'll also be talking to Claudia Mitchell, Hope's former court clerk. Seems she broke up with her fiancé recently, and skitzed out enough so that Hope had to fire her."

"Both of you are going to step on more than a few law enforcement toes tomorrow," Ryan said thoughtfully. "So let's keep me out of the mix to minimize the collateral damage. Give me the lists. I'll hole up and do some in-depth searches. Based on what I find, I'll put together likely scenarios for the suspects I think have not only the motive, means and opportunity, but the brain power and access to the right people to pull this off. I take it we're looking for a main player who's male and a compliant accomplice who's female."

"I think so, yes." That triggered another issue in Casey's mind. "I believe that Krissy's being held in a basement that was converted into a princess-pink bedroom. The woman who took her impersonated Hope, right down to her tailored black suit. She drugged her and took her to wherever she is. As of late afternoon, Krissy was terrified and isolated, but still alive."

"How do you know..." Ryan broke off, rolling his eyes. "You've been talking to Claire-voyant. I saw her wandering around the house. I don't know why the cops—and you—listen to her."

"Because ninety percent of the time she's right," Casey shot back. She steeled herself, and went for it, head-on. "You know

I plan to expand Forensic Instincts. I think we need a better balance to the group. We've got logic up the yin-yang. A little ethereal input would be good for us. I've done my homework, Ryan. Claire Hedgleigh's the real deal. I want to hire her."

"Ah, shit." Ryan slapped his palm on the table.

Casey ignored him, turning to Marc. "Ryan's feelings are obvious. Yours?"

Marc pursed his lips, silently weighing the question. "You know I'm not a big believer in psychics," he replied at last. "The fit's not going to be easy. But I do see your point. I know Claire's success rate. That's fact, not speculation. Do you know if she's interested?"

"Not a clue," Casey answered honestly. "I wanted to talk to the two of you before I broached the subject. So I take it you're not opposed?"

A corner of Marc's mouth lifted. "How tough is she? There's going to be a lot of infighting going on. Can she take it?"

"Not a doubt." Casey arched a brow in Ryan's direction. "Can you?"

Ryan met Casey's gaze. "I can take anything. But I'm not going easy on her. If I think she's spouting crap, I'll say so."

"Are you going to go after her on purpose?"

"I'm not in middle school, Casey. If you think she's a value-add, I won't fight you—or her—unless I disagree. Which I probably will. But I'll make it work, if it makes the group stronger."

"Good. Because I think it will." Casey rose. "Why don't the two of you go home and get some rest. We never did sleep off the Fisher case. Plus, I want to hit the ground running first thing tomorrow." She frowned. "It makes me ill that Krissy Willis is out there tonight, scared to death, and possibly being violated in some sick way."

"Sexual predators don't wait for bedtime, Casey," Marc reminded her quietly. "If that's who has her, time is what matters. Not time of day."

"I know." Casey raked a hand through her hair. "And I'd pound the pavement all night, if I thought that Peg Harrington wouldn't cut us off at the knees. We've got to play ball a little or the Feds will kick us out on our asses. They'll be out there 24/7. So I'll spend tonight reviewing my notes and seeing if something I haven't spotted yet jumps out at me."

"You get some rest, too," Ryan advised, yawning as he came to his feet. "You've got a packed day tomorrow."

"Will do."

But both guys knew that meant "won't do." Just as they knew they'd be burning the midnight oil themselves.

It was well past two in the morning when Casey's doorbell rang.

She'd been scribbling notes in the margins of her lists, and had pretty much reached a roadblock that couldn't be skirted until the morning's interviews.

She put down her pen and smiled. Only one person had the stamina, the tenacity and the incentive to show up on her doorstep at this ungodly hour.

She went down the two flights of stairs and peeked outside. Then she unlocked the door and pulled it open.

"Hi," she greeted her guest with a smug grin. "Here for breakfast?"

Hutch walked inside, kicked the door shut and dragged Casey into his arms. "Damn straight." He was already unbuttoning her shirt as he covered her mouth with his. He lifted her off the floor and turned sharply, pressing her against the wall as he continued yanking off her clothes. “First time will be right here,” he muttered, his voice rough with desire. “Then I’ll take you to bed.”

“It’s four flights,” she reminded him breathlessly, unzipping his fly. “I might not leave you with the strength.”

“Try me.”

“I plan to.”

CHAPTER SEVEN

Day Two

Krissy rolled over and hugged Oreo. She buried her face in his soft fur. Like always when it was dark. And here, it stayed dark whenever the lamp wasn't on. The night-light helped. It looked just like hers. It kept her from getting too scared.

The bed was soft. The blanket was, too. And she was wearing a nightgown now. The pajamas were gone. They'd been gone for a long time.

With her eyes shut, she could pretend she was home. She hadn't been able to do that before. Too many bad things had happened. But since she drank the milkshake, the bad things were going away. She felt warm and sleepy. She'd been happy to climb into bed. The hand that stroked her hair as she went to sleep felt like her mommy's. The voice was gentle like her mommy's. Maybe she'd dreamed the whole scary day.

Maybe when the lamp went back on, she'd be in her own bed. Then she could tell her mommy about the bad nightmare.

If her mommy had already left for work, she could always tell Ashley.

But she didn't really want to.

Not anymore.

With a huge yawn, Casey towel-dried her hair. The sun was just rising outside her bathroom window. An hour and ten minutes of sleep. Not exactly the requisite amount for a productive day. Yet Casey had never felt more energized. If it weren't for the case preying on her mind, she would have loved nothing more than to stay in bed with Hutch until noon, making up for lost time. He was an amazing lover, and with weeks, sometimes months, separating their visits, the intensity of their time together was pretty damned breath catching.

But those extra hours were not meant to be. Not this time. Not when both of them were committed to finding Krissy Willis.

Casey came out of the bathroom to find Hutch tossing aside his towel and pulling on his clothes. He glanced up as she walked across the bedroom in her terry robe, and shot her a very sexy, very sated grin.

"Thanks for the best shower I've had in ages," he said. "I barely remember getting clean."

"You did," she assured him. "I washed your back myself."

"Among other parts."

"And you returned the favor."

Hutch pulled her against him for a long, deep kiss. "To be continued tonight."

"It's a date."

"By the way," he told her, shrugging into his shirt and buttoning it. "I brought you a present."

Casey's brows rose. "Really. What is it?"

"First comes the *where.* Then the *what.*"

"Now you've really got me curious."

"Good." Hutch finished buttoning his shirt. "Then give me a half hour. I'll be back with two cups of strong coffee, and your gift."

"It's in your car?"

"Nope. But close by. And that's all I'm going to say." He gave her a sly wink. "See you in thirty."

True to his word, Hutch knocked on the door twenty-eight minutes later.

Casey opened the door, and blinked. She was expecting the cardboard tray of steaming coffee that Hutch clutched in his right hand. But she wasn't expecting the leash wrapped around his left. Or what was at the other end—a handsome red bloodhound. The dog sat obediently by Hutch's side, his deep hazel eyes soulful and curious, his high-curved tail wagging back and forth as he stared at Casey.

"Your gift has arrived," Hutch announced.

"A bloodhound?" Stunned, Casey found herself bending down and stroking the dog's glossy head. "You brought me a bloodhound?"

"Not just any bloodhound. A human scent evidence dog. Certified, but retired. Hero drove up with Grace and me. He came straight from Quantico. He fulfilled his two-and-a-half years of training. Unfortunately, after his certification, his handler discovered that he was a terrible air traveler. Which doesn't cut it. The team hated retiring him—evidently, he was a star pupil in his training class. But they had no choice. Anyway, I spoke to the breeder and offered to find a new home for him. I knew how much you wanted a dog, particularly a bloodhound. Now you have one."

"A human scent evidence dog," Casey murmured, still stroking Hero's head. Hutch was right. She was crazy about dogs. She'd had one most of her life. And bloodhounds were a particular passion of hers. She and Target, her last bloodhound, had gone through tracking and trailing classes together, right up to the time when he'd passed away at the ripe old age of twelve. She missed those classes terribly. But the time commitment was too extensive for her to continue once she'd started Forensic Instincts. Still, the company was under control now, growing but settled. And bloodhounds were noble and unique—far too special to pass up. Plus, her life seemed a little empty without a canine companion.

"Like I said, he just turned three," Hutch was telling her. "He's sharp, fiercely loyal, and has an olfactory sense that's off the charts. Oh, and his instincts are keen, so he'll even fit in with your company name."

A smile curved Casey's lips. "Hey, Hero," she greeted him, scratching his long ears. "I love your name. And I have a gut feeling it suits you."

In response, Hero crossed the threshold and began slobbering enthusiastically at Casey's face.

"I take it you know they drool," Hutch commented.

"Profusely." Casey laughed. "And they're stubborn as hell. Sounds like most men."

"Very cute."

"I thought so." Casey turned her attention back to Hero. "We have only a small backyard for you. The good news is that the fence is so high, you won't be taking off." Casey sprawled on the floor so she could rub Hero's white underbelly. "Also,

Tribeca has a couple of fabulous parks that would give us room to maintain your trailing skills. Plus, I could take you out for a morning and an evening jog. You won't even have time to be lonely. Marc and Ryan are in and out all day, and they'd be thrilled to have you join the team. They're both stubborn, too, yes, so you'll have your work cut out for you. Between the two of them and me, you'll have plenty of play pals. How's that sound, Hero?"

"And, whenever you can't be around, Casey, there's a great place just a few blocks from here that offers everything from doggie day care to five-star hotel service," Hutch added. "Believe me, I saw it firsthand. That's where Hero spent the night. His accommodations made mine look like a Dumpster."

Casey tilted back her head and gazed up at Hutch. "You knew I couldn't say no to this gift, didn't you?"

"I was pretty sure, yeah." He grinned. "I have a crate, food and a bunch of other essentials in my car. The rest is up to you. So, what's the verdict? Does Hero have a new home?"

Hero perked up at the sound of his name. He looked so erect and professional that Casey could swear he was applying for a job.

"Welcome to Forensic Instincts, Hero," Casey said in response. She massaged his jowls, then scrambled to her feet. "Let's get you settled. Then we'll give Ryan a call and ask him to pop up here ASAP. You two need to meet, since both Marc and I have a ton of interviews to conduct and Ryan can do everything from here today."

"Sounds like a plan." Hutch gulped his coffee. "I'll get Hero's gear from my car. Then I've got to run. Grace and I have to get over to the Willis place."

"And I'm starting out at Krissy's school. Maybe her little

friends know something they don't even realize they know. Someone hanging around the school, or pulling up in a car to talk to Krissy. I've got a zillion bases to cover."

"As do I." Hutch gave her a quick kiss and Hero a quick scratch behind the ears. "I'm sorry for an abrupt end to a great night."

"You'll make it up to me," Casey assured him with a twinkle in her eye. "You've already made a down payment by bringing me my new best friend."

Casey called Hope as she drove up to Armonk. "Any news?"

"Nothing." Hope sounded like she was about to shatter. "The FBI task force has been working all night, crossing names off the suspect list, establishing alibis and manning the phones. I'm a mess. My mother's due here in an hour, and I don't know how I'm going to keep it together for her."

"Where's your husband?"

"At the office." A pause. "He was going crazy sitting around here, waiting for a ransom call or a breakthrough. But he's ready to come home at the drop of a hat," she added quickly in his defense.

Casey refrained from responding. "I'm on my way to Krissy's school. Then I'm checking out some of the parents on the losing end in your courtroom, as well as Claudia Mitchell."

"Claudia?" Hope sounded horrified. "I know she was hurt and angry when I let her go. But do you really think she's capable of kidnapping a child?"

"I don't know. But no one's above suspicion, and I'm leaving no stone unturned. My whole team is on the move. I'll stop by the house later. In the meantime, call me with any updates."

"I will."

★ ★ ★

Claire Hedgleigh circled the area in the school parking lot where the car that had taken Krissy away had picked her up. The vibes here were dark. Something ugly had definitely happened. And it had taken Krissy totally by surprise. By the time she understood what was going on, it was too late.

With a heavy heart, Claire squatted down and touched the pavement, willing herself to sense more.

Nothing.

"Claire?" Casey walked out of the school, spotted Claire and approached her.

"Hi, Casey." Claire rose and turned around to face her. "This is the spot where Krissy was kidnapped. It took less than ten seconds for the automatic door locks to close her in and the handkerchief to cover Krissy's nose and mouth. Another ten seconds and the car was speeding off. Krissy never had time to react."

Chilling though it was, none of that information surprised Casey. She joined Claire precisely where she stood, and peered over her shoulder. "A well-chosen spot. Out of the surveillance cameras' field of view."

Claire followed her gaze. "I didn't think of that. Obviously, we have an intelligent kidnapper on our hands."

"You said you sensed Krissy. Is she still alive?"

A helpless shrug. "I don't know. I haven't connected with her since you and I last spoke. I'm trying to pick up on something—anything. Last night, I took home one of Krissy's favorite T-shirts. But, so far, nothing. That doesn't mean she's alive, or that she's not. It just means that I can't will these connections to come. They just do." Claire gave Casey a measured look. "Unless you're one of those people who secretly thinks I'm either crazy or a fraud."

"Nope." Casey shook her head. "I have the greatest respect for your abilities. In fact, that's what I wanted to talk to you about. I know you enjoy working for law enforcement. But I'm eager to hire you away. I want you on board at Forensic Instincts."

Claire started at the blunt and unexpected invitation. "You want to hire me?"

"Uh-huh. On a permanent basis, salary, benefits and all."

"But you know almost nothing about me."

"To the contrary, I know a lot about you, starting with your impressive educational background. I know how many cases you've worked on. I know your success ratio. I know that you hate the term *psychic,* because you see it as clichéd and commercial. So do I, by the way. I know that you attribute your metaphysical abilities to claircognizance. I know that claircognizance is perceiving things without being able to understand or explain how or why, but just accepting that you do. I've heard you say that sometimes you awaken from a dream with a clear vision of something that's either happened or is about to happen. I've watched you hold a victim's personal items in your hands and have what others called visions. Terminology doesn't matter. Neither do nonbelievers. You use your gift as a tool to help others, and with great success. Now, do you still think I know nothing about you?"

For a long moment, Claire just stared, looking both astonished and flattered. It wasn't often that her talents were so highly regarded, and certainly not so thoroughly researched.

"I'm not sure what to say," she replied at last. "I'm a little taken aback. This is the last thing I expected when you said you wanted to talk."

"Well, now you know. I don't expect an answer on the spot. But would you consider it?"

"Probably." Claire was nothing if not honest. "I'd be lying if I said I wouldn't welcome a work environment where my abilities were fully utilized." A pause. "But I have to ask the obvious. Have you discussed this with your team? Because I seriously doubt Ryan will be all smiles about this."

"I have, and he is." Casey's lips curved. "Did he put up a fight when I brought it up? Sure. Is he skeptical? You know the answer to that. Was he pissed off when I made him pull all that research on you? Of course. But I see your differences as a plus. Healthy debate, bringing different viewpoints to the mix, is what produces the best results. Marc approaches things with an investigative and analytical eye. Ryan is more strategic and technological. I'm all about the psychological, and I tend to go with my gut. We need a spiritual eye to round things out. You'd bring balance to the team. Even Ryan didn't argue with that. He just promised to challenge you along the way."

Claire rolled her eyes. "Gee, what a surprise. Actually, I thought it would be worse. I thought he'd write me off as a freak, and threaten to quit if I joined the company."

A chuckle. "Ryan's not nearly as narrow-minded as he acts when he's around you. Give him a chance. Give the group a chance. I promise, at the very least, you'll never be bored."

"Now *that* never occurred to me," Claire responded drily. "Can you give me a day or two to think about it? Especially since I'm committed to the North Castle police on this kidnapping case."

"Of course. Right now, I don't want you to invest time in anything except finding Krissy Willis. We'll pick this conversation up after that. Oh, one more thing. You're not allergic to or afraid of dogs, are you?"

"No. Why?"

"We got a new team member as of this morning. His name's Hero, a bloodhound, trained and certified as a human scent evidence dog." Casey found herself smiling again. "In fact, Ryan's showing him the ropes this morning. I'm sure I'll have colorful stories waiting for me when I get back."

"Oh, I'm sure you will." Claire glanced over at the school building. "Did you interview teachers?"

"Teachers, custodial staff, mostly the ones who were on the scene when Krissy was taken," Casey replied. "I didn't learn anything new. And I certainly didn't get the sense that any of them was involved."

"Nor did I." Claire frowned, staring at the concrete spot where Krissy had disappeared. "The only vibes I'm getting are right here. And they leave me cold. Cold and dark."

Before Casey could respond, her cell phone rang. She scanned the number on her caller ID. "It's Hope Willis," she announced as she punched on the phone. "Yes, Hope." A pause. "I'm on my way." She turned to Claire. "A lead was called in on the toll-free tip line regarding the car that kidnapped Krissy. The tip was legit. The NYPD found the car. I'm heading over to the Willises'."

"I'll follow you."

CHAPTER EIGHT

The car used to kidnap Krissy had been dumped in a South Bronx lot, and stripped clean during its hours sitting on garbage-strewn asphalt. The task force had traced the vehicle to a car rental company at Kennedy airport. The GMC Acadia had been rented using a fake ID and credit card. The signature on the rental agreement was no more than chicken scratch. And, given the high level of activity at the company's location, most of the employees had no memory of the customer who'd rented that specific car a full day ago. One employee vaguely remembered a woman wearing a hat and sunglasses who might be the person the cops were looking for. Overall, the only thing the employees knew was that the Acadia had yet to be returned and was overdue.

At this point, it was never going back. It was disemboweled—*and* evidence in a crime.

An immediate evidentiary sweep by ERT showed nothing.

Other than some smudges, there were no discernible fingerprints on the vehicle. The offender had obviously wiped them clean before abandoning it. And the car had been ransacked by so many people that there was no way a bloodhound could differentiate the specific scent of the kidnapper. Not to mention there was very little left to smell. The Acadia was as picked clean as a Thanksgiving turkey.

So it was back to square one. Sort of.

"The kidnapper had to leave Krissy somewhere before dumping the car. She wouldn't risk taking her along," Casey said to Peg.

"Nope." Peg shook her head. "The odometer indicates she went straight to the dumping site from Krissy's school. My guess? She met the main offender there, got rid of the car and took off with him—and Krissy."

"These kidnappers aren't stupid," Casey replied, blowing out a breath. "They knew how to plan. And they know how to elude us."

"The BAU is fine-tuning their profile, and filling in the task force now. I just came from there. Feel free to go to the command center and listen, since the Willises are going to fill you in anyway. You might as well have your facts straight when you narrow down your list of suspects." Peg glanced over at Claire. "The North Castle police have invited you to attend, as well."

"Thank you."

Grace and Hutch were explaining the profile, as well as the inconsistencies of the offender or offenders who'd taken Krissy, when Casey and Claire walked in.

"Unless this is the first in an upcoming pattern of incidents, there's no evidence that we're dealing with a serial offender,"

Grace was saying. "As a result we have to treat this as an isolated event. It still could be a kidnapping for ransom, although that's looking less likely with no contact from the kidnapper. But that motive can't be ruled out, especially when the parents are notably affluent."

"Are we dealing with one offender or two?" asked one of the North Castle police detectives.

"Our guess is two, simply because of the complex way the crime was carried out and the stats. If our unsub is a child predator, he's most likely a white male in his thirties, who works with or hangs around children, maybe through coaching or volunteer work. He'd be either unattached or in a nonsexual relationship, and he'd enjoy childlike activities like building model airplanes or playing computer games. He'd probably have endured childhood abuse, and be harboring latent anger, which would flare up if anyone threatened to stand between himself and his victim. The person who kidnapped Krissy Willis was female. Could she be acting alone? Possibly. There are a small percentage of child predators who are female."

"So you're definitely thinking this is a sexual offense."

"That's certainly right up there on the list," Hutch replied. "But there are variables that just don't fit—not the offender or the victim. Normally, a child predator has a much less complicated M.O. This one went to a hell of a lot of trouble to snatch one specific child. The typical child predator operates in a simpler and more invisible way. He seeks out a withdrawn, vulnerable child. Krissy is neither of those, nor is she an easy target. Her parents are both very high-profile people, and they're both very present in their daughter's life."

"Which might give a certain type of offender a sense of power," Casey commented from the rear of the room.

Hutch angled his head in her direction and nodded. "It might. That's another gray area, both in terms of profile and motive. Whoever's running the show here is either unbothered by, or turned on by formulating a plan that's intricate and in our faces. He or she is smart. This crime was well planned and well researched. There wasn't an iota of impulsiveness about it. And it's personal. Krissy Willis is personal. Whoever took her wanted her, and her specifically. Which smacks of either a need for power or revenge."

"If that's true, this won't end as a quiet closed case," Casey responded. "The offender will want notoriety, or recognition. Krissy will turn up."

"In one form or another, yes." Hutch's tone was grim. "Our job is to find her before she 'turns up,' and to find her alive."

Marc sat calmly in the waiting room of Dr. Brian A. Pierson, flipping through the pages of a medical magazine. The renowned neurologist's office, which until several months ago had been crammed with patients, was relatively quiet. And getting a new patient appointment, which would normally mean a lengthy waiting period, had been a snap. Not a surprise, given that the doctor's name and photo had been splashed all over newspapers since he'd been charged with murdering his wife in cold blood. The evidence against him was staggering. There wasn't a doubt in Marc's mind that the SOB was guilty. And not just of murder. Through his discreet but well-informed contacts, Marc had uncovered all kinds of ugly little secrets about the renowned neurologist. Pierson should be rotting in prison, not making hundreds of dollars an hour practicing medicine.

But Edward Willis had defended him. And that was his ticket to freedom.

"Mr. Deveraux? Dr. Pierson will see you now," the receptionist informed him.

"Thank you." Marc followed her down the hall, where she motioned him into an inner sanctum the size of two adjoining lecture halls at the FBI Academy in Quantico. She left him there, shutting the door behind her.

The very recognizable Dr. Pierson rose from behind his heavy mahogany desk. "Mr. Deveraux," he said, greeting Marc with a handshake. "Please, take a seat." He gestured at a leather chair on the opposite side of the desk, simultaneously glancing down at the new patient forms Marc had filled out.

"So you're suffering from severe headaches, and your primary care physician suggested they could be migraines." Pierson's eyebrows drew together. "You didn't list the referring doctor."

"Nope. That's because there is none. And my headaches are usually from lack of food or sleep."

Every muscle in Pierson's body went rigid. "Are you a reporter? Because I'll have you arrested on charges of—"

"I'm not a reporter," Marc interrupted. "I'm a member of Forensic Instincts, a private investigative company."

"I was acquitted." Pierson rose. "Please leave."

Marc made no move to stand. "I'm not here to discuss your murder case. I'm here to discuss the kidnapping of Edward Willis's five-year-old daughter."

The neurologist started. "His daughter? When did this happen?"

"Evidently, you don't watch the news. Yesterday. After school. The Willises have hired us to find her."

"And you think *I* had something to do with it?" A pulse was working at Pierson's temple. "What motive would I have?

Edward saved me from a life sentence in a maximum security prison."

"And destroyed your reputation in the process. He's a splashy guy, made sure your story was a household word. From what I gather, you and Willis had several heated arguments about his sensationalistic strategy, especially as you watched your patient list dwindle. Not to mention that his legal fees—which he refused to reduce—pretty well wiped you out. And I didn't notice a waiting room full of patients here to tip the coffers in your favor. A hefty ransom would do wonders toward getting you back on your feet."

"I feel nothing but respect and gratitude for Edward. He did what he had to do. And I don't abduct children. Not for money. Not for anything."

"But you certainly like them."

Pierson's pupils widened. "What does *that* mean?"

"It means that your ten-year-old daughter, Melanie, went off to boarding school soon after her mother died. Or, more specifically, right before your trial."

"I didn't want her subjected to—"

"Yes, that's what Willis told the jury. But the truth is, Melanie had complained to your wife about the amount of time you were spending with her friends. Sleepover dates you encouraged, pool parties you threw on warm summer evenings—during which you spent inordinate amounts of time with the girls. Making physical contact with them when you taught them how to swim. Stopping upstairs in Melanie's bedroom when they were getting ready for bed."

"That's enough." Pierson's fist struck his desk. "I don't know where you got your information, but I could sue you for slander."

"You could. But you won't." Marc bent one leg and propped it over the other knee. "Because everything I just said is true and is documented. Sealed, but documented. So tell me, Dr. Pierson, just how fond are you of five-year-old girls?"

Pierson's breath was coming fast. "My daughter has an active imagination. I don't covet young girls, and I certainly don't lust after babies. A five-year-old? That's sick. If you plan to spread rumors that I'm a sexual predator…"

"I don't. So let's stop talking in generalizations. Let's get back to Krissy Willis."

A frosty glare. "I'm neither a kidnapper nor an extortionist, Mr. Deveraux."

No, Marc thought with revulsion. *Just a pervert and a murderer.* "Where were you yesterday from three o'clock on?" he asked.

"Right here in my office. My nurse, my receptionist and two colleagues can testify to that. I came in at ten and didn't leave until six."

"And then?"

"Then I drove straight home. Speak to my housekeeper. She cooked me dinner and cleaned up afterwards. She didn't leave until after eight."

"What about lunchtime? Did you go out?"

"I had Chinese food delivered. Do you want to see the receipt?"

"Nope. That won't be necessary." Mentally, Marc crossed Pierson off his list of suspects. He'd known it was a long shot. But every lead had to be pursued. Plus, if nothing else, Marc's visit would keep Pierson on his toes, force him to control his unnatural propensity for young girls. The last thing the neurologist needed right now was more scrutiny and scandal.

Marc would have loved to break the guy's jaw. But that wasn't in the cards—not this time.

"What about any of your wife's relatives?" he asked instead. "Or her friends? Anyone close to her who disagreed with the not-guilty verdict and who's got the temperament to act on it?"

"Fran had no living relatives," Pierson replied in a clipped tone. "And I'm not well acquainted enough with her friends to know if any of them is deranged. Talk to the prosecutor. The people you're asking about were *his* witnesses."

"I already have," Marc reassured him. "But I wanted to follow up with you. First, because I didn't think you'd want the prosecutor to hear my theories about your daughter's friends. And second, because he's a lawyer—you were a husband. Generally, they're privy to more intricate details of their spouses' lives than a stranger is."

"Fran's friends were all mothers. I can't imagine..."

"Nor can I. But it happens." Marc skimmed his notes. "I got a list of those friends. Would you object if I were to interview them?"

"No. Not that it would matter. You'd interview them with or without my permission."

"Actually, I already have." He smiled what he knew was his most irritating smile. "I just wanted to see your reaction. Clearly, none of them has a clue about your affinity for preteen girls. Which is all that matters to me. Their opinions on the murder are moot. You were acquitted. Double jeopardy applies. Plus, my job is to find Krissy Willis, not your wife's killer."

"Then talk to whomever you like. I have nothing to hide."

"Right." Marc came to his feet. "Thank you for your time,

Dr. Pierson. Glad to hear that you're innocent of murder and of sexual deviance. There's nothing like a clear conscience."

Casey had a bad feeling.

Her interview with Claudia Mitchell had never happened. She'd rung the bell a half-dozen times. No one had answered. But she knew someone was home. She'd heard the flurry of muffled footsteps, spotted the outline of a woman through the window. The woman had retreated to the kitchen and hidden behind the counter. Judging from her height and build, it was Claudia Mitchell.

So why wasn't she opening the door?

The deception raised a host of red flags. Especially since Casey had preceded her trip to Claudia's house with a visit to the White Plains courthouse where Judge Willis presided. The couple of employees Casey had tracked down who were familiar with Claudia had confirmed Hope's description of the clerk's state of mind at the time of her dismissal. Two of them, along with one of Claudia's neighbors, knew her fiancé. And, judging from their description, the couple was a classic fit for the kidnappers' profiles. Dominant man—at least with Claudia. Passive woman, with a build not dissimilar from Hope's.

Then came what Casey already knew. There was motive on both their parts. Revenge for Claudia, who was clearly bitter about Hope firing her during her hour of need. And a windfall and who knew what else for Joe, who the neighbor described as odd and more than a little antisocial. Also, when Casey peeked in the window to see if she could spot Claudia, she noted that the living room was filled with plenty of boy toys. Not the electronic gizmos that fascinated most men, but younger, more juvenile computer games.

The whole scenario screamed for further investigation. Casey would pass the info along to Peg. But she had no intention of waiting for Peg to take the necessary steps for probable cause and a search warrant. Casey was determined to get into that basement *now.* She'd come back in the evening, when Joe was at his second job and Claudia was at county college taking a class. She'd bring Marc. After hearing "suspicious sounds" from inside, Marc would pick the lock and get them in. If Krissy was there, they'd find her.

After a quick phone call to Marc setting up their evening plans, Casey headed back to see Hope and to meet Hope's mother.

Other than her gray hair, Vera Akerman resembled a small, frail sparrow. She also looked far older than her sixty-four years. It was obvious that the blow life had dealt her thirty-two years ago had taken its toll—a toll from which she'd never recovered.

After Hope had made the necessary introductions, Casey sat down across from Vera. She opened the conversation by expressing her heartfelt regrets over Krissy's kidnapping. She also explained to Vera a little bit about Forensic Instincts and how they could take a more creative and less regulated approach to solving cases than law enforcement could. She concluded by assuring Hope's mother that the entire team was working round the clock to find her granddaughter.

Vera thanked her in a tear-filled voice.

Casey was just about to tactfully broach a few questions, when the front doorbell rang. A minute later, a square-jawed man in his early sixties with a solid build and salt-and-pepper hair entered the room.

Hope rose. "Are you with the police or the FBI?"

"I'm former FBI," was the terse reply.

"Former?" Hope pressed, brow drawn. "I don't understand." Before she could continue, she heard her mother's sharp intake of breath. She turned. "Mother?"

Vera was staring at the man. Her eyes had widened, recognition erupting across her face.

"Special Agent Lynch," she managed.

CHAPTER NINE

"Hello, Mrs. Akerman. I'm glad you recognize me. And I'm sickened that you're going through this again." The former special agent shifted his gaze to Hope. "Judge Willis. My name is Patrick Lynch. I was the lead investigator thirty-two years ago when your sister was kidnapped."

"I see." Hope was visibly thrown. "I'm sorry. I don't remember you."

"I didn't expect you would. You were six when we met." He walked over and extended his hand. "I'm sorry to be here under these dire circumstances." He shook Hope's hand. "But I'm here to offer my services. Anything I can do to help, just ask."

Casey had watched the entire exchange with interest. Patrick Lynch was clearly sincere in his offer, and disturbed by Krissy's kidnapping. But there was something more here. Something personal. It didn't take a genius to figure out that he still felt responsible for Felicity's kidnapping, for coming up empty. In fact, judging from his pained expression and determined demeanor, Casey was willing to bet that he'd been plagued for years by the case's lack of resolution.

"Thank you, Agent Lynch," Hope was saying. "That's very kind of you."

"Kindness has nothing to do with it." His next words confirmed Casey's suspicions. "I can't make up for your sister's disappearance going cold. But I *can* do everything in my power to assist the Bureau and to make sure this second crime doesn't go unsolved."

"Do you have reason to believe the two kidnappings are related?" Casey asked, also coming to her feet.

"This is Casey Woods," Hope introduced her.

"From Forensic Instincts. Yes, I know. I've been following Krissy's kidnapping since the story broke yesterday. I saw on the news that you'd hired Ms. Woods's team." He shook Casey's hand. "It's nice to meet you."

"Likewise." Casey met his handshake. "You headed up the investigation into Felicity Akerman's abduction?"

A nod. "And to answer your question, I have no idea if there's a connection between the two abductions. The only common denominator is the family. But if it is a coincidence, it's a horrible one. Mrs. Akerman barely survived the loss of her daughter. Now her granddaughter…" He blew out a slow breath. "I'm an independent consultant now. But I need to be part of this."

"Anything you can contribute would be a blessing," Hope said. "I'll gladly pay you any amount…"

He waved away her offer. "Your sister's kidnapping has never stopped eating at me. Retirement from the Bureau gave me even more time to dwell on it. Believe me, participating in this investigation is as much for me as it is for you."

"What type of consulting work do you do?" Casey asked curiously.

"Mostly security, both for private companies and law enforcement. I've done a fair amount of work with the NYPD, since New York City is my home base. And I've assisted the Bureau on a couple of cases. It works well. I live in New Jersey, and my office is in lower Manhattan." Lynch met Casey's gaze, his expression one that said he was totally comfortable in his own skin. "Not to date myself, but when I started working for the Bureau, the White Plains RA was in New Rochelle, and the New York Field Office was on East Sixty-ninth at Third Avenue, not Federal Plaza."

"Which explains your heading up the investigation into Hope's twin sister's abduction." Casey nodded. "Their home was in New Rochelle."

"Exactly." Lynch turned back to Vera and Hope. "I kept my notes from the original kidnapping. Judge Willis, if your mother is up to it, and with your permission, I'd like to speak with Special Agent Harrington about digging up the cold case file. If there's any crossover in the suspect pool, or any other details that repeat themselves in the two abductions, I want to go after them."

Hope glanced quickly at her mother, who gave a brief nod. "You have my permission," she told Lynch. She paused, visibly shaken by this turn of events. "Why would anyone target my family for over thirty years?"

"It's a long shot," he told her gently. "More a process of elimination than a viable possibility. But on the off chance that it has merit, we could uncover clues to help find your daughter."

Casey couldn't restrain herself any longer. The first question she'd planned to ask Vera Akerman was still on the tip of her tongue. In light of Patrick Lynch's approach, that question was now more important than ever.

"Mrs. Akerman," she asked quietly. "When was the last time you saw or spoke to your ex-husband?"

Hope's mother looked more saddened than she did, taken aback. "At the divorce hearing. He'd been drinking, which was routine for him those days. Once the divorce decree was official and I had full custody of Hope, he vanished into thin air."

"And you?" Casey asked Hope. "Has there been any contact with your father?"

"None." Hope shook her head, a flash of pain and nostalgia crossing her face. "All I remember is how broken up he was after Felicity was kidnapped. She was definitely daddy's little girl, into sports and arcade games, just like him. He couldn't get over her disappearance. Every day she was gone, things got worse. Eventually, he stopped going to work. He drank all the time. And he and my mom cried and fought."

"Sidney and I should have grown closer because of the trauma of losing Felicity," Vera added. "But we never did. I tried. He just wouldn't let me in. It was as if the loss was entirely his. He withdrew into himself, and gave up on life. Work, family, our marriage—none of it meant anything to him anymore. Ultimately, he lost his job, and drank himself into oblivion. I was overpowered by my own grief. The whole thing became too much. Our marriage just broke into pieces."

She squeezed her eyes shut. "Poor Hope got the brunt of it. She never said a word, but I could see it in her eyes. She blamed herself for the breakup. She felt like it was her fault, like she wasn't enough reason for her father to stay. It's amazing that she came through it—a testament to her internal strength. She was only six years old, and she was going through her own hell.

She and Felicity were so close. Identical twins. Losing her twin and then her father—how could any child come through that unscathed? I should have done more—"

"Stop it, Mom," Hope interrupted. "You did everything you could. Your child had been kidnapped. That's every mother's nightmare. Now it's become my reality." Another shaky breath. "As for Dad, all that's in the past. I don't think about it anymore. And I don't think about him."

"So neither of you knows where he lives?" Casey asked, trying to repress the urge to push harder.

"Not a clue." Hope wasn't stupid. Her head came up, and her gaze darted from Casey to Lynch and back. "Why do you ask? Do you think he might know something about Krissy?"

"I think we can't afford to leave any stone unturned," Casey responded bluntly. "Sidney Akerman is Krissy's grandfather, whether or not they've met. His whereabouts are unknown. We have to change that."

"I agree," Patrick Lynch chimed in. "I remember what a mess he was after Felicity was taken. He was actively involved in every step of the investigation. He might remember something we're forgetting. We have to track him down and talk to him."

Casey whipped out her BlackBerry. "I'll get Ryan on it right away. He can find anyone." She punched in her office number and swiftly relayed the details of what she needed to Ryan. "He'll get back to me as soon as he has something," she reported, punching off her phone.

Lynch reversed his steps, turning and heading for the hall. "I'm going to pull Peg Harrington aside and tell her the situation. Then, we can get started."

Casey glanced at Hope, who was currently leaning over to soothe her mother. Using the brief window of time to her advantage, Casey walked discreetly over to Patrick Lynch, waylaying him in the doorway with a hand on his forearm.

"Mr. Lynch, before you go, I have a blunt question to ask you. Would you be willing to combine your resources with Forensic Instincts, and work in conjunction with us? The advantage is that you and my team share the same independent status. The FBI task force is inundated with avenues to pursue and potential suspects to interview. I doubt that opening up a cold case that's three decades old is high on their list."

A corner of Lynch's mouth lifted. "In other words, you want access to my notes and to the old case file."

"Precisely." Casey saw no point in playing games. "Like I said, the Bureau can't put their resources into what appears to be a long shot. But we can. Not to mention the fact that we can push the boundaries in ways the police and the FBI can't."

One dark eyebrow rose. "I agree with your first premise. The task force has to concentrate on the most promising—and current—leads. As for the boundary-pushing, I'm not interested. After thirty-five years with the Bureau, I'm a creature of habit. On the other hand, I don't miss the paperwork. So I don't mind cutting a few corners. Just don't expect me to be a maverick. If you can live with that, I'd be happy to take you up on your offer—*if* the sharing of information is mutual."

"It will be."

"Good." Lynch's tone said that he was on board. "And, by the way, the name's Patrick."

Informal. Direct. No bullshit.

Casey liked this man.

"And I'm Casey," she replied. "I'll make sure you meet my other team members, Marc and Ryan, ASAP. In the meantime, can we talk after you get the okay from Peg? That way, you can fill in some blanks for me, and I'll do the same for you. It'll eliminate my having to ask too much of Mrs. Akerman. The last thing she and Hope need is to be repeatedly dragged through the worst time of their lives. Especially now. We need to keep their hopes alive, not imply that Krissy's case will end the same way Felicity's did."

"I think that's wise." Patrick nodded. "I'll talk to Peg. Then I'll meet you outside the house in twenty minutes."

As requested, Casey gave Ryan a quick call while she was waiting outside.

"Okay, I'm alone now," she said. "What did you want to tell me?"

"I've got the names of four disgruntled fathers who lost custody of their kids in Judge Willis's courtroom during the last few months," he replied. "All who were ripping pissed when she took away their custodial rights. All whose background checks show raging tempers and questionable lifestyles. All who fit our main kidnapper's profile—right down to girlfriends with low self-esteem. And all who openly threatened Judge Willis in her courtroom. I'll text you the list."

"Let's not waste time hanging up and texting." Casey whipped out a pad and pen. "I'll write down the info and check into it." She scribbled all the specifics Ryan provided, including names, addresses, phone numbers and current employment information. "I'll pay these guys visits as soon as I've talked to Patrick Lynch. He's a real find. You'll like him."

"I'm sure. In the meantime, I'll dig up what I can on Sidney Akerman. The guy is either dead or *really* doesn't want to be found."

"Interesting." Casey digested that tidbit. "Anything else?"

"Yeah. Your canine vacuum cleaner and gauze pads got here, along with some jars and tongs. And your dog just peed on my shoe."

Casey laughed. "Then take him out. He could use the exercise. Unlike you, he doesn't have a gym membership."

"Maybe he should. He's already dragged me to the park and sniffed out every square inch." A sigh. "Fine. I'll take him out back and tire him out. I hope he's not getting a salary. He doesn't deserve it."

"He will. That's what that STU-100, canine vacuum cleaner, is for."

"Good. Then he can use his first paycheck to reimburse us for the rug—and me for my shoes. On the other hand, he's got a hell of a nose. He'd be a great navigator for adventure racing."

"You and Hero can coordinate your schedules later. And I'll explain the STU-100 to you."

"No need. This is me. Already checked the website. I know the drill. Gauze in place. Personal article on gauze. Vacuum for thirty seconds. Gauze collects smells. Jar stores gauze. Hero has Krissy's scent. Done deal."

"Nice. Concise. Now go find Sidney Akerman."

"All over it like white on rice."

Sal Diaz stopped pushing his lawn mower, and dragged a sweaty arm across his forehead. He was working at the house across the street from the elementary school. The place was crawling with cops and FBI. It was only a matter of time before they questioned him and Rita, alibis or no alibis. Sal was the Willises' gardener, and his wife was their housekeeper. They spent hours a week at the huge Willis house. The cops would definitely be asking about them. They'd dig up the facts that Sal had a history of brawling and domestic disturbances, and that he and Rita were in debt up to their asses. If the Muellers and the Kitners hadn't vouched for their whereabouts, they'd probably be in custody now.

But how long would that safety net last?

Sal had been cutting the Kitners' lawn between two and four yesterday. And Rita had been cleaning the Muellers' house.

The Willis kid had been taken by a woman. The Muellers both worked, Mrs. Mueller until three. She'd walked through her door yesterday afternoon right around the time school closed. Technically, Rita could have left the house, grabbed the kid and stashed her somewhere, then pretended to be downstairs in the laundry room if Mrs. Mueller walked in a minute before her. The timing was too damned close. And Sal's background was too damned sketchy.

He kept waiting for the other shoe to drop.

He couldn't risk putting himself and Rita in the hot seat. Not unless—or until—the cops put them there. At that point, he wouldn't have to go to them. They'd come to him.

And he'd tell them what he knew.

CHAPTER TEN

Hope stood in Krissy's bedroom, tears coursing down her cheeks as she berated herself for everything that had happened.

It was her fault. Why hadn't she left work just a little earlier yesterday? Why hadn't she surprised Krissy by picking her up at school? Why hadn't she known in her gut that something was wrong?

She was a mother. And mothers were supposed to know.

But she hadn't.

Had she told Krissy she loved her when they said goodbye that morning? Had she hugged her? Had she tucked those stubborn wisps of unruly hair behind her ears before letting her out near the kindergarten door?

Would she ever have the chance to do those simple, priceless things again?

Her precious little girl. Would she ever hold her again, hear her sweet voice, revel in her exuberance? Would she ever share her childhood, struggle through her teens, see her grow to womanhood?

Oh, God, what was that animal doing to her? Hurting her? Molesting her? Worse? Where in the name of heaven was her baby? Was she alive?

Hope sank to the carpet, a knife of pain stabbing through her heart. She broke down completely, sobbing until her body was weak and trembling, until every single tear was spent.

The bedroom door opened, and she heard Ashley's tentative, "Judge Willis? Is there anything I can do?"

"No." Hope shook her head, not even lifting it from the carpet. "I just need to be here with Krissy's things." An agonized pause. "I certainly wasn't there for *her,* not when I should have been."

Down the hall, Ashley's cell phone began playing music, signaling an incoming call. She ignored it.

"Judge Willis, you're a wonderful mother," she told Hope with all the conviction of knowing it was true, and that this, at least, was something she could give her employer. "None of this is your fault."

"It *is* my fault. I should have been there."

"You couldn't have known."

"I should have. She's my child."

The upbeat music of Ashley's cell phone continued to play, its lively tempo a flagrant antithesis to the somber mood in Krissy's bedroom.

"That's your cell." Hope voiced the obvious.

"Whoever it is will call back."

As if to confirm Ashley's words, the phone fell silent.

Ashley walked over and knelt down beside Hope. "I blame myself, too, you know," she admitted softly. "If I'd been doing yesterday's car pool, maybe I would have gotten there sooner. I definitely would have noticed Krissy's absence right away. Maybe I would have been in time to prevent all this."

"You couldn't have. Maybe none of us could. It doesn't matter. I'm dying inside, anyway."

"I know you are." Tears clogged Ashley's throat. She reached down and gripped Hope's hand.

"I don't think I can survive this, Ashley," Hope managed. "Krissy is my world. Without her…nothing else matters."

"I know that, too. But I have to believe—"

Before Ashley could continue, her cell phone burst into song again.

"Damn." She jumped to her feet. "I'll get rid of whoever that is."

"That's okay. You can talk."

"I don't want to. I want to stay in here with you. I'm turning off my phone."

She rose and sprinted down the hall.

A full minute passed. Then another.

Hope just lay where she was, riddled with pain, guilt and fear. It was as if all the life were draining out of her.

Through her onslaught of emotion, she heard Ashley return.

"Judge Willis?" Ashley whispered from the doorway.

Something about the odd note in her voice brought Hope bolting to her feet. "Is there news?"

Ashley's face was colorless. She was gripping her cell phone so tightly that her knuckles were white. Furtively, she glanced behind her, then stepped into the room and shut the door.

"On my phone," she managed, extending her hand and offering Hope her cell. "It's a weird voice. But he told me he's the kidnapper. He said he got my number from Krissy's book bag, and that he called it so the authorities couldn't trace him, and so that you wouldn't involve them. But he wants to talk to you. He has…demands."

Hope snatched the phone and put it to her ear. "This is Judge Willis."

"I have your daughter," an odd, tinny voice told her. Clearly, the kidnapper was using a voice scrambler. "If you want her back, follow my instructions exactly, and keep your mouth shut. Tell *no one* that I called. Not your husband. Not the locals. And not the FBI. If you do, your daughter dies."

"I'll do whatever you say," Hope replied instantly. "Please, please don't hurt Krissy."

"That's up to you."

"Is she all right? Can I talk to her?"

"She's fine. And, no, you can't talk to her. She's elsewhere."

"Then how do I know she's okay? How do I even know you have her?"

"Listen." There was a brief pause, a rustle, then the punch of a button.

"I'm not hungry." It was Krissy's voice, obviously recorded, obviously tear filled. "Oreo's not either. I want my mommy. I want—"

Another punch of the button and Krissy's voice vanished.

Hope squeezed her eyes shut. "Why does she sound so frightened? What are you doing to her?"

"Wear your brown trench coat," the voice instructed. "I don't want you noticed. Bring two hundred and fifty thousand dollars—cash. In Krissy's black Adidas duffel bag. Tomorrow. Five o'clock. At the Mid-County Mall. Second-floor food court. Next to the pretzel kiosk. There's a trash can. Drop the bag beside it. Then walk away. Don't pause. Don't look back. Just go."

Dear God, he'd just provided an exact description of Krissy's duffel bag. That meant he had to be watching her when she went on a Daisy Scout outing. Who knew where else he'd been scrutinizing her? Not to mention that he'd specified Hope's brown trench coat. That meant he'd been watching her, too, probably when she was with Krissy.

The nightmare just kept getting worse.

"Did you get all that?" the voice demanded.

"Yes." Hope didn't need to write down the instructions. They were engraved in her brain. "What about Krissy? Will she be at the kiosk?"

"She'll be on the second-floor parking level an hour later."

"What proof do I have of that?"

"None."

Hope barely paused. "I'll be there."

"Good. And Judge Willis? If I see anyone but you at that food court, your daughter's blood will be on your hands."

A click told Hope the call had been disconnected.

"God. Oh, God." She sagged against the wall.

"What did he say?" Ashley asked.

Another brief hesitation. "It's better that you don't know the details," Hope told her. "And, Ashley, not a word to Edward or the task force. I'm counting on you. I've got to bring Krissy home alive. Forget your cell phone ever rang. Forget anything you overheard. Plus, I'll be going out twice—once now and once tomorrow around dinnertime. I'll need you to cover for me. Will you do it?"

Ashley gave a shaky nod. "For Krissy? Yes."

Hope's mind was racing. Edward had a large amount of cash

in their home safe, mostly under-the-table payments from rich, questionable clients Hope didn't want to know about. And they had over a hundred-thousand dollars in their safe-deposit box at the bank. Between the two, she could get the necessary cash together without alerting anyone or triggering mandatory bank reports regarding large cash transactions.

Please, she prayed silently. *Please let this work. Please bring my baby home.*

The disgruntled-father angle wasn't paying off.

No surprise to Casey. As soon as the men in question heard what she wanted, she ceased to be a pretty redhead tracking them down in their various workplaces and became an intrusive pain in the ass. And they had no intentions of speaking to some outsider they had no obligation to speak to.

Casey kept her questions brief, spending most of her few precious minutes with each potential suspect studying their reactions, their body language, and separating their natural belligerence from their possible guilt.

All four guys were bullies. All four wanted to torment their ex-wives. And all four resented Judge Willis for ruling against them.

But none of them had the brains or the balls to kidnap her child. None of them had the strategic skill to plan this perfectly executed abduction, or the guts to kill a five-year-old girl. And none of them was twisted enough to be a child predator.

So Casey had to agree with the Feds on this one. A personal vendetta against Judge Willis from a custody case in her courtroom was looking like a weak possibility.

It was time to go somewhere the FBI task force *hadn't* been.

★ ★ ★

Casey was surprised to find Vera Akerman alone in the living room. She was sipping a cup of tea, perched at the edge of the sofa.

"Mrs. Akerman," Casey greeted. "Where's Hope?"

The older woman looked up, gave a faint sigh. "She went for a drive. After spending the past hour alone in Krissy's room, she needed some air. Some time by herself. To think. To pray for strength. To get away from the pandemonium. My guess? She's parked at Krissy's school, crying her eyes out."

"I understand."

"I doubt that." The words were said factually, without bitterness or accusation. Vera glanced up and met Casey's gaze. "Do you have children?"

"No, I don't."

"Then you can't possibly understand. Not the depth of love a mother feels for her child, and certainly not the unbearable pain of possibly losing her. Knowing she's out there somewhere in the hands of a monster, and there's not a thing you can do, except pray. Hope would gladly trade her own life for Krissy's. But she's not being given that choice. All she can do is wait—and die a little each minute that passes."

"You're right. I can't understand. And I apologize for my lack of sensitivity." Casey gestured toward the chair, asking permission to sit.

Vera nodded.

Casey lowered herself to the armchair. "I can't know what Hope is going through, or what you endured and are being forced to endure again. All I can do is sympathize and work my heart out to bring Krissy home."

Hope's mother set down her cup. "It's my turn to apologize.

I didn't mean to be rude. I know how hard you're working to help my daughter. My nerves are just raw. It's like reliving a nightmare."

"You don't have to explain." Mentally, Casey ran through some of the information Patrick Lynch had given her. She leaned forward. "Mrs. Akerman, I won't do anything to make this worse for you. But would you mind if I asked you a few questions?"

"About Sidney."

"More about what life was like right around the time that Felicity was taken."

A pained expression. "Beforehand I can tell you about. It's afterwards that I can't. The memories went from horrifying to numb to blurry. The doctors tell me I went through severe post-traumatic stress disorder. I call it a nervous breakdown. I got out of bed each morning and went through the motions. I had to, for Hope. But the rest—it's like I stopped living. So did Sidney. We just stopped in different ways. And now..." Vera pressed trembling hands to her cheeks. "Why is this happening again? Why is my family cursed? Why?"

Casey didn't even try to offer an answer. "Beforehand, your family was happy?"

"Very. We were an average family. Sidney had a good job. I was on the PTA. The twins were well-adjusted. Hope was the reader who loved school, and Felicity was the athlete who loved games and sports. Still, they were incredibly close. If someone hurt one of their feelings, he or she had the other twin to contend with." A reminiscent smile. "That last summer, Felicity broke her arm. She was devastated that she couldn't play soccer. Hope arranged for everyone at camp to sign her cast. And when the cast came off, Hope asked if we could give Felicity a freedom party. That's the kind of relationship they had."

"Hope must have been traumatized by her sister's kidnapping."

"More than even she realized. She was next to Felicity in bed when it happened. The kidnapper drugged both girls, then took Felicity. I still don't know if he chose her intentionally, or whether he only had time to grab one twin and get out before he was discovered." Vera's lips quivered. "All our friends, and all the mothers from camp, came over and kept vigil with me. They prayed. They brought food. Hope wouldn't even come out of her room. Not to eat. Not to talk. It was only when I—and my marriage—started to deteriorate that she forced herself to come out of her shell and became part of our lives again. She was a brave little girl, far stronger than I was. Even after her father left."

Casey made a mental note to explore the friends and camp mothers with Patrick. But it was obvious that Hope's mother had had enough.

"Mrs. Akerman, let's call it a day," she said gently. "We can talk again tomorrow. In the meantime, I have some additional avenues I want to pursue."

And she did.

Next on the agenda—meeting up with Marc and exploring every square inch of Claudia Mitchell's house.

Ashley was preparing a light dinner for the family and the on-site members of the task force, when Edward stalked into the kitchen and seized her arm.

"The detectives tell me that you spent time comforting Hope in Krissy's bedroom," he said in a hard whisper. "And Hope has been acting odd and aloof since I got home. What did you tell her during your heart-to-heart?"

Wincing, Ashley pulled her arm away. "Nothing. I'm not stupid, Edward. I haven't told a soul."

He studied her for a long moment, eyes narrowed. "You're sure?"

"Positive. The only topic we discussed was Krissy."

"Good. Keep it that way. Remember, one wrong word from you and my marriage and your job will blow up. Not to mention that we'll zoom to the top of the FBI's suspect list. Krissy's rich attorney father, his young mistress, and his precious daughter take off for parts unknown, after a brilliant plan masterminded by Edward Willis."

"I think you're overreacting." Ashley's tone was in direct contrast to the frightened expression on her face.

"Trust me, I'm not. I'm a lawyer. I know how law enforcement thinks. Don't give them food for thought. They'll gobble you up."

"I won't." Tears glistened on Ashley's lashes. "I already feel guilty enough about what we're doing to Judge Willis. And now Krissy's abduction..." She broke off, swallowing to regain her composure. "But I know the rules. And I'll play by them. With the authorities, and with your wife."

"You do that. The alternative won't be pleasant."

CHAPTER ELEVEN

Patrick Lynch was too good a former FBI agent not to know that Casey Woods's idea of pushing the boundaries and his own were very different.

He'd shared a good chunk of information on Felicity Akerman's kidnapping with her, and agreed to share his notes and the file. She, in turn, had filled him in on everything she had on Krissy Willis's abduction, and all the avenues that she and her team were pursuing—both the ones that were in conjunction with the authorities and the ones that weren't.

She'd omitted more than a few details. Then again, so had he. Trust wasn't something you developed in one conversation. It took time, and lots of it. So Lynch had kept certain cards close to his vest, and he was sure Casey was doing the same.

There wasn't a doubt in his mind that she and her team were heavily pursuing Hope Willis's former court clerk, Claudia Mitchell. He understood why. Their reasoning had merit. Their methods, on the other hand—well, those he had a hunch would be teetering on the brink of illegal.

He couldn't be a part of it.

On the other hand, there was no saying he had to stop it.

It was just after dark when Casey and Marc parked their car under a canopy of trees a half block down from Claudia Mitchell's house. They were both dressed in black sweatshirts and jeans. They looked perfectly ordinary, and were hardly noticeable in the darkness. Marc carried his tools in a sport waist pack.

They approached the front door like casual visitors and rang the bell.

As expected, there was no response.

A second ring.

This time a cat meowed from somewhere inside.

"Did you hear that?" Casey asked flatly, knowing full well that Claudia owned two yellow tabbies.

"Yeah." Marc's response was equally bland. "I wonder what it was."

"I couldn't tell if it was a cat or a child. Could you?"

"Nope. But if it's a kid, he or she can't be left alone in the house."

"Definitely not. And he or she sounds like they're in some kind of distress."

A second meow.

"That's it." Casey reached for the doorknob. "We can't risk it. We have to go in."

Marc grabbed her arm and stopped her. "Don't bother. I think it's unlocked. Let me check." He pulled out a torque wrench and pick. Inserting the flat end of the wrench, he exerted just enough pressure to the L-shaped top of the tool, which served as a lever. He then inserted the pick and carefully tapped each pin out of the way. There was a slight click and a subtle movement of the cylinder as the torque wrench acted as a substitute key, turning the entire cylinder and disengaging the lock.

With a slight push, Marc opened the door. "I was right. Unlocked. Let's check on that sound."

They crossed the threshold in a heartbeat.

"Start with the basement," Casey instructed, all sarcasm having been abandoned. "That's the room where Claire kept visualizing Krissy."

They found their way to the stairs leading down to the basement. All Casey was hoping to see was a room transformed to a bedroom, much the way Claire had described.

All she found was a bare-bones basement. Drywalled partitions. Indoor-outdoor carpet. Two pull-string fluorescent fixtures. An Alienware gaming laptop sitting on top of a small desk. The only upgrade to the decor was a leather gaming chair facing a large flat-screen TV, along with video game consoles, controllers, various accessories and all the games to go with them.

But no sign of a child.

"Dammit," Casey muttered. She flicked on one of the overhead fixtures and scanned the room.

Nothing.

"You take care of the computer," she told Marc. "I'll keep searching."

In response, Marc walked over to the laptop, which was currently turned off. He popped open the DVD drive with a paper clip and inserted the disk Ryan had given him. Closing the drive, he turned on the computer and watched as it booted from Ryan's disk. In an instant, the laptop's hard disk indicator began flashing furiously, as the program hacked into the password security tables, inserting a seemingly innocuous system account with full administrative rights and an undetectable spyware program that tracked everything. It also enabled the microphone and effectively turned the laptop into a one-way intercom, with Ryan able to listen to everything that transpired in the room.

When the program finished, it shut down the laptop as if nothing had happened.

Marc removed the disk, sliding it into his jacket pocket, and closed the drive.

While Marc was occupied, Casey walked over to the gaming setup and thumbed through the extensive selection of games. *BioShock 2: Limited Edition. Call of Duty: Modern Warfare. Batman: Arkham Asylum. Left 4 Dead 2. Resident Evil 5: Gold Edition.*

"Terrific," Casey commented in a grim tone. "Isn't *BioShock* the game where you can decide to kill little girls?"

"Sadly, yes. But it's also superpopular among normal people. The fact that Claudia's fiancé enjoys shooter games doesn't prove anything."

"Maybe not. But this guy is obviously a hard-core gamer. When Grace described the offender, she said he'd be into hobbies like model airplanes or video games. Claudia's fiancé certainly fits the bill." Another somber look. "But there's no sign of Krissy."

"They could be holding her elsewhere in the house," Marc noted, using his heavy-duty flashlight to peer around.

"Or in a different location entirely." Casey took a few photos with her cell phone, then headed for the stairs. "Let's search the rest of the place."

They were thorough, although neither of them expected to

find Krissy on the main floor of the ranch-style house. It was too open, with no private areas or secluded rooms. The basement had been their best bet. And it had come up empty.

The house's decor was country style, and decidedly feminine. No surprise, given that Joe had just moved back in. Still, it was odd that there was virtually nothing personal of Joe's to be found, other than a broken-down chest of drawers in a corner of the bedroom.

"Let's take a look inside," Casey said to Marc. "We need to get a handle on this guy. Is he just an obnoxious boyfriend and an odd duck, or is he capable of kidnapping a little girl?"

Marc was already pulling on a pair of gloves. He waited while Casey did the same. There was a big difference between responding to an alleged cry for help and ransacking a man's drawers. They had to tread very carefully.

The top three drawers held the usual: T-shirts and jeans, underwear, some construction gear. Again, no surprise. Ryan had noted that Joe worked for Bennato Construction Company, doing mostly road paving projects.

The bottom drawer had his pay stubs from work, all rubber-banded together. The amounts were consistent, and everything looked to be in order. There was a stack of papers—software receipts, game magazines, a couple of credit card slips from a local pub.

A folded diagram was sticking out from underneath the stack of papers.

"What's this?" Casey murmured. She pulled out the sheet and smoothed it out.

It was an architectural layout of Armonk's elementary school parking lot—*Krissy's* elementary school parking lot. It included the exterior of the rear side of the building, the outside lights, the surveillance cameras—everything.

"What the hell...?" Marc breathed, squatting down and shining his flashlight directly on the plans. "This is literally a map of the kidnapping scene."

"It's also probably one of Joe's workplaces," Casey mused aloud. "I remember that the parking lot at Krissy's school was newly paved, as was the playground. We should find out if Joe was on that job."

"Yeah, along with why he would have kept this layout, even after the construction work was completed."

"Right." Casey took out her phone again, and shot a couple of pictures. "Okay, let's put everything back exactly as we found it and get out of here."

Ten minutes later, they left the house, locked the door and headed back for the car.

"Ryan's turn?" Marc asked once Casey was driving, heading back to Tribeca.

"Yup." Casey gripped the steering wheel. "We sure as hell aren't leaving this one alone. A map of the crime scene, a mother-lode gaming center, and the very real possibility that they could have stashed Krissy anywhere. Besides the hack job, we need to have Ryan get a GPS tracking device on Joe's car and, hopefully, on Joe himself." She turned onto the highway. "Let's get to the office. I want to see what Ryan found on Sidney Akerman, anyway."

Before Marc could respond, Casey's cell phone rang. She punched the receive button on the steering wheel. "Casey Woods."

"So, did you get lucky?" an older masculine voice inquired through the speakerphone. "Or did you walk away frustrated and with nothing? I agree with you that you've got a strong suspect in Claudia Mitchell. She worships that boyfriend of hers, and he's a real wack job. Still, I can't get past the feeling that there's a connection between the past and the present."

"Patrick," Casey said, after a quick glance in the rearview mirror. "Are you tailing us?"

"Don't have to. I knew what you had on your agenda. What I don't know—and I *don't want* to know—is how you got in."

Casey's lips quirked. "Then I won't disappoint. Let's just say the door was open and we heard crying from inside. It turned out to be the cats."

"Of course it did."

Gesturing at Marc, Casey made the audio introduction. "Patrick Lynch, meet my passenger and associate, Marc Deveraux."

"Hey," Marc said. He looked more amused than surprised by Patrick's insightful analysis of the evening's events.

"Nice to meet you," Patrick replied. "Even by phone."

"How about in person?" Casey's mind was racing. "We're heading back to Manhattan. Ryan's in the office. Since you're keeping such great tabs on us, can you swing by and meet the rest of the team? You know—the team you'll be working closely with to solve this crime by sharing all the reasons why you think the past and the present kidnappings are connected. The team you won't be holding back any details or information from."

"That's doable." Patrick sounded as if he'd expected the invite. "I've got your address. I'll be there in an hour."

Hope's heart was pounding in her chest as she opened the safe in Edward's home office.

She was taking a huge risk doing this during evening hours. But Edward was still at work, and the task force was scattered, performing their various assignments. This was as good a time as any to check out the contents of the safe.

She wasn't planning on removing the cash now. She couldn't. If Edward had reason to look inside during the next twenty-four hours, and he found the safe cleaned out, her entire plan to recover Krissy would blow apart. And there was no way she was taking that chance.

No, now wasn't for confiscating. Now was for counting. She had to see if she had enough to add to the $128,000 she had accumulated from today's bank visits.

She'd had to go to two separate banks, and pull cash from two separate safe-deposit boxes, to avoid suspicion. She'd never realized how heavy and bulky large sums of money in small bills could be. She couldn't walk into the bank with Krissy's gigantic duffel bag—not without looking out of place. Nor could she leave the house in the middle of the day lugging it along. So she'd taken her roomiest laptop case and removed all she had from each box.

Now, she peered into her husband's open safe, grimacing in disgust at the sight. Piles of cash Edward had accumulated in ways that turned her stomach, but that right now might be her lifeline to Krissy. Quickly, she unloaded stacks of money and counted.

She stopped when she reached the magic number of $122,000. There was more than enough in this safe to cover what she needed.

Replacing everything the way she'd found it, Hope locked the safe and slipped out of Edward's office.

Ryan was glued to his computer screen, pounding away at his keyboard and eating trail mix out of a bag, when Casey and

Marc walked in. Hero was glued to Ryan's feet, crunching on the pieces of granola that were being inadvertently—and not so inadvertently—dropped.

"Well, I see that you two have developed a rapport," Casey noted aloud.

"Huh?" Ryan looked up, then glanced down at Hero as he realized what Casey had said. "Yeah, we had a talk after that peeing episode. It's been smooth sailing ever since. While we were walking to the park, he got a whiff of something and took off. We were half a block away. He nearly yanked the leash out of my hand, he was sniffing so frantically. Turns out it was the manager of that dog hotel he stayed at. She must have been great to him, because he shoved me out of the way and jumped all over her like they were supertight. Not that I blame him. She was hot. I got her phone number. But Hero got all the attention. You have to admire that kind of strategic intent."

"I do." Casey perched at the edge of Ryan's desk and filled him in on what she and Marc had found at Claudia's. "The laptop's taken care of. But I need you to find a way to track Joe Deale's movements."

"Not a problem. He's working on a bridge repair project in the Bronx. I'll arrange for a diversion at the site tomorrow morning, during which I'll plant a GPS in his car, and a tracking chip in his cell phone. I'll monitor them on my PC."

Casey nodded, folding her arms across her breasts. "Good. Now, what did you find on Sidney Akerman?"

Ryan stared at his computer screen. "He lived like a vagabond after his marriage broke up. Different towns, odd jobs—all over the Tri-State Area. He couldn't hold down any of the jobs because of his drinking. It seems he finally got it together enough to go to rehab a good decade later, somewhere in the Northwest.

He got out, joined AA—according to an Arizona newspaper article on the group—and started working as a bookkeeper for a small office supply chain in upstate New York. That didn't last long. He went back to the bottle, and vanished off the screen. I'm still trying to fill in the blanks. I get snatches of what he's been up to, and then nothing. Suffice it to say, he hasn't exactly lived a productive life."

"Where is he now?"

"The most recent address I have is in Ithaca. But it's eight years old. The one interesting thing is what his job was, and maybe still is—custodian in an elementary school."

Marc let out a low whistle. "Any indication of off-color behavior during that time? Approaching kids, talking or acting inappropriately around kids—even watching kids at the bus stop?"

Ryan shook his head, double-checking by inputting a slew of data into the computer. "Nothing documented," he reaffirmed. He called up a page, entered the print command and waited for the single sheet of paper that he snatched off the laser printer. "But here's the address of the school, and a list of the faculty. The principal's been there for ten years, so he's bound to know Sidney Akerman. And some of the faculty predate the principal. I'd say this is our best starting point." A questioning look at Casey. "Do you want me to drive upstate and check it out?"

Before Casey could respond, there was a knock at the front door.

"Hold that thought," she said, heading for the hall.

She returned a minute later, Patrick at her side.

"Marc, Ryan, this is former Special Agent Patrick Lynch, our new consultant on the Krissy Willis abduction." Casey made the introductions. "As I told you, he was the lead case agent on the Felicity Akerman investigation."

The three men shook hands.

"Good timing. We were just discussing Sidney Akerman," Casey informed Patrick, bringing him up to speed. "Ryan tracked him to upstate New York."

"Yeah," Ryan said. "And I was just asking Casey if she wanted me to drive up there and check it out."

"I'll do that," Patrick intervened. "If you picked up on Sidney Akerman's trail, I want to follow it. He was always one of my missing pieces. There was never any doubt that he was a genuine wreck when Felicity was kidnapped. But there was also no doubt that he became an angry drunk afterwards. Plus, the fact that he's been MIA for decades is a huge loose end. It's my responsibility to see it through. I'll head up to Ithaca early tomorrow."

No one argued. Patrick had supplied them with all the background on the Akerman cold case. It was his right to pursue this lead.

But Casey wanted to know a lot more about the Felicity Akerman abduction than where Sidney Akerman fit into the puzzle. After her conversation with his ex-wife earlier today, she had other people of interest to ask about.

"Patrick, let's all go upstairs to our conference room," she suggested. "That's our think tank, the place where we do our best brainstorming. Appropriate, since you and the group of us have a mountain of information to share."

"*Share* being the operative word," Patrick returned drily. "I'm not going upstairs to be interrogated."

"Then you're going to be majorly pissed off," Casey answered with her usual candor. "Because I plan on firing questions at you. I also plan on giving you ample time to do the same."

A gruff laugh. "You're quite the force to be reckoned with, aren't you, Casey Woods?"

"I like to think so. But this isn't about me trying to one-up you. Time is running out. We all know it. If we don't put our heads together and come up with some answers—and I mean *now*—we'll lose any shot of finding Krissy Willis." Casey's pause was grim. "And when we do find her…I pray she's still alive."

CHAPTER TWELVE

Day Three

The medical complex was set in a section of countryside just north of Westchester County. The grounds weren't vast, but they were well maintained, especially the colorful gardens. The buildings were kept clean, even if they appeared a bit Spartan and institutional looking.

The facility was called Sunny Gardens. And it was the best that a middle-class income could afford.

The woman sat in one of the lovely gardens overlooking the park. She gazed across the grounds, not really seeing them. Her mind was wandering to a different place and time. Sometimes her thoughts were vivid and clear, as real as if they were happening right now. Other times, the present and the past melded into one, and, try though she would, she couldn't separate them. Those days she felt very confused, and she was happy for her medication. She also needed the nurses to explain. Sometimes they were wrong. She knew it. But sometimes they were right. She just wasn't always sure when.

Today was a fairly good day. She understood where she was. She even had a good idea why. And she was certain that today was Wednesday, which meant she'd have a visitor. Her favorite visitor.

Her little girl.

She worried a lot. Maybe seeing her mama like this would frighten the child. True, she never showed signs of fear. But that didn't mean she wasn't afraid. She was always so good at hiding her emotions.

Was that what she was doing now?

The nurse was walking over, a big smile on her face. The name tag on her uniform said Marla Greene. *Marla Greene*—did she know her? She must. Because the nurse was gazing at her with familiar recognition.

"Lunchtime," she announced cheerily.

"Lunchtime?" The woman shook her head vehemently. "It can't be. My baby's not here yet."

"Maybe she's coming later today," Marla Greene suggested. "You know how much work she has."

"Yes." The woman beamed. "She's smart. I gave her extra homework to do."

"Well, that explains why she's late. So let's go inside and have some lunch. You need to keep up your strength for her."

"Of course. You're right." The woman allowed Marla Greene to help her to her feet, and to guide her back to the main facility. "I have to keep things straight in my mind, so I can keep teaching her. I'm the only one who can."

★ ★ ★

Patrick drove rapidly up the highway. Ithaca was only four hours and change from his place, and he'd left the city right after breakfast. So he'd be showing up at Plainview Elementary School by noon.

Ryan McKay was obviously damned good at what he did. For over a year after Felicity's abduction, and sporadically thereafter, Patrick had tried to find a lead on Sidney Akerman's whereabouts—and come up empty-handed. Of course, today's technology changed all that by leaps and bounds. So Patrick was cautiously optimistic that he'd locate Hope and Felicity's father.

And then what? Did the man know anything, or was he just another dead end?

Patrick thought back to the time of the original abduction. Sidney Akerman had been all over the FBI from the get-go. Half the time, he'd been inebriated, but that didn't stop his relentless quest to find Felicity. He'd cooperated fully, taken and passed his polygraph test and answered all the questions he was asked during his interview. After that, he'd insisted on being told about every lead—until time and stress wore him down and the liquor won out.

Could he have information he didn't even realize he had—information that would tie these crimes together and shed light on his granddaughter's kidnapping? Did he even know he *had* a granddaughter?

Regardless of what Patrick learned today, there was a connection between these two abductions. He didn't know what, how or why. He only knew what his gut was telling him. And he'd learned to listen to his gut.

The sign for his exit appeared just ahead. He signaled, slowed down and turned off the highway, heading directly to his destination—and, hopefully, to some answers.

Claire jerked awake, her body drenched in sweat.

She'd been up all night. She'd gone over her notes all morning. She must have drifted off.

And dreamed.

Not about Krissy. About her stuffed panda, Oreo.

Dragging her fingers through the damp strands of her hair, Claire struggled for total recall. Krissy had been a mere wisp of presence in the dream. But Oreo—Oreo had been vivid. He'd been tangled in the bedcovers. Lonely. Crying. Sad for his best friend and her pain. Wishing his other best friend was here. Maybe together they could make Krissy smile. Maybe her eyes would light up like they always did when the three of them played—after it was bedtime and the lights were out and Krissy's parents thought she was asleep.

For God's sake, Claire thought, she was personifying a stuffed animal. Ryan would be laughing his ass off at this one.

How could a toy feel? Or weep? And why had Krissy been so faint in the dream? Almost nonexistent?

Mentally, Claire reached out, trying desperately to drag back the rapidly evaporating images. But they were gone.

They weren't arbitrary. They meant something. She was sure of it.

Now she had to figure out what.

Hutch wasn't happy.

Not just because the kidnapping investigation hadn't turned up a damned thing so far. But because it looked as if this stuck-in-neutral situation wouldn't be shifting into gear anytime soon. And soon was all they had.

The facts just weren't coalescing into a viable profile. Not for a ransom kidnapping. Nothing to suggest a serial predator or an attempt at human trafficking. And, so far, no concrete evidence against any of the potential suspects who might be seeking revenge against the Willises.

To make matters worse, he had the distinct feeling that Casey was onto something—something other than her belief that Krissy's kidnapping was connected to Felicity Akerman's. The latter part she'd discussed with him. He thought it was a long shot. But he also knew that the Bureau didn't have the resources to chase after it—not when there was a five-year-old girl out there enduring Lord knows what. So in the unlikely event that Casey's long shot had merit, Hutch was comfortable leaving it in the hands of Forensic Instincts.

No, this was something more. Casey had another bee in her bonnet. He hadn't gotten a thing out of her last night in private, nor this morning in public. No surprise there. As intimate as they were, as close as they'd become over the past year, he was a Fed and she was an independent consultant. Their goals might be the same, but their methods sure as hell weren't.

Which meant nothing good. If Casey was onto something, but had no proof; if she thought her team could get what they needed through nonkosher means, she'd be off and running without a word.

And that worried him—a lot.

Casey wasn't exactly off and running, but she was keeping a close eye on behavior that had first presented itself after her team meeting last night and before Hutch's arrival at one o'clock in the morning.

As per usual, she'd checked in with Hope Willis before turning in. The phone call had been odd. Rather than pounding Casey with questions and clinging on to her every word, as Hope usually did, she'd asked very little of her. In fact, she'd been downright curt, her voice high-pitched and agitated, rather than pained and tear filled. She'd cut the conversation short, practically hanging up on Casey.

It was definitely uncharacteristic. Not unheard-of, given the circumstances. Mothers of kidnapping victims often ran through a gamut of emotions. Sometimes those phases of emotions included anger at those who were trying to help but, as yet, had come up empty. People like Casey, who was an easy target, were perfect for lashing out at. That wouldn't have been off-putting, nor would it have offended Casey in the least.

But this was different. It wasn't only *what* Hope had said, or even how she'd said it. It was what she *hadn't* said, and the veiled quality of her tone.

Something was up. And Hope wasn't ready to tell Casey what.

Had she found out about Edward and Ashley, or was it something to do with Krissy?

The question had plagued Casey all night.

She'd headed up to Armonk at a reasonable hour of the morning, right after verifying with Ryan that he'd successfully arranged for a morning fire drill at Joe's work site. A diversion that had allowed him to place the tracking device inside Joe's car and the chip in his cell phone—which Ryan's spies had revealed Joe constantly misplaced and then scrambled to find. They could now monitor all of the guy's movements.

Casey's original plan had been to further interview Vera Akerman in order to flesh out more of the details that Patrick had run by her and the team last night—including all the people who'd been in the Akermans' lives at the time that Felicity was abducted. It was the only way to get a full picture of the past.

Now, Casey had two reasons for her trip to Armonk.

The first reason fell through. Unfortunately, Vera was in no condition to talk. The stress of what was happening had taken its toll, and she was in her room, heavily medicated on doctor-prescribed sedatives, and under strict orders to rest. Hope was sitting with her, so she, too, was unavailable.

That's when things started getting weird, and the second reason for Casey's trip had taken shape.

Walking past the Florida room, she'd spotted Ashley, alone in the room, visibly overwrought as she paced back and forth. Not the way she'd been when Krissy first disappeared. Then, she'd been emotionally freaked out and in shock.

This time she was bouncing off the walls.

First, Hope. Now, Ashley.

It was more than enough.

With that in mind, Casey strolled into the Florida room. "Ashley?"

The nanny's head snapped around. "Ms. Woods. I didn't hear you come in."

"Clearly not. You look like you're vibrating. Has something happened?"

A heartbeat of a pause. "If you mean, is there any news about Krissy, then no. So if I'm vibrating, that's why." Ashley gave Casey a stricken look. "It's been way more than twenty-four hours. Whatever they're doing to that precious little girl…it makes me sick just to think about it."

Casey heard the genuine hysteria in Ashley's voice. But she also picked up on her initial pause. She also picked up on the interesting fact that Ashley spoke about Krissy's captivity without mentioning that being missing so long usually meant not just torture or sexual abuse, but death.

"Do you know something more than you're saying, Ashley?" she asked quietly. "More than you knew the last time we spoke?"

The girl glanced at her with eyes as wild as a frightened bird. "Are you back to suspecting me? Because I swear on my life, I'd never harm Krissy."

"And, as I said last time, I believe you." Casey decided it was time to win Ashley's trust. "Can we sit down for a minute?"

Sitting down with Casey looked like the last thing Ashley wanted to do. But she lowered herself dutifully onto the lounger, her back ramrod straight. Casey followed suit, making sure that she faced Ashley so as to watch her expressions, while leaving enough distance between them so the younger girl didn't feel as if her space were being invaded.

"Do you want to ask me more questions about Krissy?" Ashley began. "Because I told you everything I know and—"

"Actually, I want to reassure you," Casey interrupted. "I have no intention of sharing your secret."

Ashley turned white. "My secret?"

"Yes. I won't tell anyone—including Judge Willis."

Now Ashley looked bewildered. "What are you talking about?"

"Obviously not what you thought I was talking about. Is there some secret you and Judge Willis share? One I should know about?"

"No." Ashley answered a little too quickly. "That's why I'm confused. What secret are you referring—"

"Your relationship with Edward Willis," Casey supplied. "I know that you two are romantically involved."

"Oh God." Ashley sagged into the cushions. "How did you find out?"

You just told me, Casey thought silently. "That doesn't matter. What matters is that I know. And I'm not here to judge you. Nor to tell the authorities or Judge Willis. So you can stop freaking out."

Ashley blew out a breath. "I appreciate that more than you can imagine. I don't expect you to understand. I never wanted to hurt Judge Willis. And I'm not naive enough to believe this is going anywhere. It just happened. Once. Then again. And before I knew it…let's just say there's something incredibly compelling about Edward. His power. His passion. I do believe that what we have is real. I'm not a diversion. But I'm not a forever either. So I hold on to the moments we get, and do the best I can to shove aside my guilt."

"Like I said, I'm not judging you," Casey replied. "On the other hand, I am doing you a pretty big favor by keeping quiet. So I think I'm entitled to a favor in return. Like your telling me what's going on with Judge Willis, and how you factor into it."

Silence.

Casey rose. "I understand your loyalty to Judge Willis." That in itself was incongruous, given the girl was sleeping with Hope's husband. Casey refrained from saying that aloud—although she did pause long enough for the irony of her statement to sink in. "But consider this. I'm not prying. But I think your secret has to do with Krissy. And since I honestly believe that my team is the Willises' best chance of getting Krissy back alive, I suggest you share it with me. No one and nothing is worth protecting if it endangers that child's life. Think about it. I'll check back with you a little later."

As she walked out of the room, Casey could feel Ashley staring after her, fighting some internal battle.

Casey hoped the right side would win.

CHAPTER THIRTEEN

Sidney Akerman parked his car in a grassy area just three blocks from Plainview Elementary School. He slumped down in his seat, shutting his eyes and wondering if he'd ever escape the pain and consequences of his past. The agony and fear were excruciating.

A quick sidelong glance at his glove compartment. There was a flask of whiskey in there. He could almost taste it, feel its effects as it numbed him up. So far he'd resisted opening the top and taking that first purging gulp. The flask had sat in the same spot for the past eight days.

He didn't want to become a drunk again. He'd kept his job for almost ten years now. He liked it. He liked being around the kids. He knew all the reasons why. And he knew he'd lose it all if he took that first drink.

But the way things looked right now, he'd lose it all anyway.

He had a couple of hours before he had to get back to the

school for his afternoon maintenance work. Maybe he'd get up the guts to call his AA sponsor and get the support he needed. Maybe the story he'd told the Feds would satisfy them. Maybe he could keep his freedom after all.

Not that he'd ever be free.

Abruptly, the passenger door of his car swung open, and a solid man of about his own age hopped in.

"Hello, Akerman," he greeted him. "It's been a long time."

Sidney felt his insides go cold. Yeah, it had been a long time. But this was one face he'd never forget.

"Agent Lynch," he managed. "What are you doing here?"

"So you do recognize me."

"Of course I do. But I don't get it. I thought last week's visit had taken care of any questions the FBI had for me. And why would they send you, of all people? Just to torture me by conjuring up the worst memories of my life? Besides which, aren't you retired yet?"

Patrick's eyebrows drew together in a frown. "The Bureau spoke to you?"

"Don't look so surprised."

"I am. I didn't even know they'd tracked you down."

"A guy from the Organized Crime Squad came to my apartment. Come on, Lynch, cut it out. How else would you have found me?"

Organized Crime Squad? That was a new one to Patrick.

"It wasn't easy," he replied carefully. "But I assure you, I didn't use Bureau resources to do it. I *am* retired, just as you suspected. I'm acting as a consultant on this case."

"Why would they need a consultant? I told them everything I knew. And you were on the Violent Crime Squad. When did you make the switch?"

Patrick took a second to study Sidney Akerman's face. The man had aged terribly, thanks to the alcohol. With his stooped shoulders, heavily lined face, and bags under his eyes, he looked as if he were seventy-five, rather than in his early sixties. He also looked frazzled about the FBI hassling him. But he didn't look frantic, like a man who'd just found out that his granddaughter had been kidnapped—something Patrick would expect regardless of the estrangement between Sidney and his family.

"I never worked Organized Crime," Patrick informed him. "I'm not here about whatever new trouble you're in. I'm here about your granddaughter."

"Krissy?" Sidney jerked around to face Patrick. "What about her?"

"So you do know she exists."

"I've followed every detail of Hope's life since the day I walked away. Her appointment to the bench, her marriage, the birth of her daughter—everything. Why? What's happened to Krissy?"

The man looked so stricken that Patrick actually felt sorry for him—and for the news he was about to deliver.

"She's been kidnapped."

"Kidnapped?" Sidney choked on the word as if it were poison. "Oh God, no." He pressed his fingers to his temples. "When? When was she taken?"

"The day before yesterday. Outside her school. Someone pretending to be Hope picked her up and drove off with her. There's been no word since. All of law enforcement's involved, from the locals to the FBI. I'm surprised you didn't see the media coverage on TV."

"My TV's broken. And I'm not much of a news watcher." Sidney's robotic answers were that of a man in shock. "I can't believe this is happening—*again.* A nightmare, repeating itself. Hope must be a wreck. And Vera…that poor woman has been through hell. First, our daughter. Now our granddaughter. She had a nervous breakdown before. How is she going to survive this?"

"Not well," Patrick replied flatly. "She's heavily sedated. And your daughter is sick to death." A pause as Patrick took in the entirety of Sidney's reaction. "You really didn't know a thing about this until now." He didn't wait for an answer. "Why is the Bureau interested in talking to you? What's your connection to Organized Crime?"

Silence.

"Look, Akerman, we can do this any way you want. But I'm thirty-two years and hundreds of sleepless nights invested in this case. I'm not going away. Not until you tell me every goddamned thing you know. Because I happen to think these two kidnappings are connected." A purposeful pause—and a glint of fear and guilt in Sidney's eyes. "I can see you think so, too. So we're going to talk. About then. About now. About everything."

Patrick pulled out his copy of Krissy's photo, shoved it in Sidney's face. "Have you seen a picture of your granddaughter lately? She's a beautiful, exuberant child. Or she was, until yesterday. God only knows what's happened to her since then."

Slowly, Sidney reached out and took the photo. "She has Hope's eyes," he managed, tears gliding down his cheeks. "And her smile. The way she's wrinkling her nose—it's like seeing Felicity again. Oh Lord, what have I done?"

"What have *you* done?" Patrick was all over that like white on rice. "Why? Did you have something to do with Krissy's abduction? Did you do something to precipitate it? Does that tie into why the Bureau's Organized Crime Squad is grilling you?"

Sidney dragged his arm across his face, wiping away his tears. Then, he shoved the photo of Krissy aside and threw his hands up in the air. "I can't take this anymore. I'm done. I played Russian roulette last time, and I lost. I'm not risking it again. Do whatever the hell you want to me. Send me to prison and let me rot there. Just find Krissy." He turned to Patrick. "Ask me what you need to."

"This Organized Crime investigation—it's related to the kidnapping. Just Felicity's, or Krissy's, too?"

"Both." A ragged sigh. "Here it is, short and sweet. When you and I first met, I was the accounting and business manager for a construction company."

"I remember."

"The owner of the company, Henry Kenyon, was an old college buddy of mine—I told you that, as well. What I didn't tell you was that Henry had a major gambling problem. He was in the hole for hundreds of thousands of dollars. He paid off his debts and became partners with the wrong people."

"The mob?"

"Yup. A handful of them invested in Henry's company. Their involvement was a closely kept secret, known by only a few members of their 'family.' They kept it that way so they could fly under the FBI's radar. It worked, because it never came up in your investigation."

"So we're talking money laundering," Patrick surmised.

"Exactly." Sidney's voice quavered. "I didn't want any part of it. But Henry was close to the edge. I couldn't turn my back on him. So I did what I had to. I kept my mouth shut for as long as I could stand it. Then I told Henry I was out. He passed that along. A few days later, Felicity was kidnapped. I lost my mind. I was up your ass while you were investigating. I prayed I was wrong. Then, I got a phone call from those bastards. They said they'd killed my kid, and that I had no one but myself to blame. They threatened me, said that if I opened my mouth, Hope would be next, followed by Vera."

Patrick let out a low whistle. "So that's why you dived into a bottle and fell off the map."

"You bet. It was the only way I could think of to keep my family safe." A bitter laugh. "For all the good that did me. Here it is, over thirty years later, and the FBI just got some mob guy to flip and give them damning info from the seventies—including the lowdown on Henry's company. Henry's been dead for fifteen years, so the FBI agent came to me for confirmation. I denied everything, told them I didn't know what they were talking about, and that if Henry did anything illegal, I didn't know a thing about it."

"Saving your family, or your own ass?"

"At this point? Both." Sidney's forehead was drenched with sweat. "The mob must have thought I gave the Feds something. So they pulled a repeat performance, this time with my granddaughter." He grabbed the front of Patrick's shirt. "You've got to stop them before they hurt her. Please. Do something."

"I plan to." Patrick whipped out his cell phone. "I'm calling the task force working on Krissy's case and filling them in. I need the name of the agent who came to see you and any immediate details on the mob guys you dealt with—names, descriptions—anything. After I pass all that along, I'm getting back into my own car, following you to your apartment, and waiting while you throw a few things in a bag. You're coming back to Armonk with me."

★ ★ ★

The news about her father reached Hope via the task force right before she packed up Krissy's duffel bag and prepared the drop for the kidnappers.

Her shock and rage at this unexpected development and the part her father had played in it were secondary now, eclipsed by the white terror of what was happening to Krissy. The realization that the mob might be involved in Krissy's abduction only strengthened Hope's resolve to follow through with her plan. Time was of the essence. Action was of the essence.

She couldn't think about her father's betrayal. She couldn't allow herself to think about the fact that, if history was repeating itself, her baby could be dead. All she could think about—blindly, frantically—was that she *had* to do everything in her power to bring Krissy home, alive and safe.

So when the agreed-upon time drew near, when the whole task force was caught up in tracking down known organized crime members, getting sketch artists, and contacting other Bureau members for further information while awaiting Sidney Akerman's arrival, Hope hauled the cash-filled duffel bag into the garage, heaved it into the trunk of her SUV and drove off.

No one noticed.

No one but Casey.

CHAPTER FOURTEEN

Casey had done her ongoing review of Ryan's documentation at Hope's house all afternoon. She didn't want to leave because she was still bugged by her suspicions that something was up. Once Hope had finally emerged from her mother's bedroom, only to be given the news about her father, Casey had watched her carefully, paying close attention to her actions and reactions.

Her reaction had been odd. Yes, she'd been genuinely stunned and devastated. But then her shock had transformed into something else. A grim determination. A panicky impatience. She kept glancing at her watch, clearly waiting for something to happen.

Or to make something happen.

The hell with Ashley's lack of cooperation, and Hope's morning-long absence. Casey could sense that something was going down. And she had a pretty good idea what that something was.

Her theory was confirmed when she spotted Hope slipping

down the back stairs and out of the house with a duffel bag that looked suspiciously heavy, and with a frantic pulse throbbing at the side of her neck.

Casey didn't say a word to anyone, although she felt Hutch's probing stare as she slipped out the door. To avoid potential problems, she turned in the doorway and mouthed the words to him, *I'm just getting some air,* before she sprinted to her car. She knew he didn't buy her staged exit. He obviously assumed she'd gotten some clandestine lead. But his hands were tied. He had no way of knowing if her lead was valid, or even if she'd truly gotten one. He was deep in his investigation, with no concrete reason to follow a private consultant wherever the hell she was going. So Casey was safe, and on her own—for now.

Jumping in her car just as Hope's garage door went up, Casey ducked down behind the wheel to avoid being spotted. From her crouched position, she made a quick call to Marc, instructing him to find and follow Edward Willis, no matter where he went. Simultaneously, she watched Hope back out of the driveway and speed up the street.

That was her cue.

Easing back up, Casey turned on her own ignition and shifted into Drive, waiting until Hope's Acadia was halfway up the block before following her.

Wherever Hope was taking that stash of money, and whether she was acting alone or with Edward, Casey was about to find out.

The mall's second-floor food court was every bit as crowded as Hope had expected. Five o'clock was prime shoppers' dinner hour. Her shoulder throbbed from the weight of the duffel bag, but she made her way among the throngs of people, not stopping until she reached the trash can that was tucked inside a little alcove across from the pretzel kiosk.

Her heart was pounding like a drum. Her insides were twisted into knots. She resisted the urge to look around. Krissy's life depended on her following instructions to a tee.

She lowered the duffel bag to the tiled floor right behind the trash can, where it was half-hidden and out of the path of the main flow of traffic. Keeping her head conspicuously down, she squeezed her eyes shut for one moment, fighting a wave of sickness. Then she sucked in her breath and walked away, heading directly for the door leading to the second-floor parking lot.

Please God, she prayed. *Please let things go as planned. Please let Krissy come home to me.*

It was going to be the longest hour of her life.

Casey stood in the middle of the food court, impatiently scanning the area for Hope. There were scores of people crammed into the various tables and chairs, endless lines in front of each restaurant station, and still more shoppers milling around the kiosks. Finding Hope was going to be a major challenge.

It was a good five minutes before Casey spotted her. Wearing her generic brown trench coat, she was halfway down the corridor, moving purposefully toward her destination, despite being weighed down by the duffel bag.

Casey elbowed her way through the crowd, losing sight of Hope twice before spotting her nearing the exit door. This time there was no duffel bag on her shoulder.

Dammit.

Following her target, Casey scrutinized the passersby in the thin hope of seeing someone with the heavy duffel bag in tow.

No such luck.

She reached the exit, pushed her way out, and headed for the garage where she'd seen Hope park her Acadia not thirty minutes earlier.

The SUV was still in the same parking space. Hope was inside, sitting in the driver's seat. Her arms were folded across the steering wheel, and her face was buried in her arms. Even from a distance, Casey could see that her shoulders were shaking with sobs.

The damage had already been done. The payoff had been made. Hope was obviously waiting for her daughter's appearance—an appearance Casey knew would not be forthcoming.

But Hope had to realize that for herself. If Casey went over there now, Hope would always blame that interference as the cause for Krissy not being returned.

Casey retreated to her car, which was parked diagonally across the way, slid inside and waited.

Thirty minutes passed. Then forty-five.

Hope got out of her SUV and began pacing around, looking from her watch to the pillars at the exit door.

No one appeared.

A good hour and a half passed before Hope sagged against her car, raking her fingers through her hair and breaking down completely. She sank to the concrete floor, her knees raised as she curled forward and wept.

Casey jumped out of her car. She crossed over until she was standing beside Hope.

Hope's head jerked up, and, for one split second, there was a wealth of hope in her eyes. It was replaced by bleak realization when she saw who it was.

"You knew?" she asked in a watery voice.

"I guessed." Casey hated this part of her job. On the other

hand, she was far from ready to give up. "I came alone," she explained, putting Hope's mind at ease about the thought of a posse scaring off the kidnapper. "I didn't tell a soul. But, Hope, they're not delivering Krissy to you, no matter what they said. That's way too amateurish for such a sophisticated kidnapping. That doesn't mean they've harmed Krissy. It just means they want something more than they've gotten."

"More than a quarter of a million dollars?"

Casey winced at the large sum Hope had gambled away on nothing.

"Yes," she responded honestly. "It might be more money, although I doubt it. I'm sure they realize that, at this point, you're going to fill the authorities in on the ransom scheme. And that the FBI task force will be all over any future ransom attempts. More likely, they want to see you suffer. Especially since we know this crime is personal. The whole ransom thing gave them a ton of cash, plus the opportunity of twisting a knife in your heart." Casey paused. "It's also possible that this entire plan was orchestrated by some news junkie who conned you into supplying him or her with some quick and hefty cash."

"I didn't think of that," Hope managed. "But they had so much personal information...I just don't think so."

"Tell me the details leading up to the drop—how they reached you, what they said—everything. Then, we'll go back to the house and tell the FBI what happened."

The FBI task force was deep into their investigation of Henry Kenyon and his construction company, when Casey and Hope walked into the house.

Hutch nearly mowed down Ashley as she sprinted toward her employer.

"Where did you two disappear to?" he demanded.

Hope glanced at Casey, who nodded, urging her to tell the truth as they'd discussed.

"I got a call from the kidnappers," Hope said quietly. "I paid the ransom they asked for. They didn't return Krissy. The whole thing was a reckless dead end."

"She wasn't with them?" Ashley asked, her voice trembling.

"No. They took the duffel bag of cash. But Krissy never showed up."

Casey could see Hutch visibly controlling himself. "When did you get this call, and who knew about it?" he asked.

"I got the call yesterday." Hope wasn't hiding anything at this point. "It came in on Ashley's cell phone, so the FBI couldn't trace it. I was the only one who knew the details. Ashley just handed me the phone. I swore her to secrecy. And Casey spotted me as I was leaving the house, and followed me on a hunch. I didn't even tell Edward. I was afraid to. The kidnappers said they'd kill Krissy if I…" Hope's voice broke, and fresh tears filled her eyes. "I'm sorry," she whispered. "Have I pushed them over the edge? Is this what they wanted? Now that they have the two hundred fifty thousand dollars they asked for, will they—"

"I don't think so," Hutch interrupted her. "It doesn't fit the profile of these kidnappers. If they wanted money, and money alone, why would they wait until the FBI and the police were so heavily involved before asking for it? They'd have better luck dealing with you alone, and right away, when the first horrible realization punched you in the gut." He signaled to Grace, as well as to Peg Harrington, who both strode right over.

Hutch filled them in with a few terse sentences.

"Tell us everything you remember," Peg instructed Hope.

Once again, Hope repeated the scenario verbatim, from the details of the phone call to the specifics of the drop.

"This plan is way amateur," Grace murmured. "It doesn't fit the sophistication of the crime."

"Neither does the amount of ransom money they demanded," Hutch added. "They know that you and your husband are good for a lot more than a quarter of a million dollars. And playing you Krissy's voice on tape? That's weak. They could have recorded her anywhere and spliced her words together. Again, an amateurish move. For all we know, it was all a hoax, and whoever called you doesn't even have Krissy. Instead, they freaked you out and made themselves a nice chunk of cash."

Casey was well aware that Hutch was intentionally softening some components and leaving out some biggies. Like the fact that, if Sidney Akerman's ties to organized crime had incited Krissy's abduction, this whole extortion scheme was either a dead end or the horrific tip of the iceberg. Scoring some quick cash wouldn't cut it. The mob would want major payback, just like they had when they kidnapped Felicity—*if* they'd kidnapped Felicity. And if they had…the mob didn't deal in idle kidnapping. They dealt in human trafficking, torture and murder.

Before Casey's thought process could continue, Edward emerged from the kitchen. Spotting his wife, he went over and caught her arm. "Where were you?"

He was livid at the answer.

"What the hell were you thinking?" he snapped. "That's why we have the FBI here. Do you realize you could have gotten Krissy killed?"

"We don't believe that's the case, Mr. Willis." Casey stepped in, seeing the white fear return to Hope's eyes. "Not in such a well-planned, cleverly executed abduction. We think this was just step one, or even an unrelated act."

Edward's gaze shot to Casey, suspicion clouding his stare. "You knew about this."

"No, sir, I most certainly did not." Casey spoke as respectfully as she could. But she *really* didn't like this man. "If I had, I would have told you and the task force about it immediately. I followed Hope. I'd planned to try to stop her. I was too late. I realize how upset you are, and that emotions are running high. But, the bottom line is that Hope wasn't intentionally undermining you or the FBI. She was behaving like a terrified mother. She wasn't thinking clearly. And now she's beating herself up enough for everyone. So I suggest we not waste time with accusations, but move on to finding your daughter. I know that's what you want. Please, Mr. Willis, let's just find Krissy as quickly as possible."

Her words seemed to placate Edward a little, because his jaw snapped shut and he nodded. "Fine."

The tension was still crackling, when there was a brief knock at the open door, and Patrick stepped inside. Behind him was a nervous, weathered-looking man who had to be Sidney Akerman.

"We're here," Patrick announced. "Ready to get started."

"Sidney?" Vera Akerman rose from the living room sofa and made her way out into the hall. "My God, it *is* you." She looked torn between relief and disgust.

Hope harbored no such torn loyalties. She whirled around, facing her father with blazing eyes. "How could you?" she demanded. "How could you compromise your family like that? Felicity and I were innocent children—*your* children. And now Krissy—she barely knows of your existence, yet she's become part of your collateral damage. How can you live with yourself?"

"I can't," her father replied without flinching. "That's why I've spent my life inside a bottle. And that's why I'm here now, even knowing you hate my guts. If I can help bring Krissy home safely, I'll do *anything,* sacrifice *anything,* to make it happen."

"How valiant. Unfortunately, it's thirty-two years too late for my sister, and my daughter…my baby…" Hope's voice quavered, and she turned away.

"Hope." Vera went to her daughter, put her arms around her. "I feel what you feel. But put it aside. We have to find Krissy."

Sidney met his ex-wife's gaze, and he was clearly speaking to both her and Hope. "To tell you that I was a stupid, naive pawn would be the truth, but meaningless. It changes nothing. Please—I'm not asking you for forgiveness. I'm just asking you to accept my help. Let me look at mug shots. Let me work with a sketch artist. Let me *try* to aid this investigation."

Hope stepped away from her mother and dashed the tears off her cheeks. "That's why you're here," she informed Sidney. She gestured toward the group of waiting professionals. "It certainly isn't for a family reunion. So go see what you can do."

Sidney was entrenched in mug shots and recaps when Casey's cell phone rang.

"Hey," Ryan greeted her. "Marc called and told me what's going on. Sidney Akerman there yet?"

"He got here about an hour ago," Casey replied quietly. "I'm not sure what's going on. The FBI's not in a sharing mood. They're pissed at me about the ransom drop. By their rules, I should have shared my suspicions with them before I took off to follow Hope."

"Yeah, well, by their rules I wouldn't be calling you with this interesting bit of info."

"I'm listening."

"Henry Kenyon's construction company was bought up after he died. Guess who the buyer was? Bennato Construction, employer of one Joe Deale."

"You're kidding."

"Nope. And from what I'm pulling up, Bennato is connected—*mob* connected."

"This one I'm going to share," Casey said.

"By all means." Ryan chuckled. "It might get you back into Hutch's good graces."

"Goodbye, Ryan."

"One more thing. When the FBI wants to pick up Deale, he's at the Laketown Bridge. They're repaving."

"Thanks." Casey ended the call on her BlackBerry.

"That was one of my associates," she announced to the task force. "Evidently, the construction company Sidney worked for was bought up after the owner died."

Guy Adams shot her an impatient look. "So?"

"So the company who bought it is Bennato. I'm sure you know they're reputed to have mob connections."

"We're aware of that."

"Wait a minute." Hutch rapidly scanned his notes. "Claudia Mitchell's fiancé works for Bennato."

"Exactly," Casey replied. "Joe Deale. I doubt that's a coincidence. Nor is the fact that Bennato recently repaved the parking lot and playground of Krissy's elementary school. Joe worked on that project."

There was a long moment of silence.

"How is it you have access to all that information?" Guy asked in a clipped tone.

"That's not important. I just do. I also know he's at the Laketown Bridge right now, working on a repaving job."

"Let's bring him in—*now.*" Peg was already at the door as she spoke.

Hope was thoughtful for a moment after the handful of agents peeled out. Her brows were knit together in concentration.

"Bennato," she murmured. "Edward, didn't you represent someone by that name a while back?"

Edward cleared his throat. "More than a while. Over a decade." This was one he clearly wished his wife had forgotten.

"Was it the same Bennato as the one Casey is referring to?"

"Yes, Hope, it was. Tony Bennato. But I represented him on a domestic, not a business matter."

"What kind of domestic matter?" Casey asked at once.

"A rather complicated divorce."

"Really. That's unusual, considering you're not a matrimonial attorney."

Edward bristled. "There were some criminal charges involved. Bennato's ex was suing him on charges of assault and ongoing physical abuse. It was a high-profile case for me at the time. So I took it."

"And you won, of course."

"I did." Edward's jaw was working. "Any organized crime allegations didn't impact my defense preparation. Nor were they a factor in the trial."

"How much were you paid?" Hutch inquired. He and Grace had stayed behind to continue their behavioral analyses, while several of the CARD team members and investigative agents had taken off to bring in Joe Deale.

"How would I remember that? It was over ten years ago."

Hutch gave an offhand shrug. "I'm just curious if Tony Bennato paid you by check or cash."

Hope shifted a bit at the question, uncomfortably lowering her gaze.

Edward was far less subtle and far more vocal. "Are you accusing me of something, Agent Hutchinson?"

"No. I'm just trying to establish the nature of your business relationship with Mr. Bennato."

"I defended him," Edward said. "He was found to be innocent of all charges. Further, he walked away with most of his monetary assets. He was happy. I was happy. Our relationship ended there. And I've had no contact with him since."

"Wow," Casey commented. "That must have been some defense you mounted."

"I'm an excellent attorney, Ms. Woods. My reputation speaks for itself."

"Indeed, it does."

Casey made sure to keep the sarcasm out of her voice. Still, from the corner of her eye, she saw Ashley—who was standing in the far corner of the hallway—wince. The poor girl obviously thought Casey was making a veiled reference to Edward's infidelity. The truth was, that was the last thing on her mind. What she was thinking was what a sleazebag Edward was, and how she wouldn't dismiss the prospect of his own mob dealings.

"The fact is, Tony Bennato would have no reason to hold a grudge against me," Edward was concluding. "And, if he did, he wouldn't have shelved it for ten years. Krissy wasn't even born when I handled his case."

"Point taken," Hutch replied. "Unless there were some under-the-table payments involved. Those tend to prompt very long memories, *and* very high expectations. Wouldn't you agree?"

Edward's only response was a glittering stare.

"Well, there's only one way to find out," Hutch continued. "Unless you'd rather save us some time and tell us how you collected your legal fees from Mr. Bennato."

"I have nothing to say. Feel free to call my accountant and discuss my finances to your heart's content, Agent Hutchinson."

"Now *that* would be a waste of time, and we both know it. You're an intelligent, resourceful man. If you'd conducted any illegal or unethical transactions, you'd be sure to cover them." Hutch's expression stayed totally neutral. "Your reaction, on the other hand, has been anything *but* a waste of time. My suggestion? Don't get too comfortable. Right now, our only priority is to bring your daughter home, safe and sound. But, once that's done, I'm sure our Organized Crime division will be eager to chat with you."

CHAPTER FIFTEEN

Ashley pulled Edward aside the instant it was feasible without raising any red flags.

"I have to talk to you," she said in a low, urgent tone.

"Not now," Edward replied, teeth clenched. "Not after that interrogation."

"It might throw fuel on the fire of what lies ahead," Ashley returned, her eyes wide and frightened. "Please, Edward. Give me a minute."

Edward glanced around. Hope was talking with her mother. Sidney was working with the sketch artist. And Casey Woods was in the middle of a heated debate with Agent Hutchinson.

With a jerk of his head, Edward signaled for Ashley to follow him into the kitchen.

"What is it?" he demanded. "This is definitely *not* the time."

"Casey Woods knows about us," Ashley replied without preliminaries.

"What the hell do you mean she knows about us? That's impossible. You must have misunderstood."

"Hardly. She cornered me early today. First, she pressured me to tell her what was going on to make your wife so jumpy. She sensed that I knew something. When I refused to share what I knew, she not-so-subtly reassured me that she didn't plan on telling Judge Willis that you and I are sleeping together—*but* that she'd really appreciate if I reconsidered sharing what I knew about Judge Willis's jittery state. A sort of one hand washes the other. Does that sound to you like I misunderstood?"

"Dammit." Edward slammed his fist on the counter. "How did she find out?"

"I don't know. The same way she finds out everything. Does 'how' matter? The important thing is she wasn't fishing. She was stating a fact. Denying it would have been stupid."

"So you admitted it?" Edward had clearly reached the end of his rope today. "For God's sake, Ashley, first you keep the ransom call from me, and now you give Casey Woods confirmation that we're having an affair. Why don't you just tell her we're taking Krissy and all my undeclared cash and flying off to the Cayman Islands?"

"Because we're not."

"You and I know that. But I'm under a microscope. The FBI might not think I abducted my own daughter, but they do think I'm a criminal. Any way I turn, I'm screwed. You're in better shape. Ms. Woods thinks you're supernanny, and, undoubtedly, an innocent young woman who's been sucked in by a rich, successful older man."

"Isn't that exactly what I am?" Ashley wet her lips with the tip of her tongue, visibly reticent about what she was about to say. "And isn't that exactly what you are? Edward, I realize you don't share your business dealings with me, but I'm not stupid. I know the kind of clients you represent. Plus, I know that Judge Willis got her hands on a quarter of a million dollars in cash in record time and without tipping off anyone—not the banks or the authorities. To me, that says there's cash lying around here. Lots of cash." She waved away Edward's reply. "I don't care about that, and I don't want to discuss it. I just want to give you a heads-up about Casey Woods. If it makes you feel any better, she promised to keep her mouth shut about our secret, not just to your wife, but to the authorities."

"How comforting." Sarcasm dripped from Edward's tone. "As if I trust her. And, even if she does keep quiet, the FBI's going to be watching me like a hawk. Which reminds me, since the ransom call came in on your cell, they'll be monitoring it. I'll have to buy you a throwaway for our conversations."

A long, painful pause. "That won't be necessary."

"Meaning?"

"Edward, you know how much I love you. Just like I know that I'm just a romantic distraction for you. So this is going to hurt me a lot more than it hurts you. But I can't do this anymore. Not to Judge Willis. And not in light of what's going on. I'm sick with worry over Krissy, and sick with guilt that Casey Woods has to waste her time on us when the real kidnappers are still out there."

Edward looked stupefied. "You're breaking things off?"

"I have to. I can't stop loving you. But I can start living with myself again."

"Fine," Edward snapped, rubbing the back of his neck. "Whatever you want. Frankly, this is an absurd conversation to be having right now. My daughter's out there somewhere. I have no idea if I'll ever see her alive again. So whether or not we keep sleeping together is low on my list. So if you've said everything you have to say, I'm going back into my living room to see if that son-of-a-bitch father that old man dragged in here can identify Krissy's kidnappers."

Casey was still having it out with Hutch when Peg Harrington called the house to say that they'd brought Joe Deale into the North Castle Police Department for questioning.

Everyone mobilized ASAP. Hope and Edward grabbed their coats. The remaining members of the task force did the same, including those with Sidney Akerman. The sketch artist was already packing up to move to the police precinct. Sidney was going with him. So was Patrick, who wasn't about to miss one moment of this opportunity of hearing what Deale had to say.

Casey spoke to Peg on speakerphone. "I want to sit in on this," she requested. "I think that's fair, since I gave you the information."

"Fine. You can sit in—on the other side of the glass," Peg replied. "The police want Claire Hedgleigh to do the same. You can give us your expert opinions *after* my agents and I have interviewed him."

"Fair enough."

Once everyone dispersed, the only people remaining in the house were Special Agent Jack McHale, who was monitoring the phone, Vera Akerman, who'd gone up to her room to rest, and Ashley Lawrence, who was weeping silently in the kitchen.

Joe Deale was ready to wet his pants by the time the FBI agents walked into the interrogation room two hours later. He'd had plenty of time to think. And he had plenty to hide. No matter how he played this, he was screwed. If he spilled his guts, he'd go to jail. And, if he kept his mouth shut, there was no way the mob would believe he hadn't talked. So the options were being locked up or being killed.

Locked up seemed like the lesser of two evils.

"Hello, Joe," Peg Harrington said as she and Ken Barkley finally entered the interrogation room, armed with documents, and took their seats across from him at the table. The North Castle Police Department's building was small, since crime there was low. And the interrogation room was bare bones.

"Why am I here?" Joe demanded. "I was paving a bridge. Last I heard, that wasn't illegal."

"No, but working for organized crime is."

"I don't know what you're talking about."

"Sure you do," Ken said. "You've done all kinds of ugly little deeds for your mob friends at Bennato. Shakedowns, violent reminders of monies owed, drug deals—I could go on and on."

Sweat broke out on Joe's forehead. "You've got no proof."

"Proof is a relative thing," Ken replied. "For instance, we've got a couple of dealers who'd be delighted to identify you as their heroin connection in exchange for a lighter sentence. And one of my associates says he dug up a witness who saw you hanging around a stolen car that ultimately ended up at a Mafia-affiliated chop shop."

"Their word against mine. Those guys would trade their mothers for a lighter sentence."

"True." Peg leaned forward and took over. "But the stacks of cash taped to the underside of your chest of drawers aren't up for debate. They're very real, and very incriminating for a man who makes barely more than minimum wage."

"You were in my house?" Joe gripped the edge of the table,

trying to look outraged. But his hands were shaking. "That's illegal. It's breaking and entering."

"Not with a search warrant, it isn't. The North Castle police got one more than an hour ago. Given the circumstances, the warrant was issued faster than you can say La Cosa Nostra. We've got more than enough to hold you."

"The money is Claudia's. She asked me to keep it for her."

"Nice try." Peg folded her arms across her breasts. "Let's stop playing games, Mr. Deale. You can sit here all night while we compile the evidence we need to charge you. You can walk out of here and take your chances on the streets. Or you can talk to us now. Because, quite frankly, your two-bit dealings with the mob are a blip on our radar. This, however, is a whole lot more…."

Peg reached for the table, flipping the architectural plans for Krissy's school faceup. She shoved them across the table and practically into Joe Deale's face. "What are you doing with this?"

Joe blinked. "It was a job I worked on."

"For which you have the plans?"

"I was responsible for providing the right number of containers of tar. So the foreman made me a copy of the plans with dimensions, and I brought them to our supplier. I forgot I even had them."

"So if we questioned your foreman, he'd tell us the same story?"

"If he remembers me being there, yeah. What's so important about these plans?" Joe stared at the designs, and realization erupted across his face. "This is that school Judge Willis's little girl was kidnapped from. You still think I had something to do with that?"

"You've got to admit, it looks pretty damning. The diagrams, the cash, the connections."

"Why would Bennato want to kidnap a kid?"

"I tell you what. Why don't we send you back out there to ask him?"

Joe went sheet-white. "Please. Don't do that. I'll be dead by tonight."

"Probably. Which makes jail a much safer choice. Tell us where Krissy Willis is, and we'll put a guard outside your cell."

"I don't know!" Joe hollered. "I didn't take that kid! Neither did Claudia. She resented the hell out of Judge Willis for firing her. But she'd never hurt a child. And even if I did do all the other things you just said—which I'm not admitting I did—I never touched a kid. *Never.* I swear it!"

"He's telling the truth," Casey murmured on the opposite side of the glass. "His entire body language is screaming it. Direct eye contact. Offensive posture. Whole body aligned with his words. He's not clever enough to fake all that."

"I agree." Claire was eyeing Joe intently. "I'm picking up a fair amount of negative energy, so my guess is that the FBI is right about his ties to the mob. But I'm not sensing any real evil. He's not a sociopath. And he didn't kidnap Krissy."

"Then who did?" Casey ran her fingers through her hair in frustration. "I feel like we're speeding down streets that look promising, but coming up against one dead end after another. We know the main road is close by, but we just can't reach it. The past and the present are related. I know it—I just can't get at how."

Claire angled her head slowly until she faced Casey. "I don't know what it means, or if it's related to anything you just said. But I had the oddest dream the other night. It was about Krissy's stuffed panda."

The house is always packed with FBI agents, and the driveway is packed with cars.

Now there's only one.

There's never going to be a better time for what I have to do.

Another assignment I can't refuse. It's for Krissy. It's necessary to fill the void until the feelings alone are enough.

Selfishly, it's for me, as well. I'm afraid of the fate I'll suffer if I change my mind and turn away.

Check the driveway one more time. Still just the one. It belongs to the agent inside monitoring the phones. Everyone else has left, except for the old woman and the nanny. Both their bedroom lights are off, which means they've gone to bed.

I'm taking a huge risk, I know. But to see Krissy's face light up—it'll be worth it. She's still so traumatized.

This close, even through the window, I can hear snippets of the agent's conversation. It sounds pretty heated. Probably an argument with his superior, or a wife. Good. It's the perfect distraction.

Back door. There's nothing but wooded acreage back there, and nothing but a short hall to the backstairs inside. I can do this. I have *to do this.*

My hands have to stop shaking. Stop it. Stop it.

Key in the lock. A quiet click. No burglar alarm screaming through the halls. Good. Although I came prepared.

The agent's still on the phone, he sounds more intense. Nonetheless, my time is limited.

Silently. Carefully. One carpeted step up at a time.

Safe. And I know just where to find what I came for. Krissy talks about it all the time. It makes her feel less scared. But she hurts so for Oreo.

This will fix the problem.

Top shelf beside her bed. Nestled in a makeshift nest of straw. Ruby the Robin and her nest. Oreo's best friend.

Step one complete.

Down the hall to the master bedroom suite. The makeup table. In a simple, classy bottle. Joy. *A lovely perfume, a memorable scent.*

Now, something else. It will add to the mirage.

The jewelry box—on the dresser. The heart-shaped locket. Inside, a picture of Krissy on one side, and a picture of the woman who'd been her mother on the other. Nothing could be more perfect.

Everything back in place. Nothing looks disturbed.

Ashley was sure she'd heard a noise. A creaking sound. Footsteps? She was probably imagining things, but, after what had happened to Krissy, she wasn't in the mood of letting anything slide.

She belted her bathrobe and left her room. First, she poked her nose into Krissy's room, scanned the area. All was silent, dark and deserted. She flicked on the light. Nobody was there. She shut the door behind her, and headed down the hall, glancing into each upstairs guest room and study. Nothing. Mrs. Akerman's door was shut. Ashley pressed her ear to the door. Silent. And no light shone from underneath. Not a surprise, given that the poor woman had retired hours ago.

Completing her tour, Ashley headed down to the other end of the hall and the master bedroom suite.

The door was ajar, the way Judge Willis often left it. Pushing it open, she stepped inside and glanced around.

There was no warning, nor any chance to turn around.

A heavy object crashed down on her head, sending blinding pain vibrating through her skull, and knocking her to the ground.

She made a faint moaning sound and lost consciousness.

CHAPTER SIXTEEN

Hope and Edward were silent during their car ride home from the police precinct. Edward drove mechanically, and Hope sat in the passenger seat, her body angled away from her husband, her head resting against the cool windowpane.

It didn't take a professional to interpret their body language.

"Joe Deale didn't give us a damned thing, other than his connection to Bennato," Edward finally said.

"Neither did you. And you once had business ties to Tony Bennato, too," Hope replied bitterly.

"What is that supposed to mean?"

"It means that there are all types of criminal acts, some dirtier than others. I realize you don't work the streets. But you represented a major figure in organized crime."

Edward shot her a sideways look. "I already explained that.

Besides, I hardly see the two associations as the same. Joe Deale works for the mob. I don't."

"Not directly, no. But the clients you represent, and the way you do business..." Hope sucked in her breath. "I've turned a blind eye for so long. But your scruples, or lack thereof, really struck home when I remembered your defending Tony Bennato. No, that's not entirely true. They struck home when I opened your safe and saw the treasure chest you've accumulated. You made it very easy for me to get the cash I needed for the ransom. I doubt you won the money on lottery tickets."

"What's your point?"

"My point is you're hardly one to cast stones. Stop being so sanctimonious about my negotiating with the kidnappers. I was trying to save our daughter. I'm well aware that you don't care for my methods. I'm not particularly fond of yours." Hope inclined her head slightly in her husband's direction. "Let's put aside our dirty laundry for now and get through this crisis. Then we can deal with our differences in whatever way we see fit."

Edward's jaw tightened. "Whatever you say. But our differences aren't just professional *or* marital. They're about Krissy's abduction, as well. You're fully committed to the idea that Felicity's and Krissy's kidnappings are connected."

"And you see no merit to that theory?"

"I didn't say that. Your father's mob dealings back then, and the fact that it just now became common knowledge makes the first strong argument in favor of that idea. But it's not the only theory. The FBI is working on several."

"None of which have produced any results. Now that Forensic Instincts is focusing entirely on this angle, I feel as if we might get somewhere. Joe Deale isn't the only mob employee. Plus, he was a baby thirty-two years ago. Maybe Felicity's and Krissy's kidnapper was the same person. Maybe he's Agent Lynch's age."

"That doesn't fit the BAU's profile."

"Profiles are based on rigorous analysis of evidence. But they're not exact."

"Neither are gut instincts."

"So, once again, we agree to disagree."

"It would seem that way," Edward said with a not undetectable amount of scorn in his voice.

The silence in the car resumed.

Hope was exhausted when they arrived home. She went directly upstairs, leaving Edward to nurse his snifter of brandy. Once she was on the second floor, she stopped in Krissy's room, just as she had the past two nights. Flipping on the light, she looked around, her gaze instinctively going to the bed, where her baby would now be asleep. Her chest gave that awful squeeze, and the rush of panic surged through her.

Two days. It had been two full days since Krissy was abducted. How in the name of heaven could she still be…

No. Hope gave a hard shake of her head. She couldn't allow herself to consider the implications of her daughter being missing this long. She had to believe that Forensic Instincts, if not law enforcement, would find Krissy and bring her home, safe and sound. They had to.

She turned off Krissy's light and headed wearily down the hall to the master bedroom suite. She ached everywhere, inside and out. But she didn't have the wherewithal to soak in a tub. So she'd take a quick, hot shower and slide into bed. Then she'd lie there, her eyes burning, for yet another sleepless night.

It didn't play out that way.

Crossing the threshold, Hope didn't even have a chance to turn on a lamp before she heard a thump as she tripped over a solid object. She regained her balance and reached for the overhead light switch.

Light flooded the room.

Collapsed in a crumpled heap on the carpet just inside the doorway was Ashley.

"Oh my God." Hope dropped to her knees, shaking Ashley in a reflexive motion. "Ashley! Ashley, can you hear me?" She leaned sideways toward the door, yelling at the top of her lungs. "Help! Somebody help me!"

There was a pounding of footsteps, and Special Agent Dugan burst into the room, Edward at his heels. They both instantly saw Ashley's limp figure.

"Call 9-1-1," Dugan instructed Edward, whose entire face had gone white. The agent crouched down, gingerly examining Ashley. "I've got a pulse," he announced. "It's strong and steady. I don't see any indication of a puncture wound, and there's no pool of blood. That means no knives or guns. And no contusions around the throat, so no strangling." He paused as his hand lightly touched the back of Ashley's head, and withdrew with blood on his fingertips. "She was struck from behind with a heavy object. She's bleeding, and she's got a whopper of a bump." He paused, spotting the weighty sculpture lying on the floor. "There. That must be the weapon. No one touch it—it's evidence. In fact, don't touch anything in this room. There might be fingerprints."

Hope complied, staying perfectly still on her knees on the floor. Meanwhile, Edward was supplying the necessary information to the emergency operator.

As he hung up, Ashley gave a low moan and began to stir.

"Ashley." Very gently, Hope stroked her cheek. "Can you hear me? Are you all right?"

Slowly, groggily, Ashley opened her eyes. "Judge Willis?" she asked in confusion. She tried to sit up, and groaned in pain, her hand automatically flying to the back of her head. "My head… it's killing me." She turned white when she saw the blood on her hand. "Oh God…"

"It's okay," Hope told her soothingly. "You took a hard hit. But you'll be fine. The EMTs are on their way."

"EMTs?" Ashley blinked. "What happened?"

"You tell us," Agent Dugan instructed. "Someone obviously got into this room and assaulted you." He frowned. "Whoever it was must have come up the back stairs. I was in the living room."

"What about the burglar alarm?" Edward asked. "I thought we activated it before we went out. And, even if we didn't, all the doors were locked."

"I have no answers for you yet, Mr. Willis. But, I assure you, we'll find them."

"All I remember was hearing a noise and going to check into it," Ashley told them, her eyes squeezed shut against the pain. "Krissy's room was empty. It looked as if it hadn't been touched. When I got down here, I stepped in…and that's all I remember. No—there was a blinding explosion of pain in my skull. I saw colors, lights. I felt like I was going to throw up. After that, I must have lost consciousness."

"Did you see your assailant?"

"No." Clearly, Ashley was struggling to remember. "Out of the corner of my eye, I saw a shadow. I heard breathing. I never had the chance to turn around, or even to react." Another groan.

"I'm sorry." She held both sides of her head. "It just hurts so much."

"I'm sure you have a concussion," Dugan said.

"And maybe some internal bleeding." Edward glanced impatiently at his watch. "I wish the paramedics would get here."

As he spoke, the sound of sirens reached their ears, and a minute later the EMTs rushed in. They took Ashley's vitals, lifted her onto a stretcher and carried her out to the ambulance.

"I'll ride with you," Hope said at once.

"No." Agent Dugan stopped her. "Once ERT has checked the crime scene, I need you here to see if anything is missing."

"I'll go with Ashley," Edward offered. "I'll keep you posted on her condition. You keep me posted on what your Evidence Response Team turns up, and if the bastard who broke in here took anything that could lead us to Krissy. He sure as hell didn't risk getting caught for nothing."

"I agree. He took quite a risk." Dugan was frowning, his professional gaze scanning the room, as he pressed a speed-dial button on his phone. "Very soon we'll have a full house, and hopefully some answers."

Casey and Hutch practically collided into each other in the front doorway of the Willis house.

"So Hope Willis called you the minute she got home." Hutch's words were a statement, not a question. And it wasn't a happy one.

"Of course she did. She's my client," Casey replied curtly.

"Not now, you two," Grace said, urging them into the house. "Later, you can kill each other. Now, we have a job to do."

They went upstairs to find ERT packing up to leave, and Hope speaking to Don Owens and several CARD team members, along with SAs Peg Harrington and Will Dugan, and Sergeant Sam Bennett of the North Castle Police Department.

"I'm so glad you're here." Hope's face flooded with relief when she saw Casey. Her reaction came as no surprise. It was very common for Forensic Instincts' clients to develop a personal attachment and to cling to them as a lifeline.

"What happened?" Hutch demanded.

Dugan filled him in on the events of the evening. "ERT found no fingerprints on the jewelry box, or on any of the remaining jewelry inside. Also, none were found on the surfaces we know the intruder touched when he removed the locket and the perfume. None on the dresser. None on the makeup table. Whoever broke in here must have worn gloves. ERT double-checked everything. They took the jewelry box with them for a more extensive examination. But I doubt they'll find anything. This kidnapper knew what he wanted, maybe even the exact locations of the items in question. He came prepared. He went straight for what he needed, snatched the locket and perfume, and left."

"A bottle of perfume, and a locket," Casey murmured. "Interesting."

"What does it mean?" Hope was shaking from head to toe. "He didn't touch any of my expensive jewelry or anything else of value."

"Tell me about the locket," Hutch instructed. "Did it open? Was there a photograph inside?"

"The locket was heart shaped. There were two photos inside. One of Krissy and one of me."

"And the perfume?"

"It's my regular scent—*Joy,*" Hope supplied. "I almost always wear it. I kept the bottle in plain sight."

Hutch leaned his head back and drew a sharp breath. "He was right here under our noses while we were all at the police station."

"Quite a risk he took," Grace added thoughtfully. "A pretty daring—and desperate—act." She turned to Hope. "I know you're badly thrown by this. But there's a big upside. It tells us that Krissy is probably alive."

"I agree." Hutch nodded. "The kidnapper took personal things—things that would remind Krissy of you. That suggests he's trying to put her at ease, to soothe her. Which not only means she's alive, it means he's struggling to make her happy. That's *not* the act of a killer, not when you combine it with the risk he took coming here, knowing full well that the task force is all over this case."

"He waited until we all cleared out," Don said. "That means he's watching the house."

"We expected as much."

A nod. "He caught Will Dugan alone and on the phone. It was the only time in the past two days that he could get in and out without running into an entourage of law enforcement. Once again, it emphasizes that we're not dealing with an amateur. Every step he takes is well thought out and painstakingly executed."

Casey turned to Sergeant Bennett of the North Castle P.D. "Can I give Claire Hedgleigh a call? I know she's working for you on this case. Maybe she can pick up on something from the scene."

"Good idea." Bennett nodded. "But I'll take care of contacting her."

Claire arrived a short time later. She was still bothered by all the loose, unconnected threads of her visions, none of which she could weave into a cohesive braid. Now, she was stunned by the brazen act of the kidnapper, breaking into the Willises' house—*again*. But she was eager to get to the master bedroom to see if anything came to her—anything that would integrate her flashes of insight.

"How's Ashley?" she asked as soon as she entered the room. "Is she badly hurt?"

"No. Just a concussion," Hope supplied, visibly relieved by that aspect of the equation. "No internal injuries. Some deep cuts and a nasty lump on the back of her head, though. The doctors are keeping her overnight for monitoring, just to be on the safe side. But we'll be able to pick her up tomorrow so she can recoup at home."

"Guilt," Claire pronounced abruptly. "I'm sorry to interrupt you. But I'm picking up on an overwhelming sense of guilt in this room."

"That would be mine," Hope said grimly. "I should have been here to prevent this."

"None of this was your fault," Casey responded at once. "Nor was it Ashley's. It's too bad that Agent Dugan was on the phone. But no one could anticipate this."

"I'm pretty pissed off at myself, as well," S.A. Dugan responded. "I can't believe someone got by me."

"This is a big house and there are back stairs," Claire murmured, still half inside her own head. "But there's another energy here. A new one. The kidnapper's."

"A kidnapper with a conscience," Hutch muttered. "More personal traits."

"Not just personal—feminine," Claire amended. "My sense is that the intruder was a woman. She came specifically to get the special items that would ease Krissy's separation anxiety."

A furrowed brow. "It's a female's energy—not dense or heavy like a man's would be. More light and airy."

"So you think the alpha male who's running the show sent his female accomplice to do the dirty work." Casey pursed her lips and nodded. "It makes sense. He'd get his desired results, and he wouldn't be the one taking the risk."

Hutch was scowling. "None of this feels right. A mobster with a grudge. One who demanded, and got, ransom money, but is still not satisfied. He also doesn't seem to want an eye for an eye. He wants Krissy alive, but is showing no signs of returning her—just as Felicity Akerman was never returned *or* recovered. What's this man's end goal? Just to make Sidney Akerman's family suffer?"

There were no ready answers.

"Are you sure nothing else was taken?" Claire asked Hope as she moved slowly around the room. She paused next to the empty space on the dresser. "The jewelry box was in this spot?"

"Yes," Peg confirmed. "ERT took it for evidentiary purposes. And, according to Judge Willis, nothing else was taken other than what we've discussed."

"Just the locket was taken from the jewelry box? You're sure?"

"I'm sure," Hope verified. "I checked the box three times. All my jewelry was untouched."

"Do you have a red stone? A ring, a necklace, maybe earrings?"

Hope shook her head. "I have an opal necklace that projects a variety of colors. But none of them is red."

"A ruby." Claire stated it with certainty. "It's a ruby." She brushed her fingertips over the spot that had held the jewelry box. "And it's not in the box that was here. Do you keep jewels anywhere else in the house?"

"No. I'm not really a jewelry person."

"What about Krissy? Does she have any ruby studs, or fake stones that look like rubies?"

"She doesn't have any jewelry, much less rubies. She doesn't even like rubies, other than the name. It's the one she gave to—" Hope stopped, her breath catching in her throat. "Ruby," she whispered. "I never thought of that. I never checked…"

"Ruby?" Grace demanded.

"Krissy's stuffed robin." Hope was already halfway to the door. "She plays with her and Oreo all the time."

By the time everyone had reached Krissy's room, Hope was standing next to the shelves beside Krissy's bed and was gazing at the top one, a stricken expression on her face.

"She's gone. Nest and all." Slowly, Hope turned. "Oreo and Ruby are like an imaginary family to Krissy. Oreo and Ruby are best friends, and Krissy is their nanny, like Ashley is to her."

"That explains my dream," Claire murmured. "It's why Oreo was crying. And who he was missing. Ruby." At the puzzled glances aimed her way, Claire explained the specifics of her dream.

"Once again, an attempt to make Krissy feel less lonely, more normal," Sergeant Bennett concluded. "Nice work, Claire." He was well aware that the FBI—particularly the BAU—was on the fence about Claire's abilities. He couldn't miss this opportunity to drive home the legitimacy of her gift.

Casey spoke up. "Not just more normal, more at home. The kidnappers are trying to recreate the securities of Krissy's world. Her mother's scent. A locket with pictures of the two of them side by side. And Krissy's two closest inanimate friends in the world, the ones she keeps with her at night in the haven of her bedroom. These people want her to *want* to stay where she is, not just to tolerate it."

"A willing captive," Claire agreed. "Which she hasn't been until now. She's desperate to come home. The kidnappers are hoping to win her over."

"Oh, God." Hope sank down onto Krissy's bed. "What if they're unsuccessful? Krissy is so strong willed. What if she fights them? What if they hurt her?"

"Hope—stop." Casey sank down beside her. "Let's cling to the fact that Krissy is alive and that the kidnappers are trying to soothe her. It buys us a little time to figure things out. Let's not waste that time panicking."

"Then what do we do from here?"

"We divide and conquer."

CHAPTER SEVENTEEN

The brownstone was dark.

Hero was stretched out on the carpeted floor, enjoying a late-night snooze.

In the bed, Hutch threw back his head with a shout, every muscle in his body strained to the hilt. Then, with an exhausted groan, he shuddered and collapsed on top of Casey, his body drenched in sweat.

Casey sank into the mattress and shut her eyes, still quivering in the aftermath. Her fingertips traced a fine line down Hutch's back.

"Still mad?" she finally managed.

"Too tired to be mad—now."

A soft laugh. "You're tough to win over."

"Have your way with me a few more times. I might reconsider."

"I'll keep that in mind."

Long, silent minutes passed.

Broaching the inevitable, Hutch rolled over, throwing an arm over his head and sprawling out on his back. "It's bad enough you play by your own set of rules," he said. "But you're reckless, too. That ransom drop could have gotten ugly. We're trained to handle that. You're not."

"Point taken. But I didn't have time to arrange a posse. I had to act fast. Plus, I wasn't sure it was a ransom drop. All I was sure of was that Hope was acting weird. Then she left abruptly—right after her father showed up. I didn't think—I just took off after her." Casey tipped her head back to look up at Hutch. "That's as close to an apology as you're going to get. I hope it makes the grade."

A corner of his mouth lifted. "You really are a piece of work. Yeah, fine, it makes the grade. I'll give it a C+. But as for our methods—we're never going to have a meeting of the minds on those."

"True," Casey agreed. "The good news is that the FBI task force is now on the same page with us about the two kidnappings probably being related. Your team can drill the hell out of Sidney Akerman and Joe Deale, and my team and I can soft-pedal it."

Hutch gave her a quizzical look. "Meaning?"

"Meaning that organized crime is the FBI's forte. But there are other ways to skin a cat. There are tons of subtleties yet to explore. Law enforcement's job is clear—to chase down every viable lead, from the mob to the other suspects on your list. Which makes Forensic Instincts' job just as clear—to hunt down more subtle leads, through the more subtle sources."

"Just to clarify, you're totally abandoning the idea that Krissy's kidnapping might be an isolated event?"

"You know me better than that. I never abandon anything—not until the case is officially, and successfully, closed. I have a few avenues left to travel on the isolated kidnapping theory, although my gut tells me they won't pan out. Nothing illegal, I promise. Mostly, I want to pursue the related kidnappings theory. I plan to go over the Felicity Akerman case file with Patrick. He's going to be an invaluable resource in recreating the past—for your team and mine. I want to take in everything he tells me. Then I want to talk to Hope and, most importantly, to Vera Akerman. If Sidney was in trouble when Felicity was kidnapped, his family might know more than they realize. Hope, from a child's innocent perspective, and Vera, from a wife's real-life observations. I want to hear about friends. Business associates. Even casual acquaintances who struck an odd note."

"It sounds like you're reaching."

"Maybe we are. But we don't have a clear suspect, just a lot of muddied waters. So between your tried and true methods and our unconventional ones, we'll have all the bases covered." Casey propped herself on one elbow. "Speaking of unconventional methods, stop eyeing Claire Hedgleigh with such skepticism. She's for real, and she's good. I'm hoping to convince her to come work for my company once this case is behind us."

"Duly noted. I guess my personality and training make it hard for me to believe in psychics."

"Then think of her as a highly sensitized intuitive. She'd like that description better anyway."

"Is that the argument you used on Marc and Ryan to get them to welcome their new colleague?" Hutch asked with a grin.

"Something like that. Marc's very similar to you. He's dubious, but reasonable. Ryan's less open-minded. Then again, I think he's dying to get her into bed, and hasn't come to terms with it. She's a one-eighty from him and from the women he's used to."

"In other words, she's not climbing all over him."

"Exactly. So his reaction to having her around on a daily basis isn't entirely professional."

"Mixing business with pleasure," Hutch said drily. "It's a lousy idea."

"True." Casey's eyes twinkled. "Then again, sometimes you just can't help yourself."

"I couldn't agree more," Hutch concurred in a husky voice.

He pulled Casey over him, bringing the conversation to an abrupt close.

My doubts had been wrong, my protests in vain.

It had *been worth the risk.*

Krissy. Watching you cradle the panda and the robin makes me all the more certain that I did the right thing by following orders and breaking into your house. And spraying the robin with that perfume... Now, you're sleeping peacefully—at last.

I've got to make you willing. This plan can't work without that. Your old life must cease to exist.

Or you'll cease to exist.

Day Four

It was seven in the morning, and it was Marc's turn to walk Hero.

He didn't mind. The dog was smart as a whip, with a sniffer to match.

They returned to the brownstone with bagels and coffee for everyone. Casey and Ryan were already seated at the conference room table, so Marc and Hero completed the team.

"I brought enough for Hutch. What did he do, sneak out the back door?" Marc asked wryly.

"No." Casey was unbothered by the good-natured teasing. "He left at the crack of dawn, boldly through the front. He's meeting with Patrick and Sidney. The FBI task force gets to talk to them first. But that's okay. We have a few things to take care of in the meantime. And Patrick had copies of the Akerman case file sent to both me and to Don. So we'll be privy to the same information. I'll make photocopies for each of you."

"Good." Marc distributed breakfast, then took a seat. "That'll give me lots of reading material."

"Well, you won't be doing it today," Casey informed him. "Today you're going to be a determined husband searching for a new house. One that's in Armonk, where the school system is exceptional."

"Really." Marc's brows rose. "And who am I married to? You?"

"Nope. I'll be your Realtor. We need someone who can be overbearing to play that part. And that's yours truly. Actually, Claire has agreed to help us out. She'll be your wife. And Hero will be your dog. We'll meet at the Willis house. Bring my STU-100, the gauze pads and tongs, some latex gloves and the special glass jars I bought. I'll create a few scent pads, using some of Krissy's things as scent articles. We'll introduce a pad to Hero."

"After which, we'll be canvassing the neighborhood," Marc surmised.

"Right. Once he's familiar with Krissy's scent, Hero will be able to tell us if she was taken to any of the neighbors' houses. In the meantime, we'll be talking to the home owners, asking questions about what it's like to live there. How many kids are around and their ages, if the parents are friendly, if there's any trepidation over the recent kidnapping. I'm willing to bet we'll find out lots of gossip, tidbits that average people don't share with law enforcement. It'll give us a good perspective on anyone in the area who's considered to be 'off,' plus firsthand interaction with the folks who live here, as well. If Krissy's kidnapping is a stand-alone crime, that should help supply us with some viable suspects. Then, Ryan can run down their names and see if anything unsavory pops up."

"But you don't believe it will."

"No, I don't. I think the two crimes are connected. But this will help the Willises comfortably rule out their friends and neighbors, and give us a chance to cross some names off our list until the FBI lets us in the door to talk to Patrick. I don't want to step on their toes. I pissed them off enough already by following Hope to the ransom drop. If they try to block our access, we'll be screwed. So let's play by the rules, at least where it comes to the organized crime angle."

Ryan leaned back in his chair, eyeing Casey shrewdly. "That's not all you have on tap for today, is it?"

Casey shook her head. "I'm going to talk to Hope, get more details of her childhood. Then, if I'm lucky, I'll get to talk to Vera Akerman. I'd be willing to bet she can relay information she doesn't even know she has. At which point, you'll come in. I'm hoping to have some names to give you, some from the Willises' neighborhood, and some from their past. You're going to be a busy boy by dinnertime."

"Good. I look forward to the challenge."

"For you?" Casey arched an eyebrow. "It won't be a challenge. You could do it in your sleep."

Her cell phone sounded its upbeat ring tone. "Casey Woods."

She was quiet for a minute, listening. "I'm still in the city, but I'll be heading up to Armonk in a little while," she supplied. Another pause. "Are you in Midtown now? Fine. I'll meet you in your office in an hour." She disconnected the call.

"What was that about?" Marc asked.

"That was Edward Willis. What was it about? Ostensibly, he wants to see me in his office to discuss the status of our investigation."

"In reality, he wants to know if you plan on telling his wife that he's sleeping with Ashley Lawrence," Marc finished.

"Bingo." Casey tapped her pen on the table. "That marriage is already in trouble. Edward probably wants to keep it from blowing apart. Not good for his image. And that means covering his ass. The man is a major pig."

"What are you going to tell him?"

Casey gave Marc a tight smile. "I think I'll make him squirm."

Edward Willis was doing paperwork at his desk when his secretary showed Casey into his office. He requested privacy—door shut, no interruptions, no phone calls. The poor young woman immediately agreed, giving her boss one long, infatuated look before retreating. Casey wondered if Edward was sleeping with her, too.

"Thank you for coming, Ms. Woods," he began, once they were alone. "Would you like coffee? Tea?"

"I'll help myself, thank you." Casey poured herself a cup of regular coffee from the expensive brewing station, then took a seat across from Edward. "I didn't know you were in the office today. I thought you'd be at the hospital with Ashley, or joining your wife in driving her home."

She saw Edward's jaw visibly tighten.

"I find work to be therapeutic," he replied. "It keeps me from going crazy worrying about Krissy."

Casey studied his expression, thinking that that was probably the first completely honest statement he'd ever made to her.

"So your phone call sounded important," she began. "What was it you wanted to see me about?"

"This." Edward slid a check across the desk until it was right in front of Casey, so she could easily view it.

She didn't look down but, instead, continued watching him expectantly.

He gave her the explanation she was seeking. "When my wife hired you, I thought of you as a fledgling company with a very light proven track record. I had no idea you'd be as committed, or insightful, as you are. I'm afraid I treated you rather brusquely, and without the respect you deserve. I know that Hope is paying you well. Still, I'd like to add a bonus to that fee right now. And another if you bring my daughter home safely."

At this point, Casey glanced down at the check. It was made out to Forensic Instincts LLC, and it was in the amount of twenty-five thousand dollars.

A lovely, generous bribe.

Keeping her expression carefully blank, Casey met Edward's gaze.

"Let me tell you a few things about myself and my company, Mr. Willis. We're everything you just described and more. Someday, we're going to be known as the foremost profilers in the Tri-state Area, with the most out-of-the-box, creative approaches to solving crimes—successfully. None of those approaches is going to include gossiping or inciting family breakups. So while I appreciate your offer, I'm not too crazy about its basis. So let me put your mind at ease. Frankly, I don't care if you sleep with Ashley Lawrence and half of Manhattan. It has no bearing on Krissy's kidnapping. I'm convinced that neither you nor Ashley had anything to do with her abduction. And that's all that interests me."

Casey slid the check back across the desk. "Consequently, there's no need to buy me off. Like you said, your wife is paying us twice our normal rates. That's more than enough. On the other hand, don't tear up the check. I'll be happy to take it as a bonus, once we bring Krissy home."

Edward startled, and then, for a split second, he actually looked as if he might smile. "Very well," he agreed, picking up the check and putting it in his desk drawer. "It's clear we understand each other."

"Crystal clear."

CHAPTER EIGHTEEN

From Edward Willis's office, Casey drove up to Armonk to carry out the house-hunting charade she'd arranged with Claire and Marc.

After several hours of pounding the pavement and ringing doorbells, they collapsed on the Willises' sofa, worn-out as they discussed their findings. One thing was for sure: it was amazing the trivia you learned in a suburban neighborhood just by asking the right questions.

By the time the "happy couple," escorted by their "Realtor," had visited a ton of local residences in the Willises' community, they knew more *about* the negligent parents and more *from* the overprotective parents than any official call could ever yield. They knew the number of kids in each household, as well as their ages and genders. They knew who the career moms were, who the stay-at-home moms were, and who the moms were who constantly had housefuls of kids over. They knew which dads worked at home, which were frequently around, and which were away on perpetual business trips. And they knew which families were tight with each other, which ones were the neighborhood leaders and which ones were loners who kept to themselves.

While there were definite families who didn't make the popular list, that list was, nonetheless, devoid of people demonstrating creepy behavior or questionable actions. Everyone described the neighborhood as warm, friendly and overwhelmingly safe. The recent abduction of Krissy Willis had sent shock waves through the community. The home owners all assured Claire and Marc that nothing like this had ever happened before, nor, given the extensive neighborhood watch that had been set up, did they intend to ever let it happen again.

Most of them were certain the crime had been a personal one, given the type of people the Willises dealt with in their work, and the high-profile nature of their careers. But not even one neighbor so much as hinted at a suspicion involving someone in the community.

Casey was unsurprised by the results, as were Marc and Claire.

"I didn't pick up significant negative energy from any of our visits," Claire pronounced. "And Hero didn't pick up Krissy's scent."

"Agreed. It was just the usual affluent suburban competitiveness," Marc clarified drily. "Whose landscaping was more elaborate, who had the latest and greatest model of Mercedes SUV, and whose built-in pool was larger. Nothing unexpected. Just another reason I'm glad I'm not a rich suburbanite."

Casey gave him a half smile. "I hear you. As for what we did—or didn't—find out, that comes as no surprise. None of us expected to hit the mother lode from this adventure. But we had to try." She glanced down at her notes. "Just to tie this inquiry up with a neat little bow, I'll email Ryan the names that came up most frequently in a negative capacity. He can check them out. If they've had so much as a run-in at a Little League game, he'll find it."

She began typing names into her BlackBerry.

"The FBI has been with Sidney Akerman all day," Marc reminded her. "Do you think they found out anything?"

"I think Patrick would have let us know if they had." Casey bit her lip thoughtfully. "I'm not quite sure why, but I trust him. Maybe it's because he's not officially on any side. Or maybe it's because I sense the same maverick spirit in him as I do in us. Whatever the reason, I think he'd let us know if they were onto something. Weaving your way through the members of the mob is no easy task. They're working with the details given to them by the FBI's resident agency in upstate New York—details they obtained from the perp who cut a deal by giving them information on Sidney's run-in with the mob. They're also dealing with Tony Bennato, who bought that company. And they're dealing with Joe Deale, who's a small potato in a much bigger organization. It's not going to come together in one day. Still..." A pensive pause. "It can't hurt to be safe. Marc, you and Hutch haven't had any time to catch up. Why don't you drop by the North Castle P.D. and see if he wants to grab a drink, or a late lunch."

Marc's lips twitched. "I'm flattered. You think I can get more out of a friend and former colleague than you can out of a guy who can't stay away from you for more than a few weeks at a time."

"Damn straight, I do. Business is business. You're former BAU. You worked together. And you'd be talking guy to guy. That's about as sacred as it gets. Besides, this will give Claire and me a chance to talk to Hope and Vera. I want to get as many seemingly inconsequential details as I can. The more I get, the more Ryan has to run with."

"True." Marc rose. "Maybe I could also drop in on Joe Deale's foreman, and intimidate him a little about those architectural plans. You never know how deep he's in."

"Good point. And good luck."

"I'll check in later." Marc shot a quick wave at Claire and headed out the door, where Hero was waiting in the car.

The man-to-man stuff was underway. Time for a little woman-to-woman action.

Hope and Vera were seated in the Florida room, sipping on cups of chamomile tea, when Casey and Claire found them.

Hope jumped to her feet in a heartbeat. "Is there news?"

"Not yet," Casey replied. "But we'd like to talk. I'll fill you in on the names we've crossed off the list, and then I'd like to ask you both some questions. The questions may seem trite, but I assure you, they're anything but."

"All right." Hope resettled herself on the couch. "Whose names did you delete from our suspect list? And how?"

Quickly, Casey ran through their house-buying charade.

"That's very creative," Hope commented when Casey was through. "But the FBI and the police have already interviewed all our neighbors. So that territory has been covered."

"Yes and no. The task force did their job—very thoroughly. But police badges and FBI ID tend to intimidate people. So the interviewees automatically supply factual answers, rather than more detailed, personal ones. We took every iota of negative feedback, however small, and turned the information over to

Ryan McKay, my techno-genius. He'll do detailed searches on those people—so detailed that anything even remotely out of whack will pop up. That'll support the law enforcement investigations, and eliminate a neighborhood of suspects altogether."

Hope gave a wan smile. "I appreciate that. But it doesn't bring me much comfort."

"I agree. That's why we want to talk." Casey sat down and opened her notepad, gesturing for Claire to take a seat beside her. "I still believe that your sister and your daughter's kidnappings are related. I think you do, too. The cops are digging into your father's connection to the mob, however limited. I want to look at the past, too, but through a different route."

"Which is?"

"You. I want you to think back thirty-two years. To rack your brains to remember every single detail, person or conversation associated with the time right before and after Felicity's kidnapping. You'd be surprised how much each of us stores away in our memory that we don't even realize is there. Events, snatches of conversation, and flashes of visual images. I'm asking you to trust me, and to try this. Claire can help us. If anything you touch on triggers a feeling or insight, she'll pick up on it. Together, maybe—just maybe—we can zero in on something that can help find Krissy."

"I was six years old," Hope reminded her.

"I realize that. Were you in kindergarten? First grade? Focus on that, on the friends you remember coming over to play. That's a good place to start to initiate memories." Casey turned to Vera. "And you were Sidney's wife. You must remember the last months you were together. Things he said. The way he acted. How he reacted to Felicity's abduction—and not just the drinking. The things he harped on. What set him off. Which parts of the FBI investigation threw him the most. Any people who came by to offer their support that elicited a notable response from him. Things like that."

Vera drew a slow, painful breath. "That was a horrible time in our lives and in our marriage. I can't overlook the drinking—it consumed us. And, yes, Sidney was obsessed with the FBI investigation. Now I realize why. He felt responsible. He *was* responsible."

"Did he have any friends who supported him? Anyone who came by frequently to offer words of encouragement?"

"I understand where you're going with this," Vera replied. "But Sidney wasn't interested in support. He was a man with a mission. *I'm* the one who craved the support. I didn't get it from my husband. I was fortunate that my friends, and the mothers of Hope's and Felicity's friends, were there for me. They came by every day, bringing food and words of encouragement." She swallowed, hard. "We had a prayer vigil each evening, the entire first week that Felicity was gone."

"I remember that," Hope murmured. "Mrs. Matthews, Mrs. Tatem, all our neighbors, and a lot of other mothers I didn't know. Felicity and I had different friends. I do remember all the mothers from the camp soccer team coming over."

"Daily," Vera confirmed. "They were kind, loving…and scared to death. They were afraid the kidnapper was targeting the girls from the team. I think they felt better being close to the investigation, so they could feel reassured. I don't blame them."

"Was there any justification for their fear?" Casey asked. "Were there any seedy characters hanging around watching the girls?"

Vera shook her head. "Not that any of us knew. Of course,

now that I know the mob was involved, I can't be sure. They're good at staying hidden. But even if they were watching, there'd be no reason to scrutinize anyone but Felicity. None of the other fathers was involved with Sidney's business."

"Have you stayed in touch with any of these mothers?"

"Of course. Some of them still live in New Rochelle. Some moved, but we kept up by phone, and now, by email. Tragedy is a funny thing—it binds people together for life."

"I understand." Casey was jotting down some notes. "Are the names of all those women—from school, camp and the neighborhood—listed in the original file along with your current friends at the time? I haven't had the chance to sink my teeth into the file yet. Agent Lynch just got it to us."

"I believe all the names are in there, yes." Vera thought about it and nodded. "Special Agent Lynch was very thorough. He collected every detail. The only ones you won't find in his file are those attached to the mob connection you've only now just uncovered. Henry Kenyon's name will be in there, of course. He was Sidney's employer and friend. The FBI questioned him—evidently not thoroughly enough."

Casey lowered her pad and gazed steadily at Vera. The last thing she wanted was for the older woman to get the wrong idea about the Bureau's competence. "As you noted, Mrs. Akerman, the mob is adept at hiding. Organized Crime is very good at staying under the radar. They keep operations like the one they were running through Henry Kenyon's company small and unobtrusive." As she spoke the truth, she still knew in her gut that Patrick was undoubtedly beating himself up for missing the connection. "The FBI would have no reason to have their antennae raised about any mob involvement. Plus, technology then was a lot more limited than it is now. Computers were a new phenomenon, and certainly not standard Federal issue. So there were no internet searches, or in-depth profiles."

"We know that," Hope assured her. "I remember hearing my parents talking. They said the FBI was all but living at our house. I'm sure Special Agent Lynch did everything he could to find Felicity. He's obviously still distraught over the case. Pointing fingers would be absurd."

"I'd never do that," Vera clarified hastily. "Hope is right. Special Agent Lynch was a godsend. He led the investigation, and he dealt with Sidney. I don't know which was more of a challenge. I'm sorry if I sounded accusatory."

"You didn't," Casey reassured her. "You sounded tormented. Which you were, and now are again."

"Do you have a photo of Felicity that you could give me?" Claire inserted herself for the first time, tackling the situation via her area of expertise.

"Of course." Vera opened her purse and pulled out a photo album. A few sleeves of pictures were inside. Most of them were dated, but still clear. She handed two photos to Claire. "Both of these are from the summer before…before our world ended. The first one is just Felicity. She's beaming ear to ear because she'd just won a plaque for scoring the most goals at her camp soccer tournament. The second photo is of Felicity and Hope together." A wan smile. "Very few people could tell them apart."

"I can see why," Claire murmured, studying the photos. "I'm going to start with the one of just Felicity. I don't want to get hers and Hope's energies confused, especially since they're identical twins. If I sense anything at all from the first photo, I'll move onto the second."

She shut her eyes, touching her fingertips lightly to Felicity's image.

A few moments passed.

"I sense joy. Pride. Maybe a little smugness." Claire's lips curved. "She beat out Suzie by only two goals."

"That's right." Vera leaned forward, her eyes huge as saucers. "What else can you sense?"

"That was the last game Felicity played. Not because of the abduction. Another reason." A pensive pause. "I sense impatience, frustration and pain. A lot of it." Claire's fingers shifted slightly and came to rest near Felicity's left elbow. "Her left arm. She can't bend it. And it hurts terribly. Shooting pain."

"She broke it," Hope supplied, visibly awestruck by Claire's talent. "It was in a cast most of the next summer. The doctor gave her the green light to play again the day before she was kidnapped. I remember how excited she was."

Claire nodded without opening her eyes. "She was. She loved soccer. She loved sports." A heartbeat of a pause. "She loved sharing them with your father."

Not a flicker of envy crossed Hope's face. "Thank you for your sensitivity. But my father's enthusiasm over Felicity was common knowledge. It wasn't that he loved her more than he loved me. They just had more in common. I never felt neglected or uncared for. Besides—" Hope patted her mother's hand "—I had my mom to share my love of reading and learning with. So it all evened out."

As she thought back, tears dampened Hope's eyes. "We were a happy, well-adjusted family. Felicity and I were different, but we were best friends. Anyone who hurt one of us had to deal with the other. I adored her. She adored me. My childhood, and a chunk of my life, disappeared when she did."

On that note, Claire opened her eyes long enough to switch

photos, laying the shot of Hope and Felicity in the palm of her hand. She ran her fingers over the twins' happy images.

"I can feel the love you're describing," she said. "Not just from you. From your sister, as well. The connection between you is strong. I doubt anything could come between you. Sometimes she got scared. She didn't want anyone to know. You made it better."

A nostalgic smile touched Hope's lips. "Felicity was afraid of going to the doctor. She always associated it with getting a shot—and she was terrified of shots. Tongue depressors, too. There was no way of getting around those visits when it came to our family doctor, although we racked our brains to come up with something. But school was another matter entirely. It was easy to fool the school nurse. Felicity was not only afraid, she didn't want her friends to make fun of her. So whenever she got sick during the school day and the teacher made her go to the nurse, she went to the bathroom instead. I went to the nurse's office and pretended I was her. I complained of her symptoms and got the nurse to call our mother. Felicity stuck out the day, and I got to go home to TV and ice cream."

Hope gave a small laugh. "It's a good thing I didn't go to camp, though, because I couldn't have pulled it off there. Every time I visited Felicity at camp, or went with my parents to see her in a game, the camp nurse knew who was who. She was sweet. And she claimed that each of us had our own sparkle."

"Linda," Vera said affectionately. "She was so fond of Felicity. She was one of the women I mentioned who came to our evening prayer vigils. Even after those initial weeks, Linda and I stayed in touch. We still do, now and then. But Hope is right. Linda always could tell the girls apart. So could our next-door neighbor, Gladys Evans and Fern Chappel, the school librarian.

It seemed to be a gut feeling with some people. Of course, it was never an issue with Sidney and me. To us, each twin was unique and distinctive, physically and characteristically."

Turning, Vera arched an eyebrow at Hope. "And, by the way, I caught on to that little game you and your sister played with the school nurse. I passed the details of your trick along to her. When one of you was sick, she knew just who to tell me to pick up. She'd describe what her patient was wearing, and I'd let her know if it really was Felicity or if it was her very loyal and naughty twin."

"Oh." Hope's smile was sheepish. "We always did wonder why you sometimes got mixed up about who you were picking up and giving a sick day to."

"Well, now you know."

"Felicity wasn't the only one who was sometimes afraid," Claire pronounced.

"No, she wasn't." Hope's smile faded. "I was afraid of sleeping alone when our parents were out. So, on those nights, she made sure we stayed in the same bed. We told our parents that it was because our babysitter's talking on the phone kept me up. But it wasn't true. I was scared. That's why we were together the night of the kidnapping."

"Yes," Claire said softly. "But that night *she* was also scared for *you*. She saw the person in black go to you first. You were asleep. She saw your face get covered. She saw you go limp. She didn't know what happened to you."

"You can visualize the night of Felicity's kidnapping?" Casey asked Claire, stunned by the realization.

Claire's eyes opened. "Fragments of it, yes. The kidnapper was dressed in black. Wearing a hooded sweatshirt. And gloves. I can visualize black gloves. The handkerchief was drenched in chloroform. That's all I see. I can feel fear and confusion. I can sense a commotion. But there's nothing distinct. It's all amorphous flashes." A sigh. "I wish I could tell you more."

"It's a start," Casey said. "A good one. I think we've made some real progress today." A pause. "On several fronts."

CHAPTER NINETEEN

Oh, Krissy, we have the whole lot of them so confused. They don't know where to look first. And they'll never look here. You're *safe.*

I love watching you play with Oreo and Ruby. Your little face lights up, and you're in a world of your own imagination. Imagination is a wonderful thing. It opens doors and dreams that no one can take away from you. It makes things right when everything is wrong. How well I know that. I'll help keep you in that beautiful, magical world. I'll keep you safe, make that imaginary world a reality.

It's so precious the way you change your voice when Ruby is speaking, and then when Oreo answers. A high tweet with words intermingled, and a low but friendly growl mixed with more words.

Until today, I watched your playtime from outside the room, through the glass pane in the door. Those were my instructions. This time, everything changed. I was allowed inside. I couldn't share your game, not yet. But I could see it up close, feel as if I were a part of it.

I came in and sat down quietly. You stiffened when I walked in, and you got that flicker of uncertain fear in your eyes. But that dissipated. And you didn't cringe or wriggle away. You took the milk and cookies I brought, and you drank and ate them without hesitation. After you got that adorable milk mustache, you went into your favorite corner and started playing with your pretend friends.

You act as if I'm not here, but I know you know that I am.

Sweet Krissy. This is just the beginning. Soon you'll let me into your pretend world. Soon you'll include me. Then I'll give you the surprise pretend world I developed for you. You're smart. You're creative. You'll love it.

You need me. You don't know it yet, but you do. No one understands that better than I do. I need what you need. But my needs were, and will be, *met. And so will yours.*

We just need a little more time.

Business at the rustic Armonk pub was starting to pick up as Marc and Hutch relaxed in one of the booths, drinking their pints of Sam Adams.

"I could ask to what do I owe this honor. But we both know the answer." A corner of Hutch's mouth lifted. "Casey sent her Navy SEAL out to do reconnaissance."

Marc took a deep swallow of beer, then lowered his glass to the table. "Actually, she wanted to give you and me some catch-up time *and* for me to do reconnaissance. So it wasn't entirely divisive. Besides, she knows damn well we wouldn't be putting anything over on you by playing games. Nope. In your case, I wear my motives on my sleeve."

"Fair enough." Hutch was totally comfortable with Marc. They'd known each other for years, ever since Marc's days at the BAU, where they'd become not only colleagues but friends. Marc had worked BAU-2, which covered crimes involving adults. Hutch was thinking of putting in for a transfer to that unit. Investigating the sexual violations, kidnapping and murder of children was beginning to get to him. He'd been a cop, he was a pro, but that didn't mean he regarded life as any less precious. And kids—well, that was watching the utter decimation of innocence right before his eyes.

"Whatever you can tell me about the Sidney Akerman investigation would be appreciated." Marc didn't waste time mincing words.

"Technically, that's nothing. It's an ongoing investigation. And you're not Bureau anymore." Hutch shot Marc a wry grin. "Which is why I got my marching orders from Peg about precisely what I could and couldn't say. She's more interested in finding Krissy Willis than playing cat and mouse with Forensic Instincts. So tell me what you know, what you want to know, and I'll fill in whatever blanks I can."

"Okay," Marc agreed. "Let's start out with the biggest question. Do you know what crime family Tony Bennato works for?"

"Between what we found out from the soldier who flipped and what we got from our own informants, the Vizzini family."

"So you've got the Vizzini squad at the New York Field Office working on it."

"Yup. They're pounding the pavement right along with us. They've got their long-term goals, which will include interviewing members of the family still serving time, those on the street, even those in the witness protection program, which they'll work through the U.S. Marshals. But for now, they know what we need. We're all about finding Krissy Willis. They'll use their informants, and whatever Carl George—the seniormost member of the Vizzini case squad—can come up with. He was around in the late seventies. He may know one or more of the guys Sidney Akerman comes up with."

"In other words, who might or might not be with the Bennato Construction Company."

"Right."

"I spoke to Joe Deale's foreman earlier. Frankly, I think that he and Deale are both dead ends—unless they know something they don't realize. What they do for Bennato is small potatoes. They're sure as hell not privy to the big-league stuff."

"You're right," Hutch replied. "We've got Deale on dealing and working as an enforcer, squeezing some dirtbags who are behind on their weekly installments. But he never heard of Sidney Akerman, and he's too dumb to handle the job of kidnapping Krissy Willis in some far-fetched attempt to satisfy a thirty-two-year-old vendetta. He's clueless. Ditto for that obnoxious foreman of his. We questioned him, too. He has no idea what we're talking about. So, if Bennato is behind the kidnapping, he didn't use those two. But, like you said, there's always the chance they overheard or saw something. So we're keeping them on our radar and we're keeping Deale in custody."

"Still, this leaves the whole Bennato angle as a big question mark."

"Afraid so."

"Then what *do* you have?"

"According to Akerman, there were four guys from what he now knows was the Vizzini family who ran the original kickback scheme. Since Henry Kenyon had most of the one-on-one contacts, Akerman's names and descriptions are limited. One of the offenders was a quick match for us, because the New York squad knew him. Unfortunately, he fell off the map eleven years ago, and his body was never recovered. We might have another match, and, if that pans out, we'll have Akerman take a look at him in a lineup. We can't afford to take our time on this, not with the clock ticking on that poor little kid."

"Yeah, but thirty-two years is a long time," Marc conceded with a frown. "There are deaths. Gaps. Changes in gang structure."

"Yeah, it's a long shot, but some loyalties run deep. Sons. Nephews. We're digging as hard and as fast as we can." Hutch polished off his beer and set down his glass with a thud. "Tell Casey that's all I have for her now."

"All you have or all you can say?"

"Both."

"You'll keep us posted?"

"As best I can, sure." Hutch gave another wry grin. "And whatever I don't tell you, I'm sure Casey will worm out of Lynch. He's a free agent, and she's very good at drawing information out of people."

Marc tossed a few bills on the table. "I don't want to know how you know that."

"Sure you do. But I don't plan on telling you."

Casey spent the evening once again poring over the old case file Patrick had provided. She sat at the sweeping table in the Forensic Instincts' conference room and scrutinized every detail—from names to dates and times, to investigative leads. Patrick had gone well above and beyond the line of duty, delving into every aspect of the Akermans' lives. But, as Casey had explained to Vera, the technological resources of the FBI in the late seventies had been far more limited than they were now. Which meant that Ryan had his work cut out for him.

She'd already fed him the names Vera had mentioned tonight,

and he was running them through various databases. Again, another long shot. A support group for a grieving mother didn't scream child abduction. Casey was half hoping one of them would be married to or involved with a member of the mob. But she knew it was rarely as easy and straightforward as that.

Patrick had promised to drive down here tonight, after the meetings with Sidney Akerman broke up. Casey wanted him to fill her in—just in case Hutch had left out any details when he talked to Marc—and to flesh out any theories Patrick had entertained from the case information she was reading.

Marc showed up at the brownstone before Patrick. He climbed the stairs to the conference room, where he was greeted by an enthusiastic Hero. One leap, two slobbery licks, and Hero was sniffing at Marc's pocket.

"Not to worry," Marc assured him, unzipping the bag he carried with dog treats in it. "I know better than to challenge your olfactory skills. Here you go." He gave Hero two healthy-sized biscuits.

"You know," he said thoughtfully, watching the bloodhound chomp on the biscuits. "Hero did a great job sniffing out the neighborhood. Why don't we continue to use him? Let's go to the Willises' house tomorrow and collect some more scent articles from Krissy's room. Bring Hero. You never know where that supersniffer of his might lead."

"You're right. In the meantime, fill me in on what Hutch told you."

A half hour later and, true to his word, the doorbell rang. Casey went downstairs to open the door, and Patrick strode inside.

"This is frustrating as hell," he announced, tossing his jacket on a chair. "The sketches we were able to come up with from Akerman's descriptions were vague at best."

"I heard there was one strong lead," Casey replied.

"Yeah. Lou DeMassi. He's one of the Vizzini guys who's still alive and serving time. He was in his late twenties when Felicity Akerman was kidnapped, which means he's sixtyish now. The sketch artist aged the image Akerman came up with by three decades, and the resemblance is strong enough for us to pursue. Peg Harrington and two other members of the task force took Akerman and are on their way to the prison. He'll look at DeMassi in a lineup, and they'll interrogate the hell out of him. Whatever they can get is more than we have now. Oh, and DeMassi has a son who's tied to the Vizzini family, too. Ken Barkley and two other agents are on their way to his place."

"You think it's possible he's avenging his father in some way? Maybe because Sidney talked to the Feds? You think that's the basis for Krissy's kidnapping?"

A shrug. "Anything's possible. Frankly, Casey, I don't know what I think. Other than the fact that I could kick myself for missing the mob connection in the first place. We're now investigating a complex web with no time to do it in."

"That's not your fault. But I won't be able to convince you of that. So I won't even try. I'll just suggest we take what we've got and go from here. Ryan's in his lair downstairs. I gave him all the names from the Akermans' past that I could come up with, including a list of most of Felicity's classmates. Hope and her mother put their heads together to supply those."

Patrick started. "You think someone connected with a kid from Felicity's past played a part in Krissy's kidnapping?"

"I think we can't overlook anything. And Ryan has the software and expertise to age-enhance those kids into adulthood—not only visually, but as whatever real, living, breathing human beings they've become. Their careers, marriages, children, financial circumstances—you name it. Trust Ryan to produce it all."

At the moment, producing it all was precisely what Ryan was focused on doing. Except that the avenue he was pursuing was one of his own—one he was determined to see through before turning his attention to the project Casey had given him.

Ryan's space was an interesting combination of the many facets of his personality. Most important was the "business section": his server farm, where he was customarily stationed, staring at the two-by-two grid of screens. Located downstairs, the company's secure data center took up a third of the entire floor. It was the technological heart of Forensic Instincts, housing Ryan's custom-built servers: Lumen, Equitas and Intueri.

Then came the other sides of Ryan McKay.

In the middle of the basement was his personal gym—a self-contained masterpiece of pulleys, cables and weights, for those times he needed to release energy by working out but didn't have time to escape from his lair.

And, last, came his "stuff," which helped him focus his intricate mind on assembling complicated machinery when the answers wouldn't come. That "stuff" occupied a good chunk of the basement. In one corner was his electronics bench—a laminated rock maple tabletop with floor-to-ceiling shelves and racks, filled with electronic equipment: a dual-trace oscilloscope, computer workstation, Weller soldering station and numerous drawers of electronic parts. A high-definition monitor sat directly above the center of the workbench, able to display—with a word to Yoda—a live feed from the surveillance cameras positioned inside and outside the building, or any sporting event in the world.

In the opposite corner sat a small machine shop: compact lathe and mini vertical milling machine and welding equipment, along with a wall filled with hand tools, measuring devices and attachments for the machining equipment.

Between these two shops, he could design and build anything smaller than a go-cart. His "robots," as the team liked to call them. For larger projects, he would draw on his network of fabricators who on short notice would construct anything he requested.

And, in the center of it all—where he was now crouched—was his "arena," as *he* liked to call it: the place where he would test his latest robotic incarnation against a variety of challenges—obstacles, flames, circular saws. The swept-up pieces of those experimental designs that had failed in combat were in a neat pile in the farthest corner of the room.

The team could be as amused as they wanted. They'd be surprised as hell to learn how much playing in the arena supported his efforts at Forensic Instincts.

And, yeah, okay, it was also damned fun.

A crash caused Ryan to swivel around from what he was working on. On the floor lay a peculiar robot with suction-cup-like attachments on its feet. Ryan had been testing his latest toy—a small robot, not quite the size of a paperback book, capable of walking up walls and inside ductwork. Affectionately dubbed "Gecko" by the team, and the "little critter," by Ryan—it sported miniature video cameras and microphones.

Ryan walked over and switched off the battery pack. The little critter needed more work. But that would have to wait.

He returned to his electronics bench, soldered the last

connection and inspected his work. Pleased with the result, he walked over and reinstalled the modified hard drive assembly into the floor-standing copying machine, set the countdown timer for ten seconds, then walked back to the bench. A message flashed on the monitor: "E.T. phone home." A mosaic of images began to appear. Each image was a thumbnail of the pages copied by the photocopier and temporarily stored on the hard drive—all transmitted via the cell phone that Ryan had just hard-wired to the copier hard drive.

"Test successful," Yoda announced.

"Yeah, thanks, Yoda." Still, Ryan had to iron out a few bugs. Once the copying machine was in place, it would have to be one hundred percent reliable.

So right now, fun was the last thing on Ryan's mind. He had a job to do, a job that—between his own project and the one Casey had given him—was going to take all night.

So an all-nighter meant canceling his evening plans. There was no choice to be made. A five-year-old child's life depended on him.

And the sands of the hourglass continued to trickle down to empty.

CHAPTER TWENTY

Day Five

Claudia Mitchell was in panic mode.

Joe was being held in custody for having connections to the mob. She was pretty sure the FBI suspected him of kidnapping Krissy Willis. And there wasn't a damned thing she could do about it.

She was alone, she was unemployed and she was devastated—again. She'd just gotten Joe back. She didn't care *who* he worked for. He wasn't a bad man—he was Joe. Plus, everything else aside, they were just beginning to put the pieces back together, to make a life together.

And now this.

Damn Judge Willis.

Claudia understood that her anger at Judge Willis was irrational. But that woman had taken everything from her: her career, her income and now her man. She wanted to strike out, to make Judge Willis pay.

But, in her heart, Claudia knew that the judge was already paying—in the most heinous way possible. Her little girl was gone. She'd been taken from her, maybe forever.

Given those circumstances, it was cruel to harbor resentment. Still, Claudia couldn't squelch hers. It continued to boil inside her, like a volcano about to erupt.

Her life was in shambles.

The phone call she'd received from the employment agency was the closest thing to good news she'd had since this turmoil began. A nursing home north of Westchester County was looking for a bookkeeper and an office manager. It was a far cry, both in content and in salary, from her position as a court clerk, but it would help pay the bills. And the commute would be long, but it was doable.

Her interview was today.

She rose early, dressing in her most serious business suit, and mentally ran through prospective interview questions in her head. It had been a while, and she had to make the transition back to professional woman.

With a modicum of confidence, Claudia left the house and climbed into her car, beginning the hour-and-a-half drive up to the facility. She left herself plenty of time, since she was unfamiliar with the area and the winding, mountain roads. As it turned out, she made good time, and arrived at Sunny Gardens fifteen minutes early.

That gave her a short interval to scan the grounds from the vantage point of the administration building. From what she could see, the acreage was lovely—well manicured, serene, just the atmosphere a patient would need to enjoy the final stages of his or her life. The facility was set on rolling hills with expansive gardens. Aside from the main complex and the administration building, there was a modern clubhouse and a sprawling patio with a view of the sunrise. Claudia would have loved to stroll down to the lake, but the distance would make her arrival at the interview tight. Maybe afterward—*if* she had a shot at the job.

Which she did. The interview went beautifully. Claudia was direct and honest about her qualifications and experience. And, Ms. Babick, the human resources executive Claudia met with, was clearly aware that Claudia was overqualified. But she was also aware of the high unemployment rate, and the scarcity of good jobs. So, rather than being put off by Claudia's years clerking for a judge, she was pleased by her organizational skills and her ability to take charge.

A half hour later they shook hands, and Claudia was on her way, with the guarantee of a prompt phone call to the employment agency.

Feeling good about herself for the first time in ages, Claudia decided to take that stroll down to the lake.

The stroll turned out to be a lot more than she bargained for.

Rounding the corner of the administration building, Claudia got a full panoramic view of the facility. The first thing that stood out was that a new wing was being constructed at the farthest end of the main building. The second thing was the large sign on the fenced-in construction area.

It read: Bennato Construction Company.

She stopped dead in her tracks and stared in confused disbelief. Then, she pulled herself together. She reminded herself that Bennato was involved in construction projects all over New York

State. Any connection between Joe and them had nothing to do with her, or today's job interview.

She was overreacting. She had to be.

She turned away. That's when she was hit with her second surprise of the day.

This was no coincidence.

She considered retracing her steps and forgetting she'd ever seen what she did. But she couldn't. She was too unstrung. So she didn't think. She just marched straight into the eye of the storm. And she had the confrontation before she could chicken out and walk away.

She left the nursing home with a sense of awareness and dread that far eclipsed the positive impact of her upbeat job interview.

Hurrying to her car, she jumped in and turned over the engine. She couldn't get home fast enough. What she'd learned in her face-off could change everything.

So stunned was Claudia with her newfound, overwhelming knowledge, that she failed to spot the dark sedan following a short distance behind her.

It waited until she was a quarter mile from the sharp hairpin turn atop the mountain to pick up speed. Then, the driver floored the gas. The car flew up to Claudia's in seconds. Just as quickly, it moved to the left and astride hers. The driver lost no time, slamming the sedan's passenger side directly into Claudia's driver's side.

She screamed and clutched the wheel, swerving from side to side and trying to get out of the way. But there was nowhere to go—not with the steel divider to her right, separating her from the steep decline that plunged down from the mountaintop.

The sedan wouldn't let her go. It struck her car over again and again—hard, purposefully—nudging it closer and closer to the railing. Claudia veered wildly, trying to escape the inevitable.

She lost the fight.

With the sickening sound of tearing metal, Claudia's car tore through the divider and plummeted over the side of the mountain. It flipped over four or five times before crashing into a tree.

Seconds later, the car burst into flames.

Ryan was still at his desk when Casey came down late that morning, Hero at her heels. Ryan's five-o'clock shadow told her he'd been at it all night. The dark circles under Casey's eyes told him the same.

"Where do things stand?" she asked.

Ryan leaned back in his chair. "You look like hell."

"Thanks. So do you."

"Rough night?"

Casey shrugged. "I've been buried in the Felicity Akerman case file."

"Hutch must be pissed."

"Nope. He pulled an all-nighter of his own. The BAU is busy modifying their profile in light of the potential Vizzini connection." Casey put a lid on the chitchat about her private life and changed the subject. "What have you got for me?"

Ryan took the hint and reverted to business. "I've aged the images of all the kids you gave me to work with—Felicity's friends, the neighborhood kids she played with, the girls she went to soccer camp with. I'm in the process of tracking them down. So far, there's nothing impressive to report. No parents with mob connections. No sleazy backgrounds. Just normal middle-class families. And the kids, now men and women, are scattered around the country—different careers, different marital statuses, different lives."

He handed Casey some printed pages. "Those are the adult images I came up with. Each page has a small corner photo of that person as a child. That gives us the continuity we need when we show the pictures to Vera Akerman and Hope Willis. See if either of them recognizes a familiar face. Particularly Hope. Have her rack her brain for anyone who's been hanging around, maybe visiting as an alleged repairman or someone canvassing for a religious organization or political candidate. That would have given them access to the house and to the Willises—maybe even to Krissy. And if Hope does recognize someone, and if Vera recalls them from childhood, we might have a lead."

Casey glanced toward the center of the room, taking in the copying machine. "It looks like you've been busy working more than one lead."

"Yeah. I know we haven't gotten anything incriminating off Joe Deale's computer. And I know the guy's low on the Vizzini totem pole. So I figured we'd step up our investigation, take it to the next level—the Bennato Construction Company." Ryan walked over, patted the copier. "As of four this morning, this baby's ready to go."

Marc was in his office at the Forensic Instincts brownstone, getting ready for the visit he and Ryan had planned, when his BlackBerry rang. The call was short. But it was a shocker.

He made his way to Casey's office, calling down to Ryan to join them.

"Get this—" he said the instant the three of them were together. "Claudia Mitchell is dead. Her car went off a cliff forty miles north of here, a couple of hours ago. There were two sets of tire treads at the crime scene. This definitely wasn't an accident."

"Wow." Casey blew out a breath and sank down on the edge of her desk. "Who told you this—Hutch?"

"Yeah. He gave me a courtesy call, just so we'd have a heads-up. This sure as hell supports the mob theory. And it suggests that either Claudia knew something, or, more likely, that Joe is being delivered a message to keep his mouth shut. Which means he knows something, whether or not he realizes it."

"All the more reason for today's mission." Ryan was already dressed and ready. "Casey, you go ahead up to the Willises' place and deal with this new development. Marc and I will do our thing."

Casey was already punching a phone number into her cell. "I'm calling Patrick. The FBI might already have alerted him, but, if not, he should be a part of this. It's another indication that Sidney Akerman's illegal dealings are at the heart of Krissy's disappearance—and Felicity's."

An hour later, Marc—clad in a gray uniform with the word "Superior" printed on his shirt—pushed open the door of the Bennato Construction Company.

The reception area was cramped, filled with piles of building materials, with peeling walls, a dusty floor and a steel desk, behind which sat a young, attractive secretary. She was cracking gum, talking on the phone and reading *Cosmo* at the same time. Based on the conversation, and the juvenile notes she'd written on Post-its that were stuck to her desk, Marc knew he was not dealing with a brain trust.

All the better.

She looked up when Marc walked over. Her gaze traveled from his broad, well-built physique to his brooding, sexy stare.

"Suze?" she said into the phone. "I gotta go. There's a workman here. I'll call you back." She hung up, folding her hands and leaning forward. It was no accident that she was providing Marc with a spectacular view of her cleavage. "Can I help you?"

"Now *that's* a loaded question." Marc gave her a slow, crooked smile and a wink, making sure to scrutinize her breasts appreciatively as he spoke. "I'm sure you can—in lots of ways."

"Name them."

Oh, this was too easy.

"You got it—" Marc waited for her to introduce herself.

"Sonya."

"You got it, Sonya." Her name was a caress, as he turned his charms on full force. "But first, let's get work out of the way. My name is Danger. John Danger."

"Really." She gave a tinkling laugh. "Is that your pickup name or your real one?"

"Both." A twinkle. "I just got lucky, I guess."

"I'm sure you get lucky a lot."

"I never kiss and tell," Marc replied in a teasing tone. "Anyway, back to business—for now. I'm from Superior Office, and your copying machine has been sending intermittent alerts to our office."

"Really?" She was barely listening to him. But she *was* eyeing his crotch. "I didn't know copying machines could do that."

"They can, Sonya. Do you know the Check Engine light on your car? Same idea, except that the light is in our office instead of on your keypad. That way, we can be of best service to you." Another smile. "Is it okay if I take a look?"

That question elicited a furrow between her eyebrows. "How

much is this going to cost? I have to get my boss's okay before I spend any money."

"Won't be necessary. It's free. Service is included at no charge along with your machine."

"Free is perfect." She pointed to her left. "The copier's in the storage room. Would you like a cup of coffee? I'm making a fresh pot."

"Only if you join me."

"Just what I had in mind." She crossed the room, giving him a clear view of her tight pants and curvy ass as she did. "It'll be ready when you are."

"I can't wait."

When Sonya was at the sink, Marc strode into the storage room and opened up the copying machine as if to service it. He then slid the special piece of paper Ryan had given him into the main paper tray.

Hearing the coffee machine sputter its last drops of water, Marc called out, "I'm not seeing any error codes. Can you make a few copies for me?"

"Be right there," Sonya called back. "How do you take your coffee?"

Marc rolled his eyes. "Hot," he informed her, his voice filled with promise. "Just like my women."

Sonya sashayed into the storage room and handed Marc a cup of steaming hot coffee. Marc moved closer to her, brushing up against her.

With a sharp intake of breath, Sonya asked, "What did you ask me to do?"

"I'd like to test the machine. Can you make a couple of copies?"

"Oh. Sure. I need some timesheets anyway."

Reluctantly, she walked back to her desk, got the original and returned. Placing the page on the copier glass, she closed the cover, punched in ten copies and pressed the button that said Copy.

The machine whirred to life for a brief second, until Ryan's sheet of paper reached the hot imaging area. Instantly, the copier seized, and a vile smell permeated the office.

Sonya's head snapped around, and her eyes filled with dread. "What did I do?"

"Don't freak out," Marc soothed. "Let me see what's going on."

He slid out the imager, scowling as he pointed to the smoking drum. "Not good. It's fried."

Sonya was practically in tears. "My boss will kill me. Anytime something goes wrong in the office, he blames me."

"Shh-shh-shh." Marc pressed his index finger to her lips, then held it up in a one-minute gesture. Whipping out his cell phone, he punched in a number.

Around the corner in their van, Ryan's phone rang. He hit the talk button. "Yup," he greeted Marc.

"Hey, Jim," Marc said in his ear. "It's John. You know that machine you were going to deliver today? I need you to bring it to me here at Bennato Construction." A pause. "I don't care. Fuck 'em. They'll get their machine tomorrow." Another pause. "Fuck Eddie, too. He can kiss my ass. Just bring that copier to me now. It's an emergency. I'll handle Eddie."

Hanging up, Marc turned to face Sonya, who was staring at him, speechless.

Marc gave her a huge, sexy smile, and said, "After this, we'll work on the other things I can do for you, Sonya. *And* on the ways you can help me."

Thirty minutes later, Marc and Ryan left Bennato Construction. Marc had a bite mark on his lips and Sonya's phone number in his pocket. And the storage room had Ryan's machine in it. The copier would soon begin to "phone home," sending Ryan images of every piece of paper that went through it.

"Nice souvenir," Ryan commented drily, turning from the wheel to indicate Marc's mouth.

"Shut up." Marc tore up the phone number and tossed the scraps into the trash container.

"Maybe you should keep that. You could get laid tonight. Hell, you practically got laid ten minutes ago on the new copying machine." An approving nod. "I guess watching me in action has had a positive educational impact. You really pulled that off. I'll make sure Casey knows that you'll make a good backup when I'm otherwise occupied."

"Don't do me any favors." Marc had no desire to fill the role of hot stud. "I do just fine on my own—when it's for real. But this phony shit is not my thing, even if I am a stellar actor. I only did it this time because seductive ol' you had to make technical tweaks on your copying machine." He licked his swollen lower lip. "Damn. She almost tore off a layer of my skin, not to mention smothering me in her breasts."

"She also had about three brain cells. Not my type either." Ryan chuckled.

"Let's just hope we get something off that machine," Marc said soberly. "The spyware on Joe Deale's laptop gave us zip."

"True. We need a quick break. Claudia Mitchell is dead. Where does that leave Krissy Willis?"

"Not just as a kidnapping victim anymore." Ryan's jaw tightened.

"Yeah. But hopefully not as collateral damage."

CHAPTER TWENTY-ONE

With a tight grip on his leash, Casey led Hero into the Willis home. The bloodhound's nose was everywhere, taking in the smells of the house and the scents of the people in it.

"Great-looking guy, Casey." Grace greeted her in the living room doorway. "I knew you'd come to your senses and replace Hutch."

"Given how pissed off at him I am right now, I just might take that advice." Casey didn't pull any punches with Hutch's partner. They were a tight team, and Casey was sure that Grace was aware of the fact that Hutch had called Marc, rather than Casey, with the news about Claudia Mitchell's murder.

Casey wasn't sure which was more immature—Hutch's action, or her own reaction.

She spotted him across the room, and purposely ignored him. She had things to deal with; she'd thrash it out with Hutch later.

"What happened with Akerman and yesterday's lineup?" Casey asked. "Did Sidney recognize that guy Lou DeMassi?"

"From what Peg told me, I think that Akerman was pretty sure DeMassi was one of the mobsters squeezing Kenyon. Last I heard, Peg and Don were interrogating him. Ken went over to DeMassi's son's place, but the guy and his family seem to have magically left on a spontaneous Sicilian vacation. Ken will find him. But we're back to the same enemy—time."

"Casey—" Hope interjected, hurrying over, her lashes damp with tears. "This nightmare just keeps getting worse and worse. Why would the mob kill Claudia? Did she know something? Are they warning her boyfriend to keep his mouth shut about my baby?"

"I don't know," Casey answered honestly. "But they obviously went to great lengths to pick the right spot to commit the murder. That section of road is all hills and sharp curves. And it's countrified, so it's pretty isolated. I'm guessing they followed her up to there, waited for her return trip and did their job."

Turning back to Grace, Casey asked, "Has someone told Joe Deale about Claudia yet?"

"Yup." Grace nodded. "Peg stopped at the precinct before she and Don drove up to the medical center to question the staff. From what I heard, Deale is totally freaked out. Not so much about losing his girlfriend, but about what it suggests. He knows that he's next. He's like a rat in a maze, not knowing what he might know and not knowing how to get out."

"I finished our updated profile and released it to the entire task force." Hutch appeared out of nowhere to convey that information to Grace. "They're all running with it." He glanced at Casey. "Hey."

"Hi," she returned coolly without meeting his gaze. Instead, she addressed Hope. "I have some photos for you and your mother to look at. Is she up for it now?"

"Yes, of course. Come into the Florida room. She's resting there. It's the only place that's removed from the pandemonium, and she hasn't gotten any real sleep since Krissy..." A tremor in her voice. "Since they took Krissy. Ashley's with her."

"Good. Ashley practically lives here. It's possible that she might be able to identify someone, too." Casey began following Hope, then paused. "Is your mother okay with dogs? As I mentioned to you on the phone, I brought Hero to do some more sniffing recon."

"She's fine with them."

"Hero does slobber," Casey warned.

Hope managed a small smile. "My mother had a cocker spaniel when she was growing up. According to her, 'Slobber' was his middle name. So I wouldn't worry. Going through those photos with a fine-tooth comb is what this is all about."

"Great. What I'll do is leave the stack of photos with the three of you, explain what I'm looking for and take Hero up to Krissy's room. Okay?"

"Fine. Yes. Anything."

They continued into the Florida room, where Vera was sitting on the couch bleakly sipping a cup of tea and Ashley was pacing around, unable to sit still.

"Hi," Ashley said, stopping to look at Casey. "Did you hear the horrible news about Claudia Mitchell?"

A nod. "The authorities are all over it. Hopefully, we'll hear something soon."

Ashley's gaze dropped to Hero. "What a beautiful bloodhound. Is he yours?"

"Not only mine, but a newly inducted member of Forensic

Instincts," Casey replied. "He's a former FBI human scent evidence dog, trained and certified at Quantico. We're lucky that he went into early retirement. This way, he can work the case with us."

Casey turned back to Vera and Hope. "I have photos for you to review. Felicity's friends, aged to what they would currently look like. And their parents, as well. Hope, you study the images carefully and let me know if you've seen any of these people hanging around your house or Krissy's school. And Mrs. Akerman, I'd appreciate if you'd concentrate on seeing if you recognize the kids from childhood, and their parents from younger adulthood."

"You're searching for a clue that would tie the two kidnappings together—like the same kidnapper," Hope concluded aloud.

"Exactly," Casey said. "Ashley, you join Judge Willis in her scrutiny of the current individuals. You spend so much time here—maybe someone in the pictures will jump out at you."

"Of course." Ashley had already settled herself beside Hope, who'd sunk down on the opposite sofa, photos in hand.

"Take your time," Casey instructed. "Hero and I will go upstairs to Krissy's bedroom. I want to collect a few more of Krissy's things that have her smells. Hero's sense of smell is unbelievable. He could pick up her scent from miles away. That can only help us."

Casey was just about to head upstairs when Patrick arrived.

"Where do things stand?" he demanded.

Quickly, Casey filled him in, then suggested that he, too, review the photos and see if anyone struck him from three decades ago.

"Consider it done," he said, perching behind Vera. "If the offender is here, I'll spot him."

Once upstairs in Krissy's bedroom, Casey put on latex gloves to do her work. She'd covered half the room, scooped up Krissy's pillowcase—which she let Hero sniff—and had gathered a pair of soccer cleats and a T-shirt, which she'd packed carefully away for later scent-pad collection, when her BlackBerry rang.

A swift glance at the caller ID told her it was the office.

"Ryan?" she asked into the phone.

"Yup. I've got something for you, straight from the copying machine at Bennato Construction. And it's a doozy. Get this. You know that medical facility, Sunny Gardens, that Claudia Mitchell's calendar said she interviewed at just before her death?"

"Yes."

"Well, guess who just happens to be constructing the new wing there?"

"You're kidding."

"Bingo—Bennato. And it gets better. From the paperwork I'm seeing off their copier, Bennato is screwing them big-time. They're using substandard materials, cutting corners in construction, you name it. Plus, it looks like they're paying off the inspectors, ensuring that they look the other way. It's quite an operation Bennato's got going there."

Casey sank down in a chair, Hero beside her. "The illegalities are no surprise. But the fact that Claudia Mitchell was at the place just before she was killed, that's no coincidence. And it changes everything. I assumed her killer had followed her upstate. Now I'm wondering if this murder was more spontaneous than planned."

"My thoughts exactly. She went for an interview. She might have inadvertently seen something, or someone, she shouldn't have. Or maybe that someone saw her, and figured that she and/or Deale might be ratting Bennato out to the Feds."

"*Maybe* just doesn't cut it anymore," Casey said. "Did any of the paperwork list the foreman or any of the workers who are on this particular construction project?"

"The foreman, yes. His name's Bill Parsons. He's been working for Bennato for a dozen years."

"We need to talk to Parsons."

"Marc and I are one step ahead of you. Marc's already on his way to the construction site."

"So's the task force, Ryan."

"We know. But this is Marc we're talking about. He'll slither in and out, get what we need, and do it all without being spotted by anyone."

"True." Thank God it was Marc handling this. No one else could pull it off. They'd be screwed. Because if the FBI spotted a member of her team on the grounds, they'd demand to know how they got the information on Bennato and Parsons first. They wouldn't like the answer, and Forensic Instincts wouldn't like the consequences.

The wisest thing was to stay out of the Bureau's way on this one. Let them follow protocol. That way, whatever they uncovered would be admissible in court when they went after Bennato. Casey and her team's job was to find Krissy Willis, not to bury the Vizzini family.

"Marc will get answers out of Parsons any way he has to," she said, telling Ryan what he already knew. "I almost feel sorry for the bastard."

"Yeah. A low-level mob soldier up against a Navy SEAL. Not promising for the foreman."

Krissy. I don't know what to do.

I've followed my instructions to a tee. I've eliminated obstacles, kept us well hidden, and done everything in my power to win you over. I thought I was making headway. But nothing works.

Even the special world I created for you didn't get the reaction I'd hoped for. The software I designed is one-of-a-kind, just like you. It's better and more original than your all-time-favorite Club Penguin. And yet, even though you obeyed me and went to play with it, you did it without the sparkle in your eyes that I expected. Silently. Listlessly. Not like when you're playing with Oreo and Ruby. They're the only ones who make you smile.

At least you're eating a little better, but you're not sleeping. The room is still strange. The monsters are still terrifying.

I want to soothe them away. But you won't let me get near you, not even with the locket and perfume. You start to cry the minute you see and smell them. And you shut down when I mention the word "mommy."

Yet you call out her name and cry for her every night.

I keep telling myself how short a time it's been.

I try not to think about what's being taken from you, day after day. I try to remind myself of the instructions. But things are different. The caring is different. No one can help or protect you but me.

I've got to remember that. I've got to have patience.

But for how long?

Hutch pulled Casey aside the minute she and Hero made their way downstairs.

"What's going on?" he demanded.

She gave him a cool look. "Hero and I were just doing a once-over in Krissy's room. I wanted him to be able to sniff out—"

"I know what you were doing with Hero," Hutch interrupted. "I meant, what's with the icy treatment? What are you so pissed off about?"

Casey glanced around to ensure they were alone. "Apparently, it's okay to sleep with me, but not to give me a major heads-up like the fact that Claudia Mitchell was murdered. I'd understand if the information was classified, but it wasn't, and you had no problem calling your buddy, Marc. So you weren't keeping it from Forensic Instincts, just from me."

"*That's* what you're ripping mad about?" Hutch sounded incredulous. "Obviously, I knew Marc would tell you. Your team is tighter than our squads."

"But?" Casey prompted. "I'm not a former BAU-er? Is that it?"

"No, that's not it." It was Hutch's turn to glance around. Then, he dropped his voice to protect their privacy. "It's *because* of our personal relationship that I didn't call you directly. The Bureau understands my continued contact and loyalty towards Marc—we were once colleagues. But you and I are different. You're the private sector, earning big bucks without having to follow the rules. It's bad enough that half the world knows we're involved. The last thing I want to do is ruffle feathers to the point where the FBI stops feeling so magnanimous toward Forensic Instincts. Up until now, it's been an amenable, if rocky, road. But your team walks a fine line between acceptable and off-limits. My giving you a direct jump on Claudia Mitchell's murder would definitely rock the boat."

Casey waved her hand in frustrated disbelief. "So even though the entire task force knows that Marc is going to come straight to me with the news, it's okay because Marc is former BAU and because the two of you aren't hitting the sheets together."

Hutch's lips twitched at her succinct conclusion. "That about sums it up."

"Unbelievable." Casey dragged her fingers through her hair. "Another reminder of why I hate bureaucracy. Fine." A thoughtful pause. "You and I really have to have a talk. In retrospect, I should have anticipated this kind of thing, but, since this is the first case we've worked so closely together on, I didn't. We need to set some ground rules. Otherwise, we'll combust."

"I agree—and not just about this case. We have to get on the same page about a lot of things."

Casey didn't ask him what those "things" were. She merely nodded.

"Tonight," Hutch stated flatly. "I'll come by late, after we're both too exhausted to work. Then we can talk."

This time, Casey's eyebrows rose slightly. "That sounds productive, but not very inspiring."

"Oh, I'll be inspiring. You can count on it."

"I'll hold you to that."

CHAPTER TWENTY-TWO

This time Claire's flashes of insight didn't come in a dream.

They did come while she was in bed, however. When she was lying there, staring off in the darkened room and contemplating the idea of joining Forensic Instincts.

Her mind began to wander, drifting from one team member to the other. She envisioned her role in the company. Her relationships with the people.

Suddenly, those images were gone, replaced with the sights, sounds and smells of tragedy.

A medical facility with negative energy surrounding it.

That image faded. The darkness persisted.

White panic. A car. Veering wildly. The grinding screech of failing brakes. Tearing metal. The car, rolling over and over, spiraling downward. Thudding against the craggy terrain. A violent stop. Flames. The smell of gas. The blast of an explosion.

The icy stillness of death.

Fear. Krissy's face. Tears coursing down her cheeks. Hope's face. Pain and frustration carved into her very soul.

Krissy. Hope. Krissy. Hope.

Claire jerked into an erect position, unable to bear the onslaught of images any longer.

For a minute she sat there, pulling up her legs and wrapping her arms around her knees. She tried to make sense of what she'd experienced. Clearly, the first part was Claudia Mitchell's murder. But the second part, the harsh, alternating flashes between Krissy and Hope—that had to mean something.

Krissy was still alive.

She knew that in a flash. The child was traumatized, withdrawn, afraid.

But still alive.

Instantly, Claire reached over and picked up her phone.

Casey was in the living room of the brownstone, drinking her fifth cup of coffee of the day. She'd hung around the Willises long enough to hear what she already knew from Marc.

Peg and the task force members had returned from Sunny Gardens, where they'd spoken to Ms. Babick in Human Resources and learned about the great interview Claudia Mitchell had had that morning. The poor woman had been shocked to learn about Claudia's tragic, fatal car crash. The task force further reported that Bennato Construction was on the premises, building a new wing. They'd questioned the construction crew, particularly the foreman, who was an emotional wreck.

Casey had smiled at that part. Bill Parsons had been a wreck, all right. But not because he knew anything. Because Marc had pinned him to the wall, pressed his forearm across the guy's neck, and threatened to crush his windpipe if he didn't tell him what he knew.

Parsons had spewed all kinds of information—the names of the construction crew, the length of time they'd been working the project, the corners they'd been told to cut.

None of it gave them a clue about Krissy Willis's abduction.

But Parsons did know Joe Deale, and he had heard he was locked up. Between that, and his terror over Marc's death grip, he was more than happy to swear that he'd keep his mouth shut about Marc's little visit if the Feds came around.

Casey wasn't surprised to hear that the task force had come away with nothing. But she was interested in their subsequent interrogation of Joe Deale, where they'd squeezed out the fact that Parsons's brother Ike was one of Tony Bennato's fair-haired boys—the foreman on some of his most lucrative projects. Interesting. Marc might have another visit to pay.

As for the photos Ryan had created, neither Vera nor Hope had come up with a damned thing. Hope hadn't laid eyes on any of the grown women who'd once been Felicity's childhood friends, and Vera didn't recognize the older renditions of those children's parents.

Even Patrick was stumped, although he did remember interviewing almost all the parents in the photos. He was frustrated as hell, but not surprised. He might have missed Sidney Akerman's mob connection, but he *hadn't* missed the obvious. He'd grilled the neighborhood suspects again and again those thirty-two years ago, until they cringed every time he knocked on their doors.

Casey was still deep in thought, when her phone rang.

"Casey Woods," she said into the mouthpiece.

"Casey, it's Claire." Claire's voice was shaky but certain. "Krissy Willis is still alive."

Casey's head shot up. "You're sure?"

"As sure as I can be without seeing her in person. I just got a strong sense of her presence, and some vivid flashes of her face. She's sobbing her heart out. This experience has badly scarred her. But whoever has her didn't break her. Not yet. And they definitely didn't kill her." A stymied sigh. "Every time I get close to sensing who the kidnappers are, or what they plan to do to Krissy, the vision is eclipsed by Hope Willis's pain. I just can't get around it. I keep seeing Hope, time and again."

"That's not a shock. Hope is coming apart at the seams. And who can blame her? Her daughter's been missing for more than four days. She knows the statistics. In fact, I'm not sure whether or not I should tell her about your vision. Would it help? Or would it give her false hope?" Casey hastened to qualify her statement. "I'm not questioning your abilities. I'm relieved as hell to hear what you sensed. But to tell a mother…"

"I understand," Claire said. "And I'm not offended. Casey, no matter how strong your faith in clairvoyance is, you can't help but doubt what you can't see. Nonetheless, I'd tell Hope if I were you. She needs something to cling to. And, if by some sick twist of fate I'm wrong, the loss of her daughter won't be any less unbearable."

"You're right." Casey had to agree that what Claire said made a world of sense. "I'll call her now. There's no need to put her through another agonizing night. Not if I can ease the pain a little."

A half hour later, Casey was still feeling a sense of well-being at Hope's reaction to her phone call. How grateful she'd sounded. How many indebted tears she'd cried.

Now, Casey could only pray that the hope she'd given the Willises would be realized.

There was a knock on the door, and Hero leaped to life, barking and braying at the sound. He headed for the stairs, making his way down, ears flopping as he descended.

Casey followed behind, glancing at her watch as she did. It was ten o'clock, too late for the team, too early for Hutch.

"Who is it?" she called.

No answer.

"Who's there?" she asked, this time louder.

Again, there was no response.

Sliding the chain lock into place, Casey opened the door a crack and peered outside. Hero shoved his nose through the small opening and sniffed, growling under his breath.

There was nobody on the doorstep.

Assuming the visitor had realized he or she was at the wrong house, Casey urged Hero inside and started to shut the door. As she did, she noticed an envelope tucked under the doorjamb.

She unchained the door and opened it, reaching down and picking up the envelope. It had her name carefully printed on it in ink.

Swiftly, she glanced up and down the street. Quiet and empty.

Hero was sniffing the doorstep. He looked ready to take off in hot pursuit.

Casey nipped that in the bud. She coaxed Hero back into the house. Then she locked the door and turned, leaning back against the wall and carefully opening the envelope. On second thought, she walked into the storage room and got a pair of latex gloves, which she wriggled her hands into. If this letter had anything to do with the Willis case, she didn't want to smudge any fingerprints that might be on the page.

That done, she slid the sheet of paper out of the envelope and unfolded it.

There was one phrase scrawled there in ink: *Look closer at family.*

The note had to refer to her kidnapping investigation. But the wording was curious.

Family. Did the person mean the Vizzini family or the Willis family? And if he or she knew something, why weren't they coming forward? Were they afraid for their own safety? Were Forensic Instincts and the FBI task force getting close enough to incite more violent acts? Was murdering Claudia Mitchell only the beginning?

And why had this informant come to Casey, rather than to law enforcement? It had to be fear. Or the hope that Forensic Instincts would be willing to take some illegal path to get at the answers. Any way you looked at it, the whole thing was sleazy. And that smacked of the mob.

She was still standing there, contemplating the message, when another knock on the door sounded.

"Who is it?" she demanded.

"Me." It was Hutch's voice.

Relieved, Casey opened the door. Hutch was standing there, looking tired and stressed-out, but no less sexy.

"Hi," Casey greeted him. "I'm glad you're here. Although I didn't expect you for hours."

He stepped inside and squatted down to scratch Hero's ears. Clearly, the bloodhound was agitated by his arrival. "The team broke up early. Ken got a break on the Sicilian whereabouts of DeMassi's son. He's following up on it. Based on our assumption that the two abductions are related, the DeMassis are our strongest lead. Father and son both take orders from the Vizzini family. The time frame works—DeMassi could have kidnapped Felicity, and his son could have kidnapped Krissy. At least it's a continuum that makes sense."

"Plus, if Lou DeMassi is serving a lengthy sentence, it's an added impetus for his son to want to avenge his father's imprisonment."

Hutch nodded. "Anyway, if the lead materializes into something concrete, or if anything else surfaces tonight, I'll get a call from the task force. If not, you and I can have that talk." He frowned as Hero continued to growl under his breath. It wasn't characteristic for him to show such hostility toward Hutch.

"It's okay, fellow," Hutch soothed. "I'm the one who brought you to your new lady. Remember?"

Hero gazed past Hutch and out into the darkened street.

Raising his head, Hutch gave Casey a quizzical look. "What's going on?" he asked, picking up on the tension that was rippling through her. Simultaneously, he spotted her latex gloves, and the letter she was holding.

"This is what's going on." Casey held out the letter for him to see. "I found it outside my door a little while ago."

Hutch squinted and scanned the letter without touching it. "Do you have another pair of gloves?"

"Sure." Casey went and got him a pair.

Once his gloves were on, Hutch took the page and studied it.

"The family," he muttered. "Does that mean the Willises or the Vizzini crime family?"

"My question exactly." Casey waved her arm in noncomprehension. "I don't see how it could be the Willises. Not even slimy Edward. We've investigated the hell out of them. Your team and mine. And we've found nothing."

"Unless the writer of this message means Sidney Akerman. He's the newest piece of the puzzle *and* the one with the mob ties. Maybe those ties run deeper than we've uncovered."

"That's the only possibility I see, and it's one we'll have to address. Next question—who's giving us this tip?"

Hutch scowled. "The operative word here being *us*. The *us* in question is Forensic Instincts. Which means that whoever left that envelope at your door is someone who chooses *not* to give it to law enforcement. And *that* suggests that he or she prefers nonkosher methods be used to get at the truth."

"Or that his or her own hands aren't clean," Casey added. "I thought of both those things."

"I'm sure you did."

"Look, Hutch. As you can see, I'm not keeping any secrets from you. The FBI lab is far superior to anything we have. So go ahead and take this back to the task force ASAP so it can be analyzed. You and I will talk another time."

Hutch scrutinized Casey thoroughly, then shook his head. "That would waste precious time. I'll call Peg. I'm sure she'll authorize me to messenger this straight down to Quantico. They'll get us answers in a matter of hours. In the meantime, the task force is already deep into investigating the Bennato Construction Company, and their role in the Vizzini family. There's nothing in this note that would change that course of action. As for Sidney Akerman..."

"I can call Patrick," Casey said quickly. "He'll grill Sidney till the cows come home. No one in this investigation knows Sidney better than he does. And before you protest, Patrick Lynch is as straight as an arrow, former FBI all the way. Whenever my team crosses the line, he refuses to get involved. He's an ethical, law-abiding man." A hint of a smile. "As opposed to Forensic Instincts, the big, bad wolves of the private sector."

"Not big, bad wolves. Maybe well-meaning wolves that roam too far into dangerous territory."

"But with proven results."

"I won't argue that point. I can't agree with your methods, though."

"Fair enough."

"But speaking of big, bad wolves…" A corner of Hutch's mouth lifted. "This one thinks that, after we take care of this letter, we should set the case aside for a few hours and adjourn to the bedroom."

"Before we talk?"

"Definitely. After that, the mood might be shattered."

"True."

The two of them pulled out their cell phones and made the necessary arrangements. Then, they put the letter and envelope in a Ziploc, and packaged it for transport. That done, they pulled off their gloves and waited for the FBI messenger to arrive.

A half hour later, the evidence was on its way, and Hutch turned and pulled Casey's sweater over her head. "A couple of hours off," he murmured. "That's all I'm suggesting. We've got other people working round-the-clock to find Krissy Willis while we recharge our batteries."

"Recharge our batteries." Casey's eyes twinkled as she unbuckled Hutch's belt. "Is that what we're calling it these days?"

"With us? We call it sensory overload."

He swung her into his arms and carried her up the stairs to her fourth-floor apartment, not letting her feet slide to the floor until they were in the bedroom.

They finished tugging off each other's clothes and tumbled onto the bed, their breaths coming fast and uneven. There was a sexual pull between them that had sparked to life the instant they met, and only intensified as the months had passed.

Now was no exception.

They made love with a passion and intensity that was theirs and theirs alone. Neither of them was foolish enough to believe that a connection like this grew on trees. Their bodies moved in a rhythm that was sheer unison, escalating to a frantic need for completion.

Casey wrapped her arms and legs around Hutch, gasping his name and arching her body hard against his, taking him as deep as she could. Hutch responded by urging her legs higher up on his back, gripping the headboard and driving himself all the way inside her—and then some.

It erupted in an explosion of nearly painful pleasure, Casey crying out as she contracted all around him, and Hutch shouting her name as he poured into her. They drew out the moment as long as they could, before collapsing in each other's arms, weak and drained and utterly sated.

"Can we stay like this for a couple of weeks?" Casey mumbled into Hutch's shoulder, when she'd caught her breath.

He chuckled. "A nice thought. Shutting out the world, the job pressures and the conflicts. Just you and me and this."

"Not viable, huh?"

"Unfortunately not." Hutch propped himself on his elbows and gazed down at her. "We've never come right out and said it, but you do know that what's going on between us is about a lot more than sex, don't you?"

"Yes, of course. That's what's going to make this conversation that much harder."

"We're worth fighting for, Casey. Whatever label you want to give our relationship, we both know it doesn't happen every day. So, no matter how heated a debate we end up having, I'm not walking away. Not unless you ask me to."

"I'm not stupid." Casey traced his jaw with her fingertip. "I'm not going to end things over our careers. I'm just going to defend what I believe in."

"Which is that the end justifies the means."

"Within reason, yes. My goal here is to find Krissy Willis. I don't give a damn about the right way to go about it. Any way I find her is the right way."

Hutch rolled away and scooted to the edge of the bed. "I'm going to grab some water for this talk. You depleted all my reserves."

Casey smiled. "Now *that* I doubt. But grab a bottle for me, too. I'm parched. Plus, I think we should have this conversation with our clothes on. Otherwise, we won't talk at all."

"Agreed." Hutch yanked on his boxer briefs and pants, and headed for the kitchen. By the time he returned, Casey was belting her black silk robe and perching at the edge of the bed.

Hutch handed her a bottle of water and sat down in the armchair across from the bed. "Okay, we're both decent and ready for verbal warfare."

"Does it have to be warfare?" Casey asked. "I know we have different jobs and slightly different philosophies, but we both want the same results—ultimately."

"Ultimately."

"The good news is it's very rare that we're working on the same case. Even when the FBI and Forensic Instincts are both involved. Thankfully, this is my team's first child kidnapping case.

I'm hoping it will be our last. So you and I won't be overlapping too often. Otherwise, we'd probably kill each other."

Hutch took a swig of water. "Yeah, well, that's part of what I wanted to talk to you about. I'm seriously considering applying for a transfer to BAU-2. They haven't filled the opening Marc left when he resigned. I'd like to fill it. I've had about all I can stomach of crimes against children. It's time for a change, something I can handle in the way I was trained. If I'm emotionally vested in a case, I can't do an effective job."

"So you'd be dealing with adult crimes."

"'Fraid so."

Casey blew out a breath. "Won't that be enjoyable."

"Like you said earlier, we have to set some ground rules," Hutch said. "Starting with separating business from pleasure. It's not going to be easy—assuming I get the job. You're going to expect more of me than I'm able to give. Such as giving you a heads-up about information yet to be released to the public."

"And you're going to expect me to follow a certain path, *and* to report every discovery I make to the Bureau—to you. It's not going to happen."

"I hear you." Hutch frowned, rolling the bottle of water between his palms. "I know what your job is. What I don't know is why."

"Why what?"

"Why you're so fervent about your investigations. And I don't mean professionally. I mean personally. You read people well. But so do I. Something happened that lit an emotional fire in your belly—enough to make you go out on your own and start Forensic Instincts. What was it?"

Casey was quiet for a minute. "You do read people well. Especially me. Okay, my team knows, so why shouldn't you?

Yes, there was something that changed my life, and probably my direction." Another pause. "Do you remember how relentless I was about wrapping up the investigation my team took on right before this kidnapping?"

"The one with that psycho perv who raped and killed all those young women? Yeah, I remember. It was pretty gruesome. I also remember how single-minded you were about catching him. It went over and above the line of duty. That's what got me started thinking along these lines." Hutch studied Casey intently. "Why? Does that case hold special meaning for you?"

"Oh, yeah." Casey blew out her breath. "When I was in college, I had a close friend. Holly. She lived off campus. One day, she told me she had the feeling she was being followed. I suggested she call the police. She did. They blew her off. A week later, she was found raped and murdered, her body tossed in a Dumpster. She'd been there for days, buried in piles of garbage. The bastard who did that to her was never found. I'll never forget how I felt when I heard the news. It was like a horrible nightmare—one that will haunt me for life. It wasn't the police's fault. They had nothing to go on and no manpower to invest in an unsubstantiated complaint. What Holly needed was someone who was skilled enough to help, but not bound by bureaucracy and red tape. Someone with the mind and the resources to sift through suspects and come up with the right answer."

"Someone like Forensic Instincts."

"Exactly."

Hutch's jaw tightened. "I'm sorry you had to live through an experience like that."

"Me, too. But I'm sorrier for Holly. She was nineteen."

"Yeah." Hutch lowered his head, stared at the carpet. "Now I understand."

"Do you? You almost ripped me a new one when I followed Hope Willis to the drop site. I did that on sheer instinct, not on concrete facts I was withholding. She could have really just been going to do an errand and it would have been nothing. I realize you were worried about my safety. But you were also pissed that I didn't clue you in. I can't always do that. Just like you can't always release advance info to me." Casey tucked a strand of hair behind her ear. "I'm not naive. This is going to test us big-time. There are times when it will probably put a huge strain on us."

"Are you willing to try?" Hutch asked flatly. "Because I am. Like I said, we're about more than great sex. I'm not willing to throw it all away just because we're occasionally going to be operating at cross-purposes. We'll hash it out. We'll fight. And, yeah, sometimes we'll combust. Are you invested enough in this relationship to take that on?"

Casey didn't have to think. "Yes," she responded. "I am. But remember, I give as good as I get. I'm not going to roll over. And I'm not going to share confidential information with you, any more than you are with me. There are going to be secrets. We'll have to accept that."

"As long as those secrets aren't about us—the private us."

"Agreed."

Hutch put down his water and crossed over to the bed. "I think this conversation has come to a successful conclusion." He unbelted Casey's robe, slid open the sides. "Now it's time to celebrate our victory."

Casey smiled, leaning back on the bed and tugging Hutch down to her. "Consider this to be our toast."

CHAPTER TWENTY-THREE

Day Six

Dawn was just breaking. Most of the patients at Sunny Gardens were still asleep.

She wasn't. She was sitting up in the chair in her room, fretting because it would be days before her baby would visit. Wednesday had come and gone, as had their time together. Now it was Saturday. Or Sunday. But whichever it was, Wednesday was far away.

She could hardly remember their visit, or what they'd talked about. She'd asked Nurse Greene if she'd been there for any of it, and if her baby had given her a hug before she left.

The nurse had soothed her and assured her that their time together had been tender and warm, and the hug had been tight.

Why couldn't she remember?

She lowered her head into her hands and began to cry.

"Lorna?"

Her head came up. A plump, middle-aged nurse she didn't recognize had stepped into the room.

"What's wrong?" the nurse asked.

"Who are you?"

"I'm Nurse Amato. I heard you crying. Are you in pain?"

"I don't know you. Where's Nurse Greene?" the woman demanded.

"She hasn't come in yet." Nurse Amato walked over, put a hand on Lorna's shoulder. Lorna could see her name tag now. Denise Amato. A stranger.

She shook her hand away. "I don't know you," she repeated. "I want Nurse Greene."

Nurse Amato gave her a placating smile. "I understand that you don't want to confide in me. We don't really know each other. But I don't want to leave you sad. Would you like to take a walk? We could go to the gardens. Nurse Greene says that the flowers always cheer you up."

"She said that?"

"She certainly did."

"But it's noisy outside. Those men are always hammering and drilling."

"We won't walk toward the new wing. We'll go in the opposite direction, and walk around back. We can get to the gardens either way."

Lorna wiped away her tears. "All right, then. We can go to the gardens. But Nurse Greene always pushes me. I'm too tired to walk all that way."

"Of course you are. Wait right here."

The nurse vanished, returning a few minutes later with a wheelchair.

"Here we go," she said cheerfully. "Shall I help you?"

"No. I can get up myself." To demonstrate that she still had some measure of control over her body, Lorna rose and made her way over to the wheelchair. She gripped the arms and sat down.

"Excellent. Let's take our walk."

The gardens were lovely. Nurse Greene had been right. There were pink flowers, and purple flowers, and some pretty yellow flowers, too. She knew what those were called. She just couldn't remember. But she'd had them in a line on her front lawn. They'd grown there a while ago. She wasn't sure how long.

Nurse Amato continued to chat as they walked. Lorna only half heard what she was saying. She was watching the sun rise, wondering if her baby was seeing the same thing. Did it rise the same way everywhere? Or did it look different from different places?

A shimmering reflection caught her eye, and she snapped back to the present.

"What's that?" she asked in a high, thin voice. She already knew. She could sense it even before she saw it.

"It's the lake," Nurse Amato said cheerfully. "The water is calm and beautiful at sunrise. I thought you'd like to see it."

"No!" Lorna's heart began pounding. Sweat broke out on her body and trickled down. Scrambling wildly, she jumped out of the wheelchair, almost toppling to the ground in her haste to get away. She gripped the arm of the wheelchair to steady herself and then stumbled off toward the building.

"Lorna!" Nurse Amato rushed over and gripped her firmly around the shoulders. "Wait! You're going to hurt yourself."

"Let me go!" Lorna shook the nurse off violently, lurching forward a few steps before falling to her knees. "Let me go!" she sobbed again, trying to crawl away.

There was the sound of running footsteps, and then the welcome voice of Nurse Greene.

"What's happening here?" She knelt down and put gentle hands on Lorna's shoulders. "Shh, it's all right. Everything is all right." She looked up at Nurse Amato. "Why did you take her here?"

The other nurse was clearly baffled. "I—I don't understand," she stammered. "I thought she'd enjoy the view."

"Next time, read the file more carefully before you take charge of a patient you're unfamiliar with." Nurse Greene sounded very upset. "This patient is never, under any circumstances, to be brought to the lake. That is listed clearly at the top of her file."

"I'm sorry," the other nurse said. She looked like she wanted to say more, but didn't. And Nurse Greene didn't wait around to further discuss the issue. She just turned the wheelchair around and helped Lorna into it. "Let's head back," she said in a soft, calming voice, starting to push the wheelchair toward the facility. "I'll make you a nice cup of chamomile tea and you can drink it in the day room sitting near the big bay window you like so much. The flowers are in bloom. You'll love all the colors. Before you know it, breakfast will be served. I think I saw some croissants being delivered."

"Those are my favorite," Lorna said.

"I know. Mine, too."

Lorna was already starting to feel better. The water was behind her. It got farther away with each step. And that other nurse wasn't with them. Lorna didn't like her. She didn't know the things she should.

Her heart rate slowly returned to normal, and the sweating stopped. Most of all, the overwhelming sense of panic, the loss of control, was dissipating.

It would be all right now.

Soon, she'd be sipping tea and eating a croissant. Since she was early, she might be one of the lucky patients who got one with chocolate inside. She really liked chocolate. It always tasted sweet. And it made her happy.

She hadn't been happy before.

But she could no longer remember why.

Denise Amato waited until the two women were out of viewing range. Then she made her way across the opposite section of grounds, stopping at a trailer labeled Bennato Construction. She pulled open the door and stepped inside.

"It's done," she said.

"And?" Bill Parsons turned, his eyebrows arched in question.

"And the poor woman nearly had a coronary. If that's what Tony was looking for, he got it."

A nod. "That's what Tony was looking for. That means his information was good. And it'll point the Feds, the cops and that nutcase Navy SEAL in a different direction. Thanks, Denise. I owe you one."

Casey hadn't slept well.

Long after Hutch was out cold, his breathing deep and even, she'd been tossing and turning, trying to figure out what was bugging her. It wasn't Hutch. If anything, tonight had been an important turning point in their relationship. They'd set some boundaries, and acknowledged the depth of their involvement.

No, it was that damned note she'd been left, and its all-too-elusive meaning.

She got out of bed just after dawn, shrugged into her robe and walked across the hall to her little kitchenette, where she brewed a pot of coffee. Hutch found her there a half hour later, sitting at the counter, hunched over her cup.

"Hey, the bed was cold," he commented, tipping up her chin and kissing her lightly on the mouth. "I've obviously lost my touch if you're running away at dawn."

Casey gave him a wan smile. "You haven't lost anything. My body aches in places I never knew I had."

"But the case is eating at you."

"Yeah, it is."

"Well, I can give you more information, but it's not going to cheer you up. I just got a call from Quantico. The lab finished their results in record time. Unfortunately, those results add up to a big goose egg. Zip. Nothing."

"No fingerprints at all?"

"Oh, yeah, there were fingerprints, but they were smudged. Nothing the lab could match to an entry in CODIS. So we have no way of knowing if the DNA was that of a previous offender."

"Meaning we've got nothing."

"Maybe. Maybe not. The fingerprints didn't give us a name, but they did tell a story. They were lightly covered with dirt."

"Dirt?" Casey straightened. "What kind of dirt? The kind you find on a lawn or in a garden, or the kind you find at a construction site?"

"Hard to tell. It could have been any of the above."

"Dammit." Casey set down her coffee cup with a thud. "So we're back to square one. What family are we discussing—the Vizzini family or the Willis family?"

Hutch was quiet for a minute as he poured himself some coffee. "It's a little unusual for a mob soldier to be stupid enough not to wear gloves."

Casey's eyebrows drew together. "So you think it sounds more like a layperson than a seasoned criminal who left me that note."

"Not sure. But my gut tells me yes."

"So does mine. Maybe that's why I couldn't sleep all night. We've investigated the Willises and the Akermans from every possible angle. Yet I can't help but wonder if we're missing something. Plus, another thing occurred to me. I know that Claire isn't a scientific source of information, but not one of the visions she's had has included anything beyond Krissy and Hope. Why isn't she picking up on the mob? She got the same feeling from Deale as I did—that he was a pawn who knew nothing more than he was saying. Should we be showing her the sketches of DeMassi and his son? Would that spawn some kind of reaction?"

Hutch drew a slow breath. "I can't comment on that, Casey. You know I'm not big on the whole idea of psychics. But if you think otherwise, fine. It can't hurt to show the sketches to Claire. In my opinion, however, our best tie-in to either family is Sidney Akerman."

"The rest of the FBI team agrees with you. Peg and Don are reinterviewing Sidney this morning. Patrick's joining them." Casey inclined her head quizzically. "Want to be there? Because I sure do."

"Oh, yeah. I wouldn't miss it."

★ ★ ★

Peg, Don and Patrick were reinterviewing Sidney behind the closed doors of the first-floor den when Casey and Hutch arrived. Hutch's presence was more than welcome. Any light he could shed on what they learned would be greatly appreciated. And Peg had no issue with Casey being there. To her, the time for protocol was over. All that mattered was finding Krissy Willis.

Sidney was perched nervously in a chair, his fingers working feverishly as he addressed the questions being flung his way. He'd been ready and waiting when the others marched in. He was staying here with Hope, despite her ambivalence about having him live under her roof, however temporary. On the one hand, he was her father. On the other hand, he was probably at the heart of everything tragic that had happened to her sister, and now to her daughter. It wasn't an easy pill to swallow, but for expediting the investigation, it was a no-brainer.

Casey and Hutch settled themselves on the leather couch, while Peg and Don stood formidably in front of Sidney, and Patrick paced the floor, listening and occasionally firing an additional question Sidney's way.

"You have *no* idea who left Casey that note?" he pressed, although both Peg and Don had already asked that question—twice.

"Of course not." Sidney's reply was filled with resignation. "If I did, I'd tell all of you faster than you could ask. Krissy is my granddaughter. After the way I screwed up, I'd put my life on the line to find her."

"DeMassi's in jail, and his son's in Sicily," Peg stated aloud. "So if they're responsible for the delivery of the note, they got one of their soldiers to do it."

Don nodded, pursing his lips. "The traces of dirt suggest that it could be someone from Bennato Construction. Mr. Akerman, are you sure you didn't recognize any of the names or photos I showed you of their workers? Or, particularly, of Tony Bennato himself?"

Sidney linked his fingers behind his neck and lowered his head in frustration. "For the tenth time, I never heard of or saw any of them before. But why would I? My connection to these bastards ended three decades ago. And, even then, I barely saw anyone, and I didn't interact with any of them. Only Henry did."

"Henry's dead. You're here. Keep thinking." Patrick was at the end of his rope.

Casey's chin came up, and she made eye contact with Patrick, silently requesting that he give her a few minutes of leeway.

At his nod, she turned to Peg. "May I?" she asked respectfully.

"Please do." A sweep of the case leader's arm.

"Thanks." Casey straightened her spine and leaned forward, intentionally conveying a power stance to Sidney. "Let's tackle this from another angle, Mr. Akerman. We've explored all your direct contacts and your knowledge of what went on with your friend Henry Kenyon. Maybe we should flip this around, and start at the personal end. Rather than dissect the mob, let's discuss you and Felicity, and maybe we can get a handle on who had access to her."

"What do you mean?"

"Your ex-wife told us that Felicity was the apple of your eye, that she was very much daddy's little girl."

Pain twisted Sidney's features. "That's true. I loved both my girls, but Felicity and I had a special rapport. We both loved all kinds of sports. And we were both crazy about arcade games. Our local pizzeria was one of the first places to get Pong. We went there together every weekend and played. And Felicity was crazy about old-fashioned Skee-Ball. She beat me every time."

"So you went to the same pizzeria each time?"

"Uh-huh. But we knew the owners. They were decent, family-loving people, not mobsters."

"I checked them out," Patrick inserted. "They came up clean." A self-deprecating pause. "Then again, I missed Kenyon's mob connections. So we can check them out again. They're in the case file."

Casey nodded. "What about sports?" She continued questioning Sidney, covering all the bases. "I know Felicity was an athlete. Were you involved with that, or was it just spectator sports you shared?"

A hint of a smile, filled with nostalgia. "Both. We watched hours of sports on TV. But we shared the hands-on stuff, too. I'm sure Vera told you what an amazing soccer player Felicity was. She had daily team practices, but we practiced together on top of that. We kicked the ball around at her school, on the front lawn, every place we could set up a goal cage. And she went to soccer camp in the summer, even at her age. It was day camp, of course. She came home every afternoon. But I took off from work whenever I could, just to watch her compete. She was great. She would have gone far if..." His voice trailed off.

Casey glanced down at her case file. "Special Agent Lynch spoke to all the families on Felicity's school and camp soccer teams."

"Yes, he was very thorough. He covered the kids, the parents, the counselors and the coaches. And I'll tell you what I told him, then and now. Everyone loved Felicity. She was kind, bubbly and happy. I can't think of a single soul who'd want to hurt her. And I certainly can't imagine any of the people you just mentioned having mob affiliations."

"Your friend, Henry, was a regular guy, too," Casey pointed out. "He just got himself into a hole and chose the wrong way out. Not everyone with ties to the mob are sinister, evil people. Some are just plain desperate, and they have no concept of the potential consequences of their actions."

Hutch, who'd been silent up until now, spoke up. "Speaking of Kenyon, here's a reach. Your daughter might have been a kid, Akerman, but she was obviously a talented kid. And I know how competitive those sports camps can be. What other camps did they play against? Was there any friendly betting that went on about the games?"

Sidney blinked. "Betting? On six-year-olds?"

"I've seen worse."

Peg's eyes narrowed, and she gazed intently at Hutch. "Go on."

"Following Casey's line of reasoning, Felicity broke her arm the summer she was kidnapped. She'd just been given the go-ahead to play by her doctor. The cast was removed. Then she was abducted. Was her playing a threat to anyone's pocketbook?"

"Wow." Casey exhaled sharply. "That's one I never thought of." She inclined her head at Patrick. "I know you spoke to the staffs of all the camps Felicity's team competed with. Do you think it's possible that any of the parents or staff members could have been placing bets on the games? Did you get the feeling that anyone was hurting for cash or into gambling excessively—anyone who might have gone the same route as Henry Kenyon?"

Patrick wasn't pacing now. He was planted in place, thinking.

"We're *really* reaching now. If this was the World Cup, I'd jump on your line of thinking. But a kids' soccer game? How much cash could be exchanging hands? Enough for a mob payment? My gut says no." A pause. "Still...you make a good point about the timing. Felicity was kidnapped the night before she rejoined the camp team. Is it possible that that wasn't a coincidence? Sure. It's the why I find shaky."

"I won't disagree," Hutch said. "But let's see it through, from every vantage point." He turned back to Sidney. "How did Felicity break her arm—exactly? How long was she out of commission? And who was involved in her recuperation?"

Sidney unbuttoned the top button of his shirt. He was wrung out and beaten. "It was an internal game, just a practice for an upcoming competition with a neighboring camp. She was knocked down by a couple of other kids. It was an accident. She didn't even land that hard. She just landed wrong. She broke her forearm in two places. It took most of the summer to heal."

"And she'd just had the cast removed the day she was abducted."

"Yes."

"So someone could have been waiting for her to heal before kidnapping her." Hutch looked thoughtful. "Someone who knew her medical timetable."

"That consists of the doctor who treated her, and whoever the Akermans shared information with," Patrick replied. "The orthopedist was highly reputable and had an alibi. I can't speak for anyone the Akermans told but didn't mention to me."

"The entire crowd at soccer camp knew the cast was coming off," Sidney supplied. "So did our friends and neighbors. Felicity was so excited she practically shouted it from the rooftops."

"Was there anyone who showed an enthusiasm that seemed over the top?" Casey asked.

Sidney turned his palms up in frustrated uncertainty. "I don't know what you consider to be over the top. Her soccer coach, Ilene Stratton, was elated. So were the other parents whose kids played on the team. And, Linda Turner, the camp nurse, gave Felicity a stuffed tiger wearing a soccer uniform. She was a very kind and compassionate woman."

"Your ex-wife mentioned her when we spoke," Casey commented, glancing at her notes. "She was one of the people who could tell Hope and Felicity apart. And she was also one of the women who came to the prayer vigils after Felicity was kidnapped. Vera said that she stays in touch with her."

Sidney didn't look surprised. "I wasn't aware of that. But it makes sense. Linda's full-time job was as an E.R. nurse at the hospital where Felicity was taken after her accident. Linda rode with Felicity in the ambulance, and met us at the hospital. She facilitated things so Felicity was seen right away. Vera never forgot her kindness. And, before you ask, I doubt Linda either needed or squandered money. She was just a simple widow who spent her time helping people."

"None of the reactions you just described are over the top, or out of place." Casey ignored the touch of sarcasm in Sidney's voice. He'd been grilled constantly since he drove down to Armonk. Painful skeletons had been dredged up. He was strung out and ridden with guilt. She had to cut him some slack. "So far you've only described the people who were elated. Did anyone seem unusually subdued about Felicity's return to the soccer field? On edge? Worried?"

"Probably the other team she was about to play. Otherwise, no."

"We're not getting anywhere going down this path," Patrick interrupted. "I agree that it's peculiar that Felicity was kidnapped the day she had her cast off. But it could have been because the kidnapper thought it would be too much of a pain in the ass to deal with a kid with an injury, so he waited for the cast to come off. More important, the timing of the abduction coincides with Sidney's refusal to cooperate with the mob. That's the reason for the when and why. Not because of the timing of Felicity's recovery."

"Probably," Don concurred. "But it's interesting."

"I agree," Casey said. "I think it should be officially ruled out by widening our background checks to include anyone who was affiliated with Felicity's camp or any of the camps she competed against."

"We'll have our support team take care of that," Peg responded.

"Good. And Ryan will do it simultaneously." *He'll take care of it in a matter of hours, with no red tape to slow down his progress,* Casey thought.

"We need to see if anyone stood something to gain—like money—if Felicity was out of the picture," Don continued. "Then we need to cross match that list with related people still in Vera or Hope's life. If we find someone with a gambling or other questionable monetary problem, that someone could have been involved in Felicity's kidnapping then and is being blackmailed by his or her past now. The blackmailer could have forced them to kidnap Krissy to perpetuate the attack on Sidney's family."

"Right." Hutch nodded, considering the profile. "An act like that, committed by anyone with a shred of decency, would elicit guilt, which could have precipitated the delivery of that note to Casey's door."

Casey saw the doubt on Patrick's face. "So far, DeMassi's our only solid lead, Patrick," she said quietly. "We're running out of options. And time. Krissy's been gone nearly a week."

Lynch's lips thinned into a grim line. "Let's run with it."

CHAPTER TWENTY-FOUR

Marc was perched at the edge of a rickety chair in Ryan's lair, half-watching his colleague at work while he himself absently scratched Hero's ears. He was a stickler for details. His training had taught him to retain every one, because any of them could be significant. In this case, the aspect that was niggling at him was the total lack of balance in the investigation.

The Forensic Instincts team, like the FBI, was now fully immersed in Sidney Akerman's connection to the Vizzini family. They'd bugged Bennato Construction. They'd tracked down each mob soldier that was connected to Henry Kenyon. Now, Ryan was running background checks on every Tom, Dick and Harry who'd known Felicity Akerman while she was in camp.

It was all centered around the mob. But too many pieces were being ignored. Pieces that Marc's intuition told him mattered.

There were still the unexplained facts that a ransom call had been made. That a drop had been arranged, and successfully executed. That a quarter of a million dollars had changed hands. Maybe that scenario wasn't a smoke screen. Maybe that was a very real part of Krissy Willis's kidnapping.

Then there was the note that had been left on Casey's doorstep. Traces of dirt—a common soil found nearly everywhere—had been detected on it. That could suggest a construction site. But it could also suggest a front lawn.

Marc had never been comfortable dismissing Sal Diaz, the Willises' gardener, and his wife, Rita, their housekeeper from the suspect list. If Ryan was searching for a couple who were in debt up to their asses, the Diazes would win the prize. Plus, Sal Diaz had a history of domestic violence. He could just as easily be taking mob money as the parent of a day camper.

And he was a gardener. He worked with dirt all day. If he was freaking out about his involvement in a child abduction, he might very well have caved and left Casey that note.

There were too many clues to ignore.

Abruptly, Marc came to his feet.

"Come on, Hero," he muttered to the bloodhound. "We're going to pay a surprise visit."

While Ryan jumped on his background checks, Casey took photos of DeMassi and his son to Claire.

"Hi." Claire looked surprised to see Casey standing at her apartment door. "Has something happened?"

"I wish." Casey waved the photos in the air. "I'd like you to take a look at these, tell me if you pick up anything from them." She purposely refrained from identifying DeMassi, or giving Claire a hint as to what she should feel. This experiment had to be objective.

"Of course. Come in." Claire stood aside and let Casey in. "I had no idea you knew where I lived."

A hint of a smile. "I'm like Santa Claus. I know everything."

"In other words, you had Ryan find me."

"Exactly." Casey glanced around her. Claire's apartment was much like she'd expected it to be. Muted pastels. Wicker furniture—and not a lot of it. And paintings of sweeping landscapes decorating the walls. There was something both lovely and ethereal about the place. Just like Claire herself.

"Have a seat," Claire invited, gesturing toward the living room. "I just made a pot of green tea, and I was about to review my notes on the Willis case yet again. Care to join me?"

"On both counts, yes, thanks." Casey went in and sank down on the pale aqua-and-sand-colored cushion of the wicker sofa.

"The North Castle police called. They told me about the note that was left for you, and that Special Agent Hutchinson had sent it down to Quantico for analysis. Did anything come of it?" Claire asked, carrying in a tray of tea and scones.

"Nothing substantial. No discernible fingerprints. Just some traces of dirt on the page."

"Dirt," Claire repeated. A brief silence, while a veiled look clouded her eyes. "Whoever left that note on your stoop was frightened. They felt trapped. I…" She rubbed her forehead, trying hard to concentrate. "I'm feeling male energy. I could be wrong, though. I'm not physically at your brownstone. So I'm getting this far from the source."

"Maybe you *should* be at my brownstone." Casey took her cup of tea with a nod of thanks. "Permanently." She hurried on, shelving that discussion for later. "I know you're working for the police. But, Claire, I need anything you can give me.

My confidence is starting to waver. Krissy's been gone for too long."

"Don't let your faith sway. Krissy is still alive. I know it."

"I pray you're right. That feeling of yours is *all* Hope Willis has been clinging to."

"But it's not enough. I understand." Claire sank down and poured herself some tea. Then she glanced at the photos Casey was holding and extended her hand. "May I see them?"

"Definitely." Casey passed them over. "Take your time. Tell me anything you pick up."

Claire looked at the photographs, one at a time. There were several of each man—alone, with their families, even just the two of them.

Five minutes passed. Then, ten.

Finally, Claire raised her head and met Casey's gaze. "I'm not getting anything. Except an ugly feeling. These aren't good men. But who they are, what they've done, that I can't tell you. They're strangers to me."

Casey blew out a discouraged breath. "Any ties to Krissy? Even the vaguest sense of the younger man being in her presence?"

"Nothing." Claire's delicate eyebrows rose. "Why? Are they suspects?"

"They're members of the Vizzini crime family. Lou DeMassi and his son, Lou Junior. There's a possibility that they're connected with both kidnappings—Felicity's and Krissy's."

Claire studied Casey's face with a perceptive expression. "But you don't think that's the case."

"I don't know *what* to think. Sidney's ties to the mob can't be ignored. But I feel as if we're trying to shove a square peg into a round hole. The connection just doesn't feel right. Although I'm still convinced that the two kidnappings are related. I don't care if they are separated by thirty-two years. And Patrick agrees with me."

Claire frowned. "But if it isn't Sidney Akerman's threats from the mob, then what's the link?"

"That's the problem." Casey ran frustrated fingers through her hair. "I can't find one. And I've *got* to."

Ryan barely heard Marc leave. He was too busy cross-checking lists of prospective subjects and ranking them in order of importance before beginning his in-depth background checks. There was no point in striking out blindly. Some of these people he'd already done topical searches on. And some of them had been back-burnered when Bennato Construction had come into play.

Such as the main players in the Akermans' personal lives—players whose appearances had escalated closer to the time of Felicity's kidnapping. And players whose financial woes magically improved after the abduction.

His adrenaline pumping, Ryan's fingers flew across the keyboard, his sharp eyes and even sharper mind taking in every piece of information that surfaced.

He happened to get lucky. Based on his calculations, one of the first names on his list popped up with something shockingly powerful.

Ryan stared at the screen in surprise. Then, he went into hypermode, digging and digging until he had a good chunk of the story in place. There were still pieces missing, like where the money had come from and how much it had been. Also, what psychiatric prognosis had resulted from the treatment, and exactly what people had been part of the support network. Any one of them could have been the connection to the mob.

There were lots of questions Ryan didn't have answers to—*yet.* But he intended to find them.

In the meantime, he was already punching in Casey's cell phone number.

Sal Diaz was clipping hedges at a home that was down the street from the Willises' when Marc's car pulled up. The gardener stopped what he was doing, although he made no move to run away. He simply watched Marc climb out of the car, leash up his dog and head over. If Marc had to guess, based on Diaz's body language, it was almost as if he'd been expecting law enforcement to come knocking at his door.

"Hello, Mr. Diaz," he greeted the short, squat man with the nervous dark eyes. "We spoke a few days ago. Do you remember?"

A terse nod. "You're that guy who's not the FBI or the police. You asked me a lot of questions. Rita, too. Everyone else believed me. You didn't. I could tell. Even though my wife and I both have alibis, you still think we did something wrong." He shifted uneasily. "I don't have to talk to you."

"No you don't. But you will." Marc spoke in that tough, no-bullshit tone that made the hair on people's necks stand up. "Because if you don't, I'm going to make you very unhappy. And I'll do it where no one can see us and where there are no witnesses."

Diaz paled, but he didn't respond.

Hero had been sniffing the gardener's work boots. Now, he let out a braying bark.

Marc glanced down at him. "My dog seems to recognize you," he told Diaz. "That's interesting. Because he wasn't with me when I asked you those questions you're talking about. So how would he know you? Or, more specifically, where would he know you from?"

"I don't know." Diaz's Adam's apple rose and fell as he swallowed hard. "I never saw him before."

"Maybe not. And maybe he didn't see you either. But he sure as hell smelled you."

No reply.

"You're the person who left that note on our doorstep, aren't you?" Marc was blunt. Now wasn't the time to mince words. "Why?"

"I…I…" Diaz dragged a sleeve across his forehead.

"Look, Diaz, I don't have time to play games. A little girl is missing. The time to find her is running out. There are holes in your alibi, and your wife's. Either one of you could have gotten into the Willises' house, or driven over to their daughter's school. Jobs or not, you wouldn't have been missed. You're well aware of all this, or you wouldn't have gotten involved and tried to throw suspicion elsewhere. So you can either willingly tell me what I want to know, or I'll drag it out of you one painful word at a time. Your choice." Marc took a menacing step in Diaz's direction. He didn't need to. The power of his build and the blazing look in his eyes was enough.

Diaz capitulated without an argument.

"Yes, I left that note. My wife and I are innocent. But I knew the cops would think what you did and come after us. I can't let that happen. So I pushed you in the right direction."

Marc's mind was racing. There was no way Diaz knew about the mob. Not unless he was connected to it, which Marc would be willing to bet that he wasn't. Which meant that the family he was referring to was the Willises.

"What right direction?" he probed. "What don't we know?"

"On TV, they said that Judge Willis left the house that morning with her daughter, and didn't come back until after school. That's not true. I saw her come home around two o'clock. She went inside while her nanny was outside checking the mail. She only stayed a few minutes. Then, she left."

Marc went very still. "Are you sure it was Judge Willis?"

The gardener nodded. "I see her all the time. So, yeah, I'm sure. Her car was a little bit down the street and she was in a hurry, but the way she acted..." He paused, remembering. "No, she didn't want her nanny, or anyone else, to spot her."

"Why didn't you tell this to anyone?"

"First of all, I didn't want attention shifting to us. And second, it didn't occur to me. Not until I saw that press conference on TV, and I heard what they were saying. That's when I knew they were lying."

Dammit. This told Marc nothing of substance. As per the BAU's instructions, the press had provided only the necessary specs to the public. That the kidnapper was a woman. That she was driving a silver Acadia. That she'd coaxed Krissy into the car during school pickup time.

Not a word had been said about the offender posing as Judge Willis. So Sal Diaz had no idea that the woman he'd seen entering the Willis house was, in fact, the kidnapper.

He *had* provided them with a time frame, however. And a confirmation of how the kidnapper had gotten into the house—by slipping by Ashley Lawrence when she was outside checking the mail.

None of that added up to shit at this point. Knowing that the kidnapper had gotten inside and taken Oreo before abducting Krissy might have meant something three days ago. Now it was moot. Because nothing Diaz had said brought them any closer to Krissy Willis.

"I didn't do anything." Diaz had obviously misinterpreted Marc's silence to mean he believed the gardener was lying. "Neither did Rita. I didn't even tell her about what I saw. She's a good woman. And she's so honest. She would have gone to the police. I was afraid. I'm just a gardener. Rita's a housekeeper. And the Willises are big, important people."

Marc nodded. He knew enough about human nature to know that Diaz was telling the truth. There was no point in torturing the man—except where it might do some good.

"I believe you," he stated flatly. "But the only reason I flagged you as a suspect is because of your history. Get help. Keep your fists off your wife. Pay your bills instead of throwing your money away on booze and cards. Now convince me you plan to do all that. Because it's the only way I'll tell the FBI and the cops that I believe your story."

"Okay." Diaz was nodding furiously. He looked ready to agree to anything. "I'll do it. I swear. You can check up on me. You'll see."

"I plan to. And I'd better see."

Casey was sitting in her car, reviewing the notes from the meeting with Sidney Akerman, when her BlackBerry vibrated. She glanced down at the caller ID.

It was Ryan.

She hit the receive button and put the phone to her ear. "Talk to me."

"I may have hit the mother lode," he said flatly.

"Go on." Casey sat up straighter.

"Linda Turner, the camp nurse. She's got an interesting

history. One that, clearly, no one knows about, because it's not the kind of thing you forget to mention. She had a daughter about Felicity Akerman's age."

"Had?"

"Yeah, had. It seems the girl—Anna—drowned in a lake on their property. It happened about six months before Felicity's soccer accident. According to what I could hack into, Ms. Turner fell apart after Anna died. The hospital sent her for a psych evaluation.. After that, she took a leave of absence and went for counseling sessions twice a week for three months. She went back to the E.R. part-time as soon as she was deemed capable. She supplemented her income with the job as camp nurse at Felicity's day camp. But, according to the accounts I hacked into, she was hurting financially. There's no doubt about that."

"Wow." Casey was processing all this as quickly as she could. "I don't understand. How could she have had a child, much less lost one, and no one knew about it? Vera sure as hell didn't. She spoke of Linda as if she were childless. And there were no obituaries? No local articles about a child drowning in her own backyard?"

"Evidently, Linda was the protective type," Ryan replied. "She managed to keep everything out of the newspapers. All that exists is a police report. Even when Anna was alive, Linda homeschooled her, and kept her pretty isolated from other kids her age."

A weighty pause that Casey recognized.

Ryan was about to tell her something significant.

"Except for soccer," he reported. "Anna loved the game. So Linda let her play in a small league two towns over. It was private, exclusive—and damned expensive. But it was noncompetitive and low-key. She also had a private coach instruct her at home once a week—a *very* expensive private coach. Anna's only other love was horseback riding. Linda gave in to that. She quarter-leased a horse for her. That costs a ton. Other than that, Anna was at home with her mother. No other siblings. No other family at all."

"The father?"

"Died when she was a toddler. Linda Turner raised her daughter alone. And on a lean budget. Her husband didn't leave her much money."

"So she wasn't flush after she became a widow. And she was an E.R. nurse—an admirable but not six-figure paying profession. Where did she get the means to give her daughter private soccer lessons, an exclusive team membership *and* her own horse?"

"You tell me. Also, tell me how far she would go to get her hands on that sum of money? Or what would she owe someone who gave it to her?"

"And isn't it a coincidence that Anna's main passion was soccer, of all things? Just like Felicity's? Not to mention the timing of Anna's death in relation to Felicity's kidnapping?" Casey leaned back against her car seat, the phone anchored in the crook of her shoulder, her hands inadvertently gripping the steering wheel. "This is big, Ryan. It's the biggest break we've had. And it feels right. Where is Linda Turner now? I don't think that Vera's seen her in a while."

"And she probably won't. Linda's still listed at the same address in a rural area of Wappingers Falls, about an hour north of Westchester County. But her phone is disconnected, and there's no one living there. I called the local PD right away. They headed over there ASAP. The place is deserted—all her clothing's gone, there's no food in the fridge, the whole nine yards."

"So she cleared out."

"You got it."

"Damn." Casey slammed her palms on the steering wheel in frustration. "No friends. No address. I'll talk to Vera, but I'm sure she can't tell us anything we don't already know. She might have a photo of her in one of the camp pictures. And I'm sure she can give a description to a sketch artist."

"Plus you have me. Get me that photo and I'll use my age progression software to create a present-day image of Linda. Vera can proof it. And we can distribute it, along with her sketch, to every law enforcement agency in New York State."

"Fine, but that takes time. We've got to act now. We've got to figure out Linda's mind-set—her *real* mind-set—at the time Felicity was kidnapped." An ambivalent pause as Casey wrestled with what she wanted and what she knew was ethical. "You mentioned that Linda had counseling after her daughter died."

"Yup."

"You don't happen to know who her therapist back then was, do you?"

"Do you even need to ask?" Ryan chuckled, ignoring Casey's customary internal battle. "I've got a name and address of his current practice. And, from my cyber stalking, I learned the happy fact that Linda's shrink is a pack rat who keeps files from the year one. So somewhere in that office is his file on Linda Turner."

"And you've already thought of a way to get your hands on it."

"I repeat—do you really need to ask?"

This time Casey smiled. "Never. Not when it comes to you."

"The psychiatrist's name is Stanley Sherman. His office is in a three-story building in White Plains, not far from the courthouse where Hope presides. As soon as you and I hang up, I'll be hitting up Marc. He and Hero blew out of here a little while ago. He was a man on a mission."

"And that mission, I take it, is about to change?"

"Damn straight." Ryan was already tinkering with something in the background. Casey could hear the sounds of metal being manipulated. That meant one of Ryan's toys. And she knew exactly which one.

"The little critter?" she asked.

"Yup. Gecko is about to make his debut performance."

CHAPTER TWENTY-FIVE

Marc met Ryan inside his van at the designated spot half a block away from Dr. Sherman's building.

"Nice work with Diaz," Ryan commented after Marc had hopped in. "You didn't trust him from the beginning."

A shrug. "All we found out was that he'd left Casey the note and that he saw Krissy's abductor come and go from the Willises' house. Not much at this point. And it pales next to what you dug up." Marc glanced over his shoulder at the back of the van to see what supplies Ryan had brought with him today. There was a packed duffel bag, along with Ryan's ever-present laptop. "So how are we doing this?"

"I did a quick tour of the building while you were filling the FBI in on Diaz's story. Sherman's office is on the second floor. His receptionist is out today. So we've got that on our side. But Sherman's in with a patient. We'll have to wait for him to go to lunch."

Marc grunted. "At which point he'll lock the office door behind him."

"You'll take care of that part," Ryan continued, reaching behind him for the duffel bag. He pulled out some tools, which Marc pocketed, followed by a maintenance uniform, which he passed over to Marc. "Time to wear service coveralls again. You should be used to it by now—and they bring out your eyes. Now go in the back and put this on," he instructed. "I'll fill you in on the rest as you change."

"Done." Marc climbed into the rear section of the van and began yanking the uniform on over his clothes. "Why do I know this is going to involve your little critter robot?"

"Because it is." Ryan didn't miss a beat. "I've been dying to try him out. Now's my chance. There's a maintenance closet in the basement," he informed Marc. "That's where I found your uniform. Grab one of those carts so you can look authentic. Then we'll time this until you can do your thing with the lock. Once you're inside Sherman's office, I'll tell you what to do. More specifically, Gecko will."

Marc's fingers paused on a shirt button. "Explain."

"When I stole your uniform, I went up to the roof," Ryan said calmly. "I placed my little guy inside the air-conditioning ductwork. I'll steer him down to where we want him, inside a duct in Sherman's office. There are built-in cameras inside Gecko that'll scan the place, and a microphone that can communicate with you. So Gecko becomes your robo-lookout. And it's all connected to my trusty laptop." Ryan reached back and patted the computer. "Together you and I will find the file on Linda Turner. You'll photocopy what we need, put everything back the way you found it, and get out of there. I'll steer Gecko back to safety. And we'll hope that there's something in the file that'll lead us to our suspect."

"Got it." There wasn't a shred of surprise in Marc's response. He knew Ryan, knew the way his brilliant mind worked. He respected the hell out of him. And, tactical and physical skills combined, they worked really well together. "Do I need an earbud?"

"While you're waiting for my 'all clear' signal, yes. But, once you're inside the office, we can talk to each other through Gecko's mike. The earbuds alone wouldn't give me a visual. Besides, like I said, mostly I'm dying to try the little guy out. This is a cool way to do a trial run."

"Ready." Marc finished donning his uniform, adjusted his earbud and peered out the window. "You first, or me?"

"You. I can position Gecko in ten minutes."

"Then I'm gone."

Marc sauntered down to the maintenance closet and found a cart, which he promptly filled with mops, brooms, rags and various chemical cleaners. Then he made his way up the stairwell, avoiding the elevators so he wouldn't run into anyone who asked questions. He carried the cart ahead of him, until he'd reached the second floor. He passed a couple of women walking down to the main corridor, laughing and heading out for a coffee break. He kept his head low and his attention on his cart, although he couldn't help but chuckle silently at the man-bashing conversation. His presence didn't slow them down a bit. To them he was invisible, so they continued their chatter. Charlie—the clueless boyfriend whose head was on the chopping block—was about to be dumped. Evidently, he was an inconsiderate bastard, and lousy in bed to boot.

It was this kind of crap that made Marc glad he wasn't the heavy-relationship type.

The second-floor staircase was deserted, and Marc emerged without a hitch. The hall was a different story. There were three lawyers standing outside their offices, discussing a litigation case. Marc moved slowly past them, noting the numbers on the doors. Good. Sherman's office was around the bend. As long as the attorneys stayed where they were and Marc didn't run into anyone else, he'd be able to do his job without a problem.

Almost home free.

"He just left for lunch."

Marc heard Ryan's voice in his ear as he rounded the corner and nearly crashed into Dr. Sherman.

"No shit," Marc muttered under his breath. Aloud, he murmured a heavily accented, "Excuse me," keeping his head low. Ryan almost lost it and cracked up laughing, as he heard Sherman call Marc a clumsy idiot, before tromping off.

Marc spied Sherman's office, his name on the door in big letters. Reflexively, he gave a quick scan of the hall. Empty.

Satisfied, he pulled on a pair of latex gloves. Then, he extracted his flathead screwdriver and file, carefully inserting them in the lock and feeling his way, listening until he heard the telltale click. He pushed open the door and tucked away his tools. Dragging the maintenance cart in behind him, he yanked the door shut, walking through the reception area and into the main office behind it.

"What took you so long?" Ryan inquired through the air duct.

Marc arched a brow. "Nice warning. Timely, too. I almost flattened the shrink. What happened to not drawing attention to myself?"

"Sorry. Let's get to it. Sherman takes short lunch breaks. That gives us maybe thirty minutes tops." Ryan fell silent for a moment. "I think I see a file room in the back."

"Yup, you do. And fortunately there's no lock on the door." Marc picked up the pace, striding across the floor and shoving open the door. "Are you in here?" he asked Ryan.

"Sure am. There's an air-conditioning vent to your left. Gecko followed you in." A low whistle. "I knew Sherman was a pack rat, but this lends new meaning to the phrase. There are file cabinets everywhere."

"Lucky me." One by one, Marc scanned the labels on the cabinets, which listed the files inside by date. "These only go back twenty-five years. Shit. Where are the rest?" He scrutinized the room.

There were loose stacks of files in the far corner.

"Let me try those," he said to Ryan, pointing.

"Good idea." Ryan waited while Marc squatted down and began rummaging through the files. He was careful to keep them in the same order he'd found them.

"These are the oldies but goodies," Marc muttered, going back thirty, then thirty-plus years. "Bingo." He stopped when he saw the name: *Turner, Linda.* "I got it," he told Ryan.

"Great. The copying machine's in the reception area. I'm moving Gecko to the main corridor outside the office. He'll watch the door and the hallway."

Marc headed right for the reception room and the copying machine, which was in plain view. He turned it on, and it whirred to life. Opening Linda's file, he took out the stack of handwritten pages, and fed them into the machine.

It took about fifteen minutes to complete the job, and three minutes to return the reassembled file to its pile in the back room.

Leaving the office, Marc shut and locked the door behind him. He looked up at the vent and snapped off a salute. "See you back at the van, little guy."

I'm scared, Mommy. Please come and find me.

It's been a bunch of days. My cartoons have been reruns five times. I counted. She puts them on for me every day. And then she sits and watches me watch them.

It's creepy, Mommy. She's *creepy.*

I keep crying and crying—not when she's here, because it makes her act weird and mushy. And that's scarier than when she watches me play or tries to play with me. I only cry when I'm alone with Oreo and Ruby.

I don't want to play the stupid computer game she gave me. She said she made it. I don't care. I want my *games back. I want to play them in* my *room, on* my *computer. But every time I ask if I can go home, she says* I am *home. I don't know what she means. I'm in a pink room. She says it's my princess room. I'm afraid to tell her that it's not mine.*

She's wearing your necklace. And she smells like you. I don't know why. But it makes me want to hide.

Oreo's fur is all wet. Ruby's feathers are, too. My crying did that. But they understand because they're crying, too.

Why does she keep telling me that she's my mommy? She's not *my mommy.* You *are. But when I tell her that, she gets mad at me. She says weird stuff. I'm afraid of her. I'm afraid she'll do something bad. So I don't say it anymore.*

She keeps coming down here. I can count the stairs by the sound of her shoes. There are fourteen.

I hate that number. I hate hearing her come. I'm so happy when she goes away.

I don't know who's upstairs. But when she's up there, I can hear her talking to someone. Only they never come down. Only her.

Maybe they're scarier than she is.

I wish she'd go away forever. I don't care about the ice cream and the toys and the bubble baths. I just want to go home.

Please, Mommy. I'm scared.

Please come and take me home.

Casey met Marc and Ryan in the parking lot of an Armonk pub. She left her car and climbed into Ryan's van. There, she studied the psychiatrist's official report for the hospital's medical review board, declaring Linda fit to return to work. She also read through Linda Turner's file, line by line, even though Marc and Ryan had summed it up perfectly on the phone.

There was no doubt that the poor woman had come apart at the seams right after her daughter drowned. She was inconsolable and despondent when she'd first starting seeing Dr. Sherman. Anna had clearly been her entire world. And that world had died with Anna.

Linda had made very little progress in the first months. But after intensive therapy, and a chunk of time, she'd begun to come back. Dr. Sherman was very pleased with her progress. And, by the time he'd given her the green light to return to work, he'd been more than confident that she was ready to start rebuilding her life, one baby step at a time. Starting with work, which he believed would give her a sense of purpose and something to focus on besides her grief.

He had, however, recommended that Linda continue with her counseling sessions, at least on a weekly basis. And she had... for a while. Then, without warning, she'd stopped going. From the doctor's notes, it looked as if her insurance was no longer willing to cover the visits. Dr. Sherman had offered to work out some arrangement, perhaps a reduced rate, so that Linda could continue with her sessions. But she had respectfully turned him down, assuring him that her monetary situation was fine, as was her mental health. Things in her life were looking up.

In what way? With what money?

There were no answers to Casey's questions. Because, abruptly, the file came to an end. The progress reports stopped. So, apparently, did Linda's association with Dr. Sherman.

That in itself was a red flag.

But the chilling part was that Linda's psychiatric sessions ended two weeks before Felicity Akerman was kidnapped.

Casey tossed down the file. "This is it. The timeline and coincidences can't be ignored. And it changes everything, maybe even the focus of the investigation. We've got to act now."

"We can't take this one on alone, Casey," Marc stated flatly. "We've got to involve the FBI task force."

Ryan turned to Marc. "Since when do you worry about playing by the rules?"

"He's right, Ryan," Casey said. "This isn't about rules. It's about telling law enforcement what they need to know, and increasing our manpower. Linda Turner has to be found."

"We can't just turn over her psychiatric file," Ryan responded. He went back to punching in information on his laptop, searching at top speed for any trail of their suspect. "We got it illegally. That means we could go to jail. Plus, the Feds can't use it in court, anyway."

"We won't turn over the file," Marc said. Being former BAU, he had the greatest knowledge and the most experience with the FBI. "We'll just act as confidential informants. Based on what we know, we'll give them verbal specifics, which will convince them to act without compromising their case."

"I agree." Casey was already up and climbing out of the van, her car keys in her hand. "Let's go."

* * *

Peg, Don and Hutch—along with two other CARD team members, three agents, Sergeant Bennett of the North Castle P.D. and Patrick Lynch—gathered in the command center in the Willises' media suite, listening while Casey and her Forensic Instincts team presented the facts they'd uncovered.

The reaction was much as Ryan had suggested.

Hutch jumped in first. "Where did you get your information?"

Casey met his gaze directly, unblinking, as she replied. "From the most reliable of sources. That's all you need to know."

"You mean, that's all we'll *want* to know," Peg clarified. She rolled her eyes, torn between irritation, worry over making a potential conviction stick and the sense of urgency based on getting to a woman who might very well have Krissy. "Dammit, Casey, why do you insist on putting us in this position?"

"It's not intentional. You know that. But it's almost a week, Peg. Krissy's life is in our hands."

"Casey's right." It was Don who spoke up. CARD team or not, he wanted to find that child. "We can argue over protocol later. Casey's team hasn't compromised us by sharing physical evidence that might or might not have been illegally obtained. It's all word of mouth. We'll find a way to write this up and present it in court—later. Now we've got to pool our resources and find Linda Turner."

Peg nodded, pursing her lips. "Agreed."

"I understand the motivation for her to kidnap Felicity Akerman," Sergeant Bennett interceded. "But where does Krissy Willis come in? It's over thirty years later. Where's the connection—besides the obvious blood ties between Felicity and Krissy?"

"It could still be someone's vendetta," Lynch answered. "If DeMassi and his son, or another mob soldier is pulling the strings, the choice of victims could be theirs."

"On the other hand," Hutch interceded, "if the psychological implications Casey is suggesting are true, then Linda Turner would have filled Anna's void with Felicity. And when Felicity grew up, the void would reappear. So she wouldn't need much convincing to do a repeat performance, this time with Krissy."

"Krissy would take Felicity's place," Casey agreed aloud. "That makes sense. And Patrick, I know Sidney was our ace in the hole. But I'm no longer convinced there's a mob tie-in here. I think we might be barking up the wrong tree. Linda's motivation is emotional and psychological. She wants—needs—to replace her dead daughter. She could be acting on her own."

"Meaning Sidney was just a wrong-place, wrong-time scenario."

"Exactly." A hard swallow as Casey turned to Hutch and steeled herself for the inevitable answer to what she was about to ask. "At what age would a child like Felicity become dispensable?"

"Based on your theory—which I think holds water—when Felicity reached an age where she no longer needed a 'mommy' and/or no longer reminded Linda of Anna. Before puberty, would be my guess."

"But that doesn't make sense," Casey persisted. "Vera Akerman has been in touch with Linda over the years. And, at no point, did she go to pieces. How do you explain that?"

Hutch's jaw tightened. "There could be several reasons. Either the void in her life was filled by someone else, like a man."

"Or?"

"Or there could have been other children in between Felicity and Krissy. Children that Linda abducted on her own."

"Oh, God." Casey felt ill.

"What about the quarter of a million dollars that Hope Willis paid?" Bennett asked. "Where does the ransom money come in?"

"It was either a hoax generated by some arbitrary bastard cashing in on the Willises' panic, or a way to throw us off track," Hutch deduced. "I doubt that Linda required a payoff. Not with motives that, as Casey said, are clearly emotional and psychological." A pause. "There is one other possibility. Linda could need money to raise her 'child.' Ransom would be a way of getting it."

"Yes, it would," Casey murmured. "Especially if Linda plans on keeping Krissy for years."

A heavy silence hung in the room.

"So we're all in agreement," Peg concluded at last. "We've got to find Linda Turner." She glanced over at Ryan. "Since you've already jumped the gun, do you have anything for us on her whereabouts?"

Ryan frowned. "She's fallen off the map. When the local cops checked out her house, they found it deserted, the phone line disconnected. But there's no indication that she moved—no forwarding address, nothing on the internet, zilch. I'm not giving up. I'm going back to the office to start digging again. I'll find her." He looked at Casey. "Does Vera Akerman have a picture of Linda Turner?"

"I don't know. But I'll find out. I have to talk to her, Hope and Edward anyway, and fill them in on where things stand."

"Tell them only what you have to," Peg cautioned.

"I will."

"If you can get me a photo, I'll use my age-enhancing software to create an image of Linda as she would look today," Ryan said. "I'll email what I come up with to your BlackBerry so Hope's mother can see it and suggest whatever modifications are necessary. Once that's done, we'll have something to distribute."

"Good. Because Marc and I are heading up to Linda's house right after this meeting." Casey was frank. Even if Peg gave her a hard time, she wasn't going to lie.

"A handful of us will be up there, too," Peg replied. "We need to determine how long Linda's been gone. Logically, she's with Krissy." Peg shot Casey a warning look. "Don't impede our investigation, Casey. You've already stepped way over the line."

"We won't. When it comes to this, we know you're the experts." Casey glanced respectfully at Sergeant Bennett. "With your permission, I'd like to bring Claire with us. She might pick up on some energy that will help us. And we're bringing Hero, too. He's out in Marc's car. I want him there when ERT is collecting Linda Turner's scent—to sniff *after* they've completed their official search," she hastily added, referring to the FBI's Evidence Response Team.

"I have no problem with that," Bennett replied.

"Nor do I." Peg turned to Hutch. "You and Grace work up a new profile. Highlight the following. Female in her mid-sixties. A loner. Photo to follow. Seen with the five-year-old kidnapping victim whose picture we distributed. I want you to call a meeting of the remaining members of the task force. I want every pair of eyes on the lookout for Linda Turner, or someone or something that can lead us to her. Don, pick a few of your people. Same with the North Castle P.D. Patrick, you're welcome to join us. We're taking off now."

CHAPTER TWENTY-SIX

The wooden house looked like all the others in the area.

It was modest, with pale blue shutters and white clapboard walls. Set back from the road, the house was surrounded by several acres of woods. The grounds and gardens hadn't been tended to, and there were weeds growing all around the lake out back.

Clearly, Linda had wanted to block out the memory of what had happened there.

The task force, along with the Evidence Response Team that Peg had summoned, went inside first, checking the place for clues as to Linda's whereabouts. Casey and her team stayed outside, waiting to be allowed in. Ditto for Patrick, who stood as still as a statue, his gaze fixed on the house, his hands clasped tightly behind his back.

Claire was with them, walking the grounds, stopping occasionally to lean over and touch the dead flowers in the garden, and concentrating intently. Hero zigzagged across the lawn, sniffing, his leash clutched in Marc's hand.

Casey paced around impatiently, frustrated at being kept out. But there was nothing else she could do until ERT had finished checking for physical evidence.

Nothing but think.

She'd told Hope and Vera the basics before taking off. Edward had been at the office. Hope had come alive at the prospect of a real lead. Vera, on the other hand, had refused to believe that Linda was involved. She was stunned to learn about Anna, since she hadn't even known of her existence. But she insisted that Linda's daughter's death must have made her all the more compassionate about Felicity's abduction. Nobody should have to bear the loss of a child, she'd told Vera repeatedly. And she'd attended every one of the prayer vigils after Felicity's disappearance. How could she have faked that level of concern?

Casey viewed Linda's actions and statements in a far different light. But she'd seen reactions like Vera's before. She was in denial. Even so, Casey could see the flicker of doubt in her eyes. Somewhere inside her, Vera was afraid that what she was being told was true. And that would mean she'd befriended the very woman who'd stolen her daughter, destroyed her life and now kidnapped her granddaughter.

Having heard Casey's request for a photograph, Vera had disappeared to her room, returning to present Casey with a photo from Felicity's soccer camp. The staff was in the back row. Vera pointed at a slender, dark-haired woman with a gracious smile that didn't quite match the sober look in her eyes and told Casey that that was Linda.

Casey couldn't help but notice that Linda's height and build could easily have passed for Hope's. She didn't say that aloud. She merely thanked Vera and gave the photo to Ryan.

Vera looked ill. This potential truth was almost unbearable.

But not nearly as unbearable as it would be to hear Casey's theory about Felicity being replaced by a series of other children, all of whom would have been disposed of when they hit a certain age. A mad cycle that Krissy could very well be taking her place in.

The very thought made Casey's stomach turn.

The ringing of her cell phone interrupted her thoughts.

She answered ASAP. "Yes, Ryan?"

"Obviously, no hospital's computer records date back thirty years," he began without preamble. "But the hospital Linda Turner worked at does have archived records in storage. So I drove there, made a few friends."

"Female, no doubt," Casey inserted drily.

"Yeah, well, they just finished digging around for me. It's bizarre, Casey. There are no records of Felicity at all. Not of her E.R. visit, not of her follow-ups—nothing. There are, however, records of a girl matching Felicity's description arriving in the E.R. that day with a broken arm. All the dates and procedures match the ones Vera Akerman gave us of Felicity."

"So the hospital screwed up."

"I'd say no to that one." Ryan had that voice again, the one that said he was about to deliver a bombshell. "According to the file, the girl with the broken arm was Anna Turner."

Casey started. "Oh my God."

"It's like Felicity's existence there was wiped clean, and replaced by Linda's daughter."

* * *

Linda's house was barren. Her clothing and toiletries were gone. Her fridge was cleaned out. The evidence suggested that she hadn't been living here for some time now. Which meant she was probably living in the place she'd set up for Krissy.

They had to find her. She was the key to everything.

The key to finding Krissy.

The FBI task force canvassed the neighborhood. Using the photos Ryan had created, they showed Linda's picture to neighbors, local business owners, anyone and everyone they could think of. Clearly the woman had been a total recluse. A few neighbors who were longtime residents of the area recognized her, but none of them had seen her in as long as they could recall. The local pharmacy had never done business with her. Nor had any of the local merchants. And if she had any doctors, they weren't in this area.

A core team, including Peg and Don, continued combing the house. Casey and Marc stayed with them. So did Patrick and Claire. And, of course, Hero. Marc covered the entire house with him, letting him sniff every nook and cranny, along with the scent samples ERT had collected. Even with her personal items gone, Linda had lived here. Which meant her scent was the one thing she'd left behind.

"She didn't want to be recognized." Peg stated the obvious. "So whatever supermarkets, drugstores, or health care professionals she dealt with, they're located elsewhere."

"What about employment?" Casey asked. "She'd need a stream of income—assuming she wasn't the one who got Hope to part with the ransom money. Do we widen the search?"

"Yes." Don nodded. "We need to check neighboring towns.

She wouldn't go far, not given how reclusive she is. But we have to act fast."

"I'll get more manpower up here." Peg whipped out her phone. "We'll expand the search area. Meanwhile, let's keep exploring the house with a fine-tooth comb. There has to be something—a receipt, a paycheck stub, something—that she left behind that would give us a clue as to what she did, where she shopped, what places she frequented."

Claire was standing at the top of the basement stairs. "I need to go down there," she murmured. "I know you swept the place and found nothing. But I still need to go down there. I'm not sure why—not yet."

With that, she descended the staircase.

"I'll bet that's where Linda kept Felicity," Casey said. "People repeat patterns they're comfortable with, and Claire keeps referring to a basement. If Linda's holding Krissy in the basement of wherever she is, she must have done the same here with Felicity." Turning and speaking to Peg and Sergeant Bennett simultaneously, she asked, "May I go down with Claire?"

Neither of them had a problem with that.

So Casey hurriedly descended the steps.

Claire was standing in the middle of the room, looking around as if she were seeing something more than an empty basement with a concrete floor and cinder-block walls. From the distant expression in her eyes, she wasn't even aware of Casey's presence.

Slowly, she crossed over to the far wall, pressing her palm against the surface, then sliding it up and down.

"A bed," she said in a soft, faraway voice. "With a canopy. The bedspread has roses on it. Roses, for Briar Rose. Princess

Aurora. The bed is for her. And the canopy is embroidered with pictures of Flora, Fauna and Merryweather."

Sleeping Beauty, Casey thought. Claire was describing Sleeping Beauty.

"She doesn't feel like a princess," Claire continued in that same dreamlike tone. "She's scared. She wants her mommy, her daddy and her sister. She doesn't understand why she's here. And she doesn't understand her new name. It's not hers. She's not who she's supposed to be. She just wants it to go away. She just wants to go home."

Casey stayed frozen in place, determined not to interrupt Claire's musings. Clearly, she was talking about Felicity. This was the room in which she'd been held captive.

Claire's words were heartbreaking. There were tears on her cheeks. "She's curled close to this wall. As far away as she can get. But she knows it's not far enough. Her legs are tucked under her. She's afraid of the dark. And it's always dark down here. Except for the night-light and the little lamp on her nightstand." Claire pressed her palm hard against the wall. "It's not a fairy tale. It's a nightmare. Why did this happen to her? She doesn't understand. She doesn't want to."

An odd expression crossed Claire's face. "Pain. Resignation. Acceptance." Her eyes flickered open. "She's gone," she whispered. "Gone for good." For a long moment, she stared at her hand. Then, she let it drop to her side. She looked exhausted and utterly defeated.

"Claire?" Casey said tentatively.

Claire glanced over at her. "Felicity was here."

"I know. I could tell by what you were saying."

"This wall," Claire murmured. "She spent hours pressed against it, trying to emotionally escape. That's how I could still pick up on her presence after all these years. A residue of her energy was left behind. It's gone now." A shaky sigh. "So we know Linda Turner was the kidnapper. Or at least one of them. She kept Felicity in this basement. That's why she's repeating herself with Krissy. Another basement, another princess room."

"Do you feel Krissy's energy here, as well?" Casey asked quickly.

"No." Claire shook her head. "Krissy was never here. Either Linda moved beforehand, or she chose a different location to make sure she didn't get caught. Either way, she never brought Krissy to this house."

Casey walked over and looped an arm around Claire's shoulders. The poor woman was shaking. This experience had taken a lot out of her.

"Let's go upstairs." Casey spoke in a gentle voice. "We'll tell the task force what you felt and saw."

"Assuming they believe me," Claire replied with sad resignation.

Casey couldn't argue that one. "We'll just have to hope ERT turns up some evidence from this room."

For the first time, Casey understood the crippling frustration Claire endured in situations like this. It was bad enough to see the dubious expressions on the faces of the task force. What was worse was the utter helplessness of knowing there wasn't a damned thing they could do to utilize Claire's information. Casey didn't care about the inadmissibility of what Claire had seen and felt. She would have jumped on this anyway, unencumbered by the limitations of law enforcement. What she cared about was the fact that she had nothing concrete that could lead them to Linda Turner.

Only the confirmation that they were looking for the right person.

"Did you find anything in the house?" Casey asked Peg.

"Nothing of significance." Peg looked as frustrated as Casey felt. "A couple of take-out menus. A broken plate in the garbage. And a roll of red string in a corner of the master bedroom. We don't need any of it. ERT had more than enough to establish that Linda Turner lived here. And they dusted for prints everywhere—including the basement—for proof that Felicity Akerman had been here. But, when push comes to shove, even if all the fingerprints match up and everything Claire said was true, it means nothing. Not in the here and now. Felicity Akerman is gone. We need to find Krissy Willis."

Casey nodded. "Nothing else?"

"Scraps of paper with nothing written on them, an empty journal and an equally empty calendar. Obviously, Linda Turner wasn't keeping track of things, at least not in a place she left for us to find."

With that, Peg's phone rang.

She snatched it and answered. "Harrington."

A minute of silence, as Peg listened.

"Good. I want it analyzed yesterday. Call me back with specifics."

Casey waited, staring at Peg. Judging from the special agent's reaction, this call had yielded something that mattered.

"That was ERT," Peg said in answer to Casey's questioning look. "Evidently, when they swept the medicine cabinet in the master bath, they retrieved a pill. Turns out it's definitely a prescription med. They're having it analyzed ASAP."

"If it was a prescription, that will tell us, not only what Linda Turner was taking, but perhaps what medical condition she was being treated for. With that info as a starting point, we'll canvass all the pharmacies. Even if she used an assumed name, this will help."

"I want the pharmacy *and* the doctor," Peg replied. "Let's just hope it's a less common drug, and not something for insomnia or depression. If we can narrow things down, this could be the break we've been hoping for."

CHAPTER TWENTY-SEVEN

It didn't take long for the FBI lab to analyze the pill.

Casey, Marc, Claire, Patrick and the entourage of law enforcement had just returned to the Willises'—leaving behind a massive manhunt that spread over two counties—when Peg got the call.

The confiscated pill was a ten-milligram tablet of Memantine—a drug used to treat moderate to severe Alzheimer's disease.

"Alzheimer's?" Casey blinked. That one had come out of left field. "I don't understand. How could Linda have orchestrated all this if she were suffering from such a debilitating disease?"

"Maybe it was moderate. The beginnings of dementia," Patrick suggested.

"Nope." Peg shook her head. "According to my medical experts, ten milligrams is not an initial dosage. On the other hand, every patient is different. Linda could be lucid most of the time.

She also could have a visiting nurse who stops by, drops off prescriptions and stays for brief enough periods of time that she has no clue there's a child being held captive in the basement. We won't know any of these answers until we find Linda."

"That explains the red string we found," Casey mused aloud. "Linda probably ties it around her finger to remember things. It's a pretty common thing to do. And a necessary one, in her case."

"So we know what we're looking for," Bennett said. "We've already got law enforcement pounding the pavement, flashing pictures of Linda Turner at every pharmacy within a twenty-mile radius. Now we've got more than her face to go on. It's time to get the necessary warrants to match the drug with the patient."

Marc pulled Casey aside the minute he could speak to her in private.

"Can't Ryan hack into some drug company database or something—bypass all that crap? Especially with the new HIPAA laws. We've got to speed things up."

"Ryan can hack into anything," Casey replied, visibly distracted as she spoke. "The problem is, he'd still have a gazillion pharmacies to check out. And even then, we'd have to hope Linda Turner used her real name. It's very possible she didn't, since she doesn't want to be found. Which means we'd be right back where Sergeant Bennett just described—taking our list of pharmacies and flashing photos of Linda to every one of them that filled a Memantine prescription, hoping that a pharmacist or employee recognizes her. That would take almost as long as circumnavigating HIPAA."

"You have another idea?" Marc recognized the look on Casey's face.

"Actually, yes. I have a possible theory. And if it's got merit, we can skip a whole bunch of steps and go to the head of the class." She glanced around the room, eyeing the large number of law enforcement agents. "I can't get out of here without the entourage noticing. And Peg will have my hide if she thinks I'm up to something. Can you slip away and text Ryan? Tell him to drive up here and bring his laptop—we'll meet in his van."

"Just give me three minutes. I'll be gone and back."

Ryan made it to Armonk in record time.

But it was long enough for Casey to separate herself from the pack, many of whom had disbanded to join the manhunt.

She, Marc and Ryan clustered together in the van, Hero stretched out beside them.

"Marc filled me in on where things stand," Ryan began. "So tell us what you're thinking."

Casey blew out her breath. "My grandfather had Alzheimer's. It's a horrible, debilitating disease. If Linda Turner is taking ten milligrams of Memantine at a time, it's very likely she's taking twenty milligrams a day. And that means she's not in a good place. Also, these drugs only go so far in slowing the progression of the disease. I just can't imagine her being clearheaded and cunning enough to pull off this whole kidnapping scheme alone."

"You're saying you think she had an accomplice," Ryan said. "Are you reverting to the mob theory?"

"I don't think so," Marc interjected. "This is personal. It's got to be Linda's idea—she'd just need help with the execution."

"Agreed." Casey picked up where she'd left off. "I don't buy the whole visiting nurse idea. I think that whoever's getting Linda's medicine, making her medical arrangements and assisting in her overall health issues, is also assisting in Krissy's captivity."

"Okay, I'll buy that." Ryan inclined his head, studying Casey intently. She had more on her mind than what she'd already said. "Are you thinking of someone in particular?"

"I have no idea. But I do have an avenue I want to pursue. It could be a far-fetched dead end."

"But you don't think so."

"No." Casey raised her chin, glanced from Ryan to Marc and back. "I think we need to revisit Claudia Mitchell's murder. We've all been operating under the assumption that it was mob related. But if the mob wasn't involved in Krissy's kidnapping, then that eliminates any motive they might have had to silence Claudia."

"Which means someone else wanted or needed Claudia Mitchell dead," Marc continued for her. "Someone she surprised, rather than the premeditated murder we originally suspected. And the place where she surprised them is at the health care facility where she had her interview. Sunny Gardens. A facility that treats patients with everything from physical illnesses to dementia and Alzheimer's."

"You think Linda Turner is a patient there?" Ryan asked.

"More likely, a recent one," Casey qualified. "Which means she'd need her accomplice to come to her."

"It also means her accomplice probably did the actual kidnapping. And *that* would mean we're dealing with a female accomplice." Marc deduced what Casey already had. "Do you think it's someone in Hope Willis's circle? Someone Claudia would have recognized?"

"It makes sense, doesn't it?" Casey's reply was more a statement than a question.

Ryan let out a low whistle. "It's quite a theory. But we'd be crazy not to check it out. The question is, how? Sunny Gardens isn't going to give us squat. Law enforcement would have a hard enough time getting privileged information, and we're not law enforcement. We have zero leverage."

"We have Marc." With absolute confidence, Casey eyed her colleague. "I'd be willing to bet that, on a dime, you can come up with a plan that will get us what we need."

Marc looked thoughtful. "We need to verify that Linda Turner is actually a patient at Sunny Gardens. I'll have to scale the gates and bypass the security cameras. Get around without being noticed. Blend in and disappear…not a problem."

"I could go with you," Ryan offered. "If I can install Gecko—"

"Let me handle this one alone," Marc interrupted. "At least for now. Covert Ops is my thing. If Linda Turner's there, I'll find her. And I'll find out what name she's registered under. We'll have our answer tonight. And if we're right, *then* you and the little critter can go on a field trip together."

"You're planning something again."

Patrick came up behind Casey the minute Ryan's van and Marc's car disappeared around the bend.

Casey's head snapped around. "Where did you come from? Are you spying on me?"

"I saw Marc leave." Patrick stuck his hands in his pockets and stared her down. "Then you slipped away. I used to be a federal agent. I'm pretty good at spotting the obvious."

"My team was just meeting to discuss our options."

"And the option you picked is something you don't plan on sharing with the task force. Which means you're coloring outside the lines again."

"Coloring outside the lines?" Casey had to grin at his choice of words. "Does that mean you're going to tell on me?"

"That depends. What do I have to tell?"

"Nothing." Casey kept her expression carefully nondescript.

Patrick didn't avert his gaze. "You're a hell of a liar. I'd believe you, except that I've learned the way Forensic Instincts operates."

"Then you've also learned that it's best not to ask questions. Just accept our results with grudging admiration."

Not so much as a blink. "That puts me in an awkward position. Because I have a strong feeling that you were bugged by what we just found out, and that you meandered your way to the same possibility I did. And I have to know whether or not to share that with the task force."

Casey kept her cool. But she wasn't happy.

"What possibility are we referring to?" she asked.

Patrick's lips thinned into a narrow line. "In other words, show my hand first. Okay, fine. Normally, I wouldn't. But we're playing with a loaded gun here, and we're racing time. So I'll start. But no games, Casey. I want the truth."

"You'll get it."

"Fine. You and I are both thinking that Linda Turner is in no condition to kidnap a kid. That she has a very active accomplice—one who actually did the work for her. Am I on track?"

"Yes." Casey could read Patrick's expression as if it were a polygraph. He knew. He wasn't fishing. This was the real deal.

Time for her to give him something in return.

"I think Linda Turner is ill enough to be confined to a facility."

"And you think that facility is Sunny Gardens, the place Claudia Mitchell interviewed at. You also think that when she was there, she saw someone she shouldn't have, and was killed because of it."

"Right. And, if Claudia recognized someone with a connection to Judge Willis, it probably means that our accomplice is someone Judge Willis knows from her time on the bench." Casey was past wondering what Patrick knew and into worrying about what he planned to do about it. "I don't care how this person hooked up with Linda Turner, nor does it matter right now. We just have to find her."

"It has to be a woman," Patrick agreed. "Based on every description we got from the crime scene and from the gardener." He stiffened, and Casey could see the FBI agent surface in him. "If we figured this out, what makes you think the task force won't?"

"I'm sure they will. But they'll have hoops to jump through to get what they need. We won't." Casey let down her guard, and let her emotion come through. "Please, Patrick, just buy me some time. Let me run with this. Let my team run with this. Don't tell Peg we're following this lead. You're not impeding anything, because you don't know what we have in mind. But it might save Krissy's life. Let the task force come up with this, and pursue this, on their own. I'm not asking you to stop them. Just don't fuel the fire by ratting us out. Please. We just need a little time first, to try it our way."

Patrick watched her from beneath hooded lids. "I'd never say yes," he admitted flatly. "But I have a personal interest in this case. And I've seen how good you are. So do what you have to.

Spare me the details. Just get it done, and get it done fast. As for Peg, I won't tell her we talked. But I can't stop her from doing what she has to. I'd do the same, if I were her."

"Fair enough." Casey paused. "And I'll find a way to keep you in the loop," she added quietly. "In a way you can swallow. I know how much this case means to you."

"*Both* cases," he corrected her. "I care what happens to Krissy Willis. And I need to know what happened to Felicity Akerman."

CHAPTER TWENTY-EIGHT

Marc tucked his car discreetly in a clearing surrounded by thick bushes, a good quarter mile from Sunny Gardens. He walked the rest of the way, positioning himself across from an entrance concealed behind a row of trees. He wanted at least two good hours of daylight surveillance before he planned to scale the fence and traverse the grounds. He needed to see when the various staff members came and went. And he wanted to see the staff's routine of moving the patients from indoors to outdoors and back.

Using his military-issue binoculars, he monitored the scene and took mental notes.

First note. The security cameras. They were positioned at the main gate, and probably at the rear ones, as well. That left long lengths of iron fence that were out of viewing range. Getting in would be no problem.

Second. Bennato Construction's crew was starting to wind

down for the day. The wing they were building was already framed, and the Sheetrock was well under way. Between the slew of men working overtime, and the piles of construction materials in the area, Marc would have an easy place to blend in and hide, should it become necessary.

Marc turned his attention to the section of grounds where patients were situated. A small number of them were interacting with other patients. Most of them were sitting alone, either under the patio canopy or in the neatly manicured gardens. Some were mobile. Most were sedentary. Even the more mobile patients were being supervised by nurses or nurse's aides. And those who were unable to get around on their own were attended to more closely, many of them being wheeled back to their rooms.

For all Marc knew, Linda Turner could be sitting right across the street from him.

Ryan had done his homework. Marc was up to speed on the number of patients living there, the ratio of staff to patients, and the physical size and layout of the main building itself. Ryan had emailed him both interior and exterior photos of the place. He would have gotten Marc a complete schematic, had there been time.

Despite the urgency of their situation, Marc waited. He'd learned the importance of patience. Just as he instinctively knew the right moment to strike.

The dinner hour came and went. The night shift arrived. The day shift went home. It didn't surprise Marc that the number of those driving in was leaner than those driving out. Nighttime would be quieter. The patients would be confined to their rooms. The number of staff members would be reduced.

Making Marc's job a hell of a lot easier—and harder. He'd have less square footage to cover, and more risk of being caught in empty corridors. So he'd made provisions for both his break-in and his presence. He was dressed in black—long-sleeved shirt and jeans, as well as the backpack slung over his shoulders. But in that backpack was an authentic white orderly's coat—straight from the Forensic Instincts arsenal.

The sun had set, and the stars were coming out, when Marc stowed his night-vision goggles and shoved the case into his backpack. It was time.

Silently, he crossed over to the section of fence he'd chosen, far away from the scope of the security cameras. He was up and over the fence in a few deft motions, landing lightly on his feet. He waited a full minute to make sure he was alone.

The only sound was the crickets.

Avoiding the outside lights, Marc moved quickly until he reached the main building. Then he slipped around to the back. Sure enough, the delivery door had a lock on it that a ten-year-old could pick.

He got the door open, then jammed his foot in to keep it ajar. He pulled out his orderly uniform and a clipboard, which had printed pages of blank but authentic medical forms on it—again, thanks to Ryan. He tossed his backpack behind the bushes.

A minute later, he was inside.

It was eight o'clock—too late for dinner, too early for sleep. The patients were either in the dayroom, watching TV, or in their bedrooms, preparing for bed.

The very areas Marc planned on exploring.

He saved the dayroom for last, since that would be the most difficult place to maneuver. There was bound to be staff inside, which meant he'd have to be seen and hope that the entire staff wasn't familiar with one another and, as a result, recognize him as a stranger.

He went up a flight of stairs and down Hall B—the section Ryan had reported housed the patients with specialized medical needs—needs that an Alzheimer's victim would have. It was a crapshoot. Then again, this entire venture was a crapshoot.

He walked purposefully, clipboard in hand, as if he had someplace to be. A few staff members passed him in the hall, but no one did anything more than smile and nod. He returned the gesture. Every room he passed, he glanced quickly inside, taking an instant mental picture of the occupant. No luck. He continued around the bend and finished his search. Still nothing. He even doubled back to see if he had missed something. There wasn't a single patient who even resembled Linda Turner.

He had two choices: try another wing or risk the dayroom in that section of the facility.

Trusting Ryan's assessment, he went for the dayroom. It was situated in such a way that told him it was only for those patients who occupied Hall B.

Pushing open the door, he stepped inside.

There were half-a-dozen patients gathered around the TV, which was anchored halfway up the wall so everyone could see it. There were another half dozen sitting at the panorama of windows, staring vacantly across the dark lawn. And there were two nurses in the back, keeping a close eye on everyone.

Seeing Marc, one of the nurses spoke up immediately. "Yes?"

"Hi." Marc shot them an easy smile, his gaze sweeping the room in one comprehensive motion. "I was told to check and see if there were any new dietary restrictions I should report to the kitchen staff before breakfast."

The nurse turned to her companion, eyebrows raised quizzically. "Anything I'm not aware of?"

The other nurse shook her head. "Everything is status quo."

"Great," Marc replied. "I appreciate it." A rueful look, and another sweep of the room, this time concentrating on the patients at the window. "After a bunch of last-minute changes, it's a pleasure to find at least one status quo."

He'd found a lot more than that.

Sitting at the window, her face angled toward Marc, was Linda Turner. He recognized her instantly from Ryan's enhanced photo. The bone structure. The sharp features. The facial expression. The salt-and-pepper hair. There wasn't a doubt in his mind. They'd found the one they were looking for.

Their long shot had paid off.

"I'll be heading off for my next meal check," Marc told the nurses, exhaling a frustrated breath. "Night shifts suck."

"Tell us about it," the first nurse said drily.

With a grimace of camaraderie, Marc and his clipboard left the room.

In theory, his job here was done. Still, the more information he could give Ryan, the better.

There was a supply room across the hall. Marc slipped inside, shut the door all but an inch, and waited.

His efforts were rewarded about a half hour later, when the nurses began to escort the patients to their rooms for the night. They worked in shifts, walking some of the patients back two at a time, some of the more mobile patients in groups of three.

Linda Turner was among the second duo to be guided to her room. Marc waited until the nurses were halfway down the hall before he eased the closet door open wider. He watched carefully, counting the number of doorways the nurses passed before leading Linda into her quarters.

Sixth room on the right.

He went back into hiding, waiting until he heard the nurses' voices, chatting with each other about the great new restaurant that had opened in town, their voices growing more and more distant as they left the area and went back to the nurses' station.

When there was nothing but silence, Marc emerged.

He inched his way down the hall to Linda Turner's room and looked at the slot beside the door. Fitted in the slot was a cardboard tab with the patient's name on it. Lorna Werner.

Lorna Werner. Linda Turner. Close enough for a woman with a fading memory to respond to. But not so close as to be recognizable. Smart choice.

Marc peeked through the glass pane on the closed door. Linda Turner was moving around, talking to herself as she sniffed some bright yellow mums that were arranged in a vase on her windowsill. He wished he could make out her words. But he couldn't take any more risks than he already had.

A quick glance around the room's interior.

Mostly institutional. The only personal touches were the numerous vases of flowers and a young girl's soccer jersey hanging on the wall.

If Marc harbored even a shadow of a doubt before, he didn't now.

Five minutes later, he was in his car, on his cell phone and on his way back to the brownstone.

By the time Marc walked into the office, Ryan was already in high gear, and pages were being spit out on the laser printer. Hero was sitting beside the printer, barking to let Ryan know that his results were coming through.

"It's amazing what can be done with the right information,"

Ryan informed Marc. "A simple name. Lorna Werner. And suddenly I have the medical data the FBI is trying to track down from before Linda's move to Sunny Gardens. Her combination of medications. The dosages. Her doctor. Her pharmacy. I hacked into the Sunny Gardens system, no problem. I've got a record of when Lorna Werner was admitted. Just one short month ago. Until then, she was being treated independently."

"Does it say who admitted her?" Marc asked.

"Nope. The system has just basic specs logged in. No details."

"Well, I gave you all the details I could possibly dig up. The ball's in your court now."

"You mentioned vases of flowers in her room." Casey was perched at the edge of Ryan's desk, having mulled over Marc's covert excursion and picked out what she recognized as the highlights. "The grounds of Linda's house were neglected, but it was obvious that there was once an extensive garden there. And the lake behind the house was covered with weeds. I'd be willing to bet that, before Anna died, it was surrounded by flowers."

"Your point?" Marc asked.

"You said that some of the patients spent the afternoon sitting in the gardens. I'd be willing to bet that's where we'd find Linda...Lorna."

"Makes sense." Marc nodded.

"And that's where Gecko and I come in." Ryan leaned back in his chair and linked his fingers behind his head. "It's time for me to become CATV guy. When I'm done with my little black box, we'll have a live feed from Sunny Gardens' video cameras streaming straight to our office. And if Linda Turner spends her time in the garden, we'll be watching."

"I only half got that," Marc said. "Then again, that's usually the case when you talk geek-speak. I'll be here for whatever. Let's just hope our accomplice shows up for the closed-circuit video show."

"She will," Casey said. "She'll have to touch base with Linda. Because no matter who did the actual kidnapping, Linda is emotionally attached to Krissy, even if she's not physically with her. She'll need to feel connected. And the only person who can offer her that is her accomplice. She's Linda's stand-in. She's probably paying herself a healthy chunk—say, two-hundred-fifty-thousand dollars—to oversee Krissy. The one thing we don't know is just how ill Linda is, and how far gone her mind and memories are. It could be that her accomplice is manipulating her. For all we know, Linda thinks Krissy is somewhere at Sunny Gardens, right nearby. This is all conjecture. We've got to get at the truth."

"Next question," Marc inserted, addressing the eight-hundred-pound gorilla in the room. "When do we call Peg and the FBI task force?"

"Not now, we don't," Ryan responded quickly. "I need time to get some answers. Once we have those, you can tell the task force whatever you want."

"This is going to be tricky—and tight," Casey murmured. "I'm sure the task force is only a few steps behind us, and that's only because of the red tape of having to get warrants. Once they get them, they're going to storm Sunny Gardens like gangbusters, looking for Linda Turner. And, if she's not clearheaded enough, that could ruin any chance of finding out about her accomplice."

"Yeah, and if that accomplice knows that Linda's been made, we can kiss finding her goodbye."

"She's our only link to Krissy," Casey said fervently. "I won't let her get away. Ryan, plan on leaving for Sunny Gardens at the crack of dawn."

CHAPTER TWENTY-NINE

Day Seven

Early-morning sunlight was peeking through the trees when Ryan's van pulled up the road to Sunny Gardens. Like Marc, he left a healthy distance between his car and the facility, parking in a dirt alcove amid a wooded area where his van could blend right in. Later, he'd make a more public appearance.

The good news was that construction workers began at dawn. So when Ryan trudged across the grounds in his dirt-stained jeans and white T-shirt, carrying a large toolbox, no one gave him a second look.

He went around back, as Marc had instructed, and, also as Marc had surmised, the delivery door was unlocked. It was daytime. Security measures were more lax. And deliveries were more plentiful.

He went straight down to his destination: the basement. It

didn't take him long to navigate the various wiring and network connections, or to locate the video distribution feed that led to the main nurses' station.

He pulled out his staple gun and fired a staple directly into the jacketed wire. Ryan waited—one minute, then two. After five minutes had passed, he whipped out his cell phone and called the head nurse's station.

"Yes?" she answered in a frazzled voice.

"Hey," Ryan greeted her. "This is the security company. Are you having a problem with your closed-circuit TV?"

"How did you know? Our bank of monitors just became wavy and full of static. We can't see much of anything."

"The system monitors itself for trouble, and a message popped up in our office. You're a medical facility, so you're a priority customer. Would you like me to drive over now and take care of it?"

"Oh, God, yes." The nurse sounded as if she were being thrown a lifeline. "Thank you so much."

"Not a problem. Who should I ask for?"

"Jeri Koehler. That's me. I'm the head nurse here."

"Okay, Jeri, you hang tight," Ryan said in a reassuring tone. "I'll be there within the hour."

He hung up, placed his tools in his toolbox and left the building, strolling across the grounds and walking out the main gate.

Reaching his van, he climbed into the back and settled down. He opened the brown bag that was waiting for him, and helped himself to the protein bar and coffee he'd bought himself for breakfast. While he was eating, he checked in with the office, let them know that phase one was complete.

A half hour later, he changed into a work shirt—making sure

to leave the top few buttons undone—got out of the back of the van, opened the driver's door and sat down behind the wheel.

He drove through the front gates and parked in the main parking lot. Checking in at the front desk was a snap.

To say that Head Nurse Koehler was happy to see him would be a gross understatement. She visibly released a breath of sheer relief when he walked over. A few of the other nurses poked Jeri, asking who the hot guy was, in low undertones that Ryan wasn't supposed to hear. She answered in a no-nonsense voice that said he was here to fix their video system, and to save their flirtations for later. Then, she showed Ryan the problem and headed off to tend to a pressing medical situation.

Ryan unpacked a few things and dismantled the monitors, listening as the other nurses muttered under their breath about Nurse Koehler. He chuckled a few times, commiserating with them about uptight supervisors and turning on the charm that came so naturally to him and that he was careful to use to his advantage in situations such as this one.

He spent just enough time searching for the problem, before announcing that he needed to go down to the basement to locate the source of the weak signal. With a wink, he promised to be back ASAP.

Once downstairs, Ryan began to repair the cable he'd sabotaged an hour ago—but with modifications. He inserted a splitter, routing the second video line to his personally designed "black box"—a computer capable of streaming the closed-circuit video signal over the internet and directly to the Forensic Instincts office.

Task completed.

Ryan used his Android phone to remotely access the brownstone's video server, checking to see if his handiwork had been successful.

A nod of self-congratulations. His black box was sending the video perfectly.

Job done. He was a genius.

Ryan packed up and headed upstairs and back to the nurses' station.

"Hi, ladies," he greeted the nurses, who were still hanging around, waiting for his return. "I made a repair, but unfortunately, it's only temporary. I'll need to order a part and come back in a few days to install it. In the meantime, the good news is, you're back in business."

"Thank you so much," one of them said gratefully. "You're a lifesaver."

"Glad to be of service." Ryan gave her a broad smile, again cranking up the charm. "Now I'll just need a few minutes to reassemble your monitors and clean up the mess I left you."

"Take your time."

Ryan did, taking as much time as he could, and chatting with the nurses as he worked.

"I noticed your gardens when I drove in," he commented. "They're pretty impressive. My mother would be jealous."

"Yes, our patients love to sit out there and enjoy them," a young, pretty, blonde nurse's aide supplied.

"I figured as much." Ryan carefully fitted one of the monitors in place. "Do they get to go out there a lot?"

"As much as they want. They're finishing breakfast now. Those who want to go outdoors will be on their way soon."

Not soon enough for me, Ryan thought silently.

He straightened up and turned, dragging his arm across his forehead and giving the women a rueful look. "I know how hard you ladies work. And I promise I'm not being sexist. But would one of you mind getting me some water? I left my bottle in the van, and that basement was really dusty. My throat is so dry I can barely swallow."

"No problem." The nurse's aide scampered off, buying Ryan a little extra time.

He used it wisely, chatting up the nurses, telling them about his marathons and extreme sports adventures, and watching their eyes widen with awe. BASE jumping came in handy. You either impressed the hell out of someone, or convinced them that you were crazy.

Either way, it passed the time until the nurse's aide returned with a large cup of ice water.

"Here you go," she said, handing it to him.

"Thanks so much." He began to drink, glancing at the monitor as he did.

The patients were being helped or wheeled outside, some to the patio and others to the gardens.

Sweet.

Ryan made sure to drink his water slowly, taking a break here and there. Finally, he turned back to his work.

About eight or ten patients were being settled in each of the garden clusters. He scanned the monitors quickly. Not yet.

He continued reassembling. *Come on, come on,* he thought, glancing repeatedly at the screens. How many patients could there be going to the gardens? He couldn't stand here forever, flirting with nurses, drinking water, and looking like a moron who couldn't put a monitor back together. The minutes—and his opportunity—were slipping away.

There. Ryan's gaze snapped to the screen. Linda Turner was

just arriving, via wheelchair, at the eastern garden. She was talking animatedly with the nurse wheeling her out.

There was a red string tied around Linda's finger.

"Well, that patient certainly looks happy," Ryan noted aloud. "If all your patients start their days in that kind of mood, I just might check myself in."

The nurse's aide peered over his shoulder. "Oh, that's Lorna Werner. She loves that spot, and insists on sitting there every day. She's normally subdued. Today, she's excited because she's having a visitor this afternoon." The aide pointed at the screen. "See the red string? That's to remind her when her daughter is coming. She tells the entire place when that's happening."

Daughter? Ryan's mind was racing. So that's what they were calling kidnapping accomplices these days. He had to admit it was a clever twist on the accomplice's part. Preying on Linda's need for a child would make her all the more open to manipulation.

He paused long enough to see exactly where the nurse was positioning Linda before she headed off to tend to the other patients. Then, he quickly finished his reassembly.

With one modification. He was careful to leave his tone generator inside the panel. It was the perfect excuse for him to make an immediate return visit.

He said goodbye to all the nurses, promised to be the technician who came back with the necessary part in a couple of days and headed out. He went straight to his van, climbed inside and shut the door. He whipped out his BlackBerry and called Casey.

"Hey, we're at the edge of our seats," she greeted him. "What's going on?"

"You can now access Sunny Gardens' closed-circuit video

right there in our office," he replied. "So feel free to take a look." He proceeded to give Casey the necessary instructions. "Linda Turner is in the garden on the east side of the grounds," he continued. "I want to plant Gecko right near there. Evidently, Linda is having a visitor later today. She's wearing a red string around her finger to remind her."

"Like the red string we found at her house."

"Exactly. And guess who her visitor is? Her *daughter*."

"Daughter?" Casey echoed, momentarily stunned. "Are you telling me that Linda's accomplice is masquerading as her daughter?"

"Makes sense, doesn't it? If this woman successfully posed as Linda's grown daughter, she could get away with anything—admitting Linda to Sunny Gardens, managing her entire stay there—you name it."

"Not just managing her stay. Managing Linda, too." Casey was over her surprise and on to her analysis. "Manipulating her, getting and feeding her information, and using it all to her advantage. Remember, having a daughter is Linda's greatest desire. She could view this person as Anna grown up, and Krissy as Anna when she was a little girl. There are so many potential psychological factors here, we could go on all day. But they'll wait. What's your plan?"

"Like I said, I want to plant Gecko in the garden where Linda sits. When her visitor arrives, Gecko can pick up their conversation, both audio and video. It's well within his range to broadcast from there to my van. I'll listen in and monitor the entire interaction. We'll learn who this accomplice is. At that point, we'll find a way to tip off Peg and the task force, so they can grab her. And we'll find out where she's keeping Krissy."

"You sure as hell won't do this alone," Casey stated emphatically.

"Marc and I are driving up there. And we're bringing Hero with us. Since this *daughter* isn't showing up until afternoon, we have more than enough time to get there and join you for the show."

"I expected as much." Ryan was already gathering up what he needed. "Okay, I'm going to set Gecko up now. I'll put him in sleep mode to save power. I left one of my tools behind to justify a return trip across the grounds. I'll make a quick stop in the garden. After I'm done, I'm pulling the van out of the main parking lot and holing up in the wooded alcove diagonally across the street from the facility. Meet me there, and you can hop on in, and take in the performance with me."

CHAPTER THIRTY

Krissy. You need me here.

I'm so sorry I have to leave you alone.

It's just for a little while. Today's just an exception. It's an emergency.

I'm worried. I've seen things on the news. Maybe they're true. Maybe they're not. I have to find out. But if they are, then photographs are being shown around. To doctors. Drugstores. They haven't reached here.

But have they reached Sunny Gardens? Have they put the pieces together? I have to know. If they're figuring things out, we'll have to go.

We'll find somewhere safe.

No one will find us. I won't let them.

You belong with me.

Nothing and no one will take you away.

The construction crew was in full swing when Ryan climbed out of the van. He was still wearing his company work shirt, and he was carrying a toolbox. Gecko was tucked safely at the bottom of that box.

With all that was going on—cranes lifting building supplies, backhoes traveling back and forth across the construction site, and dozens of workmen, hammering, drilling and calling out to each other—Ryan was pretty sure he wouldn't be noticed even without a disguise. But he wasn't taking any chances. Looking like a harried serviceman, he stalked over to the requisite garden and squatted down, opening his toolbox and removing various tools.

Linda Turner was sitting ten feet away from him. It took all his control not to look her in the eye and demand to know where Krissy was. But that would destroy their entire plan and kill any chance of pulling things off without being found out and arrested. Not to mention that he had no idea if Linda was coherent enough to even know where Krissy was.

So he kept up the charade.

"Ma'am," he greeted her when she turned her head his way.

"Hello." She gazed at him with a vague expression in her eyes, and without the slightest hint of wondering who he was or what he was doing there.

"I won't disturb you," he provided, nonetheless. "I've got a few wires to check out here. Then I'll be out of your way."

"My daughter will be here later," she replied, as if she either knew Ryan or thought she should. "It's so noisy here, it's hard for us to talk. That's why she comes in the afternoon, when all those builders are going away. I hope you'll be finished by then."

"No problem. I'll be long gone."

Ryan squatted down, making sure his back was facing the main building and his side was blocking Linda's view. Then, he began rummaging through his toolbox, flinging tools to the ground in increased agitation. To any onlooker, it would seem as if he were trying to fix something but to no avail.

Amid his flurry of activity, he pulled out the top tray of his toolbox with one hand and grabbed Gecko with the other. Quickly, he turned the little critter on, and placed him just inside the raised, circular bed of shrubs surrounding the garden.

With a few muttered curses, he tossed his tools back into the box, snapped the clasp, rose and turned to Linda.

"I can't find the tool I need. So I'll be heading back to the main building. Enjoy your visit with your daughter."

Her lips curved into a smile. "Thank you."

With that, Ryan strode back to the building, a look of sheer irritation on his face.

He marched inside and straight to the head nurse's station.

Jeri Koehler was back at her post.

"Hello." She looked puzzled. "I thought you'd left."

"I did. I was halfway down the drive when I realized I'd left my tone generator somewhere in here. Would it be a big problem if I looked for it?"

"Of course not." Nurse Koehler made a wide sweep with her arm. "I'd just ask that you not interfere with our work."

Ryan flashed her a smile. "Without my tone generator, I'm screwed." He walked over to the panel of video monitors, pretending to search for about five minutes. Then, he looked under the panel, reached up and retrieved the missing tool.

"Here we go." He looked and sounded utterly relieved. "You're a gem. I can't thank you enough." He popped the tool into his toolbox. "I'll get out of your hair now. See you in a few days when I have the part I need."

With a friendly wave, Ryan made his exit.

Ruse complete. Time for Gecko to do his job.

Ryan climbed behind the wheel of the van and drove out of the parking lot. He steered diagonally across the street, returned to the alcove behind the trees and maneuvered the van into it. With Marc's eagle eye, he and Casey would find him when they drove up, no problem.

Scrambling into the back of the van, Ryan fired up his laptop and Gecko came to life. Ryan carefully repositioned him, focusing his camera and microphone directly on Linda. If she sat either a little to the left or right this afternoon, he'd readjust the little critter accordingly. But, for now, the video and audio were perfect.

He put Gecko into sleep mode to conserve power for later, when it was needed.

Then, he called Casey and asked her to detour through the nearest Mickey D's and pick up a couple of Big Macs and fries. He never ate junk food. But he'd been up since before dawn. And all this activity had made the power bar and coffee he'd downed earlier a distant memory. And, hey, a guy had to eat. So it was time to break a few rules. They weren't the first ones he'd broken today.

The SOS call to Casey done, he sat back and waited.

Krissy heard her leave.

As always, she wriggled off the bed and searched the room, wishing with all her might that the woman had forgotten her laptop or her cell phone. Krissy knew how to use both. Her mommy had showed her. She even had a very simple cell phone with big numbers on it that she brought to school. Mommy had programmed it with emergency phone numbers. She knew which button was which. And she knew her own phone number. She could call it, even with somebody else's cell phone.

But whenever the woman left Krissy alone, she always made sure to take everything with her. This time was the same. There was nothing down here. Nothing Krissy could use to call for help.

She scrambled up the long flight of steps and tried the door, pulling and pulling on the handle with every ounce of strength she possessed. But the door wouldn't budge.

Huge tears filled Krissy's eyes and rolled down her cheeks.

At the beginning, she'd known her mommy would come for her, no matter how many times the woman told her she wouldn't. The woman said that her mommy had moved on without her, that her job kept her much too busy to be with Krissy. And she'd told her over and over again that she was her mommy, and that she'd love her forever.

Krissy hadn't believed her. But lots of days had gone by. And there was still no sign of her mommy.

Could she really have wanted to send Krissy away? Was even Ashley too busy to play with her? She knew her daddy was.

What if they'd stopped looking?

No. No. No!

She ran down the steps, jumped on the bed and grabbed Oreo, clutching him with all her might.

Then she soaked him with her tears.

Marc eased his foot off the accelerator, pulling slowly up to the spot where Ryan's van was parked. He and Casey had taken Marc's Subaru Outback because it was black and would blend in better with the wooded area. Casey's red Mazda Miata would stand out like a sore thumb.

The sounds of construction pounded through the air. It was midafternoon. Clearly, the crew was making as much progress as they could before quitting time. By three o'clock, they'd be jumping out of their machinery, packing up their tools and taking off for home.

As Marc and Casey exited the car, Hero's leash wrapped around Casey's hand, the large diesel engine of a construction crane roared to life. The noise was deafening. Hero made a braying sound.

"Not now, boy," Casey told him. "I know the noise hurts your ears. Let's get into Ryan's van."

They hurried over, and Marc pounded on the back of the van. "It's us," he yelled over the tumult.

Ryan opened the double doors. "Come on in."

Hero needed no second invitation. He sniffed the air once, scanned the woods and then sprang into the van and away from construction hell. Casey released his leash to give him the freedom he needed, and followed suit, with Marc right behind her. By the time Marc slammed the doors and plunked down next to Casey, Hero was sprawled out on Ryan's sweatshirt, panting and waiting for some water. He got it ASAP, from the Hero "supplies" Ryan had started keeping in the van.

"Big Macs and fries?" Marc couldn't help ribbing him. "That's more fat and calories than a full day at the gym could burn. And you skipped this morning's workout. Careful. Lose your six-pack and you'll lose your women."

"It's a one-shot deal," Ryan retorted, taking the McDonald's bag from Casey. "And I've seen you scarf down two or three chili dogs when you're desperate enough. So cram it."

"Cut it out, you two," Casey said impatiently. "We're not here to discuss your high-protein diets. Linda's guest isn't here yet, is she?"

"Nope." Ryan shook his head. "The patients just finished lunch. Linda will be on her way out to the garden within the hour. Her *daughter* should be showing up soon after. Apparently, they try to avoid the construction chaos. And, since the crew breaks up between three and four o'clock, I'm expecting our accomplice around then."

Marc arched a brow. "You found all this out from the nurses you charmed at the front desk?"

"Some of it, yes. The rest, I found out from Linda herself."

"You *spoke* to her?"

"Yup." Ryan munched on a Big Mac while he spoke. "She was right there when I planted Gecko. She's pretty out of it. And the only thing on her mind was seeing her daughter and getting us workmen out of the way in time for her visit."

Hero was eyeing Ryan's burger and smacking his lips.

Casey gave him a chew toy to distract him and thoughtfully scratched his ears. "If she's that out of touch with the world around her, it means her accomplice is actively running the show—just as we suspected. And she's keeping Krissy around for a reason. I'm just not sure what it is."

"Unless Linda has cash reserves we don't know about," Marc proposed. "If that's the case, it would be a sweet deal for this woman. All she has to do is feed and house a five-year-old in some secret location, probably bring Linda some photos here and there, and, at the same time, masquerade as her older daughter. Maybe she got Linda to give her power of attorney, in which case, she can do whatever she wants with Linda's assets."

"I did a pretty thorough job of checking out Linda Turner's bank records—both her real and assumed names," Ryan replied. "Nothing impressive there. But that doesn't account for jewelry, antiques or anything else of value she might have. So, yeah, Marc, your theory is definitely possible." With that, he switched

Gecko out of sleep mode and into active mode. "We're about to find out."

Ten minutes ticked by.

Abruptly, Casey peered over Ryan's shoulder at the laptop monitor. "Here she comes."

A nurse was wheeling Linda Turner over to her usual spot, chatting pleasantly with her as they went. She settled her patient comfortably, promising "Lorna" that she'd send her daughter over the instant she arrived. Then, she turned and retraced her steps back to the main building.

Linda gazed peacefully around, and began to murmur the names of the various flowers surrounding her. Some she got right, some were so far-off that she might as well be speaking a foreign language. But she was happy and very excited.

Casey's cell phone rang. She frowned, staring down at it. The caller ID said "Private."

"I'd better see who this is," she said reluctantly. "If it's Peg, and I ignore her again, I'll be in deep shit." She put the phone to her ear. "Casey Woods."

"It's me," Patrick said without preamble. "Just a heads-up. Peg is pissed as hell that you're nowhere to be found, since she knows very well what that means. Meanwhile, she put the pieces together. She spoke to the woman in human resources who interviewed Claudia Mitchell. She explained the urgency of the situation and Sunny Gardens is willing to cooperate without a warrant, and with only Peg's promise to keep the information they share with her in the strictest of confidence. So it looks like your time is up."

"Dammit." Casey dragged a hand through her hair. "Is the task force on their way to Sunny Gardens?"

"Not yet. Getting the information is one thing. Questioning

the suspect is another. The North Castle cops are going for a warrant. The FBI is going to the U.S. Attorney's Office. But between Krissy Willis's kidnapping and Claudia Mitchell's murder, I doubt they'll have trouble getting what they need. Not with time being of the essence. So whatever you're doing, do it fast."

"Thank you, Patrick." Casey was truly grateful for his cooperation. "I owe you one."

"You owe me more than that," he retorted. "Peg asked me where you were. I told her you were pursuing a lead, but that you'd refused to give me the details."

"That's true."

"Yeah, but I left out a hell of a lot."

"You won't be sorry. We're a few steps ahead of the task force—and closer to finding Krissy Willis."

"That better be true. Oh, and by the way, your boyfriend is ripping mad. I wouldn't count on a candlelight dinner anytime soon."

Casey winced. She knew exactly how pissed Hutch must be. And she wasn't looking forward to the confrontation.

"No surprise," she told Patrick. "But I appreciate the heads-up. I'll be sure to polish up my suit of armor for the firing squad. In the meantime, I have to go now. Thanks again."

She disconnected the call, her gaze glued to the computer screen as she waited for the telltale moment.

Abruptly, the video feed from Gecko began to stutter. On its heels, the audio started to break up. Like an attack dog, Ryan leaped into action, promptly checking the wireless connection.

"Son of a bitch," he muttered. "The connection speed has dropped by seventy percent."

"What does that mean?" Casey asked.

"It means that, at that rate, audio and video streaming is impossible." He was already moving toward the door, crouched down so he didn't whack his head. "I've got to find out what the problem is or we're screwed."

He pushed open the van doors and climbed out, peering in the direction of the Sunny Gardens grounds.

"Shit," he exclaimed, seeing that the huge crane had moved directly between his van and Gecko, its large steel boom interfering with his wireless signal.

Without a clear line of sight, there was no way to accomplish their goal. The crane was showing no signs of moving and they couldn't risk revealing their presence in any way.

He'd have to improvise.

"Bad news," he told Casey and Marc as he boosted himself back into the van. He filled them in on the problem.

"What's the solution?" Marc asked. "We've come way too far to give up. And the FBI task force is climbing up our asses."

"There's nothing I can do about the timing. But I can do something about the problem. I have to turn off the streaming and have Gecko internally record the audio and video, which we can play back at a later time." As Ryan explained, he sent the instructions to Gecko. Gecko acknowledged, and the streaming video went blank, the audio silent.

"Later when?" Marc demanded.

"When you come back here tonight and retrieve my little critter. At that point, we can watch and listen to the events of the afternoon. And, with any luck, we'll have what we need."

CHAPTER THIRTY-ONE

Getting onto the grounds of Sunny Gardens this time was going to be a little trickier.

Marc cruised slowly by the main entrance, scanning the front lawn and pinpointing the garden where Ryan's little critter was stashed.

There was no way he could use the same section of fence as last time to gain entry. It was too far down. Last night, he'd been headed around back, to a deserted section of grounds that was shielded by the construction site. Tonight, he was aiming for dead center, the most open area of the front grounds. If he went back to the remote section of fence he'd scaled last time, it would require his making his way across the entire front lawn. The floodlights would pick him up in any one of a dozen spots.

Not feasible.

So that left the area near the front gates.

Marc's gaze shifted, focusing on the small security booth

at the entranceway. There was one guard inside. Fortunately, there was also one TV. And the guard was lounging in a chair, drinking a can of soda and staring at the screen. Judging from his reactions—an occasional display of annoyance and a few fist-clenching punches of joy in the air—Marc determined he was watching a game. The Yanks were playing the White Sox tonight. The first pitch had been thrown out by the Yankees at eight o'clock. It was nine-fifteen now.

Just to be sure, Marc pulled over in a section of trees where he could see the guard but the guard couldn't see him. Marc turned on the radio, locating the station that broadcasted Yankee baseball. He listened—and watched the guard.

Sure enough, the Yanks pulled off an expert double play that finished off the bottom of the third inning. Simultaneously, the security guard leaned forward in his chair, his smile broad, his lips forming the emphatic word *yes!*

Clearly, it was the same game.

Marc drove a short distance and made a U-turn, pulling off the road into a cluster of bushes on the same side of the street as the facility. Approximately two hundred yards before the main gate, the space was facing the direction Marc needed to go to head for home.

Last night, he'd planned on spending a block of time inside the building. Consequently, leaving his vehicle across the road and far away where it wouldn't be spotted was imperative. Tonight was a grab and go. He needed his car as close to him as possible without being visible. His only task was to find and snatch Gecko, and get the hell out of there.

Bearing that in mind, he grabbed the small backpack he'd brought along, and quietly left his car. He crept down the grassy side of the road, pausing just to the right of the security booth, where the guard's back was to him.

He waited for the next visibly exciting play of the game. The guard was at the edge of his seat, gripping his soda can tightly and staring at the screen.

Marc seized the opportunity.

He scaled the fence in a few smooth moves and dropped onto the grass inside. He squatted low, watching and waiting.

The guard was oblivious to anything but his evening entertainment.

Swiftly, without so much as a rustle, Marc sprinted across the lawn, moving between the gaps in the floodlight beams, until he reached the eastern garden. He squatted down and whipped out the penlight flashlight he kept in the pocket of his jeans. Flicking it on, he anchored it between his teeth and aimed it downward.

It took about two minutes to find the spot in the shrubbery that Ryan had described in detail. It took less time than that to retrieve Gecko, stick him in the backpack and retrace his steps to the fence.

Again, Marc remained crouched, waiting, sizing up the situation inside the security booth.

The guard was stretching. He scratched his head and looked idly around, using commercial time to do a perfunctory check of the area.

The game resumed. The guard's scrutiny of his surroundings ended, and his attention shifted back to whichever Yankee was at bat.

Marc was up and over the fence, and on his way to his car before the ump could call strike one.

★ ★ ★

It was after eleven when Marc strode into the brownstone.

Casey and Ryan were pacing the floors. They jumped on Marc the instant he stepped inside.

"Did you find Gecko?" Ryan demanded.

"Yup." Marc whipped the little critter out of his backpack and turned him over to Ryan. "Nice directions. He was right where you said he would be."

"And no one saw you?" Casey asked, already knowing the answer.

Marc arched a brow. "A half-assed guard watching a Yankee game is not exactly a major challenge. And the positions of the floodlights were predictable as hell. Let's face it, Casey, it's a medical facility, not a terrorist compound."

"I know. I wasn't worried about the employees. I was worried about the task force."

"No sign of them."

"And I haven't heard from Patrick. So, hopefully, we're still ahead of the game." Casey turned to Ryan. "What next?"

"Next we go to the conference room." Ryan was already leading the way up the stairs.

Once inside, Ryan went straight over and plugged Gecko into a specially designed connector, where he began to recharge his battery and retrieve the information stored inside the little critter's memory.

It didn't take long for the first sights and sounds to come through.

Linda, sitting in the garden. Time passing as she gazed placidly around. Then impatience, followed by eagerness.

Abruptly, her eyes lit up and she began to wave her entire arm. "I'm here, baby. Right here."

"Hi, Mama." An eerily familiar voice reached their ears. "It's so good to see you."

Linda's visitor came into view. She walked over, leaned down and hugged the older woman. Then, she straightened, and the camera got a full frontal view of her.

And all three of the Forensic Instincts team's jaws dropped.

The person visiting Linda was Hope Willis.

CHAPTER THIRTY-TWO

Day Eight

Casey called Peg first thing the next morning, as she, Marc, Ryan and Hero headed up to Armonk in Ryan's van.

"Nice of you to call," Peg said in a chilly voice. "I've been trying to reach you since yesterday."

"Peg, where are you?" Casey asked.

"At the Willises. We'll be leaving to interview a person of interest in a few minutes—*with* a warrant."

"Are the Willises with you?"

"Yes. But they won't be traveling with us."

"I know who your person of interest is. Don't go to Sunny Gardens," Casey asked fervently. "Please. Not until we get to you. It's urgent that you wait—*with* Hope and Edward. What we have for you is explosive."

"Casey, I'm not playing games with you anymore. We have a job to do."

"And you'll do it perfectly once you have the missing pieces. If not, you'll blow it all. Please stay put."

A long pause. "How far away are you?"

"We can be there in forty-five minutes. Ryan's flooring the gas."

"Fine. Forty-five minutes is all you've got. Then we're leaving."

"Fair enough. We'll be there."

Patrick was pacing on the Willises' front lawn when the van screeched up to the curb. He strode across the lawn and met Casey as she jumped out.

"What did you find?" he demanded.

"Something that will help solve both cases." Casey was already hurrying toward the house. "I don't know where Krissy is—yet. But I will. *We* will. Till then, I don't believe she's in danger."

"You'd better be right. And your information had better be good."

"I am and it is. What does the task force know?"

"Everything about Linda Turner. First of all, they drew the same conclusion we did. But they needed grounds to descend on Sunny Gardens. So they got them. Since Linda was clearly trying to keep her condition a secret, the task force got a list of doctors she'd worked with when she was employed by the hospital. In no time, they found the private practice of the semiretired doctor who was treating her. The pharmacy she used was two blocks away from his office."

"Who gave them what they needed—the doctor or the pharmacist?"

"Both. All her medical records were confidential, but Peg spoke to one pharmacist who recognized Linda, and who said they hadn't been supplying her with prescription meds for over a month. The pharmacist's impression was that Linda was moving to an on-site facility. When the task force took that information to the doctor, and impressed upon him the urgency of the situation, the doctor confirmed that he'd recommended Sunny Gardens to Linda. Between that, and the fact that Claudia Mitchell was murdered right after interviewing at that facility..."

"The task force got the warrants they needed. So they were on their way to Sunny Gardens when I called."

"Oh, yeah. They were furious about waiting. Peg put her neck on the line for you, amid lots of dissent. So, like I said, you'd better have some hard, solid evidence to give them."

"And, like I said, I do." Casey paused outside the front door. "Thank you, Patrick. I know how hard this was for you, not only because of how badly you want to solve the Felicity Akerman case, but because you strayed a hair from the straight and narrow."

His jaw tightened. "I did it for one reason—I think you're good enough to crack this without being bogged down by bullshit. That doesn't mean I approve of your methods. It means I'm desperate enough to tolerate them."

"Let's get inside." Marc had come up behind them, along with Ryan, who was carrying his laptop and the shocking video—*if* Peg chose to see it.

The whole group went inside, converging in the media room, where most of the task force, including Hutch and Grace, along with Claire, the Willises, and Vera and Sidney Akerman were waiting.

Hope practically raced forward, grabbing Casey's arm with sheer desperation. "Did you find Linda? Was she at that place Sunny Gardens?"

"Yes." Casey studied Hope intently, saw the genuine emotion in her eyes. Not that any confirmation was necessary. Still, she was relieved to get it.

"Did you talk to her? Did she tell you where Krissy was?"

Casey turned to Peg. In the process, she spotted Hutch, and tried to ignore the blazing fury in his eyes.

"Linda Turner has a new name and a surprising accomplice. Don't ask me how I know. Just accept it as a hot tip. The sooner you can act on this, the better."

"Go on," Peg said curtly.

"She was admitted under the name Lorna Werner. You would have found that out the minute you showed her picture at the front desk. You also would have found out that talking to her is useless. She drifts in and out of reality, and she didn't kidnap Krissy, although she certainly inspired it. If she has an inkling where Krissy is—which I doubt—she'd never be able to give us a coherent description, much less directions to where Krissy's being kept. Only her accomplice can."

"Is this accomplice mob related?" Sidney asked.

"No. Your mob ties had nothing to do with your granddaughter's abduction."

"So you know who Linda's accomplice is," Peg concluded.

"Yes." Casey was both frank and blunt. "I can tell you, which would be hearsay. Or I can show you, and say we found this evidence outside the gates of Sunny Gardens, where a good Samaritan must have dropped it. Your choice."

Peg glared at her. "Show me."

Ryan produced a flash drive containing the data he'd copied off Gecko. He walked over to one of the FBI computers. "May I?"

"Go ahead."

He inserted the USB drive and punched in a few commands on the keyboard.

A minute later, the video recording came up. First, Linda. Then, the familiar voice. Finally, the appearance.

A simultaneous gasp filled the room as Linda and her accomplice launched into their visit, which included some probing questions from her accomplice, obviously fishing to see if Linda had been approached by law enforcement, leading to genuine relief when she realized that she hadn't.

"Hope?" Edward turned to her, white shock on his face. "What the hell—"

"It's not your wife, Mr. Willis," Casey interrupted. "We watched this video many times and with great care. Her body language, her choice of words, her delivery—they're all completely different. That woman is impersonating Hope. But she isn't Hope. She's Felicity."

"Oh my God." Vera's legs buckled under her, and Patrick Lynch caught her before she dropped to the floor. "Oh my God," she whispered again, staring blankly at the monitor as Patrick eased her into a chair. He himself was stark-white. "Felicity is... alive?"

"Yes." Casey nodded. "She's been with Linda all these years. Once we realized that, all the pieces fell into place. Why it was so easy for the kidnapper to masquerade as Hope. Why I never saw anyone but Hope come and go at the ransom drop. How the kidnapper got in here to steal Hope's pendant and Krissy's toy—and to knock Ashley out when she surprised her."

"Felicity must have used Krissy's keys," Edward surmised, obviously shaken to the core. "They were in her backpack, along with our alarm code and Krissy's cell phone. All our numbers are programmed into that phone. That's how she managed to call Ashley's cell in order to bypass the phone taps and get to Hope for the ransom money."

"Money she was probably planning to use to raise Krissy," Casey continued. "It's also why the gardener was so convinced he saw Hope enter the house when Ashley was checking the mail. And why Claudia Mitchell had an unexpected and fatal experience at Sunny Gardens. She must have freaked out when she spotted the woman she thought had fired her. She was filled with pent-up anger—after having to apply for a job that was beneath her, and dealing with a boyfriend who was being held by the police. I'm sure she blamed Hope for the whole fiasco. My guess? She went over to confront her, only to realize it wasn't Hope after all. Talk about ammunition. We all thought it was a mob hit. But it wasn't. It was a desperate act committed by a desperate woman."

Reflectively, Don added, "The mob did everything they could to get us off their backs. How ironic. The one thing they *weren't* guilty of was the very thing that might have gotten them caught."

"So Felicity ran Claudia Mitchell off the road?" Hope asked, her voice quavering with shock and pain. "My sister is a murderer?"

Casey took Hope's hand. "She's not stable, Hope. She probably shattered completely when she thought Claudia was going to undo everything she'd done. Krissy means everything to her. She's transferred all the love she felt for Linda to Krissy. She's frantic to hold on to her. It's the only way she can hold on to herself."

"But she doesn't even know Krissy," Edward protested.

"It doesn't matter." It was Hutch who spoke up now. "Casey's right. Linda Turner was Felicity's mother for thirty-two years.

She kept Felicity isolated from the world. Linda became Felicity's lifeline. When Linda's illness made it impossible for her to continue living on her own, Felicity panicked. She was losing her mother. The only way she could survive was to repeat the cycle. It gave her a sense of completion."

"Stockholm syndrome," Patrick said.

"Exactly."

"But how did she find me…us…Krissy?" Hope asked weakly.

"That I don't know," Hutch replied. "On some level, Felicity knew who she was. She knew she had a twin. If she kept tabs on you that easily, my guess is, she isn't far away. Especially if she visits Linda every week."

"Dear God." Vera buried her face in her hands. "Linda comforted me. She became my friend. And all the time, she had my baby. My Felicity."

"That's probably *why* she inserted herself in your life," Casey said. "She wanted to stay on top of the investigation, to make sure no one suspected her."

"And no one did." Patrick's tone was grim. "Including me. I always held out hope that Felicity was alive. But not this way."

"None of us saw this coming." Peg turned to Casey. "That's why you didn't want us going to Sunny Gardens."

Casey nodded. "If you'd burst in there with a warrant, you'd risk upsetting Linda enough to call Felicity and blurt out something. Clearly, Felicity's already wary. She must have heard rumors. That's why she made that extra trip to see Linda yesterday. She customarily visits every Wednesday. But she wanted to see if law enforcement had been poking around. Right now, she's probably feeling relieved. Which means she'll have no reason to grab Krissy and run."

"Today's Tuesday," Peg said. "Wednesday's just one day from now."

"So we wait," Don qualified. "We remain patient and sit tight. Then, tomorrow, we stake out Sunny Gardens. We let Linda and Felicity have their visit. And when Felicity leaves, we follow her. She'll lead us straight to Krissy."

"How can we do that?" Hope asked, tears coursing down her cheeks. "I know that Felicity is my sister, and God help me for saying this, but we're leaving an unbalanced woman with my five-year-old child. Who knows what she's doing to her, and what she could keep doing to her until tomorrow afternoon?"

"She's not harming her." Claire spoke up for the first time. "Krissy's scared. But she's safe. Felicity's created a virtual princess suite for her. She tried to replicate the one Linda made for her all those years ago. It's her idea of a safe haven." Claire paused, sage realization flickering in her eyes. "Now I understand my visions. I kept getting images of Hope—or the person I thought was Hope—interspersed with my images of Krissy. I couldn't understand why. Or why I never got so much as a glimpse of the kidnapper. Now I realize I *was* seeing the kidnapper. Only it wasn't Hope."

"But Krissy's safe?" Hope asked Claire pleadingly. "You're sure?"

"She's frightened. And she doesn't understand why you haven't come. But she's physically unharmed."

"And psychologically?"

"Psychologically she's a lot better off enduring one more scary day than a long, scary lifetime," Hutch stated flatly. "She's only been gone a little over a week. I know that seems like a lifetime to you. But she'll recover. On the other hand, if we miss this chance, we could lose her for good."

"We don't have a choice." It was Edward who spoke, his tone hard and determined. "I want my daughter back. We lose nothing by waiting, since we have no clue where Felicity is hiding her. I don't see a choice."

Hope was still openly weeping. "She's scared, Edward. She probably thinks we've abandoned her. Plus, she sees me, yet she knows it's not me. Can you imagine how confusing and devastating that is to a child of five? Another day like that…it kills me that she has to go through this."

"Keep your eye on the prize," Casey said quietly. "It won't ease your fear or worry, but it will give you the strength to go through with this. It's the only way, Hope. The task force will surround the building. They'll alert the Sunny Gardens staff. The minute Felicity arrives, they'll know her car and her license plate. They'll put a GPS tracking device on it. There'll be plainclothes police and agents posted on the street. She'll be followed and tracked from every direction. There's no chance of her getting away."

"I want you and your team there," Hope stated flatly. It wasn't a request. It was a demand that was aimed at the task force. "And I want to go with you."

"Not a good idea, Judge Willis," Peg intervened at once. "We're perfectly capable of handling this alone. If there are too many people present, it could alert Felicity to the stakeout."

Hope's tearstained stare was unflinching. "Forensic Instincts did an extraordinary job of solving this case thus far. I'm sure they can manage to situate themselves on the scene without being spotted. As for me, I'm Krissy's mother—and Felicity's sister. I might be needed to defuse the situation. You can't force me to stay away."

"You're right. I can't. But I can strongly advise you. You're emotionally involved. You have no objectivity, much less training. You're more apt to jeopardize this operation rather than assist it."

"Peg is right, Hope," Casey inserted. "You have my word—Forensic Instincts will be there every step of the way. But she's right about you accompanying us. You're way too close to the situation. You could wind up putting yourself, and this stakeout, at risk. I agree with Peg's advice. Stay here. Be patient. We'll call you the minute we have something."

"Advice received," Hope returned without so much as a pause. "And rejected. I'd go crazy here, wondering what was happening. I don't want updates. I want to be there. And I will be. I'm paying your fee. That entitles me to occasionally call the shots. This would be one of those times. I'm going to Sunny Gardens. And you and your team are going to take me."

CHAPTER THIRTY-THREE

Day Nine

It was 2:40 p.m.

The task force, BAU and local police were positioned all around Sunny Gardens. Ryan's van containing the entire Forensic Instincts team—plus Hope Willis—was parked in the wooded alcove on the east side of the grounds near the gardens where Linda was sitting. They'd been banished there, since the task force wanted to utilize all the prime areas that gave them a full view of the front and rear parking lots.

That was just fine with Ryan, since the Sunny Gardens administration had agreed to allow minimal video surveillance, and Ryan had arranged for Gecko to be part of that surveillance. Given the little critter's range, the alcove was perfect for keeping an eye on Linda—and her guest.

Ryan made sure that Gecko was primed and ready.

The facility's senior staff had been told only that one of their visitors was a person of interest in a law enforcement matter, and that they were to say nothing to anyone about the FBI and police presence. Their instructions were issued casually, as if the basis for the inquiry was standard rather than high priority. They were to make sure there was no disruption to their patients, and no panic among the rest of the staff.

Two forty-five.

The three-o'clock shift was arriving, and the task force, along with Sunny Gardens security, was monitoring the arrival of each vehicle. The visitor lot was separate from the employee lot. Both were being heavily surveilled. Nothing seemed amiss—yet.

Inside the van, Casey slanted a quick, anxious glance at Hope. The waiting game had depleted her to the point of near-collapse. Her complexion was sallow, her eyes were haunted and she was gaunt from having eaten next to nothing all week. She'd said very little during the ride up, just sat in the backseat of the van, twisting her hands in her lap and staring out the window. But her spine was stiff, and her entire body was rigid with worry.

Casey had sat beside her, offering an occasional word of reassurance, but mostly remaining quiet, aware that nothing she could say would ease Hope's anguish. The only cure for her torment would be having her daughter home. And that's what this stakeout was all about.

The minutes ticked by, and three o'clock came and went—along with Felicity's perfect opportunity to drive through the gates and get lost in the lineup of cars. Casey's whole team was starting to get antsy, even Hero, who whined with the keen instinct of knowing something wasn't right.

"Why isn't she here yet?" Hope asked in a high, thin voice.

"The chief administrator said she always arrives between two and three."

"I don't know," Casey said honestly. "Maybe she hit traffic."

Hope swallowed hard. "Or maybe she got wind of what's going on and is staying away."

Casey wasn't happy. There was merit to Hope's concern. But there was also budding hysteria in her voice. And that could result in nothing but trouble.

"Hope, listen to me," she said quietly. "You can't allow yourself to panic. We're going to find Krissy. Think positively. And don't go to pieces on me."

A tight nod.

"We're in business," Marc suddenly announced from the passenger seat. He pointed out the window where a blue Ford Fiesta was rounding the curve. It slowed down and turned into the main parking lot. The license plate and the driver's profile told them all they needed to know.

"It's Felicity." Hope made a move toward the door, and Casey pulled her back, signaling to Marc with her eyes.

He locked the doors.

"Don't even think about it," Casey warned Hope in as gentle a tone as possible. "If Felicity sees you, it'll blow everything we've worked for. Just stay put."

"She's scanning the area," Ryan noted. He was sitting in the back of the van with his laptop, ready to send the necessary signal to Gecko.

"Maybe that's why she's late," Marc commented. "She's not a stupid woman. Even though it would be harder for *us* to spot *her* in a crowd, it's far easier for *her* to spot *us* in the quiet aftermath of a shift change. Ryan's right. She *is* scanning the area."

Clearly, both men were right. Because Felicity parked in the visitors' lot, then exited her car carrying a shopping bag, with a tote bag slung over her shoulder. She looked both ways several times, then turned to peer behind her.

Satisfied that no one was lying in wait, she picked up the pace, crossing over to the front walk and heading into the main entrance of the building.

Ryan glanced at his watch. "She should be showing up in the garden in the next five minutes." He cued Gecko up, gave him the necessary command. "All set. Now we just sit back and watch the video show from inside the van."

As he spoke, a view of the garden—and Linda—appeared on the screen. She looked tired, her head resting against the back of the chair, her gaze fixed on the red ribbon around her finger. "Soon," they heard her tell the string. "My baby will be here soon."

As if on cue, Felicity began to walk over. Even before the monitor confirmed that fact, it was apparent by Linda's reaction. She sat up straighter, smiling and waving her hand.

"Hello, Mama." Felicity leaned over and kissed her on the forehead. Then she sat down in the opposite chair and gave her the shopping bag, simultaneously placing her tote bag beside her on the grass.

"I brought you some of your favorites," she announced, gesturing at the shopping bag. "Apples straight from the apple orchard, a box of cider doughnuts and two new nightgowns, both sleeveless and nylon, just the way you like them. I also brought you some new books to read, and this month's gardening magazines."

That made Linda happy. She leaned forward, lighting up as she surveyed the contents of the bag. "You're so good to me. Such a good girl."

"Here's some more red string." Felicity reached into her tote bag and produced a large spool of it. "Make sure you have them tie a piece around your finger next Wednesday morning."

"I never forget," Linda said proudly. "I always remind them." She gazed firmly at Felicity. "Did you finish all your math homework? I can check it for you now."

"That's okay." Felicity looked like a small child seeking her mommy's approval. "I already checked the answers in the back of the book. I got most of them right. That's because you helped me last time."

"I did, didn't I?" Linda beamed. "And I know you never look at the answers before you finish. You're such a good girl."

Felicity sat up straighter. Oddly, there were tears in her eyes, as if she knew on some level that the mother she'd loved was slipping away. "Do you know what else? I got a hundred on my spelling test. I wrote down all the words you taught me and the right way to spell them. I double-checked them when I was finished. I even used the dictionary. They were all right."

"I'm so proud." Linda clapped her hands together.

Felicity reached into her tote bag again, and pulled out some computer-generated photos. "I brought you pictures of our little girl. I know how excited you are about seeing her. I duplicated the photo that came out best, and put it in a frame. It's in your shopping bag. You can keep it right beside you on your night table."

Linda took the photos excitedly, perusing them, one by one. "She looks so much like you!" she cooed. "And I'm so glad you have her so you're not lonely." A flicker of sadness. "I wish I could see her. But you mustn't take her out. Not anywhere. You know how scary the world is. And how bad things happen."

Linda leaned even closer, placing her index finger across her lips in a gesture of secrecy. "One of the nurses tried to take me down to the lake the other day. I wouldn't let her. I know I would have fallen in. I would have died. I don't want to die."

"And you're not going to," Felicity said adamantly. "I won't let you. We'll share Krissy. We'll both love her. And I'll keep her safe. I promise."

"You've kept her inside?"

"Just like you kept me. In her princess room. I even made her a special game for the computer. She likes computers, Mama. Just like me. Maybe she'll be a web designer someday, like I am. She'll get money without ever having to go out. Till then, I have the money in the big gym bag to take care of her. She'll be fine. You'll be fine. I'll take care of her, like you take care of me. And if anyone tries to find us or hurt us, I'll take her away. No one will know where we are but you."

"Oh God." Inside the van, Hope gripped the back of the seat. She'd been watching the scene over Ryan's shoulder. "She's going to run away. We've got to stop her." She made a sharp move toward the van door.

Casey put an arm across her, stopping any sudden movements. Even though Marc had locked the buttons, she had to take Hope down a notch. Otherwise, she could start pounding on the windows and making a scene.

"Don't," Casey instructed. "Please, Hope. Let us do our jobs."

Hope whirled around. "What if she takes Krissy and runs away? My daughter would be gone forever."

"That's not going to happen. The task force is prepared for anything. It's not an accident that they're letting this scene play out. If they storm in and grab Felicity, she might never reveal Krissy's location. The kind of maternal commitment she feels for Krissy would make her put her own freedom and safety at risk before she'd risk endangering the child she thinks of as her own. The best way of making sure we find Krissy is to follow Felicity and let her lead us to your daughter."

"But if that's true, how could she leave Krissy alone in that prison? Who does she think is caring for her?"

"Felicity's not thinking rationally. She'll convince herself that somehow she'll get back to her baby. We can't trust the sanity of her reactions. We have to find Krissy firsthand."

"What if Felicity panics and Krissy gets hurt?"

"Felicity is right here at Sunny Gardens, Hope. She's not with Krissy. Which means that your daughter's not in any imminent danger. Don't fall apart on me now."

"There's an awful lot of staff milling around," Ryan noted with a frown. "I don't know how much they were told, but I wish they'd go about their business. We want things to look as normal as possible."

At that moment, Felicity rose, telling Linda that she needed to use the ladies' room. She left everything—her tote bag, and the shopping bag with all the goodies she'd brought—for Linda to enjoy. She then disappeared in the direction of the main building.

"Good," Ryan said. "She's going inside. Let's use this time. I'll give Jeri Koehler, the head nurse, a call, and tell her to page some of her personnel. That way, when Felicity gets back, she won't have an audience waiting for her."

He made the phone call on the private line Jeri had given him.

Soon afterward, the area around Linda began to clear.

"Smart move," Casey praised Ryan. "We don't want Felicity catching on to the surveillance."

Fifteen minutes later, Casey wasn't so sure.

"Where the hell is she?" she muttered. "It was a trip to the bathroom, not to the supermarket."

"She might have stopped to talk to Linda's doctor," Marc suggested. "She left her tote bag, so I think we're safe. Women don't travel without their pocketbooks."

"No, they don't." Casey was scooting over to the door, her reaction the antithesis of Marc's. "Not even to the bathroom. Marc, unlock the buttons. And sit here with Hope."

He complied at once, looping around and sliding in on the opposite side of the car, so Hope had no chance of following Casey.

"Where are you going?" Hope asked Casey in alarm.

"To make sure I'm not overreacting."

She wasn't.

Because before Casey had taken her first step out of the van, she saw Peg jump out of her car and head over to Don's, leaning in the window and waving her hand as she spoke. A minute later, a handful of agents and cops got out of their cars and scattered, some scrutinizing the parking lot, others making a beeline for the front door.

The top brass met Peg there, the hospital administrator clearly distraught.

Casey raced across the street and through the gates, charging up to the front door. "What's happened?"

Peg turned to her. "One of the nurses was knocked out in the ladies' room," she replied tersely. "Her cap and uniform are missing. So are her car keys. And Felicity is nowhere to be found."

As she spoke, Bob and Hutch flung open the doors and exited the building. "The nurse's car is gone," Bob reported. "Our offender must have used the electronic button on the key fob to find it. She took off out the back door. I've got the car's make and model and the license plate."

"Dammit." Peg turned to the group of agents and cops around her. "Divide up. Guy, call the locals to cover the immediate area. Don, call the state police to patrol the highways. Will, check the closest car rentals, in case she does a dump and run like last time. And Jack, assemble a team to check the train and bus stations. She's not getting away."

Casey's features tightened. "Peg, let me collect scent samples from the tote bag and chair in the garden for Hero to sniff. He's a former Bureau dog. He'll become familiar with Felicity's scent. We might need it."

Peg gave a hard nod. "Go."

As Casey turned, a restraining hand clamped down on her forearm. She turned, staring into Hutch's blazing eyes. "You can do your thing," he bit out. "But that's all. No creative tactics. Not this time. As for Hope Willis, keep her in that van. We don't want her to leap out and screw this up. And we don't want any of our people being put in the position of having to figure out who's Hope and who's Felicity."

"I hear you loud and clear, Hutch." Casey glanced down at her arm. "Now if you'd let me go, I'll get to work."

He released her at once.

Casey turned and sprinted back to the van, yanking open the door and giving this assignment to her Navy SEAL. "Marc, take Hero and get over to the garden," she directed. "Very carefully, collect scent samples from everything Felicity touched." She made brief eye contact with Marc. They understood each other perfectly. "Go now."

"Done." He was out of the van and around back, harnessing Hero and taking off. Simultaneously, Casey jumped into the backseat, and Ryan climbed out of the rear and ran around front, sitting in the driver's seat and locking the buttons.

Hope was only frozen for an instant. Then, she turned to Casey. "Felicity's gone?"

"Yes."

"You said this couldn't happen. Your promised me that..."

The rest of Hope's sentence was swallowed up by the screaming sound of an ambulance, which raced by and veered into the entrance of Sunny Gardens.

"Who's hurt?" Hope demanded.

"A nurse. Felicity did to her the same thing she did to Ashley. Then, she stole her uniform and her car and left through the rear entrance." Casey seized Hope's hands. "I know what I promised you. And, yes, Felicity was more clever than we expected. She either spotted an agent, or noticed the unusual number of staff members nearby. I don't know. What I *do* know is that we'll find her. The entire task force is on it, plus every state and local cop within the three neighboring counties. She's only been gone five or ten minutes. She couldn't have gotten far."

"Oh, dear God." Hope shifted in her seat. "I've got to do something."

"Yes, you do. You've got to fight the urge to act. If you interfere, it could blow this entire rescue. Especially if you try to take on Felicity. The agents won't be able to tell you two apart.

That could have horrible results. Just follow my instructions. We'll get Krissy back."

They watched as the lineup of unmarked law enforcement cars took off, traveling in different directions.

A few minutes later, Marc ran Hero back to the car. He'd brought one of Felicity's scent pads from the garden so her scent would remain under Hero's nose. "Let's go. We'll navigate the local roads, and cover a five-mile radius. The streets are curvy and narrow. She couldn't have gone far."

"I'll use my new GPS," Ryan said. "It's sophisticated enough to register even the small local streets." He'd already turned on the ignition and was shifting gears, waiting only until Marc was inside the vehicle before roaring off.

As Marc had predicted, the country roads were winding and narrow. If Felicity was familiar with them, then she had a definite advantage.

They'd covered a half mile of territory, when Casey's phone rang.

She glanced down at the number as she answered. "Hutch?"

"They found the car she stole," he reported. "It was abandoned in the woods across from the railroad station, two miles west of Sunny Gardens. I figured you'd want to know."

"Thank you." Casey got it. Hutch was extending an olive branch after his harsh display at Sunny Gardens. Last time, he'd passed on the task force's update to Marc. This time he was going directly to her—furious or not. "We're on our way."

Casey hung up and shifted forward on the seat, staring at the GPS. "Head for the Garrison train station. About a mile and a half from here. There." She pointed at the railroad tracks on the GPS monitor. "She dumped the car and hopped a train."

Ryan nodded, taking off like a bat out of hell.

They arrived at the station along with a bunch of agents and cops.

"The train left ten minutes ago," Hutch informed them. "It goes from Garrison to Poughkeepsie, and makes three more stops along the way. There's no way we can reach each of those in time—the first is four minutes from here. The next is eight minutes farther. And the last, seven minutes from the previous stop. After that, it's seventeen more minutes to Poughkeepsie. The roads suck. Peg is having the transit authority hold the train in Poughkeepsie. Some of us are heading straight there. Three cars are driving, one each, to the three local stops. The agents will show photos around, hope that someone recognizes Felicity. It's a long shot. It's midday on a Wednesday, and very few people are around. But we've got to cover all our bases."

"You're going to Poughkeepsie?" Casey asked.

"Yes."

"We'll do the local stops and let Hero sniff one of Felicity's scent pads. He'll sniff out each of the areas and tell us if she got off the train. If you call and tell me that Felicity's on the train in Poughkeepsie, we'll drive straight there and let Hero take over. Hope brought along one of Krissy's T-shirts. And, as I said, we have Felicity's scent pads. This is it, Hutch. Felicity didn't just take some arbitrary train. She's going home. She plans to grab Krissy and run."

"That's not going to happen. I'll call you." Hutch strode back to his car.

Casey ran over to the train station and grabbed one of the schedules that was hanging outside. She glanced down at the locations of the stops as she returned to the van. Cold Spring. Beacon. New Hamburg.

She gestured for Ryan to lower his window. He complied. Casey leaned inside, thrust the schedule into his hand and pointed. "Map these three stops."

CHAPTER THIRTY-FOUR

Hero had finished sniffing out the station at Cold Spring, and the team was racing to Beacon when Casey's cell phone rang.

"We're in Poughkeepsie," Hutch updated her. "She's not on the train. We manned every exit, searched every car, questioned every passenger. No one noticed her. She's gone. So she had to have gotten off somewhere between Garrison and here."

"I doubt it was Cold Spring. I know you have agents here, doing their thing. But Hero hit a dead end. And we took him everywhere—inside the station, up and down the stairs, across every platform—you name it. We're on our way to Beacon."

"That means it's probably either Beacon or New Hamburg. We've got agents at both stations. They're showing Felicity's picture around, and asking questions. I'm sure you'll run into them there. Either way, keep me posted."

"You do the same." Casey ended the call and filled in her team.

A minute later, they pulled into the Beacon station.

The place was deserted, with just one person and no employees in sight. The members of the task force were walking around, trying to do their thing.

Ryan took off to start looking around. Marc harnessed Hero and began their search. And Casey, reluctantly, stayed behind to babysit Hope. She had no choice. Despite the warning Casey had given her, Hope was at the edge of her seat, craning her neck to see a signal from anyone indicating that Felicity had exited the train here. And if she got that signal—well, that would be a nightmare waiting to happen.

Casey fidgeted in her seat, wishing she could get the hell out of there and assist with the investigation.

As she contemplated her dilemma, a slew of teenagers came sauntering along, laughing and drinking sodas. It looked as if they'd been there for some time. So they'd have to be questioned. Ryan was at the other end of the station. And the kids were about to leave.

Talk about being careful what you wished for. Casey was screwed.

"Hey, you stay put," a muffled voice called from outside the van. "I'll talk to them."

Casey's head whipped around, and she blinked as she saw Patrick standing beside the van.

He gave a half smile at the stunned expression on her face. "I might not be Claire, but I have a sixth sense for knowing when I'm needed. Besides, I wanted to be a part of bringing this thirty-two-year nightmare to a close. So I drove up here. You hang out with Judge Willis. Just lower the window on her side. I'll interview the kids."

You're a lifesaver, Patrick. Casey mouthed the words, but Lynch got them. He turned and waved down the teenagers in that authoritative way of his that made people stop in their tracks. Pointing at Hope's side of the van, he fired some questions at the teens. Clearly, he was asking if they'd seen a woman who looked like the blond lady sitting in that van.

They all looked over. But there wasn't a shred of recognition on any of their faces.

Ryan had no better luck, returning to the van and shaking his head, adding that the agents and cops he'd run into were drawing the same blank as he was. A few minutes later, Marc and Hero returned, and Casey could tell by the grim expression on Marc's face that they, too, had come up empty.

Leaving the task force to continue their work, the Forensic Instincts team left the station for New Hamburg, with Patrick following behind in his car.

"This is our last chance." Hope's desperation was a palpable entity. Hysteria was bubbling up inside her and the dam was about to burst. "What if we come up with nothing in New Hamburg? What if Felicity found another way, another train, or car, or direction, to go? What if Krissy isn't even in this vicinity, and Felicity was just trying to throw us off track?"

"That's not the case, Hope." Casey spoke with as much conviction as she could muster. "Felicity's prime consideration is Krissy, not playing cat and mouse with the FBI. She's not going to leave Krissy unattended, especially not now, when she knows we're onto her. We'll be in New Hamburg in fifteen minutes. Have faith."

"Faith," Hope replied bitterly. "I'm not sure I know what that is anymore."

★ ★ ★

Krissy heard the commotion from upstairs. It was louder than it had ever been. It scared her.

She curled onto the bed, pressing herself as hard as she could against the wall, as if its solid presence could protect her. She hugged Oreo and Ruby fiercely, her terrified gaze fixed on the door.

More banging and crashing.

Was the woman angry at her? Had she done something wrong? Had the woman figured out that she'd been trying to twist off the doorknob every time she was left alone?

Was she going to hurt her?

Trembling violently, Krissy cringed farther away.

The door swung open, and the woman raced down the stairs, her heels making quick, loud clicks on each step.

"Krissy, get up," she ordered. Her voice wasn't gentle and nice the way it usually was. It was high and shrill. Her face looked strange.

"Why?" Krissy asked.

"We're moving to another house right away." The woman reached over and grabbed Krissy's hand. "Come on. We have to hurry."

"Ow, that hurts." Krissy held back, clutching Oreo and Ruby even tighter. "Where are we going?"

"Don't ask questions," the woman snapped, although she did relax her grasp. "Not now. We don't have time. I'll explain everything later. And I'll create another princess suite later. But not here." She pulled Krissy off the bed and onto her feet. "Let's go."

"No!" Krissy wrenched her hand with all her might.

It paid off. The woman wasn't ready for Krissy to fight back. Her grip had loosened. Krissy's hand was free. And so was she.

She'd run up the stairs so many times. But the door had always been locked.

Now it wasn't. It was wide open.

She raced toward the staircase as fast as she could.

"Wait!" the woman yelled. She was running now, too, coming up quickly behind Krissy.

But Krissy had youth and speed on her side. She blasted up the stairs, nearly tripping over a suitcase. She looked wildly around, finally spotting the kitchen—and the door that she saw led outside. She was through it in seconds.

Fresh air. Woods. Trees everywhere. No open spaces.

It didn't matter. Krissy didn't pause. Even if she ran smack into a bear, it would be better than this. She had to get away.

She tore off into the woods, winding her way through the clusters of trees, and vanishing from view.

The New Hamburg train station was different than the others.

There was no set of stairs or overpass connecting the two platforms, or connecting the platforms to the parking lot. Instead, there was a tunnel that all passengers had to walk through to get from place to place. That made it more difficult to locate all those who had to be interviewed.

The task force was already on it. Given the added complexity, they welcomed Ryan and Patrick's help.

As before, Marc led Hero through the parking lot, into the tunnel and on to the opening of the train station platform. He harnessed the bloodhound and let him sniff Felicity's scent pad. He kept Hero's lead taut, but let him explore at will.

They were barely inside the tunnel, when Hero started pulling Marc, sniffing the ground, straining in his harness to keep moving forward.

Marc tightened his grip on the leash, letting Hero sniff the length of the tunnel. The bloodhound moved swiftly, giving sharp, repeated barks.

It was all the confirmation Marc needed.

"Good boy," he praised. "Let's go."

He sprinted Hero back through the tunnel and across the parking lot to the van. "Success!" he called out to Casey, giving her a thumbs-up. He gestured to Ryan and to Patrick, as well as to the task force. "Felicity got off the train at this station. There's not a doubt in my mind—or in Hero's."

"That's it." Hope practically jumped off the seat. "We have to find her. I have to go."

"Not yet." Casey was already calling Hutch on speed dial. "Racing off without a strategy will only increase the time it takes to find Felicity and Krissy. We need to get organized. *Then* we'll act."

"Casey?" Hutch answered.

"It's New Hamburg. Hero picked up her scent in the tunnel and on the platform. Marc is sure. And if he's sure, then I'm sure."

"We're on our way."

Felicity's heart was pounding so hard she thought it might burst out of her chest. Her legs ached. Her throat was sore from shouting Krissy's name.

Tears filled her eyes, trickled down her cheeks. Oh, Krissy…Krissy, my baby, where are you?

She stopped running long enough to push her hair off her face and peer around. Her face was scratched and bleeding from the branches she'd shoved out of her way. How long a stretch of woods had she covered? It all looked the same. Dirt. Rocks. Trees.

But no Krissy.

Oh, Krissy, why did you run away? I told you I'd keep you safe. I told you we'd find a new home, that I'd build you a new princess suite. What were you so afraid of that made you run?

I did everything right. I know I did everything right. Mama said I did everything right.

But it's my fault. Mama kept the world away. She kept me safe.

I couldn't do that for you, Krissy. The world wouldn't leave us alone. Those horrible FBI people won't go away. They gave up when it came to me. Why won't they give up when it comes to you? Why won't they understand that you're happy? That we're both happy? That you're where you belong?

You saw me be afraid. That's why you ran. It scared you. Mothers are supposed to hide their fear. To control themselves. To be in charge. To be strong.

I didn't do that. I was weak.

It won't happen again.

Please, Krissy, let me help you. I'll make it better. I'll take you away. Mama will understand. She knows what you need. You need me. Only me.

But I can't find you. I have to find you.

Mama's leaving me. You're all I have. You're my whole world now.

And I let you down.

Gasping for breath, seized by panic, Felicity resumed tearing through the woods, zigzagging from tree to tree and shouting Krissy's name.

Nothing answered back but the wind.

CHAPTER THIRTY-FIVE

The hamlet of New Hamburg was small.

Still, the surge of law enforcement officials spread out fast, intent on covering every square inch as rapidly as possible. They were fully aware that only a short time had passed since Felicity had arrived.

But a lot could happen in that brief interval.

Patrick joined the search party, going from house to house and street to street. Ryan joined them, but he was also glued to Hope Willis's side as her appointed bodyguard and warden to make sure that she didn't take off on her own and do something stupid.

Hope fought her confinement tooth and nail. But, in the end, she had no choice. She couldn't outsmart Ryan, and she certainly couldn't overpower him. And, if it was a choice between waiting in the van or not being nearby when they did find Krissy, there was no decision to make.

Casey teamed up with Marc, took Hero and began their search. Marc had the professional rescue skills, and Casey had the trailing experience with bloodhounds. As a human scent evidence dog, Hero was the most qualified of all. The three of them made a formidable team. And they were hell-bent on finding Krissy.

"Linda kept Felicity in a quiet house in the country," Casey said as she and Marc let Hero guide them. "Felicity would want to replicate that environment as closely as possible."

"That describes most of this hamlet," Marc returned.

"True. But Ryan checked the map. There's a section of houses in wooded areas, with little visibility to neighbors. That's where I'd start."

"I'm sure that's where Ryan is starting, too."

"But he's limited by his duties as a bodyguard. We'll probably beat him there. If not, we'll all split up by street."

Hero was already pacing along, sniffing intently as he did.

"How much geographic territory can Hero's nose cover?" Marc asked.

"From what Hutch has told me and from what I've read, it's pretty awesome. He can search fifteen linear miles, maybe more, and narrow it down to half a block."

Marc whistled. "That's amazing."

"It certainly is." A half smile. "Then again, he *is* a member of Forensic Instincts."

"True," Marc said drily. "We are an extraordinary bunch."

Once they reached the wooded area Casey had described, the terrain became difficult—rocks and dirt covering the ground, the sharp branches of trees impeding their progress and scratching their faces.

Casey's cell phone rang.

"We found the house," Ryan told her. "But there's no one

here. The basement is set up just the way Claire described. And the back door is open. They definitely took off in a hurry."

"Where are you?" Casey demanded, checking the map Ryan had printed for her.

"Thirty-nine Pine Street. But there's no point in coming here. The task force called ERT. They'll examine the crime scene. We've got to get out there and find Krissy."

Casey was scanning the map. She stopped when she found Pine Street. "We're not all that far." She glanced at her handheld GPS. "We're in the woods just west of you."

"Okay, well you should be joined by a handful of agents in a matter of minutes. So don't freak out when you hear them coming. But keep looking. Felicity took Krissy in one of two directions—east or west. They're the only sections surrounding her house that are wooded. There are trees to the north and south, but they lead to the street and, eventually, to other houses. A group of local cops are covering that territory, but I doubt it'll lead to anything. Peg took a team to the east. Bob and Hutch are moving west. Patrick and I are about to join them."

"With Hope in tow?"

"No choice," Ryan replied in a clipped, coded response.

"Got it." Casey snapped to as Hero began to strain at his lead. "Ryan, I've gotta go. Hero's picked up a fresh scent trail."

"I'm on my way."

Marc was already following Hero's lead, winding his way through the woods as quietly as he could. Casey hurried until she caught up.

There was the definite crunch of footsteps in the not-too-remote distance. It could be the agents. Or it could be Felicity.

Judging from Hero's reaction, it was the latter.

Hero was most emphatically "in odor," as the FBI called it. He climbed over the rocks and weaved through the trees, pulling at the lead until Marc had to pick up speed.

"Krissy?" called out a frantic female voice just ahead of them. "Is that you? Please, princess, answer me!"

Everything happened at once.

Hero lunged forward. The pounding of a surge of footsteps raced up behind them. And a streak of movement flashed through the trees in front of them.

A woman. Blonde. Slim. Frantic.

Felicity.

"FBI! Stop where you are!" Casey heard Hutch's command even as she felt him rush by her, weapon raised. Peg and a dozen other cops and agents followed suit, forming a half circle around the immediate area.

The woman froze.

"Help me," she begged plaintively, not even trying to escape. "I can't find my daughter."

"We'll find her for you." Peg marched over to Felicity, holstering her gun and drawing Felicity's hands behind her back so she could handcuff her.

Felicity stood by docilely, her face scratched and tear streaked, her eyes glazed, damp with worry. She looked like a frail, broken doll.

"Where did you last see your…daughter?" Hutch went along with the charade, more than aware that now was not the time to slam Felicity with reality.

"In the house. She ran away. I don't know where she is. She could be hurt. Oh, God, this is all my fault. Please, please find her. I can't leave her out there. The world is ugly. And Krissy is beautiful. A princess. Save her."

"We will." Hutch turned to Marc. "Do you have anything of Krissy's with you?"

"*I* do."

Before Marc could answer, a shaken voice brought their heads around. Hope was walking slowly toward them, Krissy's T-shirt extended. She was staring at Felicity. Her mouth opened and closed several times, as if she wanted to say something but didn't know what or how.

Felicity gazed back at her, confusion and wonder flashing across her face. "Hope?" she asked in a faraway voice. "Are you real? I thought that was you at the house. Mama said it wasn't. She said I was imagining it, that I was just picturing Krissy and me together. But she was wrong, wasn't she? You're real."

"Yes, Felicity, I'm real," Hope answered in a shattered voice. She released Krissy's T-shirt into Hutch's hands, watching as he ran forward and waved it under Hero's snout.

He and Marc took off with the determined bloodhound.

Hope's stare shifted back to Felicity. She studied her sister's depleted state, her mental deterioration, and all the accusations and venom she'd been harboring drained out of her. "Did you take good care of her?" she managed, remembering the laughter of a six-year-old twin who'd been stolen from her life.

"I tried." Tears were sliding down Felicity's cheeks. "But not hard enough. She got away. I—I don't understand." She lowered her head, breaking down entirely. "I don't understand."

Hope raised her head, and her gaze met Casey's. She looked ill. "Will they find Krissy?" she managed. "Please?"

"There's not a doubt in my mind," Casey replied. "She can't be far."

★ ★ ★

Hero air-scented Krissy within minutes.

The instant he began pulling at the lead, Hutch and Marc began calling out.

"Krissy!" Hutch shouted. "We're the FBI. Policemen. We're here to help you."

There was a slight rustle from the left.

"Krissy, it's okay," Marc called out. "We caught the woman who looks like your mommy. She can't hurt you. And your real mommy is here. She wants to take you home."

"But first you have to tell us where you are." Hutch gestured to Marc, pointing at a cluster of trees diagonally ahead of them by about thirty feet.

Marc nodded.

Hero was already heading in that direction.

"Krissy?" Hutch called out again. "Where are you, honey?"

Hero rounded the circle of trees and began braying.

His outburst clearly startled Krissy, because she let out a soft cry.

"It's okay," Marc repeated, going up to the terrified child, who was cringing against the tree trunk. He squatted down so he was at her level. "This is Hero. He works with us. He's very friendly. And he *is* a hero, because he helped us find you."

The little blonde girl hugged her stuffed panda and robin, gazing at Marc with huge eyes. She had cuts on her arms and face, her clothes were torn and her hair was disheveled. But she was alive and unharmed. "Is he really a police dog?" she whispered.

"Even cooler," Hutch said, coming around the bend. "He's an FBI dog. That makes him even more famous. And he's here just for you."

"Wow." Krissy leaned forward and tentatively petted Hero, who was now quiet and rolling over to get a belly scratch, having completed his task.

The bloodhound licked her palm.

"Is that woman really gone?" Krissy asked in a small, frightened voice. "And is my mommy really here?"

"Yes and yes," Hutch supplied. He extended his hand. "Would you like to see her?"

She put her small trusting hand in his big one and nodded her tousled head, her lashes spiked with tears. "Yes."

They made their way through the trees, retracing their steps.

"Look who's here," Marc announced, as he, Hutch and Hero reappeared, walking Krissy into the clearing where Hope waited.

"Mommy!" Krissy had no trouble recognizing her mother. She ran past Felicity, giving her one terrified glance, and then dashed straight into her mother's arms, crushing Oreo and Ruby against her.

"Oh, baby. Oh, Krissy. Thank God." Hope lifted her daughter, openly sobbing as she hugged and kissed her again and again. "You're not hurt, are you?"

"My scratches burn." Krissy was sobbing, too, her words barely discernible as she buried her face against her mother's shoulder.

"But Felic—the woman who took you—she didn't hurt you, did she?"

Krissy shook her head back and forth. "She tried to hug me. But I said no. And she stopped. She wouldn't go away. But she wouldn't take me home."

"Thank God." Hope buried her lips in her daughter's hair. "I love you. I love you so much."

"I love you, too. And I missed you. I was so scared. Oreo and Ruby missed you, too." She held up the rumpled stuffed animals.

"And I missed them." Hope planted a kiss on each of their heads. "But I know they took good care of you."

"They did. They slept with me every night." Krissy leaned back, gazing at her mother for corroboration. "Are we really going home?"

"We really are." Hope looked past her daughter, taking in the entire crowd of professionals, her grateful stare lingering on Casey. "Thank you," she managed, her voice quavering with emotion. "Thank you all from the bottom of my heart."

Her gaze shifted to Felicity, who was standing there like a lost soul, pain and sorrow etched on her face.

"Krissy," Hope said to her daughter. "Would you stand right here with Agent Hutchinson? Just for a minute. I need to talk to the woman you were with."

Renewed fear flashed in Krissy's eyes. "But what if she takes you, too?"

"She can't take me. See? Her hands are chained behind her back. The police and FBI are with her. She can't take anyone." A painful pause as Hope inspected every inch of her child. "You're going to be fine, baby. We all are."

"Come on, Krissy." Ryan stepped forward, sticking out his hand. "I'm a friend of your Mommy *and* of Agent Hutchinson. I spend lots of time with Hero. How about coming with Agent Hutchinson and me so that Hero can show you some of the cool tricks he knows."

That was an excellent incentive.

Krissy let her mother lower her feet to the ground. Then, she ran over and took Ryan's hand. She went with him over to Hutch, Marc and Hero, where she squatted down to play with the bloodhound and see what amazing feats he could do.

Certain her child was in good hands, Hope walked toward Felicity, stopping when the two sisters were face-to-face.

"You *are* my twin," Felicity managed, still staring at Hope as if she were part of a fairy tale. "You aren't made-up. You're real.... Mama was wrong. The dreams I used to have are real. When I was little...when I was scared...all that really happened. Just like it happened to Krissy. I shouldn't have taken that car. I shouldn't have hurt anyone, taken anything or tried to be you. But Mama said I was confused. She said I had to do these things so I could have my princess. She said it was the only way I wouldn't be lonely when she left me forever. But it was all wrong, wasn't it? Mama made a mistake."

"Yes, Felicity, she did." Hope was holding herself together by a thread. "How did you know how to do all those things? How did you know how to be me?"

"Mama helped me plan it.... Sometimes she's not so sick. Sometimes she's Mama. And she's so smart. I'm smart, too. I take after her. She always says so. So we wrote down the plan. I had to become me. I had to take my baby. But I wasn't me, was I? I was you." Felicity gave a hard shake of her head. "I'm so confused."

"How could you not be?" Hope replied. "You were kidnapped when we were six. You've lived in another world since then. I can't imagine..." She broke off, her throat clogged with emotion. "We're going to get you help. Then you'll remember."

Felicity began twisting and tugging at her fingers. "What about Mama? She's sick. I can't desert her. She never deserted me."

"She's getting care. That won't change." Hope restrained herself from screaming out that Linda Turner was *not* Felicity's mother. That her real mother had died a thousand deaths since the kidnapping. And that both her parents would be weak with gratitude that their daughter had been restored to them, however damaged.

"Can I still visit her?" Felicity asked. "She needs to see me. I'm all she has. For all the time she has left."

Hope glanced over at Peg.

"We'll talk about that later," Peg replied.

"Thank you." Felicity bit her lip. "I know I've been bad. I didn't mean to be. I'm usually a very good girl."

"Felicity." Hope put a hand on her sister's shoulder. "It'll be all right."

"We have psychologists en route," Peg informed Hope quietly. "One who specializes in victims of childhood abductions like the one Krissy's been through. She'll meet you at your house. And a specialist for Felicity, who's definitely suffering from Stockholm syndrome. She'll be waiting at the New York Field Office when we arrive."

"I appreciate that," Hope said. "My parents will, too."

"Once Krissy understands that Felicity is her aunt, that she was also taken by someone when she was a child, and that she was in that scary situation for years and years, she'll start to feel empathy rather than fear," Casey added. "Children bounce back quickly when there's been no physical or emotional abuse. It will be tough going for a while. But Krissy is one strong little girl. She'll be fine. As for Felicity..." A slow inward breath. "She's going to need a lot of help. She's lived a lifetime like this, not a week. And, in addition to professional help, she'll need her family, especially after Linda is gone."

"She'll have us." Hope's face was damp with tears again as she turned back to her sister. "A lot of people love you," she said fervently. "None of that has changed."

A vacant expression crossed Felicity's face. "Love me?"

Hope nodded. "Yes, Felicity, love you. You're my sister. My twin. We're connected. You wanted to love Krissy as your own, not to harm her. I know you're confused. But your memories will come back. I'll remind you of the good times. I promise." She stepped away, as Peg indicated that it was time. "Go with the FBI," Hope instructed her. "I'll drive down to see you later."

"Do you promise?"

"I promise."

Felicity nodded her acceptance, pausing for a second before relinquishing herself to the task force. "I really do love Krissy," she whispered.

"I know you do."

Torn between anguish and relief, Hope watched as Felicity was led off.

For a long moment, she did nothing. Just composed herself, so she could give Krissy the love and strength she needed.

Then she turned, beckoning to Krissy, who was playing a game of tug-of-war with Hero. Her T-shirt was definitely the loser.

"Let's go, sweetheart," Hope called. "We have to call Daddy. And it's time we went home."

Krissy raced over to her instantly and glued herself to her mother's side. Hope clasped her hand securely in her own.

Then they walked slowly back to the van, and to the life they would fight to recapture.

EPILOGUE

The Forensic Instincts team sat around the brownstone's conference table, raising their glasses of champagne in triumph.

"To a job well done," Casey toasted. "And to an amazing team of pros—both our original threesome, and our two new additions—Claire and Hero." She tipped her champagne flute in Claire's direction. "Welcome. I'm so glad you decided to leave the world of the straight and narrow, and take a walk on the wild side."

"Me, too." Claire's eyes twinkled. "The straight and narrow's not all it's cracked up to be. A walk on the wild side will be very refreshing."

With a return grin, Casey lowered her gaze to the floor, where Hero was sprawled at her feet, taking a well-deserved, and much-needed, nap. "And you, my friend, are the man of the hour. A true hero."

He acknowledged her praise with a snore.

"Hero's got the right idea. Sleeping it off." Ryan gave a huge yawn. "When was the last time any of us got a full night's sleep?"

"Uh-oh." Claire rolled her eyes. "You're tired. Does that mean you're about to turn into Mr. Hyde again?"

Ryan shot her a look. "Tread carefully, Claire-voyant. I still think Casey gives way too much credit to those visions of yours. Gecko had just as big a role in this investigation as you did—and he doesn't talk back."

"He also doesn't complain. Successful, talented and a clutch performer. Careful, Ryan. Gecko might just put you out of business."

"And so it begins," Marc concluded, polishing off his champagne. "Fasten your seat belts, fellow voyagers. The bumpy ride has just shifted into hyperdrive. Be prepared for it to blast you right out of your seats."

"And to think I'm going to miss the opening fireworks." Hutch appeared in the doorway, his travel bag slung over his shoulder. He'd been upstairs in Casey's apartment, collecting the handful of personal items he'd left in her bedroom. "I'll have to get back here for a visit ASAP. Quantico's not nearly as exciting as this."

Marc's eyebrows drew together quizzically. "Are you heading out?"

"Yup. Grace is driving down to pick me up. Then, it's a long trip home. I've got to be at my desk at seven tomorrow morning."

"Sounds like hell. Hey, did you and Casey make up?" Ryan asked bluntly, looking from Casey to Hutch. "Or are you two still killing each other?"

Casey and Hutch exchanged a quick, intimate glance. The hour they'd spent together before everyone piled into the brownstone had been anything but combative. They'd ironed out their residual anger in about five minutes. Then they'd spent the rest of the time in bed, securing their pact.

"Looks like they made up," Claire determined.

Ryan eyed her speculatively. "Another psychic insight?"

"Nope. A simple observation."

"And an accurate one," Hutch confirmed. "All is well. In fact, if it's okay with you, I'd like to borrow your boss to say goodbye."

"I'm not hanging around here for another hour," Ryan warned them. He was starting to get cranky. "So make it quick, and keep it clean."

"Yes, sir." Casey snapped off a salute as she rose. "I'll walk you downstairs," she told Hutch.

The two of them descended to the first floor, where Hutch dropped his bag onto the floor and hauled Casey into his arms.

"You're one sexy pain in the ass," he murmured, kissing her.

"Right back at you." She smiled against his mouth. "Any free time coming up?"

"Not sure." He kissed her again. "How about you?"

"Not sure." She wrapped her arms around his neck. "Maybe I can sneak away for a weekend in between cases."

"Yeah, when will that be?"

"When I show up on your doorstep." She deepened their kiss. "I like to keep you on your toes."

"No worries on that score."

A horn sounded from outside.

"That must be Grace," Hutch said. "And the parking here sucks. So I'd better get going." He tunneled his fingers through

Casey's hair, gave her one more lingering kiss, then released her. "Stay out of trouble."

"I'll do my best. You do the same."

"You got it."

Casey was halfway up the stairs when the doorbell rang.

Puzzled, she retraced her path and peeked through the peephole. Not particularly surprised, she opened the door. "Hello, Patrick."

"Hey." He strode past her, pausing at the foot of the steps. "I assume your team is upstairs celebrating."

She nodded. "Second-floor conference room. You're welcome to join us."

"I plan to." He headed upstairs, Casey following right behind.

"We have a new guest," she announced, gesturing for Patrick to join the group. "Help yourself to a glass of champagne," she invited.

"Sounds good." Lynch walked over to the table, nodding his hellos and taking the champagne flute Marc proffered.

Hero picked his head up and brayed.

"Easy, boy. I'm not an intruder," Patrick assured him. "Just a friend and fellow law enforcement officer."

With a thorough sniff—and an equally thorough slobber—of Patrick's shoes, Hero seemed to be convinced. He resettled himself, closed his eyes and went back to sleep.

"Have a seat." Casey indicated one of the empty chairs around the table.

Patrick lowered himself into the chair, then raised his glass. "To all of you. For solving two cases—including one that's been haunting me for over three decades. I can't even imagine how many laws you broke, and I don't want to know. All I care about is that a little girl is home with her parents tonight. And a woman who's more a victim than an offender is about to get the help she needs. That's the best outcome we could hope for under the circumstances."

"Were you at the Willises' till now?" Marc asked. The Forensic Instincts team had stayed only long enough to witness the touching family reunion—one that gave them the rare chance to see Edward Willis break down and weep, and to see Krissy meet her grandfather. Then they'd wrapped things up with the task force, and said their goodbyes. Hope Willis had followed them outside, insistent on giving them an overly generous check right there on the spot. They'd graciously accepted, asked to be kept posted on how Krissy was doing and left.

"Yeah, I came here straight from Armonk," Patrick confirmed. "Krissy still hasn't said very much. But that's to be expected. She was with the FBI child psychologist when I left."

"Any news on the charges against Felicity and Linda?"

"Not yet." Patrick frowned. "Both situations are difficult. Both have extenuating circumstances. Neither woman is fit to stand trial. Obviously, Linda is by far the guiltier of the two, since she set this whole nightmare in motion. I'm sure she'll be transferred to a high security health facility, where she'll be treated for Alzheimer's. And Felicity will need intensive therapy, and a lot of emotional support. I hope the sentence imposed on her will reflect her lifelong trauma."

"I'm sure it will," Casey replied. "Especially given Hope's compassionate heart. She'll intervene on her sister's behalf. She's adamant that a ruined life is more than enough price for Felicity to pay."

A nod. "Oh, one interesting twist I got from Peg before she

left with Felicity. Apparently the mob was so worried that we'd dig up something unrelated but incriminating on them, that they got one of the Sunny Gardens nurses to do some preemptive damage control."

"Even though they had nothing to do with the two kidnappings?" Ryan looked amused. "Glad to make a mobster squirm, but what happened with this nurse?"

"Denise Amato," Patrick supplied. "Seems she's sleeping with Bill Parsons, Tony Bennato's construction foreman. Peg got her to talk. She didn't know a lot. Only that Bennato got inside info that warranted his ordering Parsons to try and find a way to point the Feds, the cops—" a pointed look in Marc's direction "—and I quote, 'and that nutcase Navy SEAL' in a different direction. So, on Parsons's instructions, Amato wheeled Linda Turner down to the lake, where Linda promptly went to pieces, screaming and crying and toppling her wheelchair to get away."

"I guess Bennato knew about Claudia Mitchell's confrontation with Lorna-slash-Linda, and dug up dirt on Linda's past," Marc said, trying to keep his lips from quirking.

"Yeah, and I guess you paid Parsons a less than cordial surprise visit on your own."

"Do you want me to answer that?"

"Nope."

"I didn't think so."

Patrick cleared his throat. "That brings me to the other reason I'm here."

"Gee," Ryan said, "and here I thought you just came by to tell us how awesome we are."

"Nope. Like I said, you're great at what you do. No arguments there. Your methods, however, leave a hell of a lot to be desired. You need supervision and restraint. I've decided to offer you both."

"Pardon me?" That brought Casey's head up.

"You need me. And I'm bored by the freelance assignments that come my way. So I've decided to come on board—*and* keep you out of jail."

"You want to join Forensic Instincts?" Casey had to make sure she was hearing right.

"Surprised?"

"Thrilled." Casey shot Patrick a huge grin. "You'd be the perfect counterweight to a bunch of out-of-control mavericks." She glanced around the room. "I know we ordinarily make these decisions in private," she told her team. "But since this interview—and job acceptance—were just conducted in public, and since we know that Patrick has no ego problem, how do you feel about adding another new member to the team?"

"Sweet," Ryan replied at once. "Renegade Marc and by-the-book Patrick, battling it out. I smell a comic book series. The possibilities are endless."

"And balanced," Marc added, ignoring Ryan's taunt. "I think it's a great idea. A little more structure and discipline. I can handle the infighting if you can, Patrick."

"Bring it on," Patrick replied.

"And with Claire-voyant on board, we can use another person who has his feet on the ground." Ryan slanted a look in Claire's direction. "What do you think?"

"I think Patrick's experience and *maturity*—" Claire underscored the last word "—will add a lot to the mix. I'm a newbie myself, but if my vote counts, I say, yes, absolutely."

"And the pièce de résistance—Hero likes you," Casey said with a grin. "Or, at the very least, he likes your shoes. He doesn't slobber on just anyone. If that's not a yes, I don't know what is." She extended her hand to Patrick. "Welcome to the team, former Special Agent Lynch. We're honored to have you."

"You'll be eating those words a lot," Patrick replied. But he was grinning, too, as he shook Casey's hand. "But I look forward to working with you all."

Casey lifted her glass again. "To the new and improved Forensic Instincts. Onward and upward, and may we not kill one another in the process."

★★★★★

ACKNOWLEDGMENTS

With deepest gratitude to all those amazing professionals who so graciously gave of their time and helped provide me with the authenticity I needed to write *The Girl Who Disappeared Twice*. The list is long, and in no specific order. I thank each and every one of you.

Angela Bell, Public Affairs Specialist, FBI Office of Public Affairs (Angela, you're the exception to my rule—you're always first, because you're the most extraordinary central contact I could ever hope for!)

Arthur Cummings II, Former Executive Assistant Director, FBI National Security Branch

SSA James McNamara, FBI Behavioral Analysis Unit 2

SA Konrad Motyka, FBI New York

SA James Margolin, FBI Office of Public Affairs, New York Field Office

SSA Michael Harkins, Coordinating Supervisor, Violent Crime/Gangs Branch, FBI New York Field Office

SSRA Michael Ferrandino, FBI Long Island Resident Agency

SSA Leonard Johns, Formerly of the FBI Behavioral Analysis Unit 3

SSA Thomas Lintner, Chief FBI Laboratory's Evidence Response Team Unit

SSA Rex Stockham, Program Manager for FBI Laboratory's Forensic Canine Program

SSRA Edward McCabe, FBI White Plains Resident Agency

SA Tonya DeSa, FBI Newark Division National Academy Coordinator, NCAVC Coordinator, Assistant Training Coordinator

SA Laura Robinson, Senior Team Leader, Evidence Response Team, FBI Newark Field Office

SA Maria Johnson, NCAVC Coordinator, FBI New York Field Office

Retired SA Richard DeFilippo, Violent Crimes Task Force, FBI New York Field Office

Robert D'Angelo, Chief of Police, North Castle, New York

Retired FBI SA Richard Mika

SA Ann Todd, FBI Office of Public Affairs

Retired Detective Mike Oliver, NYPD

Jennifer Michelson, New Jersey Search and Rescue Dog Task Force

Hillel Ben-Asher, M.D.

In addition, I want to thank Adam Wilson, for being a true editorial partner, and Andrea Cirillo and Christina Hogrebe, for being agents and advocates extraordinaire.

And last, but always first, I want to thank my family, who's there from start to finish...and then some. I love and appreciate you more than you'll ever know.